COUNTERCLOCKWISE

Borgo Press Books by JAMES B. JOHNSON

Counterclockwise: A Science Fiction Novel

COUNTER-CLOCKWISE

A SCIENCE FICTION NOVEL

JAMES B. JOHNSON

THE BORGO PRESS

MMXI

DEDICATION

*For the late **JEROME STERN** of Tallahassee
and The Florida State University,
and all of "Jerry's Kids" across the land—
of whom I am proud to be one.*

CONTENTS

CHAPTER ONE

The thunderstorm warning Claxton hooted and I was looking up at the sky trying to decide whether to make a run for the clubhouse or not. Before NASA satellite global mapping and imagery, this part of Florida had been the lightning capital of the world. Everybody, especially meteorologists, said so. But now, thanks to NASA, Rwanda in central Africa has the crown. Maybe it's just who's the PR guy.

But I wasn't about to argue right then. The other three of my foursome had already hightailed it to the clubhouse in their carts, and were likely even now drinking beer and comfortably watching the storm. Rain drove needles into my upturned face. Leaves and sand peppered my ears.

As usual, I'd been searching for my ball in a copse of pine trees and whacking aside brush with my 9-iron—which was probably my best stroke. You ever make a judgment, "I can make it, just gimmie a minute"?

From the #7 fairway, you can see Bent Tree Boulevard winding its way to the clubhouse. Occasionally, a car or a jogger would go by. Golf club community houses sat back under canopies of oak, palm, and pine. My house was down one of the cul de sacs.

The wind slamming across the fairway like a locomotive amuck drowned out the second insistent Claxton.

The gates of hell swung wide, and lightning flamed forth. Thunderclaps tattooed around me like I was centered amongst concussion grenades and mortars and artillery and thousand pound bombs. Then the world exploded and the fires leapt about as lightning, sheets of lightning, arcs of lightning, lances of lightning, webs of lightning danced, Mother Nature expressing her wrath. The wind crushed me against the trunk of a massive pine and my 9-iron neatly grounded me.

The strangest thing I'd remember was the smell of burning hair. Why I could smell with the wind whipping around me at supersonic speeds, I'll never know. But I will remember.

A handful of lightning the size of a golf ball tracked through the super-charged air and whacked into the left side of my head. It was yellow-orange with a maroon corona. I wanted to duck, but I was frozen in place. A hissing sound sizzled just before it struck.

Then my throat constricted as if a tourniquet was strangling me and somebody drove a spike into my left ear, through my brain, and out my right ear. At the same time, my eyeballs seemed to pop out like Wile E. Coyote's when he runs off a cliff and looks down. All the while a great crackling noise enveloped me like tinfoil in a microwave. It weaved a pattern around me even to the point of excluding the wind. My gut turned to water and as my brain shorted out, all I could think was: Somebody killed the pine tree and that they'd bury me in a pine box and my gravestone would say: ETHAN ZACHARY, HE RAN OUT OF TIME

Still extruded, my eyeballs rolled and I recall looking oddly at my frazzled Ben Hogan 9-iron and reflecting that the club never did me much good anyway. My arm holding it didn't have much hair left on the wrist and forearm and I wished I was at the clubhouse drinking a draft Bud with the other guys—even though I don't usually drink, I'd have been there in the nick of time, and a longleaf pine splintered and shattered and crashed to the ground simultaneously with me and bounced me up and down twice because of the ground rejecting it the first time and I wondered what time it was....

And then something else weird happened. I was face up on

the ground, almost unconscious. I swear what happened next was an out-of-body experience. The power of the storm abated and I could feel a presence, someone hovering over me. It had to be an angel, which was the only clarity my scrambled mind could provide. The phantom angel tapped me a couple of times and then kissed me. Was this a final and formal sendoff to whatever is next?

It had to be Doctor's Hospital. Doctor's Hospital was only a couple of miles down Bee Ridge Road, a private, for-profit hospital, but well worth the expense.

When I woke, my eyes didn't want to work. They were sore, dry and blurry, but with an effort, they steadied and focused.

Mary Lou sat in a chair, staring out of the window. At fifty-five, her legs were still fine; they were crossed and the top leg bounced impatiently as usual. She checked her watch as if not for the first time. Doubtless, she'd rather be someplace else. Shopping? She was involved with so many organizations, projects, and volunteer work. Mary Lou had sharp features everybody called beautiful, shoulder length auburn hair, and an aloof attitude that gave her an air of mystery.

If I was middle-aged and just marking time on cruise control, what was she doing? Likely her version of the same, and I couldn't blame her. I still didn't know what I wanted to be when I grew up.

The room smelled like a florist shop. Window ledge, counters, bedside tables, all overflowed with flowers. Carnations, roses, tulips, you name it.

I realized I didn't know what day it was. My left hand and arm wouldn't move, so I snaked a right hand to my chin. Perhaps a couple days' growth—

"Ah," said Mary Lou, catching the movement in her peripheral vision. She turned to me. "Do you know how many light cycles it's taking most cars to get through the intersection of Bee Ridge and Cattlemen?" She stood and walked toward me on the bed. "On the average of two." That observation was unlike her.

I was the one who hated traffic, crowded roads, and could actually do something about it. Traffic didn't bother her one bit, not even in the middle of tourist season in Sarasota, when the snowbirds flocked down here by the thousands. I didn't blame them. Shoveling my sidewalk all winter wasn't my idea of fun, either. They used to call rush hour here "rush minute," but nowadays we'd pushed past 350,000 souls in Sarasota, so maybe it was somewhere in between.

"I'm fine," I squawked. I didn't have to ask where I was. "What happened?" My fuzzy recollection was there, but I didn't want to admit it before I was forced to.

"You got hit by lightning." She shrugged as if it were an inconvenience to her only.

More like I'd been awash in a sea of it, and then drowned in more of it. I'd eaten it, swallowed it, rolled in it, smelled it, heard it, felt it, absorbed it, breathed it, and sucked it in my ears, eyes, nose, and mouth. Not to mention downloading it into my head. Hell, I almost died in it.

She placed her hands on her hips. "Maybe you shouldn't try to talk. They say you've got burns, lost some hair, broken your left arm, cracked ribs, God knows what else. They sure don't."

My head felt like I'd been at ground zero.

"Want me to call a nurse?"

"Why?" I croaked.

"I don't know. That's what they always do on television and I told you and I told you that playing golf was no damn good."

"I'm fine." My hearing wasn't up to par so I couldn't tell how bad my voice was.

"Oh. How do you feel, Ethan?" She was wearing a magnet bracelet on her wrist to fight incipient arthritis.

"Fine."

"You don't look fine."

"Thanks," I said.

Realization must have hit her. She stepped over and took my one good hand. "Oh, Ethan, I'm sorry. I was just so worried. I don't know what I'd do without you."

She held my hand to her breast dramatically. Not to mention that we were estranged. I sometimes referred to her as my "almost-ex-wife." We still lived in the same house, but for some reason she had not yet shared with me, she was talking divorce.

Glancing at my watch, I saw the gold Seiko had stopped.

She followed my gaze and her brow furrowed. "It was working all right when I put it on your wrist earlier." The second hand stood frozen. "There was only a little burn mark on it and you like that watch so much; I just naturally thought you'd want to be wearing it."

"I do, but—" Then it occurred to me that with my life what it was lately, I didn't really care about time as much as I used to. I would again, though. When you're on autopilot, it doesn't matter.

When Carrie Jean walked in the door, I was remembering her graduation from Riverview High School and thereafter. I'd followed Carrie Jean's academic career through the University of Florida up in Gainesville and the Florida State University Law School farther up in Tallahassee. There had always been a gut-level affinity between us as she was growing up. It was because of me she was a marathon runner and usually in training for some event. She was right now in between law school and her first employment with a law firm in Seattle.

Carrie Jean Billingsley came into my hospital room in Sarasota, Florida, carrying a brand new prototype Smith & Wesson 9-iron wrapped with a big, wide red bow.

"Hi, CJ," I said.

Sometimes when I see her, there is a disturbed atmosphere about her. Maybe the air is different. Mostly, around her head is a distortion in light, air, sound, somedamnthing. So I wished I was in my twenties again. So what? I might be well over fifty, but I can still dream like a boy.

Carrie Jean was slender with bold green eyes that always looked directly at you. Her dirty blond hair was usually swept into a ponytail, a legacy of growing up where she was an acrobat in Sarasota's Sailor Circus and running every day. She'd also been a trapeze artist in the FSU circus. She always corrected me when I called her hair dirty blond. "Ash blond," she'd say. It was a ritual between us. She was wearing hip hugger jeans, expensive running shoes, and a truncated sweat shirt with the sleeves cut off at the shoulders and the waist cut off just under her breasts.

Her eyes locked onto my appraising ones and I didn't even have to say it.

Concern spread through those day-glow eyes of hers and she stepped toward me. "Ethan, I—" She glanced at Mary Lou and I followed her gaze and Mary Lou had clouded up.

As I indicated, I'm currently on cruise control, not needing or wanting complications in my life. Now I was in the hospital with a broken arm and God knows what else, and this is happening. And then the complications compounded immediately.

CHAPTER TWO

I'd been in the middle of a lightning storm on the golf course; now I was in the middle of another kind of storm in the hospital room.

And the door banged open.

"Eaze! You old dog." Jack Billingsley slammed into the room like he owned the hospital.

"Daddy," said Carrie Jean.

"Jack!" said Mary Lou delightedly.

"Why me, Lord?" I said.

Tall and ruggedly good looking, Jack walked over to me eying me suspiciously. "Is it safe? Am I going to be collateral damage here?" He patted my shoulder. "I told you that you should work on your iron game." Instead of flowers, he handed me a box of Don Carlos, the Arturo Fuente cigars with Cameroon wrappers. He gets them up in Tampa at Thompson & Company over by the airport. The pink bow was incongruous and his idea of a joke.

My arm reflecting a shot of pain, I said, "Thanks." He'd been one of the foursome; and he was a scratch golfer.

Complication number two walked in. She was catalogue cute, in a tight, short dress with half-heels. Her flaming eyes darted about and locked on me. "Commissioner?" In front of people she didn't know, she always addressed me as commissioner.

Right behind her was a guy in old high-top tennis shoes, jeans, a tee shirt, and with a small news video camera at half-mast, ready to leap into action. A cable ran from his camera to his loaded belt.

To the others in the room, the cute girl said, "I'm Elena. Elena Rodríguez. With the paper and LNN?"

As if any man would forget her. She wore her long black hair loose.

"Hey, Elena," I said She was always formal at first. She was on the local government beat. Elena was articulate and methodological—not to mention photogenic; therefore, she wouldn't last long in Sarasota. She'd be moving on to bigger and better one day soon. Her background would make an intriguing book.

"Introduce me," Jack demanded. I ignored him

Mary Lou glared at Elena Rodríguez like she always does when another attractive woman is nearby. Now Mary Lou had two attractive women sharing the stage.

Not being able to help myself, I stole a look at my watch. It clicked backward one time.

The cameraman stepped in front of Carrie Jean and she furrowed her brow trying not to frown.

Elena started to speak, but Carrie Jean came back to my side. She set the new S & W 9-iron on the bed alongside my broken arm and leaned over me. She smelled good and I noticed, as I always do, the pheromones. She kissed my cheek and whispered "Good luck."

Carrie Jean stepped deftly in front of Elena, "Excuse me there, Granny."

Elena swiveled poisonous eyes following the not-all-that-much younger Carrie Jean.

Then she was gone, good-old Elena having to step aside. The door swished behind Carrie Jean. Except.

Elena was shaking hands with Jack. Jack was your original ladies' man. Four wives, currently awaiting number five. Carrie Jean was the result of his first and longest marriage.

Mary Lou laughed and watched the circus.

"Mr. Zachary?" said Elena. "Could you do an interview for LNN and The *Star-Banner*?" Too many strangers, so she was formal.

LNN was local cable news for Sarasota and Bradenton,

which is Sarasota and Manatee counties. It was a function of the *Sarasota Star-Banner*, our only newspaper.

Except: With my good hand, I'd grasped CJ's wrist as she'd pleasantly leaned over me. A quick glance showed my hand partially obscuring her fancy sports watch. I'd bought that one for her when she ran her first marathon. It had all kinds of functions throbbing all over the face, clicking away happily. Until I'd touched it. Then it froze and the digital seconds readout had gone from 32 to 31. The moment had been ephemeral and my eyes had dragged elsewhere. If you don't want to know the answer to the question, do not ask that question. I wanted to call up my injuries and pains and discomforts; but alas and alack the cold stab of fear wiped them out.

"Commissioner?" Elena was repeating. From nowhere she whipped out an inhaler and took a hit. While Elena Rodríguez was in fact good-looking in person, she came across on television as most attractive. I found this somehow comforting; I like real people more than celluloid people. And I knew Elena to be bright, because I'd read her stuff and she interviewed me regularly. Her reporting was actually fair, believe it or not. Like many newspapers these days, ours has gone with multimedia associations. LNN was owned by the newspaper and broadcast on local Comcast cable. Most of their journalists performed double duty; they reported their stories on the cable news and wrote them for the newspaper. Elena was a decent writer; she opened her stories with a capsule, and used no adjectives.

"Hey, Eaze," Jack prompted. "The young lady?"

"Could we set up for an interview, Commissioner?" Elena asked.

"Um, I'd rather not." My voice was mumbling. I glanced at my watch. It clicked backwards one time.

Elena Rodríguez's eyes widened. She wasn't used to refusal. I think the every person in the world lives to be on television, but not me. I'm uncomfortable with it, though they interview me in my job. "What?"

"My wife might see the piece and know I'm back in town," I

mumbled, trying the old joke to get out of it.

Mary Lou grunted. She'd heard it a million times. Doubtless, so had Elena.

"You don't want to be interviewed?" asked Elena. "What about your rumored run for the 13th District seat in congress?"

The cameraman had dropped his camera to his side and was scratching his beard.

My eyes shot to Mary Lou for help, but she wasn't paying attention to me.

"I don't feel up to it," I said, not having to try to make my voice weak.

"But, but…." Elena Rodríguez took another drag on her inhaler.

Feeling guilty, I closed my eyes. Elena was personable and had always given me good press.

"County political bigwig hit by lightning, survives miraculously," she said. "What a story."

"Rain check?" I said. "I owe you one, Elena."

Jack finally caught my unease. He grabbed her arm. "Hey, let's go outside. You can interview me. I was there myself. I was a witness. I had the good sense to get out of the rain." He began drawing her out the door.

The cameraman looked at me oddly as if to say nobody ever turns down being interviewed, then followed Jack and Elena out the door.

After a moment, Mary Lou said, "I'll be goddamned. You declined an interview? What about the sympathy vote? This would assure your reelection." She paused dramatically. "And give you a major plus when you run for congress."

"If I run for congress." I was thinking about it. Mary Lou really wanted me to do so. Implied somewhere therein was that she would reconcile with me and no longer pursue a divorce— which I still didn't understand.

"A quick interview, in a hospital bed, with bandages and a cast. People would remember that. You blew a one-in-a-lifetime opportunity." She shook her head. "Talk about the sympathy vote. I can see the campaign commercial now. It reminds voters of you, laid up, one lone man against nature, coming out alive. Paperwork scattered all over your hospital bed, you doing the work of the people. A good sympathy vote could be worth five percent. And it's free."

"The story will appear in the *Star-Banner.*"

"Nobody reads newspapers any more. It's all television or the Internet; and people do not check the Internet for local news, which leaves television."

What could I say? That I was more scared than I had ever been in my life?

"Mary Lou? Come over here and let me see your watch." That's what I said. It was a most difficult thing to say.

Her eyes grew quizzical as she walked over to me. The closer she got, the higher the dread level rose in me.

CHAPTER THREE

"Ethan? What is it? You look funny—strange kind of funny."

"Give me your watch." My voice was compelling.

She stripped it and handed it to me. It was a Lorus. The second hand was trucking along, clicking off seconds just like advertised. It also had three little dialy-things, round windows with their own tiny hands.

I took her Lorus and pulled it up close to my eyes to see it better. In order to cover, I glanced at my Seiko. It was still going backwards, second by second, minute by minute.

The second hand on Mary Lou's Lorus started going backward. The inset dials stopped working. My mental facilities were such that I saw, but had no idea what they were or what function they accomplished.

Like it was on fire, I handed it back to her.

"Ethan, what's wrong?"

"I guess my watch is broken," I mumbled. "I'm tired. Maybe I ought to sleep."

"Good idea," she said impatiently, kissed her hand and touched my forehead. "I'll leave you alone." Disdainfully, she took the S&W 9-iron off the bed and set it against the wall.

"Thanks." I turned my head and closed my eyes, and she was gone.

Mary Lou had been surprisingly attentive. Though we were sort-of separated, I knew she still liked me. Hell, I liked her. If I hadn't, I would never have married her in the first place. But right now she had some kind of war going on between her ears.

The awkward part was that we were still living together.

For a couple of hours, I was alone, thinking, extrapolating. That was no fun whatsoever. Not enough data, and too much emotion. Under those circumstances, extrapolation becomes an exercise in negativity. Speculation is different. When you speculate, you're likely to insert your own druthers, hopes, dreams, or somedamnthing into the equation.

When the circus had been in my room a little while ago, I reasoned, it was about nine in the morning. Fine. Mary Lou had put the watch on me while I slept or was unconscious before that oh nine hundred. Extrapolating, the backwards-moving watch would hit midnight in maybe eight hours.

Of course, at first, it was going backwards at one for one. I watched the second hand wind counterclockwise for a few minutes, counting one-thousand one, one thousand two and so on. Close enough to one to one ratio.

In the speculation mode, one of the things that was scary: suppose it started to go backwards *faster* than a second at a time?

And so what?

What did it all mean anyway?

Empirically, there was only one answer: I had some residual electricity, stray voltage, excess static electricity, something, which was screwing up watches

There was another answer, though: I was going mad.

I took little solace in the fact that going backwards would mechanically dictate that the day highlighted in the window would backup one.

Idly, I wondered if my wild time-touch would affect computers, PC's, cell phones, pagers, wall clock, wind-up clocks, sundials, cable television, cables boxes, whatever.

Maybe I was dreaming, maybe this was a parallel universe and I was another Ethan Zachary. But I knew better. I was me, here, now.

When the situation boils down to the best-case scenario being that you are stark raving mad, you're in big trouble.

I needed some answers and I needed them soon.

The hospital room smelled like a wedding.

Or a funeral.

CHAPTER FOUR

Shortly after four o'clock that afternoon, my watch ticked from one second after midnight to midnight to one second before midnight. And the day changed from the fifteenth to the fourteenth.

I told myself all that proves is that my watch was broken.

Dexter Hampton was my doctor. He was also one of my golf partners. And friend. Dexter was short, but he could drive a golf ball 300 yards consistently. He had blond curly hair all over his body. He was convinced that if everybody drank more water, their health would improve immeasurably.

He walked into the hospital room like he owned it.

"Ever heard of keraunomedicine?" He handed me a glass of water. "Drink."

"No." I was sitting up in bed. "Never heard of it." I took the glass in my good hand and sipped to humor him.

"Me, neither," he said, pacing. "Until now." He turned and came back toward the bed. "Think pathology of lightning. Studying medical aspects of injury from lightning strikes."

"What other kind of aspects are there?"

That stopped him. "It can screw up your golf game."

He had me there.

"I've given you more tests than Blue Cross allows, CAT scan, ECG, EEG—for internal injuries, heartbeat, brain waves, even the new kinds of body imaging."

"I feel fine."

"According to the literature, possibilities are passing out, vision problems, chest pain, rapid heartbeat, headaches, lots of different pains. You could have tingling in your extremities, numbness, general weakness—"

"You've made my day," I said.

"I'm trying to tell you what could happen, even much later on."

"How much later on?"

He stopped pacing. "Beats me. All the stuff I read didn't say."

"Reassurance 101, they teach you that up in Gainesville?" Dexter was a product of the University of Florida, and a damn good doctor, but not a good golfer. His short game killed him.

"Call me if any of that stuff occurs."

"You bet, Dexter."

"There might be some good stuff," he said. "Stuff" must be technical medical terminology.

"Good thing."

"Seventy or so percent of lightning survivors. They have the neuropsychiatric stuff I've been addressing; sight problems, hearing and brain related stuff which can happen to you later."

"That's good?"

"We know that happens, but I've checked you inside and out and I don't think it will. You were lucky. Most of the power— the electricity—from the lightning rushes right over your body, as opposed to going through. That's called external flashover. Other than your obvious injuries, you done good. Had you been carrying coins, for instance, that would have burned your leg through your pockets."

"Okay."

He pointed at me. "I'm getting to the lucky part. You were not wearing trousers with a big metal belt buckle." He held up his hand. "And, your shorts had no zipper."

"I see your point," I admitted.

"I've told them to observe you tonight and then release you in the morning," he continued. "Unless anything turns up. And you're the one to know that the best. I say again, do you have any of the symptoms we've been talking about?"

I thought. "My strength is coming back, I don't feel so far out in left field any longer." I looked at my watch for the thousandth time. "Um." Should I tell him?

"Um, what, Eaze?"

I had nothing to lose. "Um," I held up my watch. "Look, it's broken."

"A zillion volts," he responded. "Or maybe you're so ugly you broke it when you looked at it." Then he grinned. "Although, from the attention that Elena Rodríguez woman is paying to you, that ain't the case to the fairer sex." His grin widened. "She appears quite taken with you. The newspaper had a story and the anchor read one on LNN. Why don't you give her an interview?"

"I don't feel like it," I snapped.

He sobered. "What's up, Eaze?"

I waved my watch in his face. "It's going backwards. See?"

He stepped forward. "Like I said—"

"It was working when I put it on."

"So? Some internal part finally failed. The lightning fried it a little, and finally it went haywire."

"Look at your own watch, Dexter."

Involuntarily, he did so. "Okay."

"Gimme."

He looked at me with speculation, and then shrugged. He pulled it off and handed it to me.

It was a rectangular ESQ Swiss watch. I held it in my good hand so that both of us could see. As before, the second hand was doing its assigned duty, clocking around clockwise. Then the second hand began slowing down.

It stopped.

Then the second hand began winding backwards, counterclockwise.

"Oh, shit," said Dexter.

"Me, too."

He snatched the watch out of my hand. "You better not have ruined it. Damn thing cost me $350 at the Watch Place over at

Sarasota Square Mall."

We were both staring at the watch. The counterclockwise motion slowed, stopped, and the second hand resumed its normal course.

"Good thing," Dexter said, not meaning the accusation. He picked up my arm and stared at my watch winding backwards, second by second. "You don't feel anything abnormal?"

"Not for a guy busted up with a broken arm and all," I said. "My arm itches like a banshee, that's about all."

"It's healing already. You're a quick mend." Little did we know.

Neither of us knew what to say.

Finally, he broke the silence. "Inordinate static electricity. Stray voltage, stray current, I never heard of anything like it." He scratched his head. "Nothing in the stuff I read. I saw one case on the Internet of hyper sexuality. Some guy took a hit and claimed he couldn't get enough sex thereafter. But nothing about extra left over current or electricity. I'm a doctor, not an electrician. It makes no sense."

From what I knew about electricity, me neither. "If I had stray voltage, doubtless it would've grounded out by now."

"Yep." He sat down in the bedside lounge chair, scratching his head again.

"People don't store electricity in their bodies," I went on. "But batteries do, and bodies have chemicals that might could generate some power—"

"Nah. Not in the right combinations or concentrations." He scratched his head and held up an empty water bottle.

"I'm grasping at straws here, Dexter."

"Remember though, the human body does have its own miniature version of electricity. Neurons in your brain and your brain sending messages throughout your body."

"Then why doesn't everybody else fry their watches? Tell me that, Dexter." I thought. "Or explode gasoline when you use it, or touch off forest fires, or light your cigars with your own pointy finger?"

"Okay, okay. I get the picture. Back in a minute," he said, got up and went out.

Ten minutes later—my watch was still accurate, you just have to read it backwards or subtract—he came back with a woman in coveralls. "Over there," he pointed at me.

"Do what?" she demanded.

"Multimeter. Test him."

"You're the doctor," she said. She came over and put the pointy positive and negative contacts on my good hand. "Not much. Minus point zero eight DC." She turned a dial. "One point nine volts AC."

"Try his head, his toes, his chest."

I swung my legs out.

She followed his instructions.

"Just a flicker, a shade more than before. It hardly registers, but mostly on his head or chest. Like the indicator wants to indicate, but it just flicks around."

"Try me." Dexter held out his forearm and pulled back the sleeve of his white smock.

"About the same. A little lower than him. Random."

Dexter straightened out his sleeve.

"What are you trying to do?"

"Just an experiment," said Dexter.

"You're wearing shoes, he's in bed. Ya'll are not really grounded."

"She's right," I said, climbing out of bed. My cracked ribs were not as sore as they had been earlier.

Dexter watched me with clinical interest. "It's good for you to be up and about."

"I think I'm feeling better." I tightened the belt on the hospital gown and held out my good hand.

The maintenance technician tested again. "A little higher, now he's grounded. But the indicator is still bouncing around randomly."

Dexter sat down and pulled off his patent leather shoes and his socks. He stood, and rolled his sleeve back up once again.

"Just like him, higher, still random."She rolled up her leads after testing him.

"How reliable is your tester?" I asked.

"Very. It's a Fluke 87 True RMS Multimeter."

"Thanks a million. That's all." Dexter sat in the chair again and pulled on his shoes and socks.

She left, still mystified.

Dexter came over with a Timex. "I borrowed this. Take it."

I did. Results the same. Counterclockwise when I held it, clockwise when I did not.

"I will be dipped in shit," Dexter said, "plagiarizing your term. I've read that a very few people have inordinate static electricity. They cannot wear watches or most diabetic insulin pumps. But you are not at all like that." He sat, moving a vase of roses.

"Nope. It was probably me," I said.

"Yep."

Twenty minutes later we were still sitting there. I broke the silence. "Look, Dexter. Be this as it may, I'd soon nobody but you and me knows about this."

His eyes were knowing. "That would shoot your political career right in the ass. 'County commissioner imagining things.'"

"I prefer, 'Too Hot To Handle.'"

"You going to tell Mary Lou?"

"Hell, no."

"Wise move," he said.

Before I could figure out what he meant, the door swung open and Elena Rodríguez came in with a soft knock.

"Uh, oh," said Dexter.

CHAPTER FIVE

"Hi, Doc," Elena said.

He rose, being a gentleman, and took her hand. "Could I interest you in a glass of water?"

She looked at him strangely. She had such large eyes; you'd think they would bulge out, but such was not the case. The blue orbs tracked what they watched, much without her having to move her head. Until you got used to it, it was disconcerting.

"Doctor Hampton believes water is the cure-all for all that ails the human body," I told her.

"Maybe three-quarters of our population is clinically dehydrated," Dexter said. "If you drink even five glasses of water each and every day, you can significantly reduce your chances of getting breast cancer." He couldn't help but look at her breasts, which, because he wasn't very tall, were just below his eye level. "That goes for other cancers, too," he went on, "like colon and bladder cancer—"

"Your bladder wouldn't have time to get cancer," I pointed out, trying to alleviate the doctor-lecture stage Dexter was building. I didn't use my line about increasing your water bill.

"Lack of water and the consequent dehydration is the primary cause of daytime fatigue," he said defensively. "It also contributes significantly to a decrease in metabolism, affects short-term memory, and," he eyed me, "ten glasses a day will decrease back and joint pain in most people."

"Well, I'm sold," Elena said with a smile. Each time I saw her, I liked her more. She waved a notebook at me. "See? No television cameras. Just notes. No story for LNN; we'll just run it in the paper." Her inhaler appeared from nowhere and she inhaled a dose.

Elena had a pen out and her notebook flipped open. "How do you feel?"

"Fine."

"More words, Easy," she told me.

"Like I walked away from a train wreck and should be dead."

"That's more like the Ethan Zachary we all know and love," she said.

"Unfortunately, I don't think the experience helped my golf game—" And more light comments to show I still had my faculties.

Then we went through the obligatory questions and answers, if I were going to vote for the millage increase for property taxes to pay for the extra deputies the sheriff requested, my position on the desalinization plant study, and the city of Venice trying to annex its way into financial nirvana.

At the end, she asked the obligatory question I knew was coming. She knew I knew it and she still had to ask it. "Is there a lesson that can be drawn about following safety protocols?" Translation: The editor wants to know if you're stupid, or what? And what kind of example are you setting for our children? Typical current politically correct thinking and reporting. Give me the old days when the reporter is chain-smoking, blowing same in your face and his editor doesn't care how many children get killed by lightning—in fact, the more, the better, because it sells papers.

"Of course," I said dutifully. "Politicians should know enough to get out of the rain." A little self-deprecating humor always helps—and if you say it first, it defuses. I went on. "Seriously, the golf course has an in-place safety system. The warning goes off, head for shelter. But I'd submit that on that day, the storm and the lightning weren't reading the rule book and rolled in much faster than the system worked." Obfuscation, make me not look stupid, especially seeing the rest of my foursome had made it inside.

"I knew you'd say something like that," Elena said.

"I knew you'd ask something like that," I said.

She grinned. "We're even. In case their reporter comes back, I told the *Tampa Tribune* you were unable to talk and weren't giving interviews."

"Nice watch," I said casually. "Can I see it?"

"Sure," Elena said, "over the counter at Wal-Mart."

She handed it to me and Dexter came over and deftly slid between us, his eyes glued to the watch. The second hand slowed immediately, stopped, and starting winding counterclockwise. I gave the watch to Dexter so that by the time she got it back, it would be working properly again.

Dexter handed her the watch, but Elena was not stupid.

Slowly she moved her gaze back and forth between us. "What's up?"

Dexter couldn't hide his guilty look. I, being a politician, was professional at that sort of thing.

"Nothing, really," I said casually. "Dexter and I have a standing bet you can tell a lot about people by their watch."

Her frank gaze said she didn't believe me for a minute. "What does mine tell you?"

Dexter's glance told me, So get yourself out of this one.

Politics rule one: Think fast on your feet. Rule two: Baffle 'em with BS if you don't (or can't) use the truth.

"That you got it from Wal-Mart shows you don't have time for frivolous shopping. It's more functional than aesthetic, saying something about how no-nonsense you are. And," I held up my good hand, "the big round blue dial face augments your big round blue eyes in a perfect sort of synchronicity."

"Jeez, you're good," she said admiringly. "Pure bull shit, but good. There are rumors involving you and the 13th Congressional District seat that will be open next cycle—you're good enough to go national."

"You really think so?" I said enthusiastically. Rule number twelve or fourteen, I forget: Distract and misdirect. Change the subject.

"Don't change the subject." As I've indicated, she was bright. She stepped toward me and peered between her watch still in her fingers, and me. "What's going on here, Easy?"

I tried one last time, eyeing her always-short dress. "I'm trying to stall you here so Mary Lou will see us and be jealous."

Elena snorted in a very unlady-like fashion. "That's a given nowadays. You hear the gossip down at the courthouse like everyone else. Discount ninety-nine percent and the leftovers involve your marriage problems." Another speculative look. "If you ever…I mean, if she…rather, if something…ah, the hell with it." She drew long on her inhaler. She slipped her watch back on, wrinkled her brow, looked at the clock on the wall and her watch again, shrugged, and nodded to me. "Well, we'll pursue whatever next time." I wasn't sure whether she was referring to Mary Lou and me or to the watch business. She colored slightly, touched my good hand, avoided my eyes, and turned and left.

My emotions were conflicting into major turmoil. I didn't need all this.

Dexter shrugged and left, too.

I had problems. My career. My marriage. Not to mention the world was going inexorably forward—without me?

This was beginning to sound like a weird change-of-life soap opera.

Now that I was alone, I went over to the institutional clock on the wall. Reaching up with my good hand, I grasped the clock. It appeared to hesitate and clicked forward and did so again. As it went, the second hand pushed forward one tick, quivered, and clockwise again. I didn't realize I was holding my breath until I let go. The second hand continued lunging forward, quivering, and repeating. Naturally so, I decided.

Why?

And I certainly was not ready for what happened next.

CHAPTER SIX

One week after being discharged from the hospital, I was sitting in Dexter's office. Two x-rays glowed on the lighted screen.

"Both these fancy pictures were taken of your broken arm, then and now," Dexter said, pudgy finger stabbing at the one on the left. "Note the obvious break."

"I see it."

His hand moved to the x-ray on the right. "Same arm, same person; you. Taken today, a little while ago. Where's the break?"

"It's smudged," I pointed out.

"We took a follow-up when I couldn't find the break," he went on. "Maybe there was a glitch, a switch, whatever, so I had them do it again."

"I remember. I was there," I said.

He opened one of those tiny refrigerators on the credenza behind his desk. It was full of bottled water. He took two out and handed me one.

"What's going on, Eaze?"

Pulling the plastic off the top, I shrugged. "You tell me, Dexter." He'd already removed the cast.

"I can't."

"Maybe I'm going through the change of life for men?"

"Time to be serious, Mr. Commissioner."

"All right, doctor. How's this: Today's follow-on x-ray was correct showing the arm wasn't broken; the problem was in the original x-ray, maybe it wasn't broken at all in the first place. The original was the one in error. You put the cast on unnecessarily."

"I never thought of that." He stood and went to the x-rays on the wall. Of course, they were the same arm and he'd see through my point. "That's actually possible," he murmured. "It's about the only explanation."

I was scared. You don't completely heal a broken arm in a few days less than two weeks. And that arm had been broken: I was there. So far, Dexter had not noticed, or commented upon, the regrowth of hair on my arm and on the left side of my head.

"You're a cool one, Easy," he said, sipping the last of his water. Mine was still full. "I'm the doctor. Your arm was broken, classic case, just like in med school. But think of this. Many people use electrotherapy. To expedite healing. We know you have something electrical, for lack of better terminology, screwy within you. Do you suppose?"

"Hell no," I said, and his eyes widened. I continued, "I don't suppose. I hope. I pray. If that ain't the answer, then I don't want to hear the real answer." I didn't mind healing rapidly. What I did mind was my body doing weird things. Like healing the broken arm in record time.

"Be advised," Dexter pointed his fingers at me, "stuff like electrotherapy has been around a long time, and not all is known about it. It's used for treating cancers, chiropractic uses, Fibromyalgia, sleep disorders, depression, hangnails, you name it somebody uses it. There are a million abbreviations to legitimatize it, TENS, CES, more. A pioneer, Tesla, had lots of stuff named after him. In the hospital we use EEG's, EKG's, ECG's...."

"Dexter, I get it."

He ignored me. "So, you could draw the conclusion that electricity has been used for healing and diagnosis and you might have gotten one big jolt, healing everything." He seemed to notice something, stood and walked over to me. I was sitting in a leather easy chair in his office, not in an examination room. He took my head and turned it so the left side showed. Next, he lifted my recently broken arm and studied it. "The hair is not yet fully grown back. But you know what? It's growing fast. Could we draw the conclusion that electrical activity also aids in hair restoration?"

"Sure."

"Stand up."

I did.

Dexter felt around my cracked ribs. "Twist and bend."

I did.

"I am not going to take any more x-rays. Your ribs appear to have healed, also."

At the time, I didn't think I ought to tell him that the spot of tennis elbow I had was gone, that I was sleeping very well, that the incipient arthritis in my hands was gone, that I felt better than I had in years.

He stepped back and we sat down again. "I've something for you to think about."

When he didn't continue, I raised my hands.

"Scientific method. Do you have any weird medical history in your family."

"No. Not that I know of."

"Well, you sit down tonight and list all your relatives and call them. And ask them."

"Dexter, that's tantamount to a clarion call."

He shrugged. "Your decision."

I didn't have many relatives anyway.

I was already thinking of other things, like military service and if I had been exposed to anything like radiation, which would make me into a B-movie mutant.

"Lemme tell you what I can do, too," Dexter went on. "In most esoteric branches of medicine, there is a good-ole-boys' network. I'll sort of put out some feelers and see if I can come up with something."

"Like what?"

"Similar cases."

An extremely uneasy feeling came over me. "With utmost discretion?"

"You got it. No names. Just me."

I had to trust him. What had I to lose, anyway?

When I got home, Mary Lou was gone someplace and I wasn't ready to return to work in my office downtown. Physically, I was, but....

I took the opportunity to experiment.

Windup clocks were not affected. Spring action, I guessed.

Electrical clocks, such as the one at the hospital, had strong enough current to overcome whatever force was in me directing the counterclockwise movement.

Mary Lou had a Zen Alarm Clock, one I always hated. It rang with little tiny candy-ass chimes that I hated. It was triangular shaped and manufactured with quote non-endangered maple hardwood end quote. And quote it "helps you remember your dreams and work on affirmations while in the alpha state of sleep" end quote. I hate that clock. I always wanted to take it outside and put it on top of a garbage can and pop it with a couple of dozen BB's from my Daisy. I suspect the Zen thing was a function of the New Age stuff in which Mary Lou was currently involved. A second point: politicians are opportunists if nothing else. The opportunity was here. Put the two together and I headed for her room and grabbed the damn thing. It had something called a "Japanese wave face" and on that the clock hands ground to a stop, albeit slowly, and then began to reverse themselves. I continued my experimentation, hoping if nothing else came of all this that the Zen clock would be ruined.

The cable box and the television time functions paid me no attention. Okay, they were remotely controlled and had the 110-volt power source.

The same reason applied to the time function on the bottom right of my computer's taskbar.

Then things became more interesting. The time of day showing on a pager would sort of fade and the battery symbol would appear. Cell phones had a stronger power source and the time line faded in and out, with the recharge battery symbol coming and going.

So the answers were inconclusive. Apparently, the time-force within me had limits—or just wasn't strong enough to overcome some power sources. Especially, normal AC from Florida Power & Light.

I looked out the kitchen window, through the pool cage, to the backyard. My lighthouse sundial sat there invitingly. I thought about it.

"No, no, no, no, no," I said aloud, recognizing another question I didn't want to know the answer to. Maybe later. A lot later.

Then I got on the Internet.

Google gave me over two million hits on lightning in less than one second.

I couldn't handle that, so I started surfing with my Microsoft Internet Explorer.

And then the hair on the back of my neck stood up.

The term "Ball lightning" began popping up and I surfed around and read, all the while recalling the golf ball-sized handful of lightning I seemed to remember attacking my head. I rubbed the left side in memory. The stubble was smoother.

It was variously described from the size of a fingernail to as large as a truck, but mostly in the size of traditional balls: baseballs, grapefruits, tennis balls, and, I filled in golf balls. The word "mysterious" peppered the literature. "High density plasma" sounded good, and characterized the phenomena, but likely meant more to a physicist than to me. Some said it controlled its own internal current flow by its own magnetic field. Okay. Others compared it to a microwave radiation field. I didn't like the mention of radiation, extrapolating again, mutants. "Atmospheric physics" was beyond me. But I noticed the word "mysterious" constantly reappearing. So I performed another Google search, this time for "mysterious ball lightning" and got 48,500 hits. TMI, too much information. Maybe I should have done an advanced Google search, but it never occurred to me and I was fast becoming overwhelmed.

I tried to decide which I preferred: the mysterious or radiation mutant or genetic mutant. I decided I didn't like any of them.

I went for a swim, really stretching it. My muscles felt well, the previously broken and cracked bones giving me no problem. My ancient cat, Budweiser, lay contentedly on the patio observing me. He was sixteen and losing hair and weight. He wasn't long for the world. A gray tiger-striped feline, in addition to old age, he was suffering from feluke—feline leukemia. FELV is a retrovirus, which affects cats only. They become weak and their immune system fails. It usually strikes younger cats.

Using the opportunity, I thought about my relatives. Any genetic abnormalities? None that I knew of. Both of my parents were long gone.

Actually, while my mother had been dead for many years, she wasn't really gone. She was here, sitting on the mantle of our fireplace in a blue-gray urn. Much to Mary Lou's disgust.

When my mother passed away, I'd been in the Army in a few inaccessible places and they couldn't find me right away to bring me out for emergency leave to the states. Mother had left instructions to be cremated, and my aunt had done so. The lady had saved me mother's remains. But my aunt was scatter-brained and lost mother's written instructions. Now my aunt was elderly and didn't remember any more than she didn't remember at the time. So nobody knew what mother wanted done with her ashes. My aunt blamed it on an old Gypsy curse. Since I never had her instructions, I defaulted to the mantle of the fireplace as a compromise. I'd been hoping the instructions would turn up in a trunk from an attic or someplace one day. The instructions have never miraculously appeared and Mary Lou hates mother's urn but is deathly afraid of the aforementioned Gypsy curse. I'm not sure there is such a thing.

I had a couple of elderly aunts on my mother's side and a ton of cousins on my father's side. Reviewing all of them I remembered nothing out of the norm. I supposed I could telephone some, but I'd never done so to date, none of us being close. Most of them were in Alabama, Texas, and Colorado, none in Florida.

An inquiring phone call would raise questions to which I had no answers. So I determined not to call, except as a last resort. I climbed out of the pool after fifty laps.

I checked my watch to see if the water had affected it. Nope. But.

I ran inside and held the Seiko next to my lighthouse clock. Without touching the clock. When the clock measured off one minute, my watch had gone backwards a minute and a half.

CHAPTER SEVEN

Two weeks out of the hospital. Sitting in my office overlooking downtown Sarasota. Trying to catch up. Staring at my computer screen. In the old days, there'd be stacks of paper all over my desk. Well, stacks of paper were in fact all over my desk. But much was now electronic. I'm an advocate of any kind of technological advance; however, it seemed to only augment the paper, not just replace. And experts can trace your every key stroke, every e-mail and website you touch. Check FlashYour-Rack.com to see what's new and they could hang you. But I was still reading e-mail. And looking at my watch too often.

I should have known who it was. She never waits to be announced, just insures I'm not with someone else.

The door swished open and in walked Carrie Jean in attractive shorts, tight halter and bare midriff. She was wearing two hundred dollar Nikes. Her hair was tight into a runner's ponytail. "Hi, how about lunch?"

"You can't just barge in here," I said, not much protest in my voice. As was often the case lately, I was hungry.

"Call a cop."

"I have a workshop with the planning and zoning guys in an hour."

"Call the chaplain."

"I missed you while you were off at school."

She eyed me speculatively. "How much?"

I didn't want to address it that way. "Nobody with an attitude ever came in here and gave me a hard time."

"You going to dodge the issue or we going to go eat?"

"I really do have to review and prep for the workshop."

"Ethan?"

"Um, yes, dear?"

"Listen to yourself."

"Oops. I forgot it was you."

"You're like me in college, my friend. I never had to read anything twice or even study. I know you." She cocked her head. "We need to talk."

"We live in the same neighborhood."

Carrie Jean snorted, like she was spitting out broccoli. "Don't forget who else lives at your house."

"Mary Lou's edgy these days. Maybe the change of life or something."

"Or something."

Not many people knew Mary Lou and I were separating, including Carrie Jean.

Was Carrie Jean trying to send me a message?

I rose and grabbed for my jacket and she shook her head.

We walked down the stairs. CJ doesn't do elevators. And when we went through the lobby heads turned. Einstein lied. There is something that is faster than the speed of light: gossip, followed closely by rumor.

We cut over and walked south on Washington and I loosened my tie. We stood in line at Dairy Queen a few blocks south of the county buildings. Carrie Jean ordered twice as much as I did. "Carbo-loading" she explained.

"You invited, you pay," I told her.

"Do I look like I have any money?" she said, voice little-girl innocent.

As usual I paid. When she was home, we ate lunch sometimes, mostly downtown, and mostly at the DQ.

We sat on a picnic table shaded by an umbrella and watched traffic go by on Washington. CJ ate a couple of foot-long hot dogs and a chocolate shake.

I had a diet Coke and a hot dog, even though I was hungry.

After a few moments, I looked up and she was watching me.

I offered, "If speculation is pure gold, your eyes are filthy rich. What's up?"

She looked tentative, highly unusual for her. She squeezed a quart of ketchup onto a hot dog. She was a healthy eater. Other men watched her, too.

"Hey, Commissioner," a cop said from an open window of his car stuck in traffic, and gave me a thumbs up.

"Hey, Buddy," I waved.

Carrie Jean appeared grateful for the reprieve.

She washed five thousand calories down with half a milkshake. I reached over and wiped the chocolate mustache off her upper lip.

"Want to burp me, too?" Her voice was angry.

"Sorry. I've changed your shitty diapers, and not all that long ago. What's going on, Carrie Jean?"

"Damn if I know, so I'm here to ask you."

A lot of buildup.

She took a deep breath. "I was running this morning on the golf course. A fifteen miler. Before dawn. I ran every inch of the golf-cart path and was finishing up just after dawn."

A dread seeped over me. "Go ahead."

"And what to my wondering eyes should appear? A lonely figure out golfing well before the course opens for the day. Somebody I know."

I shrugged uncomfortably. "Just working on my swing, really. I hit a few off the driving range, and thought I'd play a couple of holes."

A flight of Harleys went by and I had a momentary respite. Two or three things I'd wanted in my life I'd never done: owned a Harley and had a daughter. Maybe one other thing I wanted, but I wasn't prepared to even admit that thing to myself.

"I need the practice." I sounded lame, even to myself. "Your S&W 9-iron works great, thank you very much."

She sat silently.

I didn't have anything to say, so I didn't say it.

A brother with a boom box blaring on his shoulder walked by, saw me, eyed Carrie Jean, made a gun of his fist and forefinger, and pretended to shoot me. A stereotype?

I smiled and waved. To break the tension, I told CJ. "That was his way of complimenting me on my lunch company." Not a stereotype. An undercover cop I knew who cared enough to do that terrible job.

"You know everybody."

"Sometimes it appears so." I smiled. "If you ever get in a bar fight or a street brawl, he's the guy to have on your side. Strangely enough, his name is María."

The ensuing silence wasn't comfortable.

"See," Carrie Jean said and sighed at the same time, "I know your arm was broken. It was bent wrong."

"You?"

"Me?"

It began to fall in place. I was beginning to understand. "You must have been jogging—"

"You jog, I run," she pointed out.

"Everybody else was in the clubhouse having a beer—"

"Where you should have been," she said.

"Well, it appears you were out there, too, my dear."

"I only had a block to go. I love to run in the rain. And the fog. And the dark. And not to mention? I wasn't under a tree in a copse of trees during a gully whomper with a ton of lightning."

"I have only a hazy wisp here in my brain. I knew there was something, something else, and somebody—an angel! That's it." My phantom angel.

"Don't bullshit me, Ethan. You were lying there. With the thunder and lightning and screaming wind and rain, I couldn't tell if you were breathing or not, it didn't look like it. I performed your basic CPR."

"Some in the Mystic Far East would say you are now responsible for my life."

Her bright-green eyes were bleeding emotion. "Goddamnit! Goddamn you! Goddamn me!" She breathed deeply for a moment, regaining her composure. "I am only going to say one thing right now. I felt electricity between us. I never felt like that in my life. I don't know what the hell you did to me then and there, but I—shit." She sank back, her shoulders slumping.

She'd gotten me breathing and then hightailed it to the club-house, called 911 and while she was on the phone, a dozen people ran out to me. When she went back in the lessening rain, she was lost in the crowd. Dexter stayed with me and rode to the hospital in the ambulance. Until now, nobody knew what all Carrie Jean had done.

I remembered times when she'd come over, stubbed toes, broken bike, something. She'd needed a little bit of attention. I'd treat her toe or fix the chain on her bicycle and she'd leave happy.

Not wanting to continue this track, I said, "Thank you, dear, for saving my life. I am not sure it is or was worth saving; but if there is one person in the world I'd want to owe, it's you."

She sort of sniffed and swiped at her eyes with her napkin and I had to reach over with mine and wipe ketchup off her forehead. "Thanks," she said and eyed me.

"But that's not what you came to see me about, is it?" I said, the dread only a little bit lower in my throat.

She scooted closer to me, put her face an inch in front of mine in a proprietary manner. "No."

Pheromones. I had to answer; it was a biological imperative. "And you aren't talking about my golf game."

"Yes and no. I said I saw you arm askew a couple of weeks ago. I saw you a week ago without your cast, using your arm like it was brand new. And now, this morning you're hitting the golf ball better than ever. Since your, ah, accident, you've seemed somehow, ah how shall I say it? Vigorous is not the word—"

"For an old geezer like me?"

"Ethan! You know damn well that's not the case. Somehow, you are different. An attitude? An aura? Maybe that's it. I don't know. But it still doesn't explain a perfectly functional but previously broken and not-yet-time-to-be-repaired arm. I think I understand what I just said."

"Me, too." Her face was still in my face and her breath washed over me. "I don't know the answers, hon. Could it be the attitude-aura thing is my way of forging ahead because I *don't* have the answers and I'm scared to death?"

Carrie Jean blinked at the vehemence in my voice. My smile to defuse the situation failed.

"Down and dirty, Freckles. My arm is as good as ever now. Or better. It was broken big time. I don't know what the hell is going on. Dexter doesn't know what the hell is going on. And you make three. Nobody else knows."

"Including good ole Mary Lou?"

"Including my gracious wife."

"Good move," Carrie Jean said, echoing Dexter.

"I'm glad you approve." My voice was chock full of sarcasm.

"I'm sorry I stepped on your over-sensitive toes," she said. "Tell me."

I was going to, honest.

"Hey, Easy!" A female voice, shouted. Tires screeched. I looked over at the street and a satellite van with LNN written all over it slid to a stop. Elena Rodríguez opened the passenger door, hopped out and rushed over to us. The cameraman leaned over from the driver's side, and grabbed her door and slammed it closed. He drove off, the *Star-Banner* and LNN offices being just down the street.

"Want some company?" Elena asked innocently.

"No," said Carrie Jean.

"Um, ah," I said diplomatically.

"Thanks," said Elena, sliding onto a seat.

CJ stood. "I have to go. Don't forget your meeting," she reminded me. "'Bye, Granny," she said to Elena and walked off down Washington toward wherever she'd parked. All male eyes present followed her. There's an old saw about not judging a woman by how she looks from behind. In the case of Carrie Jean Billingsley, you could make an exception.

"Who *is* she? And why does she keep calling me that?" Elena shook her head. But surreptitiously checked out CJ. Elena had an endearing vulnerability about her.

An assistant state's attorney I knew looked between CJ and Elena Rodríguez and shook his head. "Some guys feast, the rest of us famine."

I waved as he left shaking his head. And all this at the DQ.

"Your arm is repairing well." Everybody was interested in my health.

I moved it gingerly to send the right message.

We talked politics for a while. Elena had excellent political instincts. Her political acumen was due to her natural intellect and her job covering downtown government and political operations. She tried to draw me out on running for U.S. Congress and speculated upon whom she thought would be my primary opposition. Our current U.S. representative, Palmer T. Hibbs, was retiring.

Ever since the rumors about Palmer T. Hibbs retirement hit the street, speculation ran rampant. It was said I was heir apparent. There were a couple of other big name possibilities, but I was the target of the most speculation.

Elena reached out and gently touched my left temple. "Almost ready for the camera." Her touch was more than casual; it was a caress.

Involuntarily, my eyes went to my watch. It continued to spin counterclockwise.

I had to do something.

CHAPTER EIGHT

Sunday morning, 0400.

She just had to tweak Mary Lou.

She knew I was up and would be out soon. She could tell from outside because the light was on in the kitchen, but she knocked on the front door anyway.

I scooted over and swung the door open. "Hold your horses, you're going to wake Mary Lou."

"Fat chance," said CJ.

I finished my stretching which I never do much of anyway. Carrie Jean leaned against the doorframe. "You'll be back hours before she wakes."

I stuck my tongue out at her barb. Mary Lou knew CJ and I run fifteen miles on Sunday mornings before sunrise—when CJ is in town. Mary Lou just doesn't like it.

We went out, I closed the front door and the screen door off the front porch. No need to lock up in Bent Tree where we live.

No moon, but plenty of stars, decent visibility. Neither of us had reflective tape on but we wouldn't need it.

Apprehensively, I hit the start button on my lap timer watch.

I lit out. "Hurry up, slowpoke."

She caught up easily. She could outrun me with a broken leg and a blindfold. In a few minutes we were on Bee Ridge Road heading east toward the old landfill. On the side of the landfill "mountain", really a hill, winked the obligatory lighted natural gas pipe. At four in the morning there was no traffic. We hit Bee Ridge Extension and headed south, leaving the filled-up landfill behind. Landfills and doing away with the discarded necessities of modern life were a constant headache for municipal governments.

Finally I worked up the nerve to click the LED readout. It had an hour capacity, and was now at 38:22 then :21 then :20. "Damn," I said, thinking I'd said it to myself. It was running maybe a two to one ratio now.

"What?"

"Nothing."

"I love you, too, Ethan."

"Sorry I snapped at you. I didn't intend to. I would never snap at you."

"Sure you would," she said, voice light, "you just did. Did your sweet wife cut you off?"

"CJ? Out of bounds."

"Ooops. M'sorrreee, Ethan. It seems as if sometimes I'm the only woman in your life who cares for you. It's frustrating. I have a big mouth and...well, hell."

There was more here than I wanted to deal with.

"Back to the point you started the other day?" she said, arms swinging easily. "I couldn't help but notice your profanity just now when you checked your watch. You said you and me and Doctor Hampton know this stuff. And I've noticed your current fascination with watches and clocks. Remember the hospital?"

"Sssh." I pointed. A buck and three does got wind of us and scampered into the brush. We were just passing the gated entrance to Misty Creek, another upscale golf course and country club development.

"How's your arm?" she asked.

It was swinging in counterpoint to my other arm. "Like it was never broken."

"Give."

I talked as we ran, giving her an abbreviated account. At the end, I summarized, "And some clocks and all watches still go backward and my arm healed in days short of a couple of weeks and I feel better than I have in years. Dexter has no answers."

I failed to tell her about the accelerated backwards pace of my watches.

"The genesis seems to be the lightning strike," she pointed out.

"Or your kiss," I said before I thought it through. "I mean, um, your CPR contact."

She stepped up the pace. She was a runner and just moseying because of me. I'd guess she stepped it up to a seven-minute mile, maybe quicker.

"Ethan," she said easily, "when I was a girl of four or five, remember I promised you I'd marry you when I grew up?"

"I do. You were a cute kid."

"That was my goal, the whole time I was growing up."

Worried where this was going, I said, "I don't want to talk about it."

"We haven't talked in years, Ethan. You've been avoiding me."

"You're a full woman, now, Carrie Jean. I've grown older." Or so I thought then. "Which is easier to do than get wiser. I'm married."

"You're in a rut. I've heard the difference between a rut and a grave is only a matter of depth."

"Cute, but not applicable."

"I don't want to dance around this any longer, Ethan. Down and dirty. Do you love me?"

"Hell, yes."

"How much?"

I didn't answer.

"Everybody knows Mary Lou doesn't care about you any more. You've got women falling all over themselves for you. Look at that info-babe from the newspaper television station."

"Elena. Elena Rodríguez."

"Right. See, Ethan? They didn't teach me this in law school, but I know I need to get on with my life."

"Are you propositioning me?" I asked to get it out in the open.

An owl hooted and the brush of the breeze from its passage

wafted into my face. There are some large owls out here.

"I don't know. I don't know what I want. I'm twenty-three and I've been pledged to you my whole life, Ethan Zachary. I'm done playing little girl games."

"That twenty-three is half my age," I pointed out.

"So what?"

"Interests. Approach to life. Attitudes. If you start out with someone your own age, you grow together, make the same mistakes, and learn as you go. Mary Lou and I went through some hard times together. She's tougher than you think."

"My rival. Is she my only rival?"

"Neither. It doesn't matter. She's my wife."

"Look at your watch," Carrie Jean ordered.

I did. "In twenty seconds, it will have counted down from sixty minutes to almost zero minutes."

"I clicked mine when you did. At that time my watch will have counted up to twenty-five minutes."

"What's your point, CJ?"

"Even a broken watch is right sometimes."

"Oh." She was making her point. Bright girl.

"Elena's closer to your age than I am," she said, resuming her train of thought. "Could you ameliorate the age thing with her?"

"She's not a factor." We were going too fast for mosquitoes to land and bite, but they banged into my face. We ran through a cloud of them, likely blown in from the 30,000-acre Myakka State Park out to the east. In most parts of south Florida, you can measure growth by mosquito population. When I was young, we lived near the beach in Ft. Lauderdale. When you went outside in the mornings, you could grab a handful of mosquitoes and squeeze and you'd have a mass of protoplasm. Now, much of Florida is simply steel, glass, and concrete. It's popular to lament the loss of the old days, the land the way it was. But I will say, we don't shovel our sidewalks and heat our water pipes in the mornings before we turn on the water. And I sure don't blame anybody that wants to come down here and share this lifestyle.

"Every time I've seen her, she's sending you signals even a yak could interpret."

"Since when are you in charge of my love-life?" I went on the offense, figuring that was better than I'd been doing until now.

"I ain't," she said angrily. "But I do have a proprietary interest in you. You can't deny that."

What could I say? I don't know, but I tried to think of something.

She beat me to it. "I've heard the Chinese or French have a rule of thumb. A lover or mate should be one half the man's age plus seven years." She laughed without humor. "Stupid saying and truly chauvinistic. But if you figure it, then your good friend Elena fits that bill. I do not."

She took off, maybe a five and a half minute mile. I groaned at more than the physical exertion. We always sped up when we hit the seven-mile mark, but never this fast. I increased my own pace until I was pounding the pavement hard. But she still was pulling away from me.

Then, abruptly, she slowed. I caught up and she resumed a pace with me.

"Look, Ethan, I don't mean to be snippy, but..." She could talk easily, but I couldn't, being at almost a dead run. But, I had to admit, running was easier than it had been for years, and I was keeping up a fast pace. It felt good.

"I always had a little-girl infatuation with you, dear. It was always you there when I needed somebody. No women in my life. None of Dad's string of trophy wives. Not Mary Lou, she never had time for me, maybe that's why I'm snippy about her when she's not treating you how I think she should. It was always you and I. Remember?"

My heart bled for Carrie Jean. "I do," I managed to get out.

"I went to law school to be an attorney, just like you."

"I know."

"I'm going to finish this marathon thing off, not that I care any more, and then I'm out of here. Seattle probably, where a job waits, points west, some goddamn place. With or without you."

My watch was counting down from another sixty minutes, never mind how you count them.

And I didn't know what the hell to think.

"Look, CJ. Even if I did, um, want to take off with you, did you stop to think about things? I mean, other than the basic age difference. I have a job, a career, a marriage. I'm lodged into this community tight."

"Sounds like you got a problem or two. Sounds like you're avoiding me."

"I'm trying to think it through."

"Either you love me, or you don't. Your choice."

Trying to not hurt her, I said, "Sometimes there ain't any easy answers."

"Sure there are. Yes or no questions."

I was gasping. I could run or talk, but not both, not now, not this fast.

"It has also occurred to me," she said carefully, "that while I have long sworn to marry you, I'm grown up somewhat now. And that means what if I'm wrong?" Her face was white against the night, staring into my eyes as if she could see in the night. Green flashed off her eyes. Maybe the night gave her some courage. "It has occurred to me that I don't know what the hell I'm doing."

"That tells me you've grown a lot."

"Do not patronize me, old man."

"I'm not. I promise. Cross my heart, hope to die, call the FBI." I sucked in air and coughed out some kind of night bug. "And I'm not an old man." No matter what I've been saying, I thought to myself. "And, my dear, I still dream like a boy."

"There's hope for you yet."

We ran some more. A bat screeched on its way home. A van headed for Saddle Creek to deliver the morning paper passed us.

I didn't know what the hell was going on in my life. I didn't know I'd have to make a choice with Carrie Jean. I wasn't ready to make a choice. I wasn't ready for any of this. I wasn't ready for my life to be topsy-turvy. I had been comfortable, as much as possible. And I sure as hell wasn't ready for my body to be doing whatever the hell it was doing.

We dodged aside as a three-foot gator clumped across the road, going from one pond to another. Doubtless, the alligator had eaten all the edible turtles in his last home.

"Know what, Ethan?" Her voice was enigmatic. "Sometimes that broken watch is right more than once or twice a day." She took off again, leaving me this time, and my footfalls became lonely against State Road 72.

The eastern horizon was beginning a predawn glow, but my heart felt darker than when we'd started. '

The road made a gentle curve but Carrie Jean was out of sight. At this point, as I recalled, SR 72 had once had a hard, almost sixty-degree turn in it. Occasionally, usually drunks or speeding teenagers, used to careen off the road. There had even been a couple of fatalities. Perhaps eight, maybe ten, years ago, a young man with a little marijuana in his blood hadn't slowed enough and rolled his car, ending his too-short life. His mother and sister put up a little white cross on the spot. They requested the county and the state to fix the terrible turn. The proper transportation authorities had squirmed and muttered platitudes and sympathy but the bottom line was they didn't have the money or the inclination. Speeding high school kids and drunks were not on their priority list. CJ was a friend of the kid's sister. Somebody started plugging in additional white crosses, late at night until after a few months there were twenty or thirty crosses and pictures made the paper and television news. Then the authorities took all the crosses down and after another couple of months another two dozen crosses had popped up like mushrooms after a rain. Finally the state and the county bowed and fixed that deadly turn in the road.

Nobody ever knew who was responsible.

About the same time Carrie Jean had built a short white picket fence around her window and planted some flowers inside the fence.

I wasn't a court depending on evidentiary rules. Two plus two was good enough for me. Carrie Jean wanted something done, she did it herself, and she did it quietly. She could be silent, oblique, subtle. Now she was an attorney heading out into the world: God help them one and all. But she was not being subtle with me.

Okay. I had some problems to solve. I couldn't ignore the facts any longer. I knew full well I was no longer in synch with real time. I'd just been sitting around, doing nothing, letting it happen. It was time to pursue this. Aggressively.

Before it was too late.

CHAPTER NINE

There was no doubt now that my biological clock was running backwards.

I felt better than I had in years. All the little things pointed to it. While it was bothersome that my time-touch was making watches go screwy, I could live with that. But the realization that my body was going backwards hit me hard. That lady was indeed tap dancing on my last stretched-out nerve. When your body isn't working properly, that gets your attention real quickly. And Dexter wasn't coming up with any answers, either.

Consequently, here I was at the YMCA off Bahia Vista. I pulled on my glove and tested my racquet strings and stepped onto the court.

Palmer T. Hibbs was already inside warming up. He had a wicked low kill shot and a tough serve.

"EZ, how you doin'?" Palmer was almost square, maybe 250 pounds, no fat. His short hair was already wet with sweat. He'd beat me here so he could practice before our game.

He pushed up his safety eye-guard goggles and came over and shook my hand. "I heard you had an accident."

"You could say that, Palmer. Thanks for the note and the flowers."

"Damn, boy, you lookin' good for bein' recently fried."

Palmer was Congressman Palmer T. Hibbs, 13th District of Florida, and Chairman of the House Armed Services Committee. He had recently announced his retirement at the end of his current term. Known as a "Man of the People", you could drive past his house on Saturdays, when he was in town, and see him outside mowing his lawn. You could even stop and talk to him. And, believe me, constituents did. He was so popular; opponents hadn't bothered to run against him in the last few elections.

"I'm ready. Go ahead and warm up," he said, stepping into a back corner and tossed me a racquetball.

Donning my own goggles, I moved to the front wall and played pepper for a minute, practiced a couple of serves, and worked on my own kill shot for a minute.

Palmer moved to the backcourt. "You lost last time, you serve."

I aced him once, and then was out on his kill shot.

He served high and near the back wall so I couldn't use my own kill shot, but I scooped it backhand and dumped it in the front corner.

"Nice," he said as I moved up to the serving line. "EZ, you're a whole bunch smoother than you have been the last couple times we played."

That was a compliment and serious, not just court chatter.

"Thanks, Palmer. That's part of what I want to talk to you about."

"I figgered there was something you wanted to explore."

We played two games, Palmer winning the first, me the second in a tiebreaker. My ceiling shot was carrying my game. Sweat ran off him like he'd just gotten out of the pool. After the second game, he called time and began wiping the floor with a towel. I got mine and helped.

"You ain't played this well in years."

"Thanks," I said, still breathing hard. Palmer had run me all over the court. In racquetball, you try to stay in the center of the court and the ball comes to you. Good players make the other guy run. And that makes you tired and finally the smart player, if both are close to equal, wins. Palmer was big enough to claim the middle of the court and thus he had the advantage.

We went out for a few minutes and walked over to the water

fountain.

He drank a quart or so and wiped his face with the towel he'd just wiped the floor with. The air conditioning felt good. "Down and dirty, Ethan. You want my endorsement?"

He was also known as plainspoken and didn't beat around the bush.

"That's not what I wanted to talk to you about."

"Knock me over with a feather."

I could hear the echoes of a couple of other racquetball games going on and maybe one of handball. Two teenage girls came out of a court and we moved out of their way.

"I'm looking for information, maybe help."

"You not gonna run for my seat in congress?"

"I haven't decided yet, Palmer."

"You in trouble?"

I hesitated. "Not political trouble."

"Remember, when they're kicking you from behind, that likely means you're way out front."

Smiling, I said, "I wish."

"Mary Lou?"

"Naw, she's all right."

"What, then? You bein' evasive."

"It's awkward to say, Palmer. Look, something's, uh, not exactly right with me, medically speaking. I think it's a result of that lightning, but I need to be certain."

"What do you want from me? See a doctor." He mopped his still sweating brow. And then he crinkled that brow. "What the hell's wrong with you?"

I popped a finger up. "I don't know exactly what's wrong. Neither does Dexter Hampton. And two," I continued, holding up a second finger, "I want to know for certain if it's the lightning, and not some super secret government test I might have been part of when I was a GI but nobody told us."

"That kind of stuff is greatly overstated, Ethan. Maybe back in the fifties or forties, some of that, but not recently." He blinked sweat. "Government conspiracies, Hollywood and television couldn't exist without them." He eyed me. "You bein' mysterious, afraid of a big government conspiracy?"

"Could you check?"

"Yeah," he said, "there's an assistant to the deputy director of something or other over at the Pentagon who pays attention to past hotspots. Fax me your units, dates of service, locations, stuff like that."

"I already have it; it's in my car written down."

"Smart man."

"Can you keep my name out of it?"

He was stepping over the threshold back onto the court. "I could try, but dates, units, assignments all point to you. Don't think it'll work." He grinned. "Hell, boy, they already know your name."

"What do you mean, Palmer?"

"You chased Che Guevara. You were SOG's there in Bolivia and 'Nam." He paused. "You ever get close to Che?"

Palmer was talking highly classified stuff, but it all seemed so far away now. And the cold war was over. "Got a glimpse of him through binoculars—or somebody who looked a lot like him."

"You shoulda shot the sonofabitch." Palmer stood inside the court; I was still outside, half bent over to talk through the low door.

"My rifle wasn't accurate enough that far. By the time I rounded up my crew and we moved in and took out the camp, he or whoever it was had disappeared."

"You could've saved the free world a lot of trouble."

"He bought it later, anyway."

"If your team had got him, you'd have been national hero," Palmer said.

"And a big time target," I pointed out. "For a long time."

"You were anyway, my friend. Purple hearts, silver star."

It had been Panama. The 8th Special Forces Group (Airborne) had spawned some *ad hoc* teams. We chased around Guatemala and primarily Bolivia for Che and his guerrilla bands.

"My information was your expertise in Latin America made you a valuable quantity and they shipped you out of there over to the fine Republic of Vietnam to use that expertise."

"They did that thing to me, Palmer," I said. "Spike Recon Teams out of Da Nang and Kontum."

"I know that one," Palmer said, dry-swinging his racquet. "At that corner where South Vietnam, Laos, and Cambodia all coincide."

"That's the one." I was becoming uncomfortable with this. Palmer knew too much about me. "How is it you know all this, Palmer?"

He stared at me for a moment. "I had you vetted. I don't like surprises." His gaze was intense. "You're the logical one to take my chair in the congress when I quit and I got a proprietary attachment to it. I don't want some unworthy political hack taking it." He smiled and the intensity went away. "Now you know."

Nodding, I didn't know whether to feel flattered or apprehensive. "Let's play ball and not talk about me."

"That's not a good attitude for a politician," he told me and turned toward the court.

I followed him through, ducking through the doorway and swung the door closed.

I had to admit he was right. But I had to go through with it.

"I'll ask for their discretion. They owe me." The armed services brass did owe him. "But be advised, EZ, that from then on, somebody will know something and if you get my job, then...."

"I see your point, Palmer. I thought about it, but I have to know. I have to take the risk." I picked up the ball and bounced it.

"All of which makes me mighty curious," Palmer said, fixing me with a glare. "Especially, if whatever you got is bad enough to check twenty, thirty years back for secret military projects."

It had been apparent to me when I decided to talk to Palmer, that I'd have to tell him about it. I didn't want to; I didn't want more people knowing about weird time-touch and backwards biological clocks within me. I'd always been a private person. But I recognized this stuff was dynamite, politically and personally. However, the end state of my health should override other considerations. All this debate didn't matter. I still had to know. I gave Palmer an abbreviated version, without alluding to my backwards-spinning biological clock. I showed him my watch going counterclockwise.

"I'll be damned," he said, with skepticism. "I never heard of anything like that."

"Me, neither, Palmer. That's why I'm willing to go to these lengths."

"You know, if this gets out, your political career is down the toilet."

I nodded. "Oh the other hand, I need to figure out what's wrong with me. That's my priority right now."

In the end, he beat me, four games to three. The thing that kept me in the game was my high ceiling-front wall Z shot, which actually made him do some running. But it wasn't enough. He was still better than I. I hoped this wasn't a harbinger of things to come.

We went out to the parking lot where I got my Army service list I'd made. Removing it from my briefcase, I handed it to him. "Thanks, Palmer." Then I thought. "You already know this stuff."

He grinned. "I do, but I didn't write it down. I just need a formal list for this guy over at the Pentagon." He paused. "And I won't tell 'em what's the problem. I'll let this guy tell me if there are any possibilities. You don't remember anything out of the ordinary?"

"It was all out of the ordinary. But nothing that would have any bearing on my current condition."

"No playing with nukes or radioactive materials."

"None." I thought. "That I remember. Agent Orange exposure of course."

He scratched his still wet head. "Somebody who doesn't

know you might suggest a shrink."

He was very diplomatic.

I showed him my arm. "Note I just played racquetball with you. Less than a month ago, this arm was broken and in a cast."

"You mend quick, boy."

I held up my watch and he watched it tick backwards. He shrugged. I pointed at his watch and reluctantly he took it off and handed it to me.

Steel colored, metal band, it was an expensive looking Baume & Mercier, with three small inset dials I couldn't make out here outside. Palmer observed with interest on his face. As the second hand ground to a stop, his face froze. Then the second hand began to reverse and his face became a believer. "I need to see the shrink," he said in an uncharacteristically somber voice.

I wondered what else could go wrong.

CHAPTER TEN

Two nights later, after dinner, Mary Lou and I were sitting out by the pool. I was smoking a García y Vega and she was drinking a gin and tonic. The night was warm and a breeze blew the cigar smoke away from her.

Since she'd decided on the separation, we'd taken to having a conversation every night, like we'd done when we were young.

Something was bothering Mary Lou. Something other than our separation. We'd been through the obligatory small talk and she was still hemming and hawing, working up to something. Of course, I had an idea or two about what it was, namely me. But I'd let her get to it.

"You ought to think about growing a beard," she said enigmatically.

"Not to cover my ugly face?"

"Not ugly, Ethan. Far from it and quite the opposite. I think you know what I'm talking about."

"Not exactly."

"Well...."

And the phone rang. She always kept the mobile next to her.

"Zachary's." She handed it to me. "For you. Dexter."

"Hey, Dexter," I said. "Good news, I hope."

"It's why I called you, Easy. Nothing yet. I just got the last call back a few minutes ago. I'm thinking of charging you double-time night rates."

"Think in terms of a special taxation district for your street."

"Never mind. Listen, I've networked out everywhere I can

think of, discreetly, of course. And I still have feelers out across the land. The results are a big fat zero. I've been through tech data, medical publications, research papers, on the web, you name it. I found a few psychics who claim they can stop clocks with their minds; a couple of people who swear they can zap other people comatose with some kind of internal energy or electricity or mind force; and one unconfirmed case of spontaneous combustion."

"A real person burst into flames?"

"It's what they said, and I didn't want to know the particulars."

"Who's on fire?" asked Mary Lou.

"Nobody we know, just somebody Dexter read about."

Dexter said into my ear, "Am I interrupting something?"

"Nope. Mary Lou says hi."

"I already said hi to her. As I was saying, I'm ignoring that kind of stuff. You can check it out yourself. The Japanese have a name for the energy some people can control with their bodies and/or their minds, and it's called ki. The Chinese call it chi. Anyway, if I find anything else, I'll call. I got one lead that... well, never mind."

"What is it, Dexter?" He had a lead?

"Oops. Not exactly a lead. It's a place, a research somethingorother you just hear whispers about. I've inquired. I'll follow up if anything comes of it. How are you feeling, Easy?"

"About the same, only more so."

"Ah," he said professionally. "I interpret that to mean you are still advancing to the rear, so to speak, and do not wish to address it front of the lovely Mary Lou."

"More or less."

"I'll call you if you need anything." He always said that.

I handed the phone back to Mary Lou. She claimed the proprietary rights to it.

My cigar had gone out and I lighted it with a kitchen match.

"What is Dexter telling you?" Mary Lou asked innocently.

"Just a follow up. Checking to see if I'm okay." My words

sounded lame even to me.

"And are you okay?"

"Sure. Why wouldn't I be?"

"Aye, there's the question." She toasted me with her gin and tonic.

Not having anything constructive to say, I didn't say it.

"And clear glasses," she said.

"To go along with the beard?"

"Bright boy."

The phone rang again. She answered again, sat straighter in her chair and smiled widely. "Well, Palmer, always nice to speak to you, too. No, here he is." She handed me the phone.

Apprehension came over me, why I do not know.

Palmer T. Hibbs came right to the point. "EZ, I talked to this guy yesterday and faxed him the info."

"Any luck?"

"Only if you count elimination of hypotheses luck." Palmer could go from Florida Cracker to university professor in one sentence. I think he meant he didn't have any good news. "Your Army units went to war and so on. Nothing on you, either in Vietnam or South America. But my investigation did turn up something I never heard of: some 600 sailors involved on ships in the Pacific, 1964 to maybe 1968. VX nerve gas, an agent called sarin. Not applicable to you. Computers are a wonderful thing these days. No hits came up on his program. And he wasn't aware of any *special projects* that would apply. And he *knows* if anybody does."

"Hollywood would toss in a government conspiracy right here," I said into the phone.

"Vastly overrated, my boy. Like I said, maybe in the fifties or forties, not now. No other similar cases. And be advised, he's tapped into the VA's systems, too. That Gulf War stuff, some still ain't solved or even categorized."

"I'm running out of options, Palmer."

"The only thing he could come up with, EZ, is Agent Orange."

"Operation Ranch Hand," I said. "They were in C-123's, out

of Da Nang, they sprayed the jungles to defoliate areas to keep Charlie from hiding there. It's likely I was sprayed at some time or traveled through an infected area."

"That's it. You said it before."

"I was on the flight line near the Ranch Hand operations once waiting for a chopper and they refilled their tanks, overfilled, spilled, hell I don't remember."

"You can check the VA website. The VA has authorized treatment for certain medical conditions they've found connected so far. But, I want to tell you, none of them matches your symptoms."

"Dead end," I said.

"That it is. Listen, got a pencil?"

"For what?"

"A name and phone number."

"Tell me. I'll remember." It's one of the things I do.

He did so. "You ever heard of remote viewing?"

"Hell, yes."

I knew enough that remote viewing is like a methodological or scientific clairvoyance.

"This guy I'm talking about over at DOD knows this other guy who owns a business in remote viewing. You might call him and put him on your problem."

"I will think about it," I said, not knowing what to think about it. This was getting ridiculous. Paranormal? Not exactly. Remote viewing had been a secret Defense Intelligence Agency project from the mid-1970s through the mid-'90s. I don't recall all the stats or why the program was discontinued. I remembered that it had been pioneered at the Stanford Research Institute in California. "Think this friend of a friend can help?" I asked, trying to conceal my skepticism.

"Tell me what other choices you got, EZ."

"To be honest? None."

Mary Lou was just sitting there watching me, intelligent eyes taking everything in. Budweiser, my cat as opposed to our cat, was lying under my chair as if the umbrella of my presence was preferable to being elsewhere.

When I thanked the congressman and hung up, Mary Lou clinked the ice in her empty drink. "Has Palmer promised you his endorsement?"

"No."

"Why not?"

"He asked if I wanted it and I said I hadn't decided whether to run or not."

"What's that got to do with anything? You need to sew up his endorsement before somebody else gets it."

"He's his own man, Mary Lou. He'll endorse whomever he wants."

"Yet you played racquetball with him and talked to him on the phone tonight. Two good opportunities and you blew it."

"I don't think in terms of blowing his endorsement."

"Well, Ethan, I doubt any other potential candidates play racquetball with him or receive phone calls from him at night."

I shrugged.

She continued, still swirling her ice. "One might think that you aren't serious about running for congress."

"If I do, I will be."

"It's like a garden. You have to do a lot of work before the harvest. And this was a missed opportunity."

"I might point out that as much as you want me to run for congress, you separating from me with divorce a likely consequence, puts me in an awkward position. Divorced candidates are elected all the time. Not many undergoing divorce are."

She didn't answer, just looked at me frankly.

"So that kind of negates your interest in my political career. Does it not?"

She nodded, her eyes glued to mine. "Ethan, if you get elected to congress, we can go back to the way we were. I won't consider divorce."

"Oh." Was her desire for the status high enough to subjugate whatever bee she had in her bonnet? I still didn't know what the problem was, and Mary Lou wasn't talking at all. I guess I was supposed to figure it out on my own.

Or maybe she didn't know herself. Change of life? Midlife crisis? All I knew was that I'd been totally shut out. I knew she wouldn't follow this line now; she still had something else to address.

I studied my cigar. García y Vegas are mild and unobtrusive. She'd get to her main point soon.

She got up, went through the sliding glass door and made another drink in the kitchen. When she came back, she sat on the edge of the pool and put her feet and legs into the water. She looked up at me. "Is this mystery part of what's going on with you now?"

I wanted to play ignorant, to draw her out, but I couldn't. "Hence your comment about the beard?"

"Yes." She sat her glass on the edge of the pool and watched the condensation run off it. "Have we been married so long you think I'm blind?"

"Not at all."

"Why don't you confide in me?"

I ducked my head and looked at her with my eyes pointing like they were looking over the top edge of glasses.

"Well," she said with a self-deprecating smile. "You know what I mean. This is a separate subject. And something off-the-wall is happening. What's wrong? Why didn't you tell me something was wrong? You need to share. If you need help, maybe I'm still here."

How should I answer that one? I would like to. "I was too scared." It was an awkward reply, but close to the truth.

"Don't you think I could help? We used to talk to each other, which was good enough. It feels like we're growing apart." She certainly was sending mixed signals that I couldn't decipher.

"It does," I admitted. "We shouldn't. Not after all these years." Saying two things at once.

"You've got your life, I've got mine. It's worked out well these last few years." She nodded, agreeing with herself. "Perhaps

I've been too caught up in my own things; perhaps I've ignored you too much." She kicked water.

"We're both at fault doing that." I agreed with her. We had been growing apart, for a couple of years. That was part of the problem, but not the genesis. "I don't like it. It's not the way we made it this far." I blew a smoke ring.

"Fine with me." She fixed me with a stare, a thing at which she was highly proficient. "You haven't really needed me or my counsel for years."

"It just appears that way," I said.

She shrugged enigmatically.

"But," I said tentatively, "it appears to me that you want this congress thing a lot more than I do." Now she was interested in my career again.

"I'd kill for you to go to Washington."

"Not me, I hope."

"Back to trust, Ethan? Do you think I'm stupid?" As if we weren't separated at her insistence.

She sounded like she had a chip on her shoulder and wanted to fight, but I thought that it was deeper than that, that she was struggling with what she wanted to say. I get like that, get tongue-tied and say the wrong thing. So I waited.

"Your arm should still be in a cast. You're playing golf, racquetball, tennis, and you're running a lot more." She glared at me. "You run with that cute little lawyer wannabe twit, Jack's daughter. She's after you like a bitch in heat." She kicked her legs in the pool, shattering the surface. "You're the same, but different. Are you going to tell me what's going on?"

"Yes. It's why I'm not giving my full attention to my current and possible future public service career. Since I broke my arm and had my lightning accident, something has been happening to me."

"What?"

"I don't know."

"More, Ethan. Elucidate."

I told her about watches. "And so my biological clock seems

to be going backwards," I finished.

"Jesus. Dexter has no clues?"

"Not a one. But he's working on it, night and day. He's got medical feelers out all over the place. But nothing has turned up."

"Brief me."

I told her of all the medical tests, from body imaging to blood tests. Literature reviews. No similar cases.

"And Palmer Hibbs?"

"He's chairman of the Armed Services Committee. He checked out my military service to see if I wasn't an unknowing test subject, or some unit I was in was part of some obscure test. Like you see in the movies—"

"Or reruns of *The X-Files*."

"He found nothing. He recommended I check with some-body else he knows."

"Who is?"

I felt stupid in saying it. "A remote viewer."

"A what?"

I told her what remote viewing was. "Scientific," I finished. "A detailed procedure in which you search for detailed infor-mation remotely. From far away geographically speaking. Supposedly they can go back or forward in time. The remote viewer isolates his or her mind and information on the target allegedly flows into the remote viewer's subconscious."

"Like channeling?"

"It's not channeling."

"And you're going to put all your money on this?"

"No, I don't know if I'm even going to contact the guy." But I didn't have much choice. When you're out of options, you take the last chance. And even if remote viewing worked in this case, did I want to know the answer?

"Ethan?"

"Yes, dear?" I knew that voice.

"Do you trust me?"

"Sure." She was building up to something.

"What do you think about parapsychology? How about past-life regression? Astrology? Psychic readings. Channeling."

"Um." Jeez. She was into all that new age stuff. "For what purpose?"

"Finding answers. We can't blame a radioactive spider on this."

"I'm not certain they will help, Mary Lou."

"And this remote viewing will?"

"Hell, I don't know. I don't know much of anything right now."

"I know one thing right now. You better start growing a beard. And you're not wearing your reading glasses to read any longer. Buy some clear glasses."

"It's that obvious?"

"It's beginning to be. People will think it's the beard that makes you different these days. It'll be light like your hair. And the glasses will give the impression of age. A little misdirection."

She was right. I didn't necessarily want to conceal anything; but on the other hand, I couldn't answer any questions truthfully.

And I thought things couldn't get any worse.

CHAPTER ELEVEN

Just another day at the office.

Yeah, right.

Paperwork, meetings, phone calls.

I had to wait a couple of hours for the central time zone to get to work. Then I used my cell phone because I didn't want a public record of the number I was calling.

L. Lloyd Yaroslav had been a major in the Army and worked for the NSA and CIA in several capacities. He'd been in the remote viewing program and now owned his own remote viewing business in Dallas. FarReaching Research performed remote viewing for clients at a high price. They also ran remote viewing training programs for amateurs and professionals.

Palmer Hibbs' name got me through to Yaroslav.

"My friend at DOD told me I might be getting a call," he said.

"Here I am, Major. I have a problem and I have no answers. And there are no easy answers to be had, either."

"My services are expensive."

"Done."

"Additionally," he said, "we require waivers, signed paperwork, and the normal administrative soup you'd ascribe to this kind of thing. But, I repeat, you have friends in high places. Give me an address and I'll fax them or e-mail them and you can download them. And then return by next day mail."

"I prefer fax." I gave him my fax number.

"Do you know anything about scientific remote viewing?"

"I am familiar with it. You all travel places and in time in a non-physical form."

"Good," he said, his voice clear over the cell phone. I imagined a man in a three-piece suit with a drooping mustache. "We use a standardized methodology and go through it procedurally." He'd been in government all right. "And you would be the target?"

"I am." The assistant over at DOD had been specific to the major. This showed more interest than I wanted, but I had no choice.

"It involves you and an incident?"

"Yes. I need to know anything you can tell me about the cause, or what you-all can perceive about me in the future."

"We do a lot of sketches, but I don't think that is called for in this case."

"Right, Major."

"Ahh." He was silent for a moment. "Mr. Zachary, even without remote viewing, I sense a huge skepticism within you."

"I've never been involved in anything like this before, Major—"

My office door swung open and Vince MacLean walked in.

"That is not important," continued Yaroslav. "But I will say we are straight up, please note our credentials." He was referring to his high government contacts.

"It's fine with me," I said, non-committal because of MacLean.

"Something is going on there," Yaroslav said. "I can tell."

"You are clairvoyant."

"We hate that word." Yaroslav's voice was dry and serious.

"Right, just a second please." I looked at MacLean and didn't cover the mouthpiece. "Hey, Mac, let me get back to you in a minute, okay?"

"Cell phone, ambiguous conversation, must be a woman not your wife," MacLean said with a leer. "I'll be in my office." He left and the door closed automatically behind him.

"I'm alone again," I told the major.

"Right, chap," said the major's voice. "Be advised that we are very busy. But you have friends in high places and I can insert your case somewhere soon. Give me your e-mail address and I'll send you our charge list."

His firm was high end and he was going to work me in. Even if I had friends, this was over and above. Which led me to believe that the aforementioned friends had convinced him to take my case immediately. Which led me to wonder.

"Price is no object, and I understand this is all completely confidential."

He paused. "We cannot operate otherwise." The change in his tone told me I hadn't had to bring that up. But he knew enough about me that since I did bring it up I was asking if he would keep it from Washington. He was sort of affirming that would be the case.

"I guess we understand each other, Major. I do appreciate your helping me out on such short notice." I was telling him, Okay, I trust you not to tell your friends what you've found out about me. It was as good as I was going to get.

"And I suppose you do not wish to put this on paper or in an e-mail?"

"You're good, Major." Not paper or electronic trail. I gave him my credit card number. The fax had to be okay.

"Okay, Mr. Zachary. Our protocols, you understand, might not turn up something useful to you; on the other hand, they might." He laughed, telling me he knew something about my problem already, which likely violated his protocols. "We can talk about it somewhat, since I will not be the remote viewer on this one. We'll select one of my people randomly as we always do. I just don't usually handle this preliminary set-up. The first info we'll get will be rough, and then as we get into the thing, we pick up sounds, visuals, whatever we can. Our procedures lead us to higher level target contact, such as geographical and so on."

"I already suspect where and when it happened."

"All right, let's talk."

When I was finished talking with the major, I went in to Vince MacLean's office. So as to not be like him, I called him on the intercom and told him I was coming in.

He was sitting behind his desk, a great big, ugly thing with mahogany and curlicues and western designs.

"Did you get the report on Midnight Pass?" He pulled his center desk drawer out a couple of inches and shoved it back to the fully closed position. That was one of his maddening habits.

"No, is the engineering firm done with it?"

He nodded. "We need to talk about it."

"Let us not violate the Sunshine Law," I pointed out.

He frowned. "Look, Commissioner, let's get this over and done with. It's going to cost too much."

"Let me read the report first, Mac. You got a copy?"

He shook his head. "They sent it to me as an e-mail attachment."

"So you receive things in advance," I said.

He grinned. I don't want to characterize his grin as evil, because it wasn't. It was, though, sort of "What did you expect?" and I shrugged.

"Gotta stay ahead of the curve," he said. "The actual report won't be here for a week or so in snail-mail, but I can send you a copy on my machine." He turned to an equally ornate credenza behind him, and hit the on switch on his computer.

When the screen came up, he typed in his password with two fingers and the asterisks filled the space. Of course, it wasn't hard to read as he typed, ignoring me. I didn't really care what his password was but it was easy to follow as he typed it in. NUMBER1. It figured. Likely, he was usually careful with his password, but I had my own and he was with a peer and didn't worry about it. And most people assume others are forgetful.

"We can't discuss it until the formal report arrives," I said.

"I want you to be ready and we'll finish this mess off," he said smugly, sure of himself. The report must help validate his position.

"Be prepared," he admonished me. Then he cocked his brown eyes up at me. "You hot after that little Cuban?" Elena.

"I'm not hot after anybody, Mac."

"There was another hot babe seen with you in your office the other day," he said salaciously. He moved his center desk drawer in and out. He was referring to Carrie Jean Billingsley.

"An old friend."

"Not old at all, Zach. For a man of your years. Way to go."

"Leave it alone, Mac."

"How about Mary Lou? Is she aware of your dalliances?"

I just shook my head and walked out of his office. I heard his desk drawer slam closed as the door swung shut. Sometimes I didn't like this job at all.

Elena Rodríguez was knocking on my door.

"Hi," I said from behind her. The view was as good from behind as from in front. While that is a sexist statement and I ought to be shot for thinking it, I will say that my eyes ain't broke and they needed exercise to keep them in shape.

Startled, she turned. But she recovered quickly. She shook out her thick, long and dark hair and her eyes flashed. "Got a minute?"

"Is this official?"

"No, sir, Ethan. Private."

Damn. "Come on in."

MacLean came out of his office donning his Stetson and stopped when he saw us.

Damn.

His wicked grin was your basic "I told you so." He moved down the corridor smiling.

We went in. "Have a seat."

"I don't have time. I just need to ask a favor."

She stood in front of me with a wistful look on her face. "There's a press awards banquet. I need an escort. Would you be it?"

Damn.

I grimaced. "Elena, it wouldn't look good, me being married

and all."

Her smile was sad. "You said that so nicely." Then she shrugged. "Well, I tried." Then she broke into an endearing grin. "Am I being too obvious?"

"Enough to make me wish I was young and single again."

She stood back and regarded me. "My Cuban heritage, well, fine men with wisdom and those who carry their years well, they are to be prized by women of any age." Again her eyes searched me up and down. "However, it is evident you carry your years so very well."

This was becoming uncomfortable. "Are you going to receive one of the awards?" The old divert their attention trick.

"They won't tell us."

"I've read your stuff and you deserve it."

"Why, thank you sir. You're too kind."

She still exhibited some of the Olde World courtesy you don't find anymore.

"Tell me when and where. Perhaps I can make it." Mary Lou had dropped the gauntlet.

"I will write it down and remind you."

"I don't have to write things down."

"Oh, yes, I forgot for a moment."

So had Vince MacLean.

CHAPTER TWELVE

The next day, Elena Rodríguez caught me on the way into a formal County Commission meeting. She attended all the meetings, and knew the politics backwards and forwards. You need to know something political, or some politician's motive for doing something, she'll figure it out immediately.

"A heads up, Easy. I was down in the newspaper's library this morning looking something up about Midnight Pass and there were two strangers down there."

"Okay."

"Sydney, she runs the library? She told me they had credentials from some newspaper in Greensboro, North Carolina, and somebody gave them reciprocal courtesy and turned them loose down there."

Elena would get to the point eventually.

"They were going through the archives, hard copy, newspapers, microfilm, stories and all on disk. About you."

"Oh, good. Why, though?" A feeling of dread came over me. My sense of danger started waving flags.

"I don't know, Ethan. They weren't very friendly, either."

"Describe them."

"One male, one female. Male, maybe thirty, thirty-five. Close cropped hair, sunglasses even inside. Like a Hollywood star concealing his identity. Female, tall, stunning, maybe six feet, an inch or two shorter than you, auburn hair in a pile atop her head. Half heels, gray type female business type slacks, white shirt tucked in."

My first thought was: government. The Defense Department couldn't resist, if for no other reason, then to check me out for future reference. But why would they use press credentials?

"Thanks a bunch, Elena." I touched her hand in appreciation and headed for the meeting.

Elena grasped my hand. "Sydney owes me. She'll let me know if anything else turns up. Or she learns anything."

My scalp was prickling like it was full of itching powder.

Elena was still holding my hand; but here gaze had fixed on my face. "Easy? Is that you?"

I'd gotten a lot of that lately. My incipient beard. I rubbed my face with my other hand and gave her a grimacing smile. "It's me. Don't I look more distinguished?"

She reached up and stroked my cheek, an unusually familiar gesture on her part. "Well, maybe in the scruffy stage of distinguished. It's kind of cute—now. Like your curly hair. I can't envision you with a full beard." Her fingers lingered on my cheek and I didn't know what to do.

Vince MacLean, commissioner from the Venice area district, broke up the awkward moment. "Come on, Zachary. Stop wasting the taxpayers' money flirting with the press."

"Hey, Mac," I said. "On the way."

Elena jerked her hand away as if stung. She looked at the floor, color flushing her face, and then fumbled in a pocket for her inhaler to cover.

I chucked her under the chin, which made it us against him, and she smiled her appreciation and stepped away. Mac was always the last one to the meetings. Infamously so. He had two hard and fast rules: First thing in the morning when he arrives at work, he goes straight to his bathroom for his "constitutional"; all the secretaries and staff know not to bother him until after. And just before each commission meeting, he does the same thing—that's why he's always the last to arrive.

Vincent MacLean III was a wealthy rancher down in South County, and my chief rival. He was chair of the county commission this year. Generally speaking, if I was for something, he was against it and vice versa. The genesis of his enmity was that I had defeated his protégé to gain my seat on the county commission. He hated being called Mac; therefore, I did so. He always wore formal rancher garb to these occasions. A big wide, white Stetson, a string tie, and highly polished boots. He owned a bunch of land he wanted to develop—not necessarily a bad thing, but it had to be done right so the taxpayer didn't pick up the tab on the entire infrastructure. I'd blocked a couple of his moves on that one, not so difficult because he had to recuse himself from voting on those matters since he had a financial interest. Had his protégé been in office, the measure would have carried. He, of course, blamed me. Some rumors had him running for Palmer's seat. Some of those same rumors had him running against me.

My pet project was reopening Midnight Pass, a cut in between two keys (read barrier islands, but to chambers of commerce, keys sounds better). Midnight Pass had closed naturally because the county let the wrong seawalls and other under-the-bay terrain changes occur. Toss in storms and bang, Siesta Key and Casey key were now connected and the bay had lost its closest source of renourishment. MacLean had blocked my efforts successfully, the last time by pushing it off on another study. Another difference in styles between him and me was that I usually was the one who initiated whereas he merely reacted, hardly ever starting anything on his own. Why they voted him in is a mystery. I guess money and slick talking do account for much in politics.

As we walked into the big room and took our seats, he said, "There ought to be a dress code. Most of us shave before we come to these formal meetings."

"Elena Rodríguez thinks my beard is cute," I told him to irritate him further.

"Are you stepping out on Mary Lou?"

Mac was sharp, he'd set a trap for me and I walked right into it.

"Not at all, Mac. Just screwing with you." I kept my voice

down and checked to see if my microphone was on. I was safe. The proceedings would go out over cable access. Elena was the political reporter for the paper and LNN and would have a condensed summary of anything of significance that we did this day. Some cynics would say that nothing government does has any significance; and theoretically, they might be right, but we can take their money and spend it however we want. That doesn't sound right, but it's the way things work. There has to be a better way.

The county attorney stepped between MacLean's seat and mine and turned to me. He thunked my mike with his pointy finger to insure it was still off. "EZ, what's going on with you?"

I pawed my jaw line. "It's my new look, Miles."

"That's not what I'm referring to. You're getting a background check from the feds. What's up?" Miles Tonchot was bright and ambitious. But he hadn't taken the steps I had to play out his ambitions. He would one day and all his training at the county level would pay off. We got along so well because generally we agreed on most of the issues. And we both had a healthy dislike for Vince MacLean.

My plate was already full of dread for several obvious reasons. Now it runneth over. "Tell me what you're talking about Miles?"

"An older guy, I don't remember his name. Federal credentials, asking around about you."

"I never heard of federal credentials. FBI or Treasury or INS." I was stalling for time, trying to think, and not getting very far.

"Maybe it was DOD, hell, they didn't tell me. That's all I know. I'll try and find out."

"Palmer Hibbs is a member of several subcommittees; he said something about testimony. I don't recall for which subcommittee."

Miles pulled his glasses off and looked down at me. "Bull shit, Easy. You don't forget anything, not ever." His voice was still a whisper.

"I remember now," I said lightly. "It was about lightning strikes and some National Safety Council position." I had an idea. "Suppose they get me appointed to some fancy bureaucracy; then I won't run for Palmer's seat. That way Vince MacLean can get his guy back in this county commission seat and he can take the thirteenth district. A full sweep."

Miles waved his granny glasses. "That, Easy, is positively Machiavellian. It's worthy of what they'd do to get both seats. So the Feds are vetting you."

"Could be." I'd almost convinced myself.

"Would you take it?"

"Beats me." I wanted to be noncommittal about everything.

He eyed me closely. "You might have to shave. That stubble makes you look like a crook." He waved his glasses. "I know, I know. The definition of a politician. Your views are well known." He paused. "I'd think Hibbs' seat in congress would be more suited to you than some high level bureaucrat job." He put his glasses on. "You have that younger male look they talk about these days. Curly hair, no gray. Good-looking candidate, and that never hurts. That way they won't say you're too old for the job and would retire before you could get enough seniority to help the district and the state. And if they do say so, your looks would defuse that attack." Meaning my new younger image. I suppose when someone sees you, they assume that's how your appearance has been without thinking, in my case, that I actually did look younger because I was in fact becoming younger. I think.

Miles was always thinking. Which he was, I suddenly realized. This was a multi-layered conversation. Miles was aiming for something and I thought I knew what it was.

I stood so no one could hear. I whispered to him. "You're good enough to be a campaign manager, Miles."

He grinned. "I knew you were the right man for the job. I'd be available, and I've plenty of contacts for raising money."

It all came clear to me then. He had political aspirations, but no guts. He'd satisfy them vicariously through me. The train of logic here was that he'd be a successful campaign manager, and then translate that into chief of staff for an up and coming congressman. And doubtless he'd already handicapped our two U.S. senators, when the first would retire or be vulnerable, and projected me running for that seat after four or six years. The offer was sitting right there in front of us. The thing was, though, that Miles was good enough to run on his own for the seat. He was bright and had the right instincts and his political bent matched well with the local electorate. Maybe he was thinking of hustling me into the senate from the platform of the 13th district seat, and then he could jump into the water for the then open 13th congressional seat.

Vince MacLean was clearing his throat and everybody in the auditorium became quiet. It also wouldn't surprise me if Mac actually did enter into the competition for Hibbs' job; but I think he knew if it were me against him, he'd lose. He always came across too smug, glib and condescending. How he keeps getting elected is beyond me.

I had to give Miles something. "Very attractive proposition, Miles. Cover my back like you've been doing and I'm certain things will work out for both of us." Everybody was looking at us now. Miles nodded happily and made his way to his seat. The political silly season was beginning to kick in. My next move, read here my future, would start the dominoes falling. It was intriguing that Miles had just declared himself. It meant that suddenly a political demarcation was occurring; now there were two camps, where before it was mere political sniping and squabbling. Miles was a highly astute and ambitious young attorney: it was time for him to move on and up; and that vehicle he selected was me.

Leaning back, I wondered. Reporters from North Carolina and an investigator from Washington? As if I didn't already have enough problems. But now Miles was on my team and he's an effective political combatant. Not to mention, as the Sarasota County Attorney, he was in a perfect position to assist. I thought about it and decided I needed to know who these people were and what the hell was going on.

Or did I?

The old saw, if you don't want to know the answer to the question, don't ask that question.

After the meeting and back in my office, I made a few phone calls. I didn't want to, but I did.

I asked Elena Rodríguez to see if the two reporters from Greensboro were still anywhere around the newspaper and if so, tell them to come and see me or call me.

I did the same with Miles about the so-called federal investigator, trying to keep both low key.

Nothing happened. Nobody called or came to see me. I didn't want to give the researchers, if that's what they could be called, too much significance, so I couldn't call around asking about them, nor could I call Elena or Miles and see if they'd had any success. Apparently they had none, anyway. Maybe those seeking information about me had found what they were looking for and returned to wherever they had come from.

Not likely, not with my current string of luck.

Which turned worse when I got home later that afternoon.

CHAPTER THIRTEEN

Mary Lou had been dabbling in astrology for a while. I'd ignored it, of course, figuring it would go away. I'd never had any use for physic insight, New Age, old age, any damn age stuff.

"I'm only trying to help," she said.

The physic was sitting in the dining room laying out cards on the dining room table.

"She's going to tell my fortune?"

"She projects what the future has to offer." Mary Lou was insistent. Was she hiding something?

"How is this trying to help me?" I asked softly, not wanting my voice to carry.

"Maybe, just maybe, Dolly can figure out what's wrong with you."

"By flipping cards?"

"Yes." Defensively.

"I'd do better playing poker with her."

"Don't be flippant." Mary Lou was going on the offensive.

"It's, it's—" I had no words. "I don't need this kind of help."

"You need something. What can this hurt, Ethan?"

"My political career you seem so locked-on about. That's what it can hurt. Just envision the headlines: 'Candidate consults psychic.' Nancy Reagan got laughed at for the same thing. And there goes the election."

Fear streaked across Mary Lou's face; her one goal in life now threatened. "No, no, Ethan. This is very private. All Dolly's clients are confidential. All the sessions are confidential.

Nobody will ever know."

"*I* will know."

"Do I recall that you are going to do something called remote viewing? Isn't that psychic?"

"It's scientific, methodological," I said trying to keep the defensiveness out of my voice.

"Do this for us, Ethan? For me?" She wrung my hand and a couple of tears leaked from her eyes. Did the "for us" part mean our marriage? I didn't want to ask. It must be real important for her, I thought, else wise she wouldn't have brought Dolly over, nor would she be pushing this with so much vigor. I hoped she didn't really believe in reading the future from cards as much as this was leading me to think she believed.

How could I say no to her pleading? Women get all emotional and start crying and I'm flat out one hundred percent lost, out of my element, and at major disadvantage.

I tried one last time. "I say again, Mary Lou. If this got out, my political career is a goner. I don't want to trivialize the future, but even if I haven't decided to continue in politics, I shouldn't jeopardize it now. Not only that, but I don't believe in this crap."

Mary Lou's voice turned harsh. "What else can I do? You don't need me for anything, not anymore. You never ask my opinion anymore. You never consult with me. You never share your problems, not anymore. Goddamnitall, this is what I do, this is what I know. Knock, knock, Ethan. Let me in." More tears.

And suddenly I knew that even if it meant the end of the world, I had to do this. I had no choice. Not after what she had just said. Nor did I want to admit to myself that within her words were things I'd damn well better address, and soon.

"Okay, okay. Look, don't get emotional. I'll do it." My devious political mind kicked in. "Here's what I want you to do. Say these words: 'Ethan, I dare you to get your future read. I will mow the yard this week if you do.' Say that."

She scrunched up her face, thinking quickly. "Bastard. You've covered your political ass and made me pay a price, too."

I grinned. At least she wasn't crying any longer. "I'm waiting."

"Ethan, I dare you to have Dolly read your future. If you accept this dare, I will mow the grass."

"This week, not just some unnamed later date."

"Yeah, sure." She nodded acceptance. It must have been really important to her, because she, to my knowledge, had never used a lawn mower in her life. When I was in the hospital, she'd hired a neighborhood kid to mow.

"Cross your heart, hope to die, stick a pin in your eye?"

"I promise. I said I would, damn it. Don't run it into the ground."

"Let us go and do that thing, then." I still wasn't happy, but I'd won a small battle, maybe not the war. And, I was afraid to admit to myself, I'd learned something about Mary Lou and me. I'd be calling Dr. Laura next.

Dolly was not a gypsy with a wrap around skirt and white silk shirt and a scarf headdress like Deion Sanders' durag. She did not fit the stereotype.

Dolly stood when we entered the dining room.

Mary Lou introduced us without using last names. If Mary Lou knew Dolly well enough to bring her to our house, I wondered if Dolly knew any of my circumstances.

Turning to Mary Lou, I asked, "Have you told Dolly anything?"

"And possibly taint her reading? I should think not." It was as if I'd insulted her integrity.

Dolly said, "I know nothing, Ethan. Just what I read in the *Star-Banner*. But that shouldn't make any difference. Please let us sit down."

She sat. Dolly wore jeans and a smiley-face sweatshirt. She was maybe thirty, with real blond hair draped to her shoulders. Nope, no stereotype she. I sat across from her and Mary Lou disappeared.

Dolly picked up her deck of Tarot cards and held them out to me. "Seventy-eight of them, Ethan. Twenty-two are key. These are called the major arcana; the suit cards are minor arcana.

Sometimes only the twenty-two are used, or maybe fifty-four. Surely we can learn something?"

Taking the cards, I nodded, non-committal to the end. I glanced at them. Not your basic Bicycle poker deck.

Dolly said, "Usually the client has something specific they want to ask about their future." Her eyes were dark and hard to read.

"Mary Lou didn't already set that up?"

"No, sir. Just shuffle them softly while I run through my relaxation technique." Dolly closed her eyes and visibly relaxed. She rotated her head on her neck and slumped into the chair for a moment then was quite still. Her breathing became audible and regular.

Not wanting to seem a voyeur, I looked at the cards and shuffled them absently.

Dolly's hazel eyes popped open and she sat up straight. "Questions?"

Having no experience in this or any idea, I sort of shrugged it off. I thought of asking if the Tampa Bay Buccaneers would win the Super Bowl again this year, but doubted she'd appreciate the male-centric joke.

Her attention was focused. She took the cards and started laying them out. Some were face up, some face down. Maybe half and half. "Reversals," she said, reading my mind. "That negates the meaning or changes it to read backward."

She was all business, eyes flowing across the table. "Your questions?"

"I have none specifically. About the future?" I glanced at my watch winding merrily backwards. I certainly wasn't going to ask about that.

Her mouth pursed. "The Magician." The card she indicated was red and white. The sword was prominent and I saw the infinity symbol.

Her brow furrowed. "The Sword of intellect," she intoned

Well, I wasn't stupid, but I'd never been known as an intellectual. Was this reading just "Give him the old number twenty-three reading"?

"I...I don't understand." Dolly shook her head. "There's a Mystery whether the Magician can come up with the tools—" She shrugged. "This doesn't usually happen to me. I know my stuff." She studied the cards below the Magician. "Of the minor arcana, the aces are a basic force. The ace of Swords here with the Magician points to you being ready for new roads, but what now? Scientists? Troubles? Nightmares? There are explanations, but I'm not going to invent one just to fill in the blanks." She looked up at me and captured my eyes, hers glowing. "I can make the language pretty and acceptable, but such is not my way."

At least she was being honest. While I remained skeptical, I think I was beginning to like her; she wasn't trying to dazzle me with BS.

"And over here," she pointed. "The Sun. As they lie here. Rebirth."

Jeez, she was beginning to scare me.

Additionally, the card showed two naked children, a boy and a girl, and, I guess sunflowers. It didn't escape my attention that I was heading quickly toward the child stage. There was a wall on the card, too. That was probably the most prescient part of this whole thing: I kept running into walls; maybe even banging my head into them. But I wasn't the one supposed to be reading the cards.

"A youthful energy," she said, "and with the other cards here in the spread, children could be in your future."

That chilled me. "I'm too old," I said lamely.

She must have taken me seriously. "It is not clear. But one thing I learned to say in this business, and I quote almost exactly a well-used line. The new you, they taught me to say, a child lives within you."

"If I was female, maybe." I took in a breath. "Though," I said thoughtfully, "I usually am wont to repeat that I might be an older man now, but I sure dream like a boy."

Dolly ignored my words. "I read you here. Healthy, maybe

fresh. Muddy in the mind becoming clear...." She sat back and shook her hair out. "Ethan, some of this is right out of the textbook. But some of it is strange. Back with the Magician," she pointed, "I get thoughts of the old mantras. Chalice of Love, Ward of Ambition, and something to do with the medicine man...I have a strong sense...that your readings are not exactly the traditional interpretations that I've read about. We learn to follow our intuition, for that's why we're in it in the first place. This Magician thing and the Mystery of tools—I just don't know. Well, I do know, but what is difficult is how it all applies to you."

"Does any of this interface with your readings for Mary Lou?"

She looked up at me sharply. "All of my readings and sessions are confidential."

"That fails to answer my question."

"Right."

I got the feeling I'd sort of trashed the moment.

She had more, but it seemed all rote. Different suits, cards, so on.

Dolly addressed children in a couple of different ways, saying, "These are my interpretations." She must have read my mind. "I was always sensitive. I was taught how to read these cards, but after that, it's mostly up to the reader herself. What you feel when you're turning over the cards, what you can project using them. Experience is necessary. After a few thousand sessions, you sort of know. The cards fall almost as you expect—except today. Like it's gone off the charts."

"You did fine, Dolly," I said, trying to soothe her and keep her away from the truth. How could I tell her that the "children" part was me growing younger by the minute?

Unconsciously, I glanced at my watch. No longer a slow minute hand winding its way clockwise unconcernedly. It was trucking counterclockwise like a runaway train. I thought about the sense of urgency and subordinated it to the courtesy of the moment.

Dolly slipped the cards into her purse. "Maybe I need a new deck." She correctly interpreted my look. "There are hundreds of tarot decks, I just use what's comfortable for me. In fact, readers often design their own. That's become a cottage industry."

I was going to show Dolly out, but Mary Lou materialized out of nowhere and ushered her out. They stood out by Dolly's car for a while.

So I went and got a Don Tomás, a San Vicente, an excellent cigar made down in Honduras. I knew we were going to do some talking. I checked my watch for the millionth time. No change.

By the time I lighted up with a big kitchen match and settled into my chair on the patio, Mary Lou appeared with her gin and tonic.

"So you had a nice little visit?"

"I guess you could say that," I answered.

"Dolly was somewhat disconcerted."

"Ah," I said, figuring some of the clues. "Dolly told me her readings were confidential. Yet obviously she told you all about mine."

"You're missing something important, Ethan. You were the subject, but *I* was the client."

"And they accuse us lawyers of parsing the language too much."

Mary Lou was gazing at me without interruption. It's a thing a wife can do, specifically as opposed to staring at me. "Dolly didn't have any real answers."

"I'll be damned."

"Ethan, this is serious."

"Okay."

"Think about channeling."

"Swimming from England to France?"

"No, silly. It's like communicating with spirits to see what they know."

"I'll pass. I miss my mom, but I don't think I have anything to say to her dead self."

"It's not necessarily family, it's anybody, any spirit rather, and who can help."

"No way, Mary Lou."

"I didn't think so." She looked wistful. "Dolly said something which resonated with me. When they read the cards for you, their purpose usually is to divine the past, the near future, your personality traits which influence those things." She just stopped talking.

"And?" I prompted.

"It's sort of like what I've been hitting my head against. Dolly said she could read your immediate personality, maybe the surface, but when she really got into it, she said there was a dark veil that blocked her. As if your dark side was in the way of everything."

Budweiser wandered over from somewhere mysterious, gave Mary Lou a wide berth, and parked himself under my chair as usual. Poor old thing didn't have long to go. Maybe he knew Mary Lou had proposed putting him out of his misery. No way I was going to have Budweiser's life artificially shortened, even if he was in some pain. He couldn't speak for himself, and if you know cats, doubtless he would opt for staying alive. There is always hope.

"Altered states of consciousness—" Mary Lou was continuing.

"You're trying to sneak one in one me, hon. What you just said is a form of channeling."

"Ah ha," she almost cried. "You already know this stuff."

"My eyes ain't broke. I can read."

"You do that thing, I will grant you. You'd rather have a good book than a good woman."

"Say that again, only make sense this time." Was she trying to tell me something? Or just being catty?

"No." She looked around then back at me. "I was also thinking you could go into past-life regression therapy." She locked onto my eyes hopefully.

"I will be dipped in spit. You do not believe this shit. God, tell me you don't believe this shit."

"An earlier character could have become dominant and is somehow controlling your present life issues."

"I have been neglecting you terribly, haven't I?" I shook my head sadly. "I can't believe you believe this shit."

Her jaw locked. "Ethan Zachary, I never said I believed it."

"You don't believe it? Then why do you want me to undergo these things?"

"I didn't say I don't believe it, either. These are the only approaches I know to help."

I actually believed her then.

"And I haven't even suggested herbal treatments—yet." A tentative smile. The old Mary Lou I was missing more and more lately. "What do you think?"

"None of the above."

"How about a clairvoyant."

"Nah," I said automatically, not even thinking. I should have.

"Yet remote viewing is a form of clairvoyance."

"You tricked me," I accused to stall for time.

"I set you up; you tricked yourself."

"Um, remote viewing is a scientific approach, it's very methodological." I kept saying that. Maybe I was trying to convince myself.

"It's clairvoyance, Ethan."

"I thought maybe I couldn't lose anything by trying it. Strangers out of town do it. Nobody local. Nobody who knows us."

"It's still clairvoyance. And nothing to lose by trying it? That could be said about all the above I've been bringing up to address."

"Your point is taken. I still ain't doing none of that stuff." I puffed on my cigar, just barely saving it from going out. Cigars are economical smokes: don't puff on 'em, they don't burn. I thought about doing some of the things Mary Lou was suggesting. But I just knew it wouldn't be worth my time. I flat out don't believe in those kinds of things. I wasn't certain

I believed in remote viewing, either. However, it was scientific, and it has shown some good results. Military and CIA used it for a while, they never used tarot cards. And rational adults trying to keep a scientific and methodological process, even sometimes done in the double blind method, do it. Nope, none of the junk stuff for me, just the scientific junk stuff. One overriding factor was that I was taking charge now, not just floating with the flow. I was making decisions and deciding upon a plan of action. I studied the long ash on the Don Tomás. Well rounded and uniform. Excellent.

A determined look came over Mary Lou. "Another thing we could do. Astrology." This was apparently what she was building up to. Maybe all the foregoing had been a diversion just to get me to agree to this one thing. Then again, knowing Mary Lou, maybe not. I was finding that she and I had grown more apart than I'd been thinking. Perhaps our problem was that she recognized that fact long before I figured it out.

"Astrology would help," she said, trying to soothe me.

I didn't say anything. Especially what I was thinking. Not after Dolly and having my fortune read by a bunch of non-Bicycle, non-poker-deck cards with weird images all over them.

"I already got the exact time and location of your birth in Ft. Lauderdale from your birth certificate. One of the things about astrology people don't know is that once you've got your fate pretty well figured out or what all's going to happen to you as you go along, you can have an impact to change it."

My gut froze. I don't think I could speak.

She dropped her gaze and tried to obfuscate. "With that information, you establish a center point. And chart from there. It's just another form of divination. Gives you a shot at changing...." Her voice trailed off.

I inhaled the Don Tomás down to my toes. I now knew.

And she knew that I knew.

CHAPTER FOURTEEN

The phone rang and, having for once forgotten the mobile, she was off like a thirsty GI after free beer. Avoidance lent her wings.

She brought the mobile out. There was some relief in her voice. "Dexter, for you."

"Easy? Listen, I just got an enquiry from a friend of a friend of a fraternity brother. They wouldn't talk, but the network they came through to contact me is encouraging. What's your blood type?"

"Don't you know?" I couldn't believe he didn't look in my records.

"Listen, dadgumit, I'm trying to remember. I'm on my cell phone and at a celebrity auction right now. These people are heavy hitters and they want an answer now. I don't have time to run to my office."

I told him, "O positive."

"Thanks. It's not like you're my only patient, you know."

"Yeah, I'm sorry, Dexter. What's up with this thing?"

"I just told you all I know, Easy. Remember I was talking about sending out discreet inquiries through the good ole boys doctor network?"

"I do."

"I finally got a bite. When I know more, I'll tell you anything I know."

"Fine, Dexter. Thanks."

After I handed her the phone—Mary Lou requires her to be

the person in control of that instrument—she asked with her eyes.

"Dexter didn't know anything. He's been discreetly networking about the national medical community—"

"With your name?"

"Not unless he had to use it. Anyway, he's looking for any medical guys who ever heard of anything like my problem. He asked in the right places and was vague about it. Apparently he got something, because one of his sources called and asked my blood type."

"What difference would your blood type make?"

"It—" I paused. "Hell, I don't know. That is curious."

"And he remembers your phone number but not your blood type and he is a leading physician?"

"Golfing partners have auto-dial programmed in." You don't have to remember any phone numbers, even though I do.

"Oh." She took my hand.

I was still waiting for the explanation she was dodging.

"But a lead, Ethan, think of it!" She squeezed my hand.

"Saved by the bell?" I said and regretted it immediately.

Her face fell and she dropped my hand.

"I'm sorry," I said. "That kind of personal shot isn't my thing, and you know that." I took her hand that had squeezed mine. "But, please note, you're the one who's initiated this separation business. And now comes a seminal moment in our marriage. I find that astrology has told you to make a change in your life, obviously in your marriage, and you—"

And the damn phone rang again and Mary Lou jerked her hand out of mine and snatched up the telephone.

"Who?" she demanded. Her face made a quizzical look at me. "You know a guy named María?"

I grabbed the phone from her. "What's up?"

"Ethan Allen?"

"It's me, buddy."

"Those two so-called reporters you lookin' for?"

I'd put out the word to a select few friends and associates.

Some owed me favors, others were part of a select group of people who help each other out when necessary. Others were just friends in the right places. While I was a county commissioner, María was a Sarasota city cop, and not connected to the county law enforcement unit, the sheriff's department.

"You got a fix on them?" I moved to the edge of my seat.

"I followed them to the Ritz Carlton. They have a room upstairs."

"Together?"

"They do."

I glanced at my watch and cursed silently. Hell, I didn't know what time it was. I shot a glance to the clock on the wall near the deep end of the pool. It was still early.

"María, are you on a cell phone?"

He gave me the number, knowing I didn't need to write it down.

"I'm on the way. When I get downtown I'll call you and meet up." I gave him my cell phone number.

"Done," he said and disconnected.

I handed Mary Lou the phone and took a last puff on my cigar. The Don Tomás was smooth and tasty. On second thought, I sat it down to let it go out.

Standing, I said, "I've got to go downtown. But when I get back, maybe we can discuss astrology and why that thing has made you my-almost wife sleeping in the guest bedroom?"

"If I'm still here."

"I'm not sure I want to know what that means."

She stood and faced me. "You're running off when we were going to finally talk out our problems—"

"This is an emergency. I have to."

"Thanks for letting me in on it."

Damn. "Listen, Mary Lou, it's about those two people who are investigating me behind my back. We've got a line on them."

She shrugged. "Sure."

It did not escape my attention that she was evading my scrutiny. And seemingly blaming me.

"Just hold on for a couple of hours."

"Yes, sir."

"Look, Mary Lou. These people know something. I cannot ignore the opportunity." I waved my watch in her face. "I'm going to hell in a time machine and a problem not of my making. I am going to do something about it. Nobody else is going to, it has to be me."

Hurrying inside, I changed into jeans and a pull over shirt. On the way out I grabbed my now cool Don Tomás. That and my scruffy face and shaggy hair would give me a more threatening appearance.

Driving my pickup downtown, more than once I wondered if Mary Lou would be there when I got home. I guessed mowing the yard was out.

CHAPTER FIFTEEN

Cruising west on Fruitville, I passed the library visible a block to the south. Nice new and large building, but expensive. They'd spent a ton of money on the new building when the old one had been fine. They could have spent the money on upgrades and books. Not a chance. So they moved it south a few blocks and suddenly the new library became downtown renourishment. That's the way government works these days.

I called María on his cell phone and he had followed the two to St. Armand's Key, just over John Ringling Causeway from downtown Sarasota. St. Armand's is an exclusive shopping district spiraling out from a central traffic circle. Of course, John Ringling helped put Sarasota on the map a century give or take ago. His residence up by the airport had been turned into a museum.

María was sitting on a park bench in the middle of a traffic circle. "They're eating supper." He pointed to the famous Columbia restaurant on the corner. Traffic flowed around the circle for a change. "They got a rental car parked a couple blocks over." He pointed northeast.

"Good job. I appreciate this."

"It's nothin', man, I owe you anyway."

I sat beside him and drew air through my unlit Don Tomás.

"What we gonna do?" María had a couple of plain gold earrings in the helix of his right ear and one in the earlobe. The upscale shopping area was lighted well enough to run a third-world country.

Jaguars, Caddies, Mercedes, all drove around the circle, some more than once, incapable of exiting where they wanted. Because of traffic and, frankly, many people can't handle traffic circles. The engineers were always trying to get us to approve a traffic circle here or there; however, I always voted against them. Traffic circles might work elsewhere, especially Britain, but not here. Most of the cars were headed north to another bridge to Longboat Key. Others were going on to Lido Key and that beach community.

"If we can get them out of the public spotlight, I'd like to talk to them."

"I need to know why?"

"They've been asking around town about me. I want to know why."

"Whyn't you just ask them, Ethan Allen?"

"I didn't know who they are or where to find them."

"Makes sense, Ethan Allen."

"How'd you find them?" I wanted to know.

"I just went over to the newspaper and asked Sydney in the library."

"Oh."

"She told me their names and I checked hotels."

"Oh."

"That's me. A highly skilled professional." He brushed his fingernails off on his shirt. After a dramatic pause, he said, "I suspect they're both doctors."

"They're doctors?"

"They told Sydney they were reporters and showed her a press pass or some damn thing. The Ritz Carlton got 'em registered as Doctor and Mrs. Doctor R. Fielding Smith."

"Difficult names to hide."

"And I thought I was the professional," María said. "We gonna hassle 'em?"

"We were, now I don't know."

"You better figger something out because here they come." María must have eyes in the back of his head. He didn't nod or point. In fact, he looked away. He was professional.

Doctors? I could understand interest in me and my condition. But why dig around behind my back? Why not just come and talk to me? And why pretend to be reporters? "Maybe they are reporters and doctors, both," I said.

"Nah," said María, "that offend some natural law." He moved his head as if watching this good-looking woman who was walking in front of us hustling a poodle on a leash. "They ain't walkin' to their car, man."

We watched them window shop around part of the circle then they continued west. Likely, they were heading for the beach, a block or so away on Lido Key.

"They ain't been checkin' behind themselves," said María. "We safe to wander along behind if you want."

"Let's go."

"People here, they think you and I salt-and-pepper gay guys."

We followed the two doctor reporters. He was tall and well built like he worked out. He had short-cropped blonde hair. She was almost as tall as he was, bouncy brunette hair, and enough curves and angles to put her in a men's magazine. She wore glasses and carried a heavy purse.

"Though all them hot babes I seen you with lately, you crazy if you be gay. And you be married, too. She older, but she still a finey." Doubtless María was referring to Mary Lou.

"Thanks for the commentary."

"And, Ethan Allen, you look like shit tonight. You ain't shaved lately. You runnin' around with major babes and one at home, and two doctor types are investigatin' you and nobody tole you. Kind of makes a man wonder."

"You *are* a professional."

"Nothin' gets by me." He glanced up. "No moon yet tonight. We get 'em on North beach, we cool."

"And you got a degree from University of Alabama," I said. "In English?"

"Pre-law," he said. "Look, Ethan, you want to tell me, fine. If not, never mind. Circumstances are strange with you and it leads to natural curiosity."

He was going to hear anything I said to the doctors. If they were, in fact, doctors. "Lemme get this straight with these two first," I stalled.

The sidewalk curved around to follow the beach to the south. The two doctors had taken off their shoes and were walking down the beach to the water. They turned north hand in hand.

"Ain't love grand?" María said. "This gonna make it tough to beat the truth out of them."

I didn't answer. I didn't think I could justify any strong-arm stuff. Hell, I was an elected official and María was a sworn police officer. It didn't make the job any easier.

The tide was out giving us hardpan sand to walk on. I was in jogging Nikes so it was easy. They each carried their shoes. As they walked north along the beach, I increased our pace to catch up. As if we were just a couple of guys walking the beach faster than they were.

"Every female you involved with look good from behind," María noted quietly.

As we got closer we swung to the dune side of them as if to walk past. The man was talking casually and absently put his right hand in his jacket pocket. It must have been awkward, because he had dropped his wife's hand and shifted his shoes to that now-free hand. Then he was withdrawing his right hand from the jacket pocket when María twirled in the sand, a difficult thing to do, and stepped away from me, swinging his left leg wide and high. Some kind of savate or karate kick. His foot slammed into the man's hand coming out of his jacket pocket.

María was good, I'll say that again and again.

A light little .25 automatic flew into the softly lapping waves.

The two froze, squared off against each other. Doctor Smith, the man, had known we were following him and made his move at the best possible opportunity. But María had been better.

While the two of them were very good at this, I was no slouch either. My attention naturally should have been on them, where the action was. And my attention was focused on them. But if the man was that aware, then it occurred to me that the woman was worthy of watching, too. So as the man and María were doing their macho dance, I saw peripherally that the woman had dropped her shoes. The fact that her bag was obviously heavy struck me in context. Especially as her hand darted therein.

My kick wasn't as pretty as María's. But it sent the purse flying, spinning in the air, female stuff spewing out, along with a PDA, a couple of similar sized electronic gizmos, and a small .22 revolver. The revolver that her hand had been clutching out of her purse.

Since there was nothing to do, nobody did it. It's really good when you have adults being adults, not cowboys. And it was night with no beach walkers near enough to observe the action.

The male Doctor Smith said, "If you touch my wife, I will kill you."

"I tole you ain't love grand," said María conversationally. "Looks like a Mexican standoff, no ethnic insult intended."

"I concur," said the male Doctor Smith and forcibly relaxed himself.

María followed suit.

Both of them were comfortable in this game.

The lady Doctor Smith eyed me. "Are you going to kick me again?" She was wearing a wraparound skirt and a silk blouse.

"Chill out lady, I did not kick you the first time." I had to fight doing a double take. Looking at her made me want to be young and single again. Oops, maybe I was on the way to both—

"Shall we act civilized?" asked Mister Doctor Smith.

María kept his eye on the man, but asked me, "You cool with that, boss?" He was telling me it was my play. He didn't use my name, not tipping our hand. María had one hand on his hip nonchalantly. Of course, his weapon was under his shirt right behind his hand at the small of his back.

Everybody was looking at me now. I released the tension in my shoulders and noticed my right hand was cocked for a follow-up. I dropped it. I didn't want to like these people, and I don't think I did. But the male Doctor Smith's fatal concern for his wife did get my attention. And María's, too. Smith would've gone after me, leaving himself open to the far more professional María.

"Okay," I said, "if you promise not to wave guns around."

Nobody said anything. María bent over and began retrieving things off the sand. He popped the clip out of the dripping .25 auto and jacked the shell out of the chamber. Even I noted that it had been cocked and ready. María continued to pick things up. He flipped the cylinder out of the .22 and dropped the five rounds into his hand. He put both weapons into the lady's purse and handed the shells and the .25 clip to the man. He policed up a hairbrush, makeup mirror, and other stuff from the sand and dropped them into the purse. He showed me a small electronic item.

"This a micro bug detector. Jammin' unit. Picks up video, video transmitters, computer signals, telephone and body bugs, and more. Beep tone gets louder as you get nearer the RF source." It had different signal lights for different levels, whatever that meant. He put that one in the purse and showed me another.

All I could see was a digital readout.

"Phone and fax bug deactivator," María said. "Works five or six ways. Power comes from the telephone line itself. Tells you about eavesdroppers, it's got a special muting circuit, an anti-VOX system. It's a fine line analyzer, just watch the voltage readout." He dropped it in the big purse and found the PDA and looked at me.

"Let them keep it," I said.

"Betcha lotta shit worth lookin' at in here," María said and shrugged. He dropped the PDA in the purse and handed it to the woman.

"Your move," said the man.

Damn if I knew. "What's the 'R' for?" I asked.

It threw him off.

"Raleigh," said the missus.

"Do you have a first name?" I asked her.

"Rhonda," she said. Her eyes were bright and intelligent, I could tell, even at night and beneath glasses.

"It figgers," said María, referring to the "R" Fielding Smith. Two R's.

"Raleigh and Rhonda," I said. "From North Carolina."

"If you like," she said, still cool, rearranging her purse. "You would be Commissioner Zachary." Not a question, but a statement. "Your press photo does not do you justice."

"He need a shave bad," said María.

I pulled the saliva soaked cigar butt out of my mouth and paused to light it with a kitchen match.

"Could we cut to the bottom line," I said. "Word's gotten back to me that you are investigating me. Frankly, I don't know why, but would like to."

"He polite, too," María said. But I noted he was always within striking distance of Raleigh Smith.

Rhonda looked at Raleigh who shrugged. "He has to know sooner or later."

"In short, we're representatives and were checking out your bona fides."

"That tells me nothing." I inhaled smoke for a change. It felt good all the way down.

"Do you want us to talk in front of the hired help?" Raleigh said, indicating María.

And I had liked him a bit. "He's not help. He's my friend." I guessed Raleigh was giving me an opportunity to send María off. While I thought I could handle it now, I wouldn't diss María that way. Then it occurred to me that Raleigh was trying to stir the pot and change the subject from them. So, Raleigh wasn't dissing María on purpose, he was simply gaining whatever advantage he could. After all, they'd been smoked out and bettered.

María obviously had already figured this out and not taken offense.

I sighed. "Whom do you represent? And what about me were you checking out? And, most of all, why?"

Rhonda took over. "We're not prepared to disclose our principal without authorization. We were checking public records about you."

"Good thing you in government already," said María, "you understand bureaucrat. These people they say a lot, but they ain't said nothin'."

"Yeah, I noticed." To her, I said, "Could you be a little more clear?"

"Yes, it seems there is something unique about your physical condition."

"He a hot babe magnet," María said appreciatively, eyeing Rhonda.

"So what's your interest?" I said, knowing the answer.

"Medical."

"They doctors and all," said María. He seemed to realize he was being intrusive and stepped back and nodded at me.

"This is like pulling teeth," I said. "What can you tell me? Hell, I can extrapolate as well as anybody."

"We sort of know your condition," Raleigh took over. "But we have to okay it with the boss to make you an offer. And, quite frankly, I—we would like to examine you and make our own determination."

María was as if an outsider now. He knew the conversation was beyond him.

"What kind of an offer?" I wanted to know.

"That if you have a problem," Rhonda said judiciously, "we have been engaged in research which might or might not have a bearing. Again quite frankly, we have not read a medical diagnosis. All we have is on-line and telephone whispers and hints. Your doctor is very guarded."

"But obviously you've read between the lines."

"We have," she said and smiled for the first time. María even seemed to melt a little at her charm, even here at night.

"Whyn't you just call him up on the phone?" María asked I was just going to ask the same question. Then he held up his hands and mimicked her voice. "No authorization."

"Right," said Rhonda.

Raleigh looked at Rhonda, then me. "Can you give us some confirmation of your condition?"

Rhonda nodded approvingly.

María looked at me strangely, all the word dancing making a point.

"Can you confirm that you two are alone in this?" I asked.

They looked at each other, obviously not understanding.

"An older man than you two," I said. "Checking around town about me."

"Damn," said Rhonda.

"You a important person, Ethan Allen." María hadn't heard of the alleged government snoop.

"Commissioner," said Raleigh, "you're telling us that someone else is pursuing a background check on you also?"

"I am." The Don Tomás was burning the fingers holding it. Reluctantly, I tossed the remnants into the Gulf of Mexico.

Dr. Raleigh Smith shook his head. "We've got to advance our timetable." His wife nodded agreement. "All right, Zachary, here's the thumbnail sketch. We represent the Justyn Tyme, Tyme with a 'y', Institute. We, ah, do research and applications of aging. Your case has come to our attention through a high level network."

María was looking between us. "This beyond my pay grade."

"So?" I said, my voice harsh. I started to look at my watch but didn't. The sense of urgency I'd existed on lately came to the surface and I fought it.

"You have a problem, I'd guess," said Rhonda.

María said, "You treat him like a radioactive mutate."

It occurred to me that if my problem was their only concern, they'd sure traveled a long way and gone to a great deal of trouble to help me out because of the goodness of their hearts. What was their angle? Why the big time interest? But it did mean I had some bargaining position. It didn't take being an attorney and politician to realize that.

"Whether or not I have a problem, what's it to you?" I

demanded. Two armed doctors, professional at strong-arm tactics, were investigating my past and present.

"We suspect we can be of mutual benefit to each other," Rhonda went on. She was sharp. She knew I expected them to have some kind of stake in this game; it was only logical given these strange conditions. So she was going to be upfront with that.

"What's the benefit to you?"

"Frankly, your unique condition could provide some, um, answers to a line of research in which we're currently engaged."

They weren't going to answer with a lot of specifics.

"I need more information."

"Do you?" Rhonda stepped to me. Clouds scuttled away from the stars, and she stared closely at my face. "Do you?" she said again. Slowly she touched my face and rubbed the scrub on my chin. "How old are you, Ethan? Forty?"

I kept my eyes fixed on hers. "If you didn't already know, you wouldn't have asked."

"So you're a big, strong, tough guy," she said. She turned my head with two fingers on my chin, eyes locked on mine the whole time. "I see no panic in your eyes, Ethan."

That was because I was busy hiding it as I'd been day after day after day. She couldn't know any particulars. Who else knew anything? Dexter, Mary Lou, Carrie Jean. Mary Lou hadn't had time to tell anybody and have it get out. Dexter had been discreet, or said he had, and I'd known him too long. Not him. Carrie Jean, even if pissed at me, wouldn't talk even under torture. All of which meant that they'd picked up somehow on Dexter's discreet inquiries, and it meant something significant enough to them to hop a plane down here and investigate me. And from what had happened tonight with them and us and what they'd said, they must've extrapolated my situation with some high degree of accuracy. I needed to do the same. However, I had one advantage: I had no other options other than to play this hand out.

I took a deep breath, thankful as usual for that fresh sea

smell. "Have you-all encountered this condition before?"

The Doctors Smith looked at each other, and Rhonda dropped her hand from my chin.

She grimaced. "No, but we have been searching for it."

Whatever that meant.

"You have merely extrapolated my condition."

She nodded again, auburn hair bouncing. "It's what we do well, Ethan. A few days of research on you, big changes in your public profile and appearance, tied in with the whispered inquires we received. Not a difficult thing."

The tide was coming in and a small wave wandered around my running shoes and the tiny crest swarmed over her more than shapely ankles.

"What is it you would want from me?" Not that it was difficult to guess myself. Tyme Institute. And doubtless it was a well-endowed institute. Even then I knew what a myriad of sins an institute could cover.

"Go over your medical records. Do some tests. We'd like to run more tests on you than they do on the president for his physical."

"Do you have any—or are there any techniques or medicines you can use to arrest my condition or reverse it?" I thought about anything impinging on my theoretical congressional run and career. I had no choice. Go for it.

"We won't know until we run the tests," Rhonda said smoothly.

"What's in it for you?" I knew because of their interest it wouldn't cost me anything. Blue Cross would laugh in their face anyway.

"Ethan, Ethan, surely you know."

For a change, I was the one who nodded. "Guinea pig."

"Poor word choice," Rhonda said. "Point of reference would be better terminology. Our equipment is the most advanced in the world; it's years beyond quote state of the art end quote. So, too, is our expertise and research. Our facilities are world class. If anyone anywhere can help you, the Tyme Institute can."

I pulled out my cell phone and hit Dexter's cell number on the auto dial.

"Ethan, what's up? I'm at a charity thing at Michael's On East."

"Dexter, have you ever heard of the Tyme Institute?"

"Can't say I have. Why?"

"I have two of their representatives here with me now. They want to make a deal with me."

"Jesus, I can only guess. Listen, this is a cell call and I'm in the middle of this auction. I need to do some calling around tonight. Meet me at my office in the morning?"

I looked at Rhonda. "My doctor's office, early?"

"Dexter Hampton," she said. "Fine reputation in the field. University of Florida trained. The earlier the better." More homework done on their part. The Doctors Smith were in a hurry, too. Good, that was to my benefit. The rate I was going, I'd be in Pampers too soon.

"We'll be there," I said.

"Early, seven, before office hours."

"Thanks, Dexter." I hit the disconnect and pocketed the instrument. High tech has made the mechanics of modern life so much easier.

To the Doctors Smith, I said, "Dexter's office, seven tomorrow. It's over in—"

"We know," said Raleigh.

"I think we can help, I really do, Ethan," Rhonda said, voice couched to be reassuring. She thrust her purse at Raleigh and it clanked. "Here, you carry this heavy damn thing for a while."

"One more thing?" I asked.

"That is?" asked Raleigh.

"Where did you-all attend med school?"

"What difference does that make?"

"None at all," I said. "Just curious. It's something I like to know about people, about doctors." Like hell.

Raleigh smiled this time. "UCSD. University of California at San Diego. We matriculated together."

"Well, Raleigh, you are a lucky man."

Rhonda gave me another reassuring smile and took her husband by the arm and they picked up their shoes and continued their walk north on the beach.

Actually, it did make a difference. Now I knew. Now I could check *them* out.

María and I walked back to the road. "What an ass on that babe," he said.

"Maybe I owe you an explanation, María." I kicked sand.

"You don't owe me nothing. You covered my ass and saved me some jail time and I still got my job. I owe you."

"Okay, then."

"And I don't care if you are day-glow green," he said. "You still be my friend. When you become a congressman, you still be my friend. When you a high and mighty senator, you still be my friend. Maybe you get me a cushy country-club job with the Secret Service or Capitol Police Force or something."

"Done." Apparently everybody except me knew I was going to be a congressman and then senator.

He glanced at me. "You bitchin' under fire. Immediate action like you done, just the right thing, and that damn cee-gar never budged outa your mouth. Way cool, man. For a politician, anyway. But what you got, it ain't contagious, right?"

CHAPTER SIXTEEN

María and I went to a place over on Tallevast where you could sit outside on a picnic table and drink a beer. They had a few cigars in a glass on the counter and I bought one.

María had a Colt .45 malt liquor and I had a Budweiser. I don't ordinarily drink, a glass of wine or draft beer occasionally and that's about it. I have nothing against alcohol; I just never developed a taste for it.

It was after midnight and it didn't occur to me then what day it was.

Cigar smoke and the late hour kept the mosquitoes away.

There were six other customers outside, all black and middle aged or older and curious about María and me. I recognized one who worked for the City of Sarasota, but I didn't remember what office. I smiled and nodded and he acknowledged me and after that I was okay. They were more hostile to María.

I'd bought the beer and we sat down and I handed María his Colt .45. "You're going to stereotype yourself."

It took him a minute to get the joke. He looked around uncomfortably. We were against the building in the shadows.

"You okay here?" I asked.

"I guess." Nobody could hear us as long as we weren't loud. "It's my cover I'm worried about."

"So I'm just another county commissioner out making a buy from a dealer."

"Small-time," he acknowledged. "It's okay here. Nobody knows, nobody says anything." He shrugged. "It's your reputation. What do I care?"

His language had become normal. I guess he didn't need his public persona here.

"You got some kind of problem, Ethan Allen."

"I do. I owe you an explanation."

"You don't owe me squat. Matter of fact, I ain't altogether sure I want to know, now you mention it."

The cigar was something called a Miami-Havana. Allegedly hand made from genuine Cuban seed. First one I'd had and it wasn't half bad.

"You want I should hunt down the other party investigating on you?" María asked.

Thinking about it, I shook my head. "Word out is this other guy is a fed."

"Jesus. A fed? You trip over your dick big time, Ethan Allen?"

"That's the whole goddamn thing, María, I did nothing. I don't know what these people want."

"They're doctors. Maybe they want your blood." María shook his head sadly. I should have listened to him. "Though I don't know about the fed. They badass mother fuckers. You don't want to get involved with 'em."

"Hell, I don't want to get involved with anybody, let me tell you. It ain't my fault, either. They just won't leave me alone."

He drained his brew. "Upon great reflection, I think I don't want to know anything about you and your problem."

"Fine. Think about this: Two doctors, carrying handguns, and using newspaper credentials. What's wrong with this picture?"

He frowned. "I'm a college educated and trained investigator, Ethan Allen, and I missed that discrepancy."

"It wasn't the right time for me to brace them with that. So I didn't."

He rose. "Nice dealing with you tonight, Ethan Allen. There's a *Star Trek: The Next Generation* all-night festival on the Science Fiction Channel I gotta go home and tape."

His way of saying it's late. I had to agree. He faded into the night and I got into my truck and headed home. It was past two in the morning now.

I needed time to figure out what was going on and how I fit into whatever it was. But I wasn't going to get time to reflect. It was strange to see time progress properly on the dashboard of my truck. But one glance at my watch renewed my sense of urgency. It was fairly spinning backwards. Rhonda had said, "Forty."

Throughout history, people have searched for a fountain of youth, and not found it. Once aging, they've wanted to grow younger. No such luck. Only one person as far as I knew had accomplished that thing: me. And contrary to popular opinion, it wasn't any fun.

Driving home I was on the phone again.

A deputy on nighttime desk duty owed me a favor or two. "Gotta have it by in the morning, Sarge. Anything you can come up with. Call me, never mind the time."

"You got it, Easy. Nothing going on tonight so far." He was accommodating. He'd run an NCIC check and whatever else he could. The National Crime Information Center was an excellent database, and compiled info from nationwide.

Dexter was finished with his charity auction and on his computer.

"I'll be online most of the night," he complained.

"Exhaustion will help your golf game," I said. "But I do appreciate everything, Dexter. You're really helping out."

"Yeah, sure. You're my patient, I know, I know. When you turn me loose, I'll have one hell of an article in the *AMA Journal*."

I was going to be tired by the time I got to Dexter's office. I noted the time was getting late as I cruised up Bee Ridge Road. Of course, now I was younger and could deal with it better.

A sheriff's deputy assigned to patrol this zone recognized my truck and flashed his lights at me. I got through the Cattlemen-Bee Ridge intersection in one light cycle, nobody around after two in the morning. Of course, it was late and Sarasota was an early to bed town.

On the northwest corner of that intersection was Doctors Hospital and their adjoining medical building where Dexter had his office. The prospect of having something concrete to do about my condition was exciting. Until now, there had been really nothing I could do. I hadn't even had a direction to investigate. Now, there actually was a tunnel; I wasn't sure about any lights at the end. Whatever the Tyme Institute was.

Of course, all of this meant I was avoiding thinking of Mary Lou and what I would tell her. I thought about it some. She was in on the problem now, more or less, and when in doubt, tell the truth. Even a politician should do that.

Thinking about being a politician, I had to admit that I actually liked doing that thing. I liked the give and take and the chess moves, and the rush when you win a significant power play. While I was telling one and all I had not yet decided to run for Palmer's seat in congress, I pretty much wanted to do so. It was an intriguing goal. I'd needed something different and become a county commissioner; now I was hooked. I wanted to climb the ladder. There were many issues I'd like to address on a higher level than Sarasota County. But I couldn't make one step toward running for congress until I'd solved my reverse aging.

If.

One thing I had pushed into the back of my mind: This could be fatal. As long as I was an adult, I could handle it physically. I wondered if I'd get the reverse of Alzheimer's and become smarter, remember more, and improve my concentration, as I grew younger.

I wondered if I'd become eligible for the draft again. Though I'd served my time, it raised an interesting question.

Another interesting question: how old would I be at my birthday? Being fifty-seven at this time—on the calendar, would I be fifty-eight? Or would I be fifty-six? And if I was fifty-six, should I be younger because I'd grown much younger than fifty-six. Rhonda Smith had said forty. Was she trying to get under my skin? No, she had no reason to.

Uh, oh. Rhonda. She'd actually said the word "forty." She'd done her research. Tomorrow—make that today, I thought, glancing at the clock on the dash—was my birthday. So just how old was I?

Too much going on, I'd simply forgotten. And Mary Lou hadn't reminded me. That was my usual trigger. It's part of a wife's job description to keep track of important dates and anniversaries.

I dimmed my lights as I went past the rent-a-cop in his hut at the entrance to Bent Tree. He waved his appreciation.

In a couple of minutes I swung onto our cul de sac and pulled into my driveway.

Sometimes life ain't easy.

There in my front yard, caught like a deer in headlights, was Carrie Jean Billingsley. She stood amongst maybe fifty plastic pink flamingoes and gray rabbits stuck into the yard. At her feet were, without counting I guessed, seven more, and one in her hand ready to shove into the ground.

I didn't want to hit the clicker to open the garage door in case it would wake Mary Lou. I'd leave the truck out tonight, even though that dastardly unneighborly action was against the deed restrictions. A rent-a-cop patrol would leave me a note.

I hopped out of the truck and went over to Carrie Jean. She was just outside the pool of light from the yard pole light next to the entrance walk, but there was plenty of starlight. She wore very low hip-hugger jeans just barely over her hips and a loose top, showing midriff from well below her belly button.

"*Goddamn* your sorry ass, Ethan Zachary. What the fuck are you doing here—?"

"I live here."

"Shit, you scared the hell out of me. You out cattin' around?"

"I'm saving myself for you," I said joking and without thinking. "Um, would it be too much trouble to ask what you're up to?" Though I had it figured out.

"Happy birthday," she said. "Damn your soul. I wanted to surprise you. You'd wake up and come out and get the paper and lo and goddamn behold, surprise."

"Yes, I would've been shocked."

"Not any more, you rat bastard." The gray rabbits were stand-up tall, like Bugs Bunny on his two feet.

"Sorry I upset you. Thanks for thinking of me." Suddenly, I understood the purpose of the gray rabbits. They were hares. A few gray hares amongst the rest.

"It was the least I could do," she said, trying to shake off her pique. "Here, I'll be damned if I'm gonna let all this be for naught."

"You pick that language up in law school or on your own?"

"Shove it, Ethan. You scared the shit out of me and fucked up my goddamn surprise, damn your sorry hide." She jammed the flamingo in and let go and the plastic figure quivered in the night.

I plugged in a few and she finished the rest.

"There," she said. "Happy friggin' birthday."

Lately, I couldn't seem to please anybody. Including myself. I felt like an innocent bystander hit by a truck. "You make me feel like my dog died," I pointed out.

"You don't own a dog. You own a cat."

"You ought to be a lawyer. And people don't own cats."

"And the last time I saw Budweiser, he wasn't doing very well."

"I'm glad we got that out of the way," I said. I picked up some twine that had come with the flamingoes and threw it in the bed of my truck. "CJ?"

"What?" she demanded.

"Thanks for thinking of me on my birthday."

"Yes, dear," she said. "Hell, I think of you every damn day."

"This isn't the time or place to go over this again."

"It has occurred to me that pretty soon you're going to be my age."

"God help me," I said. I leaned back against the truck.

CJ stepped up to me and cupped my face in both her hands. "Even in the dark you're so much younger. I'm worried about you, Ethan. What's going to happen to you?" A plaintive note crept into her voice.

"Damfino," I said. "I've an appointment at Dexter's in about four hours."

"Something wrong?" Her voice was worried.

"Not any more than it already is," I said. "But I've encountered something offbeat—"

"Any more weird and we're in the Twilight Zone."

I told her about the Doctors Raleigh and Rhonda Smith.

"He really threatened to kill you?"

"That he did."

"That's kind of touching. He's protecting his woman." CJ was still rubbing my face and leaning against me. Something I should have moved away from, but it felt so good that I was loathe to break the contact. Something awakened within me. I stole a glance at the front window, imagining Mary Lou standing there holding an edge of the curtains aside, watching us.

"This is becoming too familiar, too close," I said hoarsely.

"I'll show you close." She jammed her hard body against me. "I'll show you familiar." Her hands went from my face to around my neck and pulled my face down into hers. The kiss was warm, moist, and startling. I didn't know when I was going to finally die, tomorrow or in a hundred years. But I'd remember that kiss. And it kept going. My hands went to her bare waist atavistically. Finally, I took her arms in my hands and gently broke the contact.

"Happy birthday, Ethan," she said.

"Jesus," I said.

"You taste like a good cigar. And you taste like a real man. Even all scruffy."

Until now, I'd sort of humored Carrie Jean in her assault on me. I'd known her since she was born; and we were so easy with each other I hadn't really taken her as seriously as I should. Hell, attention from her was flattering to an older guy. It gave me a sense of importance to myself. Now I was going to have to deal with her.

Which scared the hell out of me. I didn't know what to do.

"CJ, I need to discourage you, hon." Even to me it sounded half-hearted.

"Not any more. We've been through this."

"I've got a probably fatal disease, and likely it won't be long now." Something I hadn't even wanted to admit to myself, though it had been lurking right below the surface. And that fact was why I would cooperate with the Doctors Smith and the Tyme Institute. A drowning man doesn't care where the rope comes from. Well, that sounded good at the time. "I'm chronologically challenged," I added trying to divert by humor. It didn't work.

"You changed my diapers, I'll change yours."

"We've argued this before. I don't want to do it again."

"Me neither. I gave you an ultimatum. Remember?"

"Yes."

"I withdraw it. That kind of thing isn't fair."

Suddenly, I was weary. I looked at my watch out of habit. Counterclockwise, too much, too fast.

CJ surveyed the flamingoes in the yard. "Ninny nanny boo boo. Happy birthday, sugar. Leave them up for a few days, huh?"

"If it'll make you happy, I will," I said.

"It will. But it'll piss off Mary Lou." CJ grinned.

I groaned. "This yin and yang of life sucks."

"Suddenly I feel better," said Carrie Jean. She kissed the tips of the fingers on her right hand and touched it to my lips. "Later, gator." She weaved her way through flamingoes to the street, got into her own pickup parked on the street and started it.

As she drove off, she blew the horn twice. Doubtless, she wanted to wake up Mary Lou. Small wonder they didn't like each other.

I glanced at my watch again, not having a clue what time it really was. But I hoped to have some answers in a couple of hours.

I got the unfinished cigar out of the ashtray in my truck, lighted it and pulled down the tailgate of the truck. I sat on that thing and smoked.

Cigars make me think. That's why I like them. They put me in a channel where I think in different avenues. Outside the box. I even inhale sometimes.

I thought over the events of the evening. Maybe I was having an epiphany.

For the first time I realized I really was dying from this—condition. The odd circumstance of my body running counterclockwise was killing me. My time on Earth was now finitely limited. I gazed at the glowing tip. It didn't burn as evenly as an expensive cigar; but I liked the taste of the Miami-Havana. If I was going to live through this, I was going to have to fight this thing with all the energy I had. And all the mental energy I could muster.

Not to mention I needed to reconcile my love life. Hell, I needed to reconcile my life, period. Or whatever was left of my life.

I'd been running on cruise control, confident the Carrie Jean problem would solve itself. Many problems are like that—better off left without tinkering. Especially if it's me and the tinkering likely will aggravate the problem. CJ's growing infatuation might be just that: a girl's crush, here today, gone tomorrow. I inhaled the cigar to my toes trying to erase the phantom feel of her pressed against me.

It also did not escape my attention that Elena Rodríguez was making a play for me. Now there was one hell of a woman. I thought that her ubiquitous use of an inhaler was even an endearing quality. It gave her character. Not to mention that she was the most attractive woman on television. And bright, too. Along with every other man, I was strongly aware when she came into my presence. We were intellectually compatible.

And there was good old Mary Lou who obviously wasn't very happy these days. That state had existed long before the onset of my physical problems. I wondered what the initial spark of her discontent was. Maybe I'd never know, for she certainly wasn't telling me. Was I supposed to figure it out? Or was I supposed to know? Well, I sure as hell didn't. I had a suspicion, but I doubted the suspicion was the original causal factor. Maybe the kickoff was time itself. Maybe she'd just grown discontented with me and my "I still don't know what I want to do when I grow up" routine. She'd been supportive for all these years. Yet I'd never dissed her, never been unfaithful. My eyes weren't broke, but you could say that about all men. And Mary Lou was tied into some kind of psychic network and trying to drag me into it, too. No thanks. But what had driven her to that point? I was trying to avoid thinking about "that point." Was it a desperation point? Had I missed something significant and thus lost my chance to help her? Could her disaffection with me be her own version of "I don't know what I want to do when I grow up"? Maybe she was just tired of the same old same old as I had been. I sold my lucrative law practice and went into politics. And I therefore didn't have the more time to spend with her as we aged as we'd sort of looked forward to as life went on for us. And she was still doing the same thing; I wasn't. Maybe she needed a change, too. Maybe the human animal needs change to keep the batteries charged. Doubtless there is a medical or scientific term to fit that thought.

The thought of me being a battery was disquieting. It could be that she needed to be more intellectually challenged. She was highly intelligent. I'd had the daily intellectual challenge all attorneys enjoy, if you could call it enjoyment, but not Mary Lou. As our lives became easier, existence took less and less of her intellectual capacity and intellectual energy. Finally, I knew that menopause did make changes physically and mentally in a woman. I didn't know if these changes were chemical or psychic or what, but I knew changes could abound. And she'd gone through a several-year long menopause. I didn't know if it was finished yet, either. Hormones or some other chemical result could well have changed things around inside her. Now I wished I hadn't slept through physiology class. That well could be the genesis of her/our problems. Or, as any good manager can tell you, a combination or all of the above could be the genesis of our current situation. Sometimes there ain't no easy answers. Good thing that, or we'd all be mind-numbed robots mimicking a six billion element insect colony. And all those lady insects would look the same and life wouldn't be interesting at all.

A minefield, that's what I faced. And if I made it through that minefield? I still faced falling off the edge of the Earth. My head was going to burst with the metaphor soup.

The cigar was now a cold, saliva soaked butt. I tossed it away in disgust. It clipped the head of a three-foot tall pink flamingo and bounced into the grass.

The bottom line? Damn if I knew. All things being equal, I was still loyal to Mary Lou. Elena was intriguing to say the least and sure made a man think of all the possibilities. And Carrie Jean? Lord help me.

In quick succession two trucks and two vans whipped by my house, swish plop, swish plop. I believe in reading at least two newspapers a day. And I get all of them home delivered if I can. I was receiving local papers and *The Wall Street Journal,* and *USA Today.* I read more online, but I prefer actual paper in my hands. Elena's employer failed to cover national news and state-wide Florida news very well. The *Tampa Tribune* was excellent for those two things, but they'd stopped delivering to Sarasota County. So if I wanted to read more in depth about something, I could go online and look up any number of stories. Not to mention political columns of all stripes. And, most importantly, *Calvin and Hobbes.* Universal Press Syndicate ran old Calvin strips one a day on their U-Comics website, even though Bill Waterson had stopped drawing Calvin years ago.

Each newspaper delivery vehicle usually cruised by, tossed the paper, continued on and hung a U-turn at the end of the cul de sac, and cruised on out. Not today.

There I was sitting on my tailgate doing apparently nothing, amidst fifty-eight tacky plastic flamingoes and rabbits. All slowed significantly, and then blinked their lights in response to my wave.

Except the last van, who hit his horn.

As I was gathering the newspapers, the outside spotlights switched on and I went inside to face the music.

CHAPTER SEVENTEEN

Why, I don't know, but I did it.

I shaved.

After two hours of sleep, I was up, had a quick swim, and got ready for the Doctors Smith.

When I came out, Mary Lou was still up from earlier. The coffee pot was almost empty. But fresh coffee always smelled so good.

"Hello, Mary Lou." My traditional morning greeting.

"When is your girlfriend going to remove her plastic birds?"

"She's not my girlfriend and I don't know. I suspect she'll milk it as long as she can." Especially if she knew Mary Lou would react as she had, and doubtless Carrie Jean had calculated that thing along with the birthday part.

"The lawn will have to be mowed soon."

"Your turn, darlin'. You promised."

That shut her up. She knew I had her.

As usual, I crosschecked my watch with the cable television box. As was currently usual, my watch was going haywire backwards.

"Your beard! Where's your facial hair?" Mary Lou stood up.

"I did away with it. I was sick of it. I'm not used to a beard. It itches. I was still asleep and wasn't thinking."

"You certainly were not thinking." Mary Lou took my chin and tilted my head so she could see a different angle. Seemed as if a lot of women were grabbing my face lately.

"Jesus God, Ethan. *What* is happening to you?"

Actually, while I had been tired and sleepy, I'd had an adrenaline boost when I looked in the mirror after rinsing off the shaving cream.

Now I was scared and actually looked forward to a fight with Mary Lou. That would distract my attention and kill some of those iron butterflies dog fighting in my stomach.

When I came inside earlier, I'd explained about my trip to Lido Key and the Doctors Smith. I'm not certain Mary Lou fully believed me.

I ate a banana. Another worry: my phone had failed to ring yet this morning.

Mary Lou refilled her coffee cup. She was dressed attractively in shorts and a halter-top. She had on a pair of sandals she'd gotten mail order from Italy.

"Would it bother you if I pulled up those damn birds?"

"Not at all, hon." I smiled. "Likely, it's what Carrie Jean wants you to have to do."

"Oh, yeah." She opened a cabinet and pulled out an envelope and handed it to me. "Happy birthday."

I opened the card. Snoopy. I'm not a big fan of Snoopy. Garfield now, that's better. Garfield's arrogant, selfish, and fat. How can Snoopy compare to that?

"You remembered," I said brightly. "Thanks." I kissed her cheek, which seemed to surprise her.

"How could I forget?" Her voice was grumpy.

The old Mary Lou, the very intelligent Mary Lou, the one from an earlier life, would have launched into the mental gymnastics about my real age. Fifty-eight? Fifty-six? What? Talk about your intellectual conundrum.

Purposefully, I had not followed up on my realization that she was pursuing our separation and/or divorce because of some kind of screwy psychic reason or phenomenon. That was at the top of my list for when we could sit down and talk again.

Of course, that was predicated on the possibility that I'd be alive soon, and not aging myself backwards right out of existence. A premature baby in an oxygen tent? A splat of sperm and ova? These possibilities would go against some law of physics about conversion of energy and matter or $E=MC_2$ or whatever, I fell asleep in that lecture.

It was getting on toward seven and I had a five-minute drive to Dexter's office. I couldn't wait any longer for the phone call. I'd have to wing it this time. One of the things about me is that I like to be prepared. Even with a surprise.

I grabbed a Diet Coke, popped it, and headed for my truck. Of course, there was a little note from the rent-a-cop under the driver's side windshield wiper telling me to park my vehicle in the garage overnight.

Mary Lou followed me out. As I climbed into the truck, she kicked at one of the flamingoes, clipped it, and her Italian sandal went flying into the midst of the flock. She looked like she wanted to cry.

As I started my truck, she walked over to my window, limping slightly from wearing only one sandal.

"Ethan? I hope it works out for you." That sounded too final and I didn't say anything in response.

She continued. "I do love you, you know. In my own way. And happy birthday, too." She smiled gamely and patted me on the arm. Then she turned and limped into the house, ignoring her lost sandal surrounded by enemy flamingoes.

"Damn," I said out loud as I drove off.

In five minutes I was driving through the intersection of Cattlemen and Bee Ridge Road. If you reviewed my life, it would appear I spent half of it at this interchange. I turned left at Arby's and headed for the parking lot. As I pulled into a space in the vacant lot, my cell phone rang.

Checking the caller ID I sighed in relief. "Hey, Sarge," I said clicking on.

"Mister Commissioner," he said with a grandiose voice.

"What do you have, Sarge? I'm on the way into the meeting now."

"Easy, I spent all night on-line. Slim pickings, my friend. I've been with the AMA, and UCSD, FBI and the NCIC. Something funny here."

"University of California, San Diego?" I climbed out of the truck and locked it with the door locks instead of the doohickey on the key ring. A pickup ought not to have anything that fancy.

"Right, boss. Both of 'em got their medical degree and their Ph.D.'s at UCSD. In cellular and molecular biology. They both are licensed to practice in California, North Carolina and, strangely, Texas."

"Anything else?"

"No, and that's the problem, Easy. I should have been able to come up with a lot more. Not even an employer. I plugged in this Tyme Institute and got nothing. Well, I did a couple web searches, and it was mentioned in passing in a couple of logged in official e-mails from some study, but they didn't say anything at all. I say again, it is strange, very strange because of the lack of information."

"You done me good, Sarge. I owe you one." I was walking along the sidewalk to the building. I thanked him and disconnected. Recorded owl screeches rang out periodically from a speaker under the eaves of the top floor. It was bothersome, but the system kept other birds from sitting around up there and pooping all over the entranceway. Some architect hadn't thought it through for Sarasota, left coast of Florida.

Dexter looked haggard.

"Been up all night," he told me. "I'm gonna do my patient load, blow off golf this afternoon, and take a serious nap." He handed me a bottle of water. None of his nurses or office crew was here yet.

He sat behind his desk. "What the hell is going on?"

"Tyme Institute. Agents or doctors or something thereof."

"You told me on the phone. I've been on the phone and on-line all night. Nothing. Their names appear on a couple of lists at the AMA, but nothing significant, nothing that tells us anything whatsoever."

"I've heard that already this morning."

"Did you get a haircut? Lose weight?"

"I shaved."

"You look chipper this morning. No," he went on thoughtfully, "you look *younger* this morning. Come with me."

Dutifully, I followed him into an examination room, stripped my shirt, and suffered blood pressure cuff. His stethoscope was cold in the morning air conditioning. He thumped my chest.

As he worked, he talked. "Tyme Institute. Absolutely nothing I could find on-line. I woke a hell of a lot of people up last night. Good thing I got cheap long distance. I did links with them, like you do on-line, you know? One person would refer me to another or to several others. Found maybe two people who had even heard of Tyme Institute. One led to the other. The last one, head of a department up at Pittsburgh, he heard of it but wouldn't say much, not knowing me. But the guy referred me to him was a fraternity brother and this guy in Pittsburgh told me if I really wanted, he would contact Tyme and *they* would call me. You can get dressed now." He swallowed half a bottle of water. "I said maybe later. And you are healthy as the proverbial horse."

"I feel like the south end of the horse."

"Get some sleep. Are you having some problem I don't know about?" His eyelids rose.

"Lack of sleep."

"Me, too."

While we were heading down the hall back to his office, the front door opened and closed. "Dexter?" a voice called.

I followed Dexter to the waiting room.

A very nattily dressed man wearing a five hundred dollar navy blue suit stood there waiting. He appeared the kind of guy who gets a haircut every week and has his nails done then, too. He didn't wait for Dexter to introduce us, though I'd met him before in passing. I tried to recall his name, but couldn't. Politicians generally remember names easily. Especially me. However, the problem is that we have too many to remember and it takes repetition to reinforce memory. What I did not need was to worry that this backwards-aging thing was robbing my memory, too.

"Half of the board of directors of the hospital woke me at five this morning," he said severely. "Guess why?"

"Beats me," Dexter said, refusing to play his game.

"With instructions. To give you and a couple of visiting fireman doctors from North Carolina access to all the labs, equipment and facilities we have. And do this on a priority basis today. This morning."

Dexter was too tired to take the bait. "Fine, thanks for telling me."

The hospital chief executive, I suddenly realized. But I couldn't come up with his name.

The administrator waited for Dexter to fill in the blanks, but Dexter said nothing.

"Okay, then." His voice was acid. "So be it, Dexter." He bowed low and extended an arm. "So be it. We're *all* at your convenience." He turned and stormed out.

"So what was that about?"

"Two plus two plus two equals six," I said.

"This Tyme Institute thing. They have power and connections." I didn't say but I did think it ominous that we could find nothing about Tyme Institute, but they could pull these kinds of strings before business hours.

The door swung open and the Doctors Smith walked in, both carrying briefcases, and Raleigh carrying a laptop computer.

"Good morning," said Rhonda, too cheerful for the circumstances. Her eyes sought me immediately and locked onto my face. "Newspaper clips don't do you justice." She was wearing a tan skirt with matching jacket over a silk blouse.

Dexter was staring at her.

I made introductions.

Raleigh went around behind the receptionist's desk and opened his briefcase. He pulled out the two electronic units that María had found and outlined last night. Raleigh blew off an imaginary grain of sand from one and started scanning the phone line.

"Can't be too careful."

"I'd like to see Ethan's medical records," Rhonda said.

"No." Dexter's voice was defiant.

Raleigh came around the counter and stood next to his wife. "No?"

"I want to know what's going on." Dexter held both his hands up. "This is a runaway train. I'm Easy's doctor and I control these things. Why do you want his medical jacket?"

"Why, to read it, of course," said Rhonda. She was wearing contacts today. Her eyes were even lighter blue than I'd thought, like sapphires.

"You've credentials?"

Husband and wife looked at each other. Rhonda smiled. "Do we ever. But we don't carry diplomas around with us."

"Med school at UCSD," I said, "along with a Ph. D. in biomedical sciences specializing in cellular and molecular biology."

Both of them stared at me. As I said, I like to be prepared.

It was getting so I could read Rhonda somewhat. A technique an attorney must have and a politician usually screws up; but I had it. Rhonda glanced at me with a new sense of appreciation. Her husband watched me with speculation.

"Did you meet there, in San Diego? Or in Texas?" I asked. My advance knowledge meant nothing really, but it did put them a bit off balance. Now there would always be a subtext of them wondering what I knew and didn't know. From their approach thus far, it figured that I would need some advantage in the near future. It did occur to me that I did not possess a distant future.

"No. We were high school sweethearts," Rhonda said. "In San Antonio, Texas. Shall we get to work?"

"In aid of what?" I said, and observed Rhonda trying to figure me out.

"In aid of you," she said.

"Fine. What's in it for you?"

Neither answered.

"Extrapolation again," I said. "You both have invested a few days coming down here and checking me out. You don't come cheap, that's easy to tell. You're very professional, with some kind of maybe law enforcement training, or something similar." I touched the heavy purse sitting on the counter. "Not to mention Doctors Hospital has some marching orders from your boss or somebody in high places. And these marching orders coming well after close of business and before start of business in the morning. You have been very busy. You-all have a sense of urgency about you."

Dexter sat in a lounge chair and sipped on his water.

Rhonda and Raleigh glanced between each other and me.

"Doubtless you're fine people, but I don't think all this is because you like me and I'm a real good guy. You're not afraid to touch me so I don't think I'm contagious. Tell me. Why?"

Raleigh said, "You're pressing your luck, Zachary. We can help you."

Rhonda put her hand on his arm. "Let me handle it, darling. Ethan. You're right. You have a problem. We have a problem. If we can solve your problem, we might solve our problem. It's as simple as that."

"What other choice do you have?" asked Raleigh.

"Frankly? None right now. So what's in it for you?" What was their problem that I could help solve?

Rhonda smiled. "You bargain with no chips. That's admirable. You ought to be a politician." She smiled, trying to disarm us all.

"Hell, lady," Dexter interjected. "That's old Easy Zachary himself. He's always been that way. He'd challenge the devil with no ammunition. And tack Jell-O to the walls of hell afterwards." He laughed. "The only thing he's never been able to best is a 9-iron."

Rhonda smiled obligingly. At least she was diplomatic. "Let us reach an accommodation. Ethan, we've heard you have a problem, sort of confirmed last night. The Tyme Institute is engaged in research on aging. Hands-on research. We have facilities and knowledge to do more than any medical facility in the world."

"What's in it for me?" I said, knowing the answer, but trying to get more out of them. "And especially, what's in it for you?"

"Fair and balanced question," she said. "For you, help, if we can. For us, your case can contribute significantly to our knowledge and understanding."

That was about all I was going to get. I knew this because she had yet to address my spoken and unspoken queries about their sense of urgency. However, both of our goals might be the same. And their urgency certainly was to my benefit. I avoided looking at my watch.

Besides, I had no other options to pursue.

"Done," I said.

She didn't belabor the point. "We've heard and guessed much, and by observation I can guess a problem with your biological clock."

I showed her my watch. Raleigh leaned over and shrugged. "Means nothing."

"Gimme yours." Three watches mimicked mine and a clock radio slowed down significantly—maybe my electrical condition was getting stronger. They were already believers, but good scientists have to be shown.

"Today you are fifty-eight-years old," Rhonda said. "Last night I would've guessed forty." She pushed on my cheek, another woman touching my face, and tilted my head up and down. "But this morning, I'd guess younger than forty."

"I'm aging counterclockwise," I explained. "I look younger, I feel younger. Hell, I'm convinced I am younger." I paused. "And the pace is accelerating."

Dexter went into his office and returned, handing Raleigh my records.

Raleigh began scanning them. "My God," he said. "Jackpot."

"Raleigh," Rhonda warned.

Raleigh looked up. "Medical enthusiasm."

"I wonder why your names didn't come up with any publication credits," I said conversationally.

Raleigh snorted. "We're past that," he said enigmatically.

Rhonda looked at me. "Ethan. Can we stop playing word

games? You're not going to trick us into any revelations. We'll tell you more when we can tell you more, and not before."

"Internal alliteration," I pointed out.

I wasn't getting any points for wise cracking so I shut up.

A cell phone rang and Raleigh pulled it out of his briefcase. "Smith." Pause. "You made good time." He glanced at his watch. "We're at the medical building alongside Doctors Hospital, corner of Bee Ridge and Cattlemen. Meet us in the parking lot." He snapped the instrument closed. Then he looked at Rhonda with an intensity I hadn't seen before now. "They're here. We're a go."

"Let us get with the program then." She turned to me.

"What are your intentions?" I really wanted to know.

"We have to catch a plane," she said. "So we'll lay our cards on the table. In order for us to help you—and..."—she held up her hand catching the look on my face—"...you to help us, we must satisfy ourselves about your reverse aging condition. That is, prove it, buster." She gestured at Dexter and the office. "We know it's not a hoax, but we must convince ourselves the diagnosis is correct." She shot a look at Dexter.

Dexter said, "My dear, if you think I'm funning you, to hell with you." Then he laughed. "But you'll find I have not yet diagnosed Easy's condition. In the records I've made some guarded entries about accelerated healing and obvious signs of good health where not warranted by past events, but that's it." He grinned at me. "You've only Easy's word for it." Then he amended, "And my witness; I shan't document until I understand."

Raleigh was running his finger over lines in my records and flipping pages.

Rhonda said, "What is it you do think, Doctor Hampton?"

Dexter stood and came over to her. "Me? Easy has been my friend and patient for a hundred years. He's a fifty something, almost sixty, and was involved in one or more lightning strike incidents a few weeks ago. Since that time he has made remarkable, almost miraculous recoveries of broken ribs and arms and other body repairs. His current state of heath is consistent with a man much younger than he is. His appearance has changed significantly in that time."

Raleigh had stopped reading and was watching us now.

Dexter went on. "Ethan Zachary has a unique medical condition, one with which I am not familiar. It has occurred since the lightning incident; however that may or may not be the causal factor. It could in fact be the trigger for this amazing transformation; which leaves the causal factor to yet be discovered. That's what I think. And Easy ought to learn when to come in out of the rain."

"Thank you, Doctor Hampton. Your summary confirms our projections." Rhonda turned to me. "To finish up. You've a condition. We might be able to help each other. For us to do so, we need to tear you apart metaphorically speaking. We'll run some tests on you, first to insure no contagion, but certainly Doctor Hampton has done that?"

"More or less."

"Then we'll investigate for other causes. If all ends up as it appears to be right now, we want you to return with us to the Tyme Institute where we have facilities and equipment which are far in advance of current state of the art."

"Where's that?" I asked.

"North Carolina."

"Near Greensboro?"

"Close enough." No surprise this time.

"And when there?" I pushed.

"More tests, data comparisons. We come up with a tentative diagnosis and see if we can treat it."

I couldn't help but say it again. "Fine. You do all this. What do you get out of it?" My refrain.

Raleigh snorted. "Take it or leave it, Zachary."

"No, no," Rhonda soothed. "The answer is very simple. We are researching aging. You no longer are aging, ostensibly. You're aging backwards. Can you not see the research coup we have?"

I could. But it didn't explain their urgency. I raised an eyebrow. "Your hurry?"

Sometimes you're blind about yourself? I know I am. My mind doesn't want to accept something so it ignores that something.

"The answer is too simple," Rhonda said with a grimace. "If you continue to age in reverse, or counterclockwise as you put it, and at the accelerated pace, we won't have you for very long as a research subject."

"The more you talk," Raleigh said, "the closer you are to death."

I'd even admitted it to myself and my brain was starting to reconcile the possibility. But my heart wasn't.

On the other hand, I didn't believe them. They'd flown down here on a whispered rumor, a guarded request for information. Dexter had made his discreet inquiries and they were the result. An unbelievable situation, me going counterclockwise, and they'd hopped the first airplane down here? And gone through all the background checks on me? Yeah, right. They had another agenda, or a simultaneous agenda. But, I thought then, that it could only benefit me.

What other choice did I have?

Soon, I'd end up in some teaching hospital, an animal in a zoo, with millions of experts poking me and taking my temperature and wringing their hands while I wasted away in some regressive fashion.

"Your quick thumbnail diagnosis is that I'm dying, am going to die, will die, of this whatever?" I said, holding my voice tightly so the panic wouldn't creep into it.

"Life's a bitch, then you die," said Raleigh.

"Beats me," Rhonda said cheerfully. "But I'm going to die of impatience if we don't get going."

"I've been faced with my own mortality before, specifically, on behalf of Uncle Sam over in the Mystic Far East." And elsewhere, but I didn't say that part. I could do something about that: I had options and weapons to fight with. Now, I had none.

Sometimes a feeling of helplessness washed over me and I had to fight it. I was an attorney and a politician, and thus had trained myself to not react emotionally, not show any emotion if I didn't want to. So I didn't give away anything. Maybe they thought I was a cold fish, or just another political asshole. But now I had the opportunity of doing something, anything would be better than nothing.

"I am at your disposal," I said formally.

"Good," Rhonda replied. "Doctor Hampton, can we borrow an examination room?"

"This way, my dear." Dexter had fallen under her spell. Not hard to see why.

Raleigh was at Dexter's copier burning copies of each page and lab test insert in my records jacket.

I stripped for Rhonda. While she was a lady, I'd much rather deal with her than her husband.

She had a notebook out and a hand held Dictaphone; she used both, but mostly whispered into the Dictaphone. Occasionally, she'd ask me a question.

"Bullet hole?" she asked, fingering a scar above my left kidney.

"AK-47 round." I fingered it. "7.62 mm."

She gently rubbed the cicatrix of scars on the back of my right shoulder. "This?"

"Machete and maybe bayonet scars. I never want to see another tetanus shot."

Penlight glaring into my right eye, she asked, "While I'm thinking of it, I want you to tell me if you've ever had anything weird happen to you. Any other out-of-the-ordinary incidents, medical conditions."

"Charlie hit me with a Russian 122 rocket, concussion and residual vision flashes, but that's all gone. Whatever exotic diseases they had over there for a year and change."

"No UFO abductions?" She was half serious.

"God, no. Nobody would believe me anyway."

"Gypsy curses?" She was only half joking.

"Well—yes. Though I don't know much about it and don't believe in them. It's likely more of an urban family myth with little or no basis." Mary Lou was exploring my psychic side and I hoped Rhonda the doctor and scientist wouldn't get too interested in that. Fortunately, she didn't.

"Close your left eye and follow my finger with your right." As I did so, so continued. "At some point we want to know every where you've lived your entire life; we need an inclusive history. So when we're at your house in a little while, find that information if you cannot remember it. Addresses, military units and addresses. Schools. Transcripts if you have them."

"My house?"

She smiled. "Don't worry, you'll have plenty of time to find the information and pack."

Little did I guess.

And I'd already guessed the packing part.

But I did guess that if this mysterious counterclockwise condition didn't kill me, Mary Lou would.

"Well, hell, happy birthday, Ethan," I muttered to myself. Even if it might be my last.

"What did you say?"

"Just talking to myself."

"What's this?" she wanted to know.

A pair of small faded scars on the inside of my left thumb. Rhonda was thorough.

"Rattlesnake strike."

"An odd place."

"I was too slow."

"Remember I said tell me everything?"

"I do." I hadn't thought about this for years.

"This is important. Suppose your condition is a result of a combination of several factors. Think about this. Suppose you are the only person in the world who has a combination of factors, snake venom, shrapnel, specific blood type, and a lightning strike."

"Got it. Not one, but more than one. And perhaps in that

certain sequence, too," I said.

"Very good. I keep telling Raleigh not to underestimate you."

I said nothing, wondering why I must be estimated, either over or under. Generally, that categorization is reserved for antagonists.

"Bend over and spread 'em," she said, pulling on a surgeon's glove. "Unless you'd be more comfortable with Raleigh doing this one?"

Raleigh would kill me. "No, I trust you." My words were emphatic.

CHAPTER EIGHTEEN

When they were finished, I felt flushed.

Rhonda and I were back in Dexter's office to pick up her stuff. Raleigh was still in the hospital gathering and printing out info, and developing x-rays et al. Some of the data he was transferring digitally by phone.

"I'll ride with you," Rhonda said as we got out of the elevator. "When Raleigh completes his tasks, he'll join us."

His absence was fine with me. "Should I tell him how to get there? Or maybe you could call him when he's ready." Not that I wanted Raleigh at my house.

"No need."

"Okay." That was a measure of how well prepared these people were. Raleigh already knew where I lived. And, apparently, how to get there. More than GPS. This thought led to other questions I wasn't ready to ask or even address.

Out in the parking lot I led her from under the portico and pointed at my truck. "Over there."

The valet parking attendant gave her an appreciative glance. She stopped in the middle of the parking lot and waved at a four men standing in front of two rental vans. One gave a thumbs-up and they climbed in the vans and drove off. The call Raleigh had taken.

At my truck, I opened her side door and helped her up.

"A gentleman," she said.

"Give me a minute," I told her, and went around the tailgate and got in the driver's side. From the sun visor, I pulled a García y Vega miniature and began unwrapping it. "Do you mind? I'll leave the windows open."

"I like the smell," Rhonda said.

It had been a harrowing morning. I sucked in an illicit lungful and exhaled appreciatively. Then I started the truck and backed out of the parking space. A young guy in a blue '85 Pontiac slipped into the spot.

I was holding the smoke out the window out of common courtesy.

"May I?" Rhonda pointed at it.

"Sure." I handed the miniature cigar to her and watched her inhale deeper than I had.

She held the smoke in, blew it out and seemed to relax all over. She took another puff, blew that out the window and handed the thing back to me.

I pulled out onto Cattlemen Road and got into the turn lane for Bee Ridge. As usual the lights cycle was against me. We sat in traffic waiting. I puffed again not worrying about sharing the smoke with Rhonda, and handed it back to her.

"If you mention this to Raleigh, next time think in terms of proctology big time." But her smile belied her words.

We shared the smoke all the way to my house. When we turned down my street, she pulled out a stick of cinnamon gum and started chewing it. As a second thought, she offered me one and I took it. Cinnamon is another of my vices.

When she saw my house and the plastic flamingoes and hares, she said, "Happy birthday," as if this were an everyday occurrence. Her eyes even danced a little. "Your wife has good taste. A present with a smile."

"Not exactly."

Rhonda looked at me with frank appraisal. I shrugged and responded no further.

The two vans had parked in the street and I pulled into the driveway. The four men were pulling on loose fitting red sterile suits. The men worked their way into the red suits from the back and helped each other Velcro-close. And they stared at the yard full of pink flamingoes and gray hares.

"We're not afraid they'll catch anything, Ethan," Rhonda said. "We don't want them to contaminate the samples they take."

Mary Lou was standing just outside the front door with her hands on her hips.

I introduced Rhonda and Mary Lou wasn't warm and friendly. The widow across the street was watching this unfold from behind her curtains.

"Just exactly what the hell is going on here?" Mary Lou demanded.

I explained. "They have to check everything," I said, finishing up.

Mary Lou's hand waved at the yard. "First, all these tacky, tacky *things* in my yard and now this."

Rhonda shifted her gaze between us quizzically. She stood aside to make room.

The four red-suited men went into the house. They were carrying dozens of different sized plastic bags.

"Red is more anti-static," Rhonda pointed out.

They seemed to know what they were doing. Rhonda directed matters and Mary Lou went out on the pool patio to sulk. But one of the men followed her out there and took a sample of the pool water.

Budweiser scurried across the floor and caught Rhonda's attention. She pointed at the cat and one of the crew came over. "Where's the litter box?" I indicated a door, which was the laundry room. He went in there and dumped the whole box into a large bag and sealed it. I went and replaced the kitty litter. It was my cat.

Rhonda knelt by the cat and caressed him. He fell immediately for her and rubbed up against her knees. She stood and held her hand out to the man returning from the laundry room. He opened a small baggie and she brushed off a few cat hairs into it. He sealed it and wrote on it with a marker. Then he put the baggie into a new U-Haul dish pack box they'd placed in the kitchen.

It was interesting to watch them operate. They split the house and took samples of almost everything you could think of. From dust in the corner and off of books from the numerous bookcases to samples of food from the pantry, refrigerator and freezer. And samples I couldn't even see from corners of the refrigerator, closet, pantry, garage, everything. The refrigerator had an ice and water dispenser from which they took samples. They removed the water filter and put the whole cylinder in a bag and I got a new one out to replace it.

One of the crew filled bottles with tap water from each faucet and the hot water heater.

They took samples of each one of Mary Lou's makeup items. They asked and I okayed them taking one each of her medications. The hormone replacement I knew about, the Prozac I did not.

It was as thorough as an anthrax investigation; and with them dressed similarly, it resembled a CDC team going through a building. While watching their thoroughness, it occurred to me that this was amazing. Overnight, and from somewhere far away, they had assembled this team, and flown it down here between the time María and I had confronted the Doctors Smith and this morning. The logistics and resources involved were scary. Somebody was spending a ton of money. Not to mention the Doctors Smith. All the above finally hit me. Something significant was happening. Someone somewhere was reacting to me, to my condition, with alacrity, money, and pure power.

This gave me pause to think.

The team scraped with precision instruments. They collected with tiny vacuums like you see when people work on computers.

They went through the garage taking samples of all poisons, yard fertilizers and chemicals, chemicals for the pool, paints, everything. One of them climbed into the attic and took insulation samples. And then he clambered around up there for a while longer.

Mary Lou came into the garage and faced Rhonda and me.

"They're tearing up my house, now all that climbing around in the attic."

Rhonda explained. "He's sampling from inside the walls for mold and spores. It's one way to do so without cutting into a wall."

"Great, just great," said Mary Lou and went back into the house.

When he came down from the attic, he combed through Mary Lou's car and my truck, including the ashtray. Then he dug soil samples from different sections of the yard. Plant samples, grass samples, bits of bark from trees all went into sample bags and then into more assembled U-Haul boxes. The plants Rhonda or the crewmember couldn't identify, she got Mary Lou to assist and tell her what they were. The names and types were duly noted on the collection bag.

A man in a red sterile suit wandering around the yard collecting samples of course drew attention from the neighbors who were home at the time, and a couple who drove by during the process. But I didn't explain. Mary Lou kept darting glances up and down the street while she was outside.

When Mary Lou stormed back inside, Rhonda came over to me. "I tried to get her involved, but it didn't work. She said she feels violated."

"Thanks," I told Rhonda. I was beginning to hope we wouldn't see Raleigh any time soon. Two sourpusses together? I had enough problems as it was.

Before they finished, crewmembers went through the whole house with a couple of electronic devices.

"Radiac meter and radon detector," Rhonda said. "We don't expect to find anything, but we must eliminate what possibilities we can." Another walked through with a small video for about twenty minutes.

Another came from the bedroom I'd made into an office and spoke with Rhonda.

"We need to check your computer in there," Rhonda said to me.

"Why?"

"Something you might have forgotten. Weird websites of people who might have locked onto you and are stalking you, staking you out, doing something we won't know unless we check it out."

For a moment I thought. With the resources these people had, they could just turn it on, connect to an Internet site, and suck the guts right off my hard drive. But I had little or nothing to hide. What would they find? All my personal files, e-mails, and history of each keystroke. Uncomfortable and awkward but damning? Then it occurred to me that if they could follow each keystroke, and there was no doubt they had the ability, then they'd trace my research and contact with the remote viewing people at FarReaching Research.

Nothing I thought in the computer or my history on the Internet would help them.

They'd find a history of aperiodic e-mails to Carrie Jean when she was off at college.

"I don't see where we'd gain anything," I said, my voice casual.

"But—" said Rhonda.

Shrugging, I went on. "I've some confidential stuff regarding Sarasota County government I just don't feel right about sharing."

Rhonda agreed reluctantly, apparently not wanting to be pushy about it.

One of the team who carried around electronics came over to us. His Radiac meter was in a pouch about the size of a brick. A coiled wire led to the probe, a rectangular unit five or six inches long.

Rhonda stepped back. "Go ahead."

He scanned me like the guy at the airport with a metal detector wand. It didn't go "clickity-clickity-clickity" like Geiger counters in the movies. It reminded me of Dr. McCoy on *Star Trek* with his tricorder. The probe had a hinged lid and he opened it and closed it.

"If I remember," said Rhonda, "it picks up alpha and beta waves when it's open, and gamma rays when that thing's closed."

"It didn't pick up nothing," said the guy reading his display.

"Well, that's good," I said lightly.

Nobody laughed.

Then I felt violated when Rhonda herself opened my humidor and took tobacco samples from several cigars and dust and residual tobacco from the bottom of the humidor.

Next came the final blow. One of the suited guys came over carrying the urn containing my mother's remains.

"What's this?" he asked as he peered inside.

I snatched the top from his hand and put it back on. "It's the cremated ashes of my mother."

Rhonda shot me an inquiring look.

"Might be the old Gypsy curse," I said. "I was overseas and unavailable. My aunt knew mother wanted to be cremated, but had misplaced mother's instructions on what to do with her ashes."

The guy looked at Rhonda for instructions.

"Sorry," Rhonda said, apology serious. "Here." She took the urn and removed the cap. The guy held open a plastic bag and shortly some of my mother's remains slipped into the bag. They didn't look like the ashes from a real fire. They were more like burned sand.

Feeling frustrated without being able to do anything about it, I turned away. Rhonda squeezed my shoulder in sympathy and I think she meant it.

The guy with the Radiac meter stuck the probe into my stereo cabinet and called, "Hey, Doctor Rhonda, Mister Zachary got an April Stevens CD like you." I felt more violated. I was glad I'd prevented them from invading my computer and its files and e-mails. They'd already invaded my body with the most extensive physical examination I'd ever had. They'd searched my house and belongings in more detail than the FBI could have. And now April Stevens? Her voice was made to listen to while you smoked an expensive cigar.

But the search must go on. I was trying really, really hard not to think of all this as an effort to save my life. And when that leaked in to my mind, I tried really, really hard not to think of the term "last ditch" as applied to that effort to save my life.

I backed my golf cart out of the garage and one of the crew got on. But I insisted that he remove his sterile suit and Rhonda intervened and he did so. I didn't want to cause a panic at the golf course. Budweiser, having followed me to the garage, hopped on. He loved to ride in the golf cart. He didn't like to ride for the hours it took to play a round of golf, but I sometimes took him on short trips around the neighborhood. We motored to the copse of trees where the lightning and I had had our contretemps. About all we could collect were a few soil and foliage samples. The crewman shrugged a put a couple of rocks into a baggie. "Can't hurt," he said. Budweiser jumped out and marked his territory like a dog. As I've said, Bud was getting old and his kidneys reacted to even that short ride. Fortunately, nobody was in the area looking for a lost ball. Most everybody knew me and I didn't want to answer any questions.

When we got back Mary Lou was walking around, sulking. I didn't blame her. Her home, her privacy, was being invaded in every sense of the word.

I was beginning to regret agreeing to this. But somewhere in the back of my mind I told myself, "You're going to die and die soon. Whatever they do doesn't matter. Nothing matters now." Well, I disagreed, some things still mattered. However, I did have a sense of time fretting away and my life slipping away like a ticking clock. Backwards.

It had been a long day. All of the morning and a couple of hours into the afternoon at Dexter's office and Doctors Hospital going through all the tests. Now this. It was past five in the afternoon. Thankfully nothing was going on downtown. There were no formal meetings or events to attend today. However, appointments and paperwork were accumulating, and I should be at work dealing with them.

They were about done when Rhonda came over to me. "We

need to go over to your office."

"And do the same thing as here?" I asked.

"Yes."

"No."

"We've got to, Ethan," she said, voice smooth, making strong eye contact.

I felt drawn. But.

"Listen. Do you know what it will look like when six of us show up and four guys in those fancy suits start taking the place apart?"

"I can imagine, Ethan. We simply *have* to obtain samples from there. We can't not do so. It would negate all our work here. I don't think we'll discover anything, but we must eliminate every possibility. You do understand, don't you?"

I nodded. "We're talking about an office here. One man can handle the chores." I thought some more. "And so many people go in and out, if he didn't wear the contamination suit it might not matter."

She glanced at her watch. "You're actually making sense." At least her watch was going clockwise. She continued, "I want to be out of here by dark."

"I need a few minutes to pack," I said.

CHAPTER NINETEEN

One of the team named Bo, Rhonda and I drove downtown in my pickup. Driving west on Bee Ridge, I thought I saw Raleigh in their rental car heading east of Bee Ridge. Rhonda didn't notice, as she was busy sucking on a García y Vega miniature she'd plucked off my sun visor. She shot a warning glare at her subordinate who merely shrugged as if this weren't the first time. So I cranked one myself and he coughed a little to show his disgust.

It was after six when we got to my office. I thought we were safe from observation, it being so late and this being a government operation.

The crewmember carried a case, about twice the size of a briefcase, with sample bags, bottles, the vacuum in one and the electronics. I got us into my office relatively unnoticed and he went to work.

"You were right," Rhonda told me. "It isn't going to take long. We could be airborne by eight." She eyed me.

Pointing to a guest chair, I sank onto my own desk chair. She sat.

"How long will I be up there?" I asked.

"As long as it takes. If you thought today's medical evaluations were exhaustive, you ain't seen nothin' yet."

Occasionally, the vacuum would whirr momentarily. The technician went into my bathroom and took a water sample.

I was typing an e-mail note to all the other county commissioners and the administrative staff telling them I'd been called out of town unexpectedly when Vince MacLean walked in the door. I might have known if anybody were to interrupt, it would be my nemesis on the county commission. His polished cowboy boots probably had never been in stirrups. His ranch garb was cut in western fashion.

"Zachary, I heard you came up this way…." He caught sight of Rhonda and stopped. "Every time I see you lately you're with a different beautiful woman. And this one's a grown-up, what do you know?"

I sighed and introduced him to Rhonda as Doctor Smith.

"Does Mary Lou Zachary know about you?" Mac asked, voice innocent.

"We spent the afternoon together," Rhonda replied with sweetness thick in her voice. Apparently her snap judgment of people was pretty good.

MacLean turned to me. "You've changed or something."

"I shaved."

He nodded once. "There is more to it. You been on a diet?"

"No."

"Ah, got it. You dyed your hair."

"No."

Rhonda was watching the exchange with amusement in her eyes.

"Viagra?"

Suddenly, the bathroom door swung open and the technician walked out with the radon detector in front of him.

He stopped and looked at Rhonda.

She spoke immediately. "Go ahead and finish your test, Bo."

"What are you doing, Zachary?" asked MacLean.

Rhonda spoke before I could. "We're testing a few large public buildings for a study, Commissioner. Radon."

"Sarasota County won't incur any liability?" he asked. He was intelligent, after all.

"No."

"Just some random locations," I said. "And if it picks up anything we'll at least know." Thank God Rhonda hadn't used anthrax; if you want to panic a government—local, state, or federal—just mention the word anthrax.

"Yeah, sure," Mac said, as if already dismissing it as below his station. "I do not wish to violate the 'Government in the Sunshine Law', Zachary, and I'm not, really, but there are a couple of things in your in-basket we need you to sign off on. And you have not been around lately. You've been absent quite a lot."

"You the hall monitor today, Mac?"

The Sunshine Law was passed so that public officials couldn't discuss in private any item they might possibly vote on or have an influence on at any time. Among other things, this precluded collusion. For instance, Mac and I couldn't sit down right now and discuss Midnight Pass because we were going to eventually vote on it. But they've pushed it too much, so much now that officials don't even socialize privately together. You look over your shoulder if two of you are outside having a smoke and shooting the breeze about the Tampa Bay Buccaneers.

Mac looked at me as if I were a snake. Then he stepped closer to me. "There is something with you. You do look different. I'll figure it out." Then he smiled widely. "If I don't, that federal investigator will."

"Have you talked to him?" I asked. Hell, I wanted to know.

"Damn straight."

I wasn't going to give Mac the pleasure of me asking him what the investigator asked about.

"What does the CDC want with you, EZ?" asked Mac. I think he genuinely wanted to know. But now, Rhonda and I knew the genesis of the investigator. And now I knew the real reason MacLean had hunted me down. He wanted to rub my nose in it.

He ground his chin with his hand. "Let me see. The CDC. Now some ostensible study involving radon? Are you contagious or something?" He had figured there was a connection but he couldn't put it together.

"I doubt the connection," I said. "But I'll look into it." It occurred to me to tell him I was going to be gone for a few days to change the subject, but he'd just pick that to death, too. Well, I thought it'd be only a few days. "Do you remember his name?"

It wasn't hard to guess what the Center for Disease Control wanted. I could see Rhonda putting it together, also. The investigator's presence told me that Washington couldn't ignore me, couldn't ignore whatever the hell it was that I had. I doubted the source was Palmer Hibbs. Most likely it was Palmer's DOD contact, or somebody in the chain the DOD contact had encountered chasing down the information for me. Or, more accurately, the lack of information. No matter how the questions had been phrased, they'd still generate interest. And in the new environment, the government couldn't ignore my case and me.

"I forgot. Pinball, Pinella, something like that." He frowned. "Last I saw, he was outside grabbing a smoke." You'd think somebody from the CDC wouldn't smoke.

"Maybe I'll go find him and talk to him."

Mac nodded at Rhonda and winked at me. "Do that paperwork, hear?"

"Sure."

He left as Bo the technician walked around the room. He stopped in front of a series of bookshelves and glanced at me. "What is it with you and books?"

Rhonda produced her cell phone and hit a preset number.

I followed Mac out and went downstairs.

He was short, maybe five five, and leaning against a light pole watching traffic go by, and smoking a filtered cigarette.

"Hey there," I said as I approached him.

He looked startled. He glanced at his cigarette and then back at me.

"I hear you've been asking around about me?" I stood in front of him, closer than courtesy dictates, aiming for a little intimidation.

"I've seen your photograph," he said in a higher voice than I would have expected him to have.

"Maybe you could tell me about it?"

"Maybe, maybe not."

"Or you could have just come and asked me what it is you want to know."

"Maybe."

"Your name Pinella?"

"Yes." Pinella had watery eyes.

"Government officials have identification."

"I do." He puffed his cigarette and did nothing else.

"Harassment." I pointed at the traffic signal down Ringling Boulevard. A city police patrol car was waiting for the light to change.

"Is that a threat?"

"You bet."

"I am a civil servant," he said, his voice telling me he didn't care one way or the other. He dug out a thin, worn wallet and pulled out his ID. A handful of credit cards fell to the ground. "Shit," he said, and bent to retrieve them. He gathered them up and shuffled them. He handed me his ID card and put the credit cards back in the wallet.

As I was starting to read his identification, Rhonda and Bo came out the doors behind us and walked over to where we were standing.

Rhonda looked down at Pinella. She was holding her cell phone. "Mister Pinella? C. Roger Pinella?"

"That's me."

I glanced at the identification card. C. Roger Pinella all right. Then C. Roger snatched the laminated card from my hand before I could read it. Though, these days, ID cards are largely irrelevant. With computer programs and Internet websites abounding with fakes, anybody can produce a legitimate looking ID. Laminating machines are everywhere. Good ID's have the microchip, but you can't usually read them standing around in the street.

Rhonda held her cell phone out to C. Roger. "Your boss wants to talk to you."

"Who the hell are you?" he demanded, sneering.

Bo moved around Rhonda and began crowding C. Roger.

"You don't talk to the doc that way, Shorty." I wanted to look for cameras, this fast becoming a B-movie and all.

Angrily, C. Roger took the phone. "Yeah." He listened. "Yes, Ma'am." He listened a minute longer.

Again I wondered at the power of Rhonda and her employer. All she'd had was the last name of Pinella at the CDC, and it was after business hours, and a few minutes later she'd gotten some honcho from the CDC on the line, so to speak. And I was the focus of that power.

"Yes, Ma'am, right away." He flipped the phone closed and handed it back to Rhonda. "Who the *hell* are you people?"

Rhonda didn't answer; she just put her phone in her purse.

"That wasn't my boss," C. Roger said, apparently trying to be funny. "It was my boss's boss."

"Why were you investigating my background?" I asked.

C. Rodger looked up at me for a moment. "I guess it doesn't really matter now, does it?" His voice was disgusted. He turned and walked down Ringling Boulevard.

Bo said, "That whiny voice bothers me."

Rhonda patted him on the arm. "No longer. He's gone. Recalled." She turned to me. "Shall we be going?"

Bo hefted his case and we headed for my truck. A lady lawyer I knew was going home late and waved at me. This part of Sarasota was as full of lawyers as a country dog was full of fleas.

Rhonda was lighting up a García y Vega before we got in and Bo just shook his head and climbed into the bed of the pickup. I helped Rhonda up and closed the passenger side door. As I went around to get in the driver's side, I saw Vince MacLean standing outside the county building, briefcase in one hand, wide and white Stetson in the other. You just knew he had to be a good guy—his hat was white. He was watching us intently. And there was no telling how long he'd been standing there and whether he'd heard any of our conversation. Rhonda glanced at the back covers of a couple of Adam Hall novels I was carrying around and rereading when I got the chance.

As I turned onto Washington to cut over to Fruitville Road, Rhonda noticed I wasn't smoking and checked the pack. "Empty," she said and offered me a puff. I took two quick drags and returned the cigar to her. "Ethan, have you told your wife you are going with us tonight?"

The sun was setting behind us over the Gulf of Mexico. "No."

"Methinks you have a problem." She blew smoke at the windshield contentedly.

"Rhonda? I could make a crack about you and marriage counseling, but somehow I don't feel like it." Rhonda didn't respond, nor did she seem to notice the familiarity with which I'd called her by her first name for the first time.

We shared the smoke for a few minutes while I drove east of Fruitville toward I-75.

Then she said, "Sometimes I just don't like my job. Does that ever happen to you?"

I took the García y Vega from her and liked the taste of it and of her together. "It did. So I bailed. That's why I ran for county commissioner. After so many years in the law firm. Uggh. I liked it, but it was time to move on. And the attorney business? Sometimes I don't like us."

"I am reminded of animals eating their young," she observed.

We passed Honore Avenue. Bertha Honore Palmer showed up in Sarasota circa 1910 and is generally credited for highlighting Sarasota enough to put it on the map. She'd been from Chicago, a big time socialite and businesswoman. And carried on the tradition in Sarasota. She owned purchased thousands of acres hereabouts, and drained swamps and built places and raised cattle.

"And cannibals eat their brothers."

"Perhaps when we became civilized, we were doomed to return to that point?" Rhonda said.

"Sort of like going back in time?" I pointed out.

"Ooops." She inspected the ash on the cigar. "Last night I couldn't sleep. I wondered what I would do if the circumstances were mine instead of yours." She inhaled. "I came face to face with my own mortality." She studied the cigar again seriously.

"Poor baby."

Her face pursed up and she looked at me as if I were on display at a zoo. Then she laughed like a man. "Your point, Ethan. Thanks for bringing me back to Earth." She stuck her tongue out at me and handed me the butt. "Not much left," she said, "but it's all nicotine."

Inhaling the last of it, I wondered about life. Briefly. Then I tossed the remains out the window and was driving onto the interstate and accelerating. I glanced in the inside rearview mirror. Bo didn't seem to mind.

Last year we were hard into a drought and wildfires and you'd get a ticket for tossing lit butts out, but this year was chock full of rain and nobody cared. Cigars were biodegradable anyway. I was helping the environment.

Bo's teammates were drinking soda and sitting in my front yard amongst a graveyard of plastic gray hares and pink flamingoes. Raleigh's rental car was in my place in the driveway.

Rhonda and I went in and found Raleigh and Mary Lou sitting together on the pool patio. Raleigh's eyes lighted up when he saw Rhonda.

So there was one positive aspect about the son of a bitch. He was drinking a glass of iced tea and Mary Lou had a glass of gin, likely.

Budweiser the cat scurried over to Rhonda and did the rub-a-leg thing, and then to me for more of the same.

Mary Lou raised her glass to us as if toasting. "Raleigh tells me you are leaving with them tonight." You have to know her well to pick up that tiny bit of accusation in her voice. I did, they didn't. Raleigh must be a charmer. Well, look, he got Rhonda.

For a change, I said something intelligent. "Well, I gotta go pack. What?"

"Not much," Rhonda said. Slacks, shirts, nothing formal. Maybe a pair of jeans? Hiking boots, we're in the mountains."

"I'm a flatlander," I said. I'd never owned hiking boots in my life. But I had some good running shoes that should suffice.

"Excuse me, and I'll throw some stuff in a bag."

The sun had gone down and dark was falling quickly. Mary Lou had the pool light on. I went in to pack and she followed me.

"How long will you be gone?"

"I don't know. It's a medical investigation."

"Raleigh told me."

"All right." I had a sports bag from the closet and was rolling jeans and socks.

"Ethan, I don't like this. I feel so—unneeded."

"Nothing you can do," I said. "Hell, nothing I can do, either."

She sat on the bed. "Remember Dolly?"

Unfortunately. "I do. She tells your future by reading her cards."

"If you say so. I had her do a reading for me and it didn't look good."

"What did she say?"

"I'd rather not tell you now. But, well, it was cloudy."

"Just a minute." I went into my office and raided my humidor for cigars and brought them back and put them into the bag, along with a few boxes of matches. I prefer a wood match—and the sulfur enhances the first taste. "If you're not going to tell me what Dolly said, then why did you bring it up?" I tried to keep the irritation out of my voice.

"Because I need something, dammit, and I don't know what and that's what I know so I did it, okay?"

"Jeez, Mary Lou. Listen to us."

"Yeah. Happy birthday. I didn't get you anything like we don't get each other anything and that damn brat got you all those horrid things on the front lawn and when is she going to get them the hell out of there?"

"I dunno. Maybe tonight. Don't worry about it. I didn't want anything. You did fine."

"No I did not. You know? I'm sounding like a nagging whiny wife who doesn't have a brain of her own. And that is not me."

"No, it isn't. This ordeal is just wearing you down." Me, too,

I thought.

She didn't say anything.

I went on packing.

"I hope they find out what's wrong with you, Ethan. Raleigh seems like a fine doctor." She looked over at me, her eyes hooded. "You have changed, you know. You are really different."

"Well, I'm the same on the inside here." My attempt at humor did not touch her. But it did make me long for the routine, boring days. Go to work, come home, eat, sleep, play golf. Those things were shrinking from my life like they belonged to a different person. I was going to look at my watch wistfully, but I didn't want to start feeling sorry for myself right then.

Rhonda's voice talking to Raleigh drifted into the bedroom and I did think at least her crew was very thorough and professional. From what they'd shown me up to now, I guess I couldn't be in better hands. The nagging key thought being that I probably didn't matter to them one way or another, alive or dead, just the fact that I existed and was a unique research subject was likely the significant point to them. Well, that's what I thought then, and it did make sense from everything I knew.

Being a proponent of the Boy Scout Motto, I went back into my office for more cigars. On the way out I noted that my lighthouse screen saver was flipping through the picturesque shots of lighthouses I loved and wondered briefly why the machine was on screen saver, not hibernate. I hadn't used it today. Perhaps Mary Lou had checked her e-mail. It was changing from Kewaunee Peirhead Light on Lake Michigan to West Quoddy Head Light in Maine—allegedly the easternmost point in the United States. Even though I was from Florida, I had to admire the coast of Maine. I had an urge to drop everything and visit every lighthouse along the Maine coast, climb them, and sit atop them one at a time at sunset and smoke an expensive cigar and cogitate upon the world. If ever I had the time, I vowed to do that thing. Sighing, I reached to turn off the computer.

Which made me wonder about something. Moving the latest copy of *Gould's Legal Guidelines & Legislative Highlights of*

Florida out of the way, I sat and logged on. Nothing from CJ for a change. I sat down and typed her a quick note to come and get her gray hares and pink flamingoes and that I'd been called out of town suddenly.

Then I sent Mary Lou a note: "HELLO MARY LOU, GOODBYE HEART." Thanks to Ricky Nelson. Mary Lou would read it tomorrow and know I was thinking of her. I'd been ignoring her too much during this ordeal. Which was probably contributing to the strained relations between us.

As I logged off and turned off Windows and all, it seemed to me that Carrie Jean was already angry enough with me and that a generic e-mail I'd sent would set her off once again. I grabbed a phone and called her cell, not wanting to call her house and talk to Jack Billingsley. Thinking about CJ took my focus away; had I been thinking clearly at the time, I should have been more suspicious and checked history in Internet Explorer.

She didn't answer, so when the voice told me to leave a message, I said, "CJ, sorry I missed you. I'm heading to North Carolina. Some doctors think they can help me and they appear to be pretty well connected in the right areas. Sorry I missed you. Please retrieve your flamingoes and rabbits before my lovely wife launches them into orbit thank you very much. Consider my tongue sticking out at you now. See you when I get back."

I thought about taking my laptop, for no other reason than to keep in touch via e-mail. I could coordinate with work and home. On the other hand, I wanted to travel light and could do the same with my cell phone. So I left the laptop in my office.

We shuffled cars out of my driveway and I put my pickup in the garage. The two vans had already left for the airport.

I tossed my bag in the rental car's trunk. Raleigh and Rhonda had gotten into the front seat and the right rear door was open waiting for me.

Mary Lou was standing with me.

"Bye," I said brightly. "Wish me luck."

"Will I ever see you again?"

"Jesus, Mary Lou. Who's filling your head with that kind of

crap?"

Something streaked across her face and instantly I regretted my words. "Hey, I'm sorry. I didn't mean to—"

She shook her head. "It doesn't matter, Ethan." She turned to stare at the yard full of plastic gray hares and pink flamingoes. Then she looked back to me. "Happy birthday and good luck."

Raleigh had the engine running and gunned it.

"I'm coming," I said. I went to kiss Mary Lou goodbye and she dodged her shoulders aside, stepped away from me off the driveway, walked around a pink flamingo banging her hip against the beak, and went inside.

I closed the right rear door and went around and got in the left rear, behind Raleigh, so I could at least talk to Rhonda and maybe Raleigh would ignore me. Once on I-75, I directed Raleigh to take University Parkway to the airport.

"I don't want to pry," I said, "but I sure want to know why you were using newspaper credentials. A couple of doctors?"

"They are legitimate," Rhonda said. "Those credentials and others certainly facilitate research."

"We like to facilitate," Raleigh said.

"You must like to facilitate with guns, too." I was tired and my voice was nastier than I'd intended.

"Our employer is very security conscious," Rhonda put in. "The gun wasn't my own personal choice. Everybody's paranoid these days."

"I will say though," Raleigh said proudly, "that Texas girl can shoot."

Rhonda dimpled cutely. "Thank you, dear. You aren't bad, yourself." Then she frowned. "I wish all this gun stuff would go away. Why does everybody have to be armed all the time?"

"Rhonda." Raleigh was obviously warning her to get off the subject.

We drove to Dolphin Aviation, off the Tamiami Trail side of the airport.

Out on the flight line sat a Boeing 737 with just the identification tail number on it, no logo, no airline, nothing. Rhonda's crew was loading their equipment from the two rental vans. Lights from ground equipment lighted the entire area. Flying insects dodged here and there, seemingly more here than there. Our security check was simple. The pilot stood by the gate to the flight line and told the security guy we belonged to him and his aircraft. Thus the Doctors Smith were able to get their weapons onto the aircraft. Soon I was climbing the stairs into the 737. The VIP 737, I amended, once I went inside.

In about twenty minutes we were airborne and leveling off. Rhonda's crew scattered throughout and she and her husband sat together. I was across the aisle in a single seat, a luxurious captain's type seat. As soon as we leveled off, I reclined my chair and fell asleep.

It had been an exhausting and long day.

And God only knew what was in store tomorrow.

CHAPTER TWENTY

The interesting thing about Tri-City airport near Greensboro is that we did not go through security. We parked at what I guess they call the executive part of the ramp and walked a hundred feet, giving way for a fuel truck, and got into a sleek Bell 430 helicopter. Rhonda, Raleigh, and I did, that is. Their crew was tossing boxes and duffels onto a baggage cart.

Near us at the edge of the flight line perched a hangar with TYME, INC. painted discreetly on the side.

The chopper had no markings, either, except for the tail number.

"What's our destination?" I asked Raleigh.

"No name, just a place in the mountains," he said, obviously not wanting me to learn anything more than I already knew.

The time being still before dawn, a few bugs whirled around the lights. Nothing personal to that part of North Carolina, but Florida has insects; these were nothing.

This was no "chopper." The Bell 430 is a luxurious corporate machine. Inside were half a dozen leather recliners, not just regular aircraft seats. The carpet was a deep pile, in a rustic blue.

I sat and watched out of the window. I'd flown out in helicopters before and had to walk back, so out of habit I tried to pay attention to terrain. Some dying moonlight aided me, but I'd have preferred daylight. The lights of the city spread out below as the pilot steadied the chopper and then ascended. We were heading generally west. And there was Winston-Salem passing under us. The time still well before dawn, there wasn't much traffic below to gauge the roads. I fought sleep, somehow feeling I needed to pay attention.

But I felt displaced. I was no longer in Florida, my body knew that. But my body wasn't yet oriented properly. It needed some time on solid ground, in the open air, with the sun wandering around above like it's supposed to.

We flew for maybe an hour and began descending. I could tell we were way away from anywhere. Scattered lights on the ground had grown fewer and more far between. And they'd been obviously on different elevations.

We dropped into what I'd term a bowl in the mountains. Maybe cartographers would call it a valley, since the mountains surrounded the place. A glare rose from the target: a helipad with circular lighting built into the concrete waited invitingly. I could catalogue the terrain in daylight. I always liked knowing where I was, what the circumstances were. I don't even like being in strange buildings where I'm not familiar with all the entrances and exits. My wild guess was that the current elevation was somewhere between three and four thousand feet. And we were way in the hell and gone from anywhere.

The pilot touched down softly.

Once the engine wound down and the blades coasted to a stop, the copilot opened the hatch and we climbed out.

Stretching, I noticed the quiet. Not many night insects making obligatory noises like in Florida. No frogs, cicadas, night birds that I could hear. The only sounds were just the pinging of expanding metal from the helicopter settling down to rest.

The valley or the bowl loomed around and above. I could see a couple of dozen buildings set on three sides of the valley, rising from ground level where we were standing. Terraces, it came to me. Offset from the helipad was a gravel parking lot where several vehicles sat. They were mostly pickups and SUV's.

The buildings appeared connected by a series of well-lighted and covered walkways. I had much to survey in the light of day.

Raleigh Smith was fussing with Rhonda over the fact that he could carry more and she was a woman and shouldn't have to do the toting. He was a man full of contradictions.

The aircrew was securing the helicopter, doing their post flight inspection.

Two golf carts sped across the parking lot and came to a stop alongside of us.

Men with short hair and khaki slacks and white pullover shirts with collars drove both. "Hey, Doctor Smith," said the taller one. "And you, too, Doctor Smith." He grabbed the bags and grips from Raleigh and tossed them into the elongated rear rack of the cart.

"Hey, fellas," said Raleigh.

The tall guy came over to me and peered at me. "This him?" Something was wrong with his right eye.

"He's the one," Raleigh replied. "Put him in his quarters. Are you hungry, Mr. Zachary?"

"Sleepy."

"Fine. Do so and we will see you in a few hours."

"And then?"

"More of the same, only a lot more."

The tall guy took my sports bag and put it on the other cart. "Come on, I'll run you up there."

I stepped onto the cart and sat in the passenger seat. Tall Guy drove through the parking lot, fat tires crunching on gravel, and then onto a wide sidewalk and up a ramp. The temperature was in the mid or upper fifties, quite a pleasant contrast to oppressive Florida humidity. However, I was a flatlander and preferred ninety-five degrees temperature and humidity.

Ramps led from level to level. They were covered and well lighted with florescent lights. The sidewalks running in front of the buildings were just as wide and similarly covered; leading me to conclude the preferred means of travel was by golf cart on these walkways. Owning one myself, I noted that these were either E Z Go from Textron or John Deere machines. The latter extended to different kinds of utility vehicles, battery and small horsepower operated.

We zipped up ramps past buildings built into the sides of the mountain. Some were two and three stories. At a one of the buildings, about halfway up, a pickup was offloading food.

"Hungry?" asked Tall Guy.

"No, thanks."

"When you wake up, just go down there and eat, or you can eat in your room. They deliver to the patients who are laid up."

"Patients?"

He shrugged.

"Where is this place anyway?"

We were still threading our way up ramps.

"They didn't tell you?"

"Not since we landed in Greensboro."

"Oh. It's not really a secret," he said easily, "but then again, I ain't in charge."

So that meant he wasn't going to tell me. Which, of course, made me wonder why. I was already more than curious, keeping in mind the mysterious Doctors Smith and their electronic sweeping gizmos and their guns. And especially keeping in mind their particular penchant for not providing information, either. All of which in turn told me that there was more than one simple context involved here. Ostensibly, they wanted me for information, for what was happening to me, to learn what they could. In turn, they'd try to help me using all their alleged "new & improved" techniques, equipment or knowledge or whatever it was they were slyly hinting at.

Taking a deep breath of the cool air, I sat back. What the hell, it wasn't like I had a lot of choice. Both my watch and my personal clock were unwinding with uncomfortable speed.

We chugged up the central ramp. As we climbed the mountain, big, wide walkways split off the main artery at different levels or tiers on the mountain. Finally Tall Guy took a left off the ramp and drove along the walkway. The valley spread out below, buildings connected by lighted walkways in a web-like pattern. Another cart was whipping up the central ramp, and I assumed that was Raleigh and Rhonda. At the bottom, the helicopter pad lights still beckoned. The two crewmembers were finishing up their post flight inspection.

On the far side of the parking lot, a pair of lights appeared through the trees. This was at the side of the valley without buildings. The way in and out. All down at the foot of these mountains in the valley. Doubtless in the daylight, quite picturesque. Occasionally, golf carts sat aside next to buildings.

Tall Guy pulled up to a single story building. "They want you in the corner apartment," he said. It looked like a motel building with four units, but was larger than you'd think necessary to contain four rooms.

"Fine."

Tall guy got out and waited for me to grab my bag. He indicated a rocky path to the side of my apartment. "The path winds through the woods above, and then follows along the top of the ridge line. The old man had it built for walking and exercise. Stay on the path. On the other side of the ridge is a long drop, almost a cliff. Where it's not a dangerous fall, we've put in fences—for security." He shook his head. "Only way in or out is on the road." He pointed down the valley at the road I'd identified.

Of course, by now that didn't surprise me.

He opened the door without a key and led me inside. Turning on the overhead lights, he said, "They'll find you when they want you. Like I said, if they don't get you and you're hungry, just go eat." He went out and closed the door after him.

Surprisingly, the room was a cross between a hospital room and a motel suite. The front portion was a sitting room and a kitchenette. Behind that was a large bedroom and bathroom. The bed was a hospital bed with the rails down and all the appropriate controls. Alongside the bed, but pushed into corners, was the obligatory hospital room equipment. Oxygen access, computer terminal with keyboard and monitor, another monitor hitched up to the blood pressure cuffs and other wires and tubes. In another corner sat one of those racks they hang blood bags and IV's from. On the bedside table was a telephone with a laminated placard. Apparently, I had two choices. The "Duty Nurse Station" or the "Café." At the bottom of the card was a note in caps: THIS IS NOT AN OUTGOING OR INCOMING TELEPHONE.

Checking the sitting room, I found the same laminated page. So they didn't necessarily want me to have outside communications? Surely they knew most people carried cell phones these days. And, surely if I had a laptop, I could plug it in the wall phone jack and communicate. Or could I? I didn't know if that made any difference or not. I was at their mercy and convenience for now, anyway. Then it occurred to me that as important a place as this was shaping up to be, it would probably have a wireless capability.

Thinking on all this, I put my stuff in the dresser, what little there was of it, and hung up a couple of pairs of slacks and shirts. I tried the television and ran it through the channels on the remote. Satellite, a couple of hundred channels. Not that I cared. I'd brought a copy of *Guns, Germs, and Steel*, Jared Diamond's tying together of the different human societies for the last ten or fifteen thousand years. Sounds boring, but was actually fascinating, explaining many aspects of human development. Carrie Jean had given the book to me so that we could discuss it on our long runs.

The suite was decorated more to the luxury side than the hospital or motel room style, and there was a fancy clock radio on the bedside table. Checking the time, I found it just after five in the morning. I guessed I had time for a couple of hours of sleep.

Nonchalantly, I dragged a chair to the middle of the bedroom by the foot of the bed and sat down on it, pulling off my shoes. I took off my slacks and shirt and folded them over the back of the chair. Until I figured how long I was going to be here, I'd best be careful or find a laundry building. Doing a final walk-through of the rooms, I found the same shadow in the overhead light in the sitting room. We'll see, I thought.

I took a shower and turned out all the lights. It was pretty dark. I turned on the radio and WBT 1130 AM was on a talk show. Being a radio person, I knew the station, out of Charlotte. I also turned off the illumination light on the radio and the room became almost pitch black. I turned the radio volume up to hide any sounds I might be making.

Feeling my way slowly to the chair I'd casually placed in the middle of the floor, right under the overhead light, I stepped onto it quietly. Touching the rim of the cover, I felt the still hot bulbs. But where I'd seen the out-of-place shadow, I felt the plastic and shape of a miniature camera. Still being quiet, I climbed down and eased myself into bed. The sitting room would have one or more cameras or listening devices, too.

I fiddled with the radio to give cacophonous noises to further misdirect any possible listeners.

Was this mere security? Was it a sign of the new times? Or was it more sinister?

It was even possible that the cameras were installed but not in use. There, just in case. You never could tell. But somehow I doubted that the spy devices were installed and not being used.

What would this day bring? Judging by my experiences lately, probably nothing I could anticipate.

Not having any answers, I fell asleep.

CHAPTER TWENTY-ONE

In about four hours I was up and did the only logical thing for me.

I went running.

In athletic shorts, tee shirt and running shoes, I headed up the path Tall Guy had pointed out. I assumed my stuff would be safe, for I certainly had no key to the room, nor was there one lying around. Again attributable to the hospital motif?

On the walkway a young man was pushing an old man in a wheelchair. The young man was dressed in khaki slacks and pullover white shirt. The old man had to be ninety and looked familiar. He looked to me like an older version of that southern senator who had always been in the news maybe twenty-five or thirty years ago. The institutionally dressed young man nodded pleasantly and kept them going; the old guy merely glanced at me. I smiled like I knew what I was doing.

A few quick stretches later, I was climbing the mountain path. Hard clay and gravel, maybe five feet wide, it made a nice morning walk. When it leveled off above in the trees, I began running. It extended into the woods on the right and the left. I chose the left fork. Must stay in character. Trees, brush, rock outcroppings. The path rose and dipped. The path wound through woods and occasionally overlooked the valley below. While I was interested in that, of course, I also wanted to check out the other side of the mountain. With the uneasy feeling I'd had since this started and which had compounded since I arrived earlier this morning, I wanted to know what was where, where I was, how to get out of here, what the circumstances were.

Some of the trees still dripped from the morning mist. Varieties of hickory and maple dominated. I recognized ash, dogwood, and white pine. I was better at recognizing fauna than I was at flora. Generally speaking, a tree's a tree. In Florida we have oak, palm, pine. If it's flora and in a swamp or underwater, I recognize it fine. Every so often, I saw a thorny kind of tree, a locust maybe.

After the past few days full of stress, the running felt good. I had Mary Lou and Carrie Jean hard on my case. Down at work, things generally were going to hell. And I was growing younger faster, my biological clock tripping out big time, to employ the current idiom. My future was going down the toilet even if I lived through this. I kicked up the speed another notch.

And in about half a mile the trail died.

It came to an end alongside a wild cherry tree sitting atop a lookout point. The valley sloped down from here.

In the daylight, my observation that the elevation must have been between three and four thousand feet looked about right. I still hesitated to term it a valley in the mountains because it wasn't big enough. But, I supposed, valleys probably don't have an exact size requirement to be called valleys. It was practically a bowl in the mountains. Maybe a couple of hundred acres, the terrain was uneven, but was arranged in a series of offset terraces. At the bottom sat the helipad like a central target. Up one terrace level was the gravel parking lot with a dozen pickups and SUV's. I got the impression that the main method of travel in and out of this place was by helicopter.

There was one entrance to this place where a road wound through a cut in a ridge leading to the parking lot. Access to this valley wouldn't be difficult to control.

From the parking area up the mountains on three sides like a horseshoe, the buildings sprawled. As I'd observed last night, covered walkways, ramps, and stairs between the terraces connected most of the buildings. I'd seen the concept before, only before it was rice paddies.

The buildings were painted a uniform white and throughout the terraces and on the side of the surrounding mountains were thick with trees and brush. The ridges around the bowl were another five hundred feet above the highest terrace. The walking path I was on wound in and out of sight, both below and on top of the ridgeline.

The impression I got was isolation. Then it struck me. I could see no indication of what this place was, no signs, no lettering on the vehicles, no clues. Just like the private 737 and the choppers.

Turning away, I began running again. Occasionally I'd stop to look at certain things, most specifically the terrain away from the valley. Where the terrain allowed you to climb up from the trail, an eight-foot chain link fence ran adjacent. If there were a precipitous drop off, the fence dead-ended and restarted again. Where I could actually see a ways, the lay of the land appeared to be more mountains, more forest, more rock, drop-offs, clay, hillsides, mountainsides, but no habitation.

At the halfway point, I passed the access trail and kept going. The hiking path wound its way through the mountainside and trees for another mile and ended on the other side of the U from the first overlook. I went to swat a large insect but it turned out to be a hummingbird. The far end of the trail died also, but the overlook was wider and I could see the entrance to the valley.

Standing maybe a thousand feet above the valley on the other side of our quaint little valley, I could finally put this place in some kind of perspective. In that next valley, a small road wandered along from one end to the other. The position of the sun told me that next-door valley was directly east. That valley was also not inhabited, except for a fence line alongside of the road. The cut in the mountain which led from our valley to that valley led to the top of a hill and the road from the parking lot ran straight to the county road over there. Where the two intersected, our gravel road had what appeared to be a cattle guard and a gate in the fence line. A small block building sat just inside the fence line. It gave every impression of one of those lonely cold war outposts. I expected a couple of gray uniformed guards in great coats with rifles slung over their shoulders to step out of the building. I wondered why they had a cattle guard when I didn't see any cattle. Of course, that could be a relic from earlier times, I thought.

Whatever, the cool weather felt different than my Florida. I did not dislike what some people called our oppressive humidity and excessive heat. On the other hand, this was an enjoyable change. I decided I was hungry and ran back down the path.

When I returned to my room, Tall Guy was driving his cart up the path above the buildings. "Hey, Mr. Zachary, they're looking for you."

"Let me take a quick shower and change."

Instead of riding with him, I continued down the path and then went into my room. He followed me in the golf cart and pulled up on the walkway in front of my room. "I'll wait for you."

"Thanks." I thought.

Quickly showering, I hurried through dressing. I chose a pair of slacks and a light blue button up shirt. Pocketing my cell phone, I hurried outside. This activity helped me keep my mind off my condition and any hope that it would be solved immediately: meaning I didn't want to jinx my luck by hoping.

When I stepped onto the golf cart and sat down next to him, I said, "You have weird hours." He was driving an electric John Deere without a top.

He grimaced. One of his eyes didn't open all the way. "I don't work shift. I live here." He pointed to a building below on the parking lot level. "We'll get you some breakfast first, Mr. Zachary."

"Most people call me Easy."

"Yessir, Mr. Zachary. Most of our clients don't dress so formally. Did you bring any jeans?"

I nodded. "What's your name?"

"Hallelujah. Hallelujah Gertz." His right eye drooped.

"I bet there is a story behind it."

"Yessir. I was such a big baby that's what my momma said when I came out of her." He spat off the walk onto the ground and turned right onto the down ramp. "She also said that when I left home as soon's I turned eighteen." He studied me with his bad eye. "I don't regret it a damn bit, neither. I been working here ever since. Old Mr. Tyme, he had me get a GED, too."

"Mr. Tyme?"

Hallelujah laughed. "Christ, they didn't tell you nothin', did they? They jumped through their ass to get down to you and get you back and didn't tell you nothin'. Well, it ain't surprisin'." He had the requisite North Carolina twang. He kept driving down levels. "Never mind what they say, old Mr. Tyme, he ain't a bad guy. So you know that thing, Mr. Zachary." He turned onto a level and stopped immediately at the building we'd passed earlier this morning where the pickup truck offloaded.

We went into the center door and it was not at all like a hospital cafeteria.

There were a dozen tables in the room all covered with white table cloths, and already set at four places with cloth napkins and silverware, not flatware. Two large plate glass windows looked down upon the rest of the valley and across the valley to the far side. This was pretty country, green and wavy in the wind. The rear of the dining room had a waist high counter with a sliding panel. It was open.

Hallelujah went to the counter and said, "Hey, Emeril, you got customers out here."

A short guy with thick glasses popped up. "Hey, Hal. Hello, sir. You must be the guy from Florida."

"I am."

"Still got oatmeal on, and I could come up with almost anything you want. Breakfast or lunch. Sandwiches, meal. Gimmie an idea what you're looking for. Fruit? How about some coffee?"

"Maybe some oatmeal, a banana and a large glass of water."

"No coffee?" He gestured at a pot on the counter.

"Diet Coke." A bit of caffeine would do.

"You're easy. Be right out."

"That's me."

Hallelujah poured himself coffee into a large mug. "Sit down anywhere."

I selected a window table so I could observe what was going on and eye the territory. Hallelujah Gertz sat down with me. "He'll bring it out in a minute. We're pretty informal around here. Except some of the clients get real VIP treatment."

Not me, I guessed.

He correctly interpreted my look. "You're ambulatory and not a jillionaire. Or one of them hoity toidy celebrities."

The cook came out with my breakfast on a silver platter. The banana was already peeled and lay on a bed of lettuce with a side of mayonnaise. The oatmeal was in a fancy bowl with butter and cream separate. "Thanks, got any peanut butter?"

"Certainly. Crunchy?"

Nodding, I began eating and he came right back with a bowl, not a jar, of crunchy peanut butter. I split the banana and spread some peanut butter and mayonnaise on the banana. Still always hungry.

The cook watched with interest. "Good move," he said and returned to the kitchen.

"What can you tell me?" I asked Hallelujah Gertz.

"They want you to know, they'll tell you. It ain't a big secret. Tyme, Inc. is exclusive."

"Who are they?"

"The chief of staff and the docs, they run this place. They got an administrative staff, but the administrator, she's in charge. The docs run the medical side."

"Raleigh and Rhonda Smith?"

"And a couple of others. Of course, Mr. Tyme, he's the man. But he don't bother with the day to day stuff much anymore." Gertz glanced out the window to the farther side of the valley. On our central level, a more ornate building stood out. "Tyme's quarters?" I asked.

"*Mister* Tyme," he corrected.

Right then I castigated myself for not doing enough home-work. I'd known the name Tyme, extrapolated from Tyme, Inc. I could have done quick research or had somebody do it for me. But Dexter had tried and failed.

A golf cart sped along the walkway spoke just below us, charged up the ramp, swung next to our cart and stopped. Rhonda stepped out and pushed the door open. She was wearing a basic doctor hospital type smock that fell below her waist. Under that she wore a pair of dark slacks.

"We're waiting," she said without preamble. She was wearing glasses this day. But her sharp, sapphire eyes cut through the glass.

"Hi yourself," I said conversationally.

Hallelujah Gertz was standing now, as if he were at attention. "He was out running on the hiking trail and—"

"We know, Hal, thanks. I'll take him from here."

How'd she know I'd been running? Word obviously trav-eled fast at this place. Or the electronic surveillance was more extensive than outwardly apparent. Maybe that was something I should check out more in depth the next time I was out on the hiking trail.

I stood and drained my Coke. I started to gather up the dishes.

"Not your job, Mr. Zachary," said Hallelujah Gertz, obvi-ously happy to have some other event interfere with the spot-light upon him.

"Come with me." Rhonda turned and went out the door. The golf cart was rolling before I took my seat. She went down one level and sped down the walkway. She was strangely silent, so I didn't say anything either.

She pulled up in front of a large building with double doors. Beside a green ash was a concrete apron. Several green John Deere golf carts were already parked there. She swerved over there and slid to a stop. She looked at me. "Are you ready, Ethan?"

"I suppose. Could you tell me a little about this place? Who's who, what's what?"

"Ah, the organizational inquiring mind wants to know. Okay, I'll brief you as we go along so we don't waste time."

"Rhonda? I really have to know something."

"And that is?"

"You are now and have been in a great hurry. I've referred before to your sense of urgency. The question: Do you know something I should about my condition? Am I going to die off soon? Is that the reason for all this expediting?"

"Ethan, I pray you brought some of those delicious little cigars. The answer? I have never before encountered a condition such as you exhibit. Nor has Raleigh. Nor has our research turned up any other legitimate cases."

She didn't answer my question, of course. But I expected no less.

Then I was trailing her inside. I wasn't sure I liked this all-business Rhonda.

The double doors had a motion sensor and swung open inwardly.

I followed Rhonda into the utilitarian lobby. It gave every appearance of being the hub of a medical complex. Next to the sole elevator, a directory window box listed rooms with medical terminology, X-ray, CT scan, laboratory, Dr. Smith, Raleigh, Dr. Smith, Rhonda, that kind of thing. I didn't get as long as I needed to study the listing as Rhonda dragged me up a flight of stairs. A young man who could have been a nurse or a technician passed us on the stairs and said hi to Rhonda. He looked at me with interest, but kept on going. I suspected every new client or patient in that place invited inspection.

Rhonda's was one of several on the second floor. In her suite were several more rooms. We passed an examination room out of *Star Trek*, an office with a desk and files and books shelves. We went into a well-appointed sitting room. A plate glass window filled the front wall. The view was a panorama of the valley. It reinforced my opinion that Rhonda was high up in whatever hierarchy ran this place.

She indicated for me to take a seat and I chose a modern

couch looking out. She selected a steel straight-backed chair behind a coffee table. On the coffee table were a couple of pens, a yellow legal pad, and a remote control.

Rhonda picked up the remote control and touched a button.

I saw no televisions, recorders, VCR's, anything.

She pointed above her head. Hanging from the ceiling was a miniature camera.

"We're recording this session so that we have it for reference and won't have to repeat ourselves."

I thought of all the privacy laws and knew the rules were different here.

"Fine. Where's old Raleigh this morning?" I don't know why I said that. Maybe I just had to throw in a monkey wrench, get her off balance, establish myself. I felt somewhat stupid. Maybe I somewhere in my subconscious I didn't want to be a plain old every day medical subject. I didn't want to be a patient. Hell, I didn't want to be here to start with.

"He has other things to do." She checked her watch and frowned. I got the impression she was telling me to stop being snide and personal, that we were being recorded—and/or observed, it occurred to me. On the coffee table sat a sheaf of papers. She pushed them over to me. "Releases. Sign where the sticky notes say sign and initial where they say initial."

I followed her instructions. Being a lawyer, I recognized some basic wording. But a highly proficient attorney had designed this liability release specifically for me. I felt important. I thought about questioning it, but didn't. I scanned most of it. It didn't matter. This was quickly becoming my last chance—an idea I shied away from for the reason that if this failed to help, then I was dead and just waiting for it to happen. So without a peep, I signed and initialed.

"This is necessarily exhaustive. You realize we can now impregnate you with a yak and you have no recourse."

"You'll recall I'm an attorney."

"Just wanted you to know. Listen, Ethan, we're going to start at the beginning and go through it all. We've got to make sure we don't miss anything."

Maybe I just wanted to establish myself period. Maybe I didn't appreciate feeling like a pawn or an object of study and investigation. And the more I thought about it, the more I thought that maybe others were watching this interview.

"Rhonda, maybe you could tell me a little bit about this place? Nobody wants to talk to me." I waved my hand to include the whole valley. "Lots of effort. Lots of money. Lots of facilities. All way the hell away from anywhere. People are all closed mouthed. I won't tell, I promise." I gave my most winning smile. I was ready to quit cooperating.

Her glasses were at the end of her nose and she looked over the top of the lenses at me and sighed. "This is the Tyme Institute. Justyn Tyme, both names with a 'y', founded it many years ago for the purpose of research into the aging process. It has evolved into a clinic for wealthy clients. We apply science, medicine, and nutrition to the elderly clients who—"

Footsteps sounded in the corridor and then Raleigh Smith walked in. He had a single rose in his hand. "Hi, hon. Excuse me. It's time?"

"Of course," she said rising. "We were running late."

"My fault," I said jokingly but nobody laughed.

Raleigh handed her the rose. "For you."

"Thank you." She favored him with a smile. She clicked the remote, formally ending the session. She leaned forward and pushed a button on a telephone.

Raleigh did not look mean-spirited this morning; he appeared distracted.

A forty-something woman in a nurse's outfit came in the door silently. She had a big smile and her front teeth poked out when she did so. "Hello, young man, I'm ready for you."

It took me a surprised moment to realize this woman who was probably fifteen years my junior was reacting as if I were younger than she.

She seemed to realize something similar. She looked me up and down and nodded as if confirming something to herself.

Her hair was blond, almost as blond as Raleigh's, and shorter than his.

Rhonda said, "This is Sis. She's my assistant and she'll take you around for tests." She saw my frown. "You will remember in Sarasota that I told you there'd be more of the same and some tests they've never heard of."

I groaned but got no sympathy.

Sis asked Rhonda, "How's he doing this morning?"

"Better, now that we're home." They weren't talking about me. Probably this Justyn Tyme with a 'y'. I wondered briefly about somebody named that who'd founded a place like this on aging. However, stranger things have happened. Just look at me.

"Come with me, Mr. Zachary." Sis took me by the arm and dragged me out of the office and down the stairs. "We believe in exercise here," she said. "Nobody takes the elevator. Those are for people in wheelchairs and hospital beds. And they constructed the hiking trail up the mountain, too." She sort of pointed up the mountainside. "Though they wanted you here earlier, when they saw you were going to go running, they let you do that because we believe in exercise. Aren't you glad?"

"I guess."

Downstairs, she led me into a corridor and then into another room with electronic equipment. I recognized the one where they stick you into a giant barrel and zapped you with kryptonite. Or something.

"CT scan," Sis said. "Computerized tomography. Tomography is from *tomos*, which is Greek for 'section.' The machine is going to look at your insides."

"I'm all happy," I said.

Nobody was laughing at my jokes today.

She stuck me in that machine and their computer went to work. Actually, I laid on a table in front of this impressive machine with a big hole in the front and she sat at a computer station and started the process. "This is the same as a CAT scan. It's all part of what we call 'Diagnostic Radiology.' But don't worry; you won't be exposed to much radiation. It's a patient friendly exam."

"I was worried."

"They performed the body scan in Sarasota; we will do it again to make sure. But we're also going to concentrate on your head. With this and other tests, we will find something if it's there. I mean disease or tumor or whatever. We'll see your brain cavities, sinuses, if you have blood clots, aneurysms, other stuff."

"Great."

"Have you been having headaches?"

"No."

"Maybe that's good. If nothing appears here, the doctors might not want to take a biopsy."

"You mean stick a giant needle into my head?"

"Badly put, but yes."

"Great."

"And after this, we have other equipment we're going to get into. The next one will be functional magnetic resonance imaging. Now we're going to use x-rays in this CT scan. The fMRI uses a magnetic field and radio waves."

One way or the other, I was going to be nuked.

"That one will show small metabolic changes in your brain, among other things."

Later, when we got to the MRI, she put me on the sliding table in a head brace. The big cylindrical machine loomed over me. She checked a sheet of paper. "Ah, good to know. You had shrapnel and bullets."

"Well, not all that many—"

"But it's important to know because any residue could skew the results. Did they remove all the metal?"

"I guess."

As she was performing an MRI of my head, she made me hold still for several seconds. "This is a new unit, more patient-friendly. It's called a 'short-bore' system and doesn't fully enclose you."

"I feel so much better."

I had to drink ill tasting stuff and get x-rayed or scanned or z-rayed, whatever.

She also took several test tubes of blood. Occasionally, another technician helped her out.

She made me do dozens of tests that day and the next two days. They even checked my eyes; echocardiogram, which is an ultrasound of my heart; other ultrasounds; exercise stress test, a treadmill with wires attached all over my body; I swallowed barium for upper gastrointestinal series; a thyroid scan; a colonoscopy, God help me; throat cultures; more x-rays, and x-rays with dye; allergy tests; oxygen saturation; pulmonary function tests, which was breathing through tubes connected to machines; electrocardiogram, your basic EKG; electromyography, where they stick needles into your body to analyze nerves and muscles; pee in a cup; something called a PET scan (positron emission tomography) using some kind of "tracer" which emitted something called "positrons" which somehow produced gamma rays picked up by the ring-like machine through which the table I was lying on passed and showed images of specific organ's metabolism and other esoteric stuff I don't understand; and more.

During a break I called Mary Lou on my cell phone. She wasn't there so I talked to the answering machine. "Hi, it's me. Just calling to check in. We've been doing tests seemingly forever. Hope you're doing okay. Talk to you later." I never have been good at talking to machines for later hearing.

Sis instructed me to not eat after midnight. The next day, they gave me a spinal tap and more blood tests. I had to lie on my side and curl up they numbed my back and took fluid from my spine with a big damn needle. I didn't think they expected to find anything, but they were gathering data and excluding as much as they could. That procedure took an hour by itself.

Another lengthy process worthy of remark turned out to be a bone marrow biopsy. Sis told me they scheduled it for the last test of the second day. I found I had to recover from it. And Raleigh Smith was the one to extract my bone marrow. They had me to lie on my face and they numbed the area above my buttock and made a cut into it so they could insert the biopsy needle. A big damn needle with a big damn handle on it. Raleigh inserted it and I felt movement in my backside. I felt the needle hit the bone of my pelvis, or I guessed that's what it hit, and then he almost screwed it into my bone.

"Ah, we're into the bone. Give me the syringe," he told Sis.

I could imagine him inserting the syringe into the big damn needle. When he withdrew the syringe, I felt pain even though they'd numbed the area and given me oral pain medication.

After that, he screwed the needle in farther. "This part is known as the core biopsy," he told me. "The first part we took some liquid, now I'm getting solid tissue from the bone. We just push it out of the needle when I withdraw it." He did that thing and I felt it all the way. "Hold this pad on with pressure," he told Sis, "for a few minutes. Zachary, you'd be better off to lie down for a couple of hours and let the medication wear off." He was right. Somebody even had Hallelujah Gertz come by and drive me to my room.

I slept until maybe 10:30 and went down to the café to see if I could get any food. Emeril gave me some cold fried chicken. "Usually, I got more here, but I'm settin' up for the big birthday party tomorrow." He said it like I should know what he was talking about, so I just sat and ate and then went for a walk and a smoke. Later, I read some of Diamond's *Guns, Germs, and Steel* I'd brought. It made me think that anthropologists have all the fun. Then I thought that maybe, while they did interesting stuff, they dealt a lot with dead people, just like morticians. Politicians and attorneys deal with real live people—more or less.

Thinking I needed contact with the real world, I thought that I would call Carrie Jean and share these observations with her. And my intentions were to check in with Mary Lou, too. I got a miniature cigar. I'd have a smoke and call outside. I didn't want to share my phone conversations with whoever was listening and watching electronically.

Except I couldn't find my cell phone. I thought I'd had it earlier today when I was undergoing those extensive tests. Maybe I'd left it in my room instead, but it wasn't here. I remember being half drugged, medicated, and beat upon, and stuck through and through with medical paraphernalia so much that I'd been punch drunk if nothing else. Doubtless, I thought, I'd left the cell phone somewhere along the way. I trusted everyone here. Sis and her technician friends would not find the phone and run up a long bill. I knew I'd be down in those same offices and buildings tomorrow and look for it. If it was lost, so be it. I could use the Institute's phone—though I remembered there wasn't an outgoing phone in my room.

So I went outside and had the smoke anyway. It occurred to me that since my reverse aging had begun, I'd been smoking a whole lot more than I usually did. The night was turning cold and quiet and the smoke hung there in front of me and then gradually broke up. The stars seemed more defined in this crisp air then they did in the humid Florida atmosphere. Fireflies blinked in the valley below, a sight I hadn't seen in Florida for years and years.

They were about out of tests and by now some of the results should be coming in. Many of the tests, the MRI's, the x-rays, that sort of thing, they already had the results. And probably they could perform some or most of the blood and fluid tests here. I still had to go over my medical history and so on with Rhonda.

Would the results be sufficient to give them some idea of a possible treatment for my condition? I prayed so. What else did I have left? Remote viewing? That seemed more and more remote, so to speak, from this perspective.

I was walking along the walkway on the level where my room was. When I finished the miniature cigar I headed back for my room.

Just as I arrived, a golf cart whished up and Hal said "Hey, Mister Zachary. I saw your light on and thought I'd come up for a second."

"Hal, I don't want to be so formal. Most people call me Easy.

Or Ethan."

He shrugged. "It don't matter, Mr. Z., we gotta use client's last names, it's the rules." He held up a cell phone. "This was in my cart. I guess it's yours."

"I did lose it. Thanks. I owe you a beer."

"No, thank you anyhow. I only got one kidney and I don't drink. Drinking ain't a big thing up here. Some do it, but not many. We got liquor and beer and wine and the like for the clients if they want, but that's about it."

"Well, I don't drink either."

"And you a lawyer and all."

"Life is strange sometimes," I said and flipped the phone open to check the time. Generally, it worked, unlike my watch. Although the display usually dimmed when I held it. But now the display window remained dark.

Hal leaned over with his bad eye and looked as I was shaking the phone in my hand. "Maybe it needs charging."

"Not usually. But I'll do it."

He drew back his head. "I never had any use for them things."

"It's the way of the world now, Hal. Pretty soon nobody will have regular phones. They'll all be like this."

"Don't matter to me. I been here for so long, I live here, I don't need one. I'll be here 'til I die, I won't need one."

"Sounds like you have good job security."

He nodded vigorously. "I do that. Mr. Tyme, he took care of me. Even after he passes, I'll be here. It's in his will."

"Must be nice."

"He took me in and I take care of him and he takes care of me. Me and him, we're like that." He held up crossed fingers. He seemed to realize it was late. "Well, I gotta go and let you get to sleep. Got a big birthday party I gotta help Emeril set up tomorrow."

"Whose party?"

"Nobody told you?"

"Not a thing. Emeril mentioned it but...."

He shrugged again. "I guess they didn't think to. You'll be

here, so you're invited. That famous actress and that ex-senator, they'll be there."

"Whose birthday?" I asked, expecting what I'd been sort of expecting since I arrived. Justyn Tyme and his eightieth birthday. Whoever Justyn Tyme was.

"Oh. Well, uh, it's the kid. Doctor Rhonda and Doctor Raleigh. It's their son." The way he said it left something unsaid. But he didn't tell me. He continued, "That Emeril, he really worked hard. His name ain't Emeril, you know. Everybody, we just call him that after the cheft on teevee. That makes him feel good." Hal looked around. "Hey, Mr. Z., it's late, I got a couple things left to do, so I gotta go. G'night."

"Tomorrow then."

He zipped off.

I went inside and plugged the cell phone in. The clock on the wall told me it was very late, but I thought I'd give Mary Lou a call anyway. Especially since she hadn't called me. I thought I could call while the phone was plugged in; it should have plenty of power.

But the display remained blank. I punched buttons and arrow keys, but still nothing registered. I supposed my personal screwy electricity had finally zapped the phone. If that were the case, I thought, then why hadn't I been killing other electronic items? The other side of the coin occurred to me: with the acceleration of my counterclockwise aging, did that also mean I was becoming more and more charged with whatever electrical force was buried in my body? Did it mean that inimical force was now raging within me?

Frankly, the next thing I did made me feel like a damn fool.

After my shower, I shaved as usual and purposefully nicked myself so that I was bleeding slightly. I turned out all the lights and stood naked in front of the mirror. Thankfully, the blood failed to glow. I opened my eyes and mouth wide; I rubbed my hands together; I twisted and turned. Nothing. Not one spark, not one arc of electricity. My eyes weren't glowing like a werewolf's in a movie. I held up my hand and spread my fingers wide.

No glow from the thin skin of the web between my fingers. So much for scientific method.

I fell asleep thinking about bone marrow and busted cell phones.

CHAPTER TWENTY-TWO

In the morning, I decided to test their limits, discover some parameters so I could figure out what really was happening here.

I needed to wring out my system anyway.

Before I left, I checked the cell phone. Still nothing showing in the display. It acted as if it were a blown electronic unit. I thought wryly that it was obvious. The phone companies put time and date and almost everything else on your phone nowadays that the phone knows how many days have elapsed since they activated the phone and the current date. Meaning, of course, that the warranty had expired two days ago. Sometimes the most obvious answers are the correct answers.

Running shorts felt better on my upper buttocks—or lower small of the back, because they didn't rub the bandage from the bone marrow biopsy. The incision point looked all right in the mirror, so I could take the bandage off any time.

At the parking lot, I did a few stretches in case those in charge of watching me didn't notice me making my way down the ramps. The morning was chilly and, being a Floridian, I wished for more than a flimsy tee shirt, the one CJ had given me with a smiley face, which had a bullet hole in the forehead with blood trickling out. Was I making a statement? Beats me. But I felt like wearing it. Carrie Jean could think up some off-the-wall things, I reflected.

Some vehicles were in the parking lot, a half dozen which would be company vehicles, and others obviously personal vehicles of workers. SUV's and pickups, most with North Carolina tags, but two with Virginia plates. It stood to reason this was very north North Carolina. In Florida most of the license plates identified the county, but North Carolina just had the little Wright Brothers biplane and told the world that North Carolina was "FIRST IN FLIGHT."

Done stretching, I jogged off. I'd start with a nine minute mile, do a couple of eights, and then turn it on—depending on the terrain and running surface.

It felt good running up the short hill through the cut in the mountains. Here the ends of the U of the valley met. Craning my neck, I could see one of the lookout points above. All these mountains reconfirmed the fact that I was indeed a flatlander.

Coasting down the hill, I could see the ribbon of the county road running through the adjoining valley. And I could also see the intersection of this gravel road with that one. The lone sign of human habitation was the building at the cattle guard entrance to the paved road. While this gravel was okay to run on and better on my knees than pavement, I still preferred the evenness of concrete or asphalt.

When I came trotting up, feet grating noisily on the gravel, a man stepped out of the door near the cattle guard and gate.

"Good morning, sir," he said. He wore the traditional Tyme garb, Khaki trousers and a pullover shirt, this one with "TYME, INC." printed on the left chest.

"Good morning, sir." This time, his voice contained a warning.

The gate being closed, I ground to a stop.

"Can I help you?"

"No, thanks. Just let me out the gate. Or do you want me to climb over."

"Are you authorized to leave?"

"Authorized?" My voice was louder than I'd intended.

"Yes, sir. You're not supposed to leave without them telling me to let you." He took off his camouflaged baseball cap revealing unkempt hair.

"You got a gun to stop me?" Anger drove my mouth and I

struggled to control it.

He glanced in the open door. "Only if I need it." Inside in the shadows I could see a set of monitors and I recognized sections of the gravel road I'd just run. I also saw both of us standing here.

"Well, get your gun out and shoot me," I said. Then I pointed to my body. "Does it look like I'm stealing all the silverware? Am I escaping? Where the hell would I go?"

"I don't know, Mr. Zachary. I only do what I'm told." It appeared everybody knew my name.

"By whom?"

"Our boss."

"Justyn Tyme?"

"Well, he's the boss's boss. The chief of staff. She's in charge."

I was going to tell this fellow to tell the chief of staff to shove it, but this guy was just following orders. It wasn't his call. I think that's half the trouble with the world. People just do what they're told.

"Never mind. I'll be back in an hour or so." Just to plant a seed, I asked, "Which way to town?"

He didn't fall for it, but his eyes shifted to the right, that is the south, for a nano-second.

I smiled and stepped around the cattle guard and pushed on the gate. It was locked and I noted it had an electrical motor to open and close it. I put one hand on the top rail at chest level and levered myself over feet first without touching. Not bad for an older guy. Well, maybe I was, maybe I wasn't. I turned right and started running. Glancing back, I saw the sentry standing in the doorway of the building talking on a telephone.

The running felt good. There was no traffic, not yet anyway. The road surface was asphalt, but deteriorating on the edges.

Feeling better, I cranked it up to a seven-minute mile pace. It was wringing cobwebs out of my mind and stiffness out of my body. I felt really alive. It was difficult to believe that I was dying. Now warmed up, a small sweat broke out on my shoulders and forehead.

Soon I was out of the valley adjoining Tyme, Inc., and cruising along as the asphalt wound through the mountains. In about two miles, this road intersected with another more formal looking thoroughfare. Still two lanes, this one ran east and west at this point. And a farmhouse sat upon a hill down the road. A sign with an arrow said LANSING. I knew Lansing was in North Carolina, right close to the northwestern most point, just under Virginia. The Blue Ridge Parkway was up there somewhere.

I turned around here and headed back, determined to see if I'd kicked over the anthill. In a little while, I approached the entrance to Tyme's valley and kept on going. The sentry was leaning against the building and took off his cap and waved it at me. None of the army ants were swarming out of the anthill: so much for my heightened sense of self-importance. Waving back, I increased my pace to slightly over a six-minute mile. I couldn't keep that up long and I wasn't trying to impress Carrie Jean by staying with her, so as soon as I rounded the corner of a slope, I slowed.

An old man in an old pickup slowly drove past me. In the bed of the pickup was a giant roll of hay. I don't know how he got it on there or how it stayed, but it did. He waved and watched me for a moment. Interpretation: Nobody ever sees runners up here in the remote mountains and I was an anomaly.

The contrast keyed my memory and I wondered about Rhonda's son. Rhonda and Raleigh, I amended. The Tyme Institute in the isolated valley didn't appear to me to be a place where children lived or even visited. I hadn't seen even one child. I was becoming proficient at developing questions without answers.

The morning had warmed and I was feeling good about it, so I found a straightaway and sprinted for about two minutes on and off doing some interval training. Running takes the edge off hunger, but I knew I needed food, so I headed back under sharp blue skies. It did not escape my attention that up to a couple of months ago, I was in nowhere near this fine a physical condition. While that thought didn't ameliorate the fact that I was probably dying, I felt good about it.

It was a fine day. I heard a helicopter and soon one appeared from the east and swooped down into the valley out of my sight.

The guy at the gate saw me coming and opened the gate for me. I waved and he tipped his hat as I trotted by. I was barely jogging when I crested the hill in the cut between the mountains, and I slowed to a walk to cool off by the time I reached my room.

Above me the valley opened. I could see the buildings dotted about on the rising terraces. There were colored balloons everywhere, mostly tied to the posts holding up the walkway coverings. The Tyme residence that had been pointed out to me was especially festooned. At the hub, about the midway café location, the decorations were heaviest. Different colored strands of bunting stretched from post to post. In front of the café, smoke rose from an outside cooking grill.

As I started up the ramps, a cart scuttled alongside me. Hal drove with left leg hanging outside, foot almost skimming the ramp surface. Two twenty pound bags of Kingsford charcoal were in the back. "Hey, Mr. Z. You have a good run?"

"I did." Everybody also knew what I was doing and when I did it.

"How about a ride."

"No thanks. I need to walk it off."

"The party starts in a few minutes. You're invited, and it's the onliest place you gonna get fed right now."

"Thanks."

"Mr. Tyme's 'poda be here."

People were starting to wander outside and I noted most were dressed more informally for the party, so after my shower, I put on jeans and a fresh pair of running shoes. I had a Richard Petty shirt I'd brought to run in, so I pulled it on considering this was North Carolina, home of the king and hotbed of stockcar racing. All the time, of course, I'd been wondering about the star of the party, Rhonda and Raleigh's offspring.

Reflecting on the festive atmosphere, I stuck a cigar in my

back pocket, reminding myself not to sit down on it.

When I made my way down to the center level, the party was well under way.

Emeril was in front of the long grill tossing hamburgers and hot dogs. Hal stood behind a table with three large tubs full of ice. He was pulling dripping cans and bottles out of the ice and setting them on the table. People took whatever they wanted. I saw no alcohol, no beer, just soft drinks, juice, and bottled water. I took one of the latter to rehydrate after my long run, finished that, and took another. They even had separate garbage cans set up for metal and plastic recyclables.

Most of the people looked like employees. I'd seen many of them in passing during my short stay. Others still had all or part of their khaki and Tyme, Inc. uniform on.

I saw Rhonda and Raleigh amongst a small crowd farther down the walkway. Since Raleigh was there, I turned away from them. Set against the wall of the café stood a wide table and thereon sat a cake, a huge birthday cake, flat with enough icing to kill off a herd of diabetics. HAPPY BIRTHDAY ROLLY went across it in script. The cake was probably three feet by three feet in size. Seven large unlighted candles poked out of the cake in the center. Walking past Emeril, I turned to him.

"Did you make the cake?"

He pointed down the mountainside to the helicopter resting there. "I could have made it, Mr. Zachary, but they special-ordered it."

I kept going, trying to get out of the main thoroughfare. I nodded at the chopper pilot. "Hello, Mr. Zachary," he said.

"You must be a new client," a voice said behind me.

I turned. The old man I'd previously recognized sat there in his wheelchair. The senator, from Georgia if I recalled my political history. "Hello, Senator," I said.

"You know me?"

"I do. Retired just before Watergate. From Athens." Which made him maybe two hundred years old.

The senator beamed. "Smart boy," he said to his companion.

"Who are you?" he asked me.

Extending my hand, I said, "Ethan Zachary."

He shook it weakly. I raised my water bottle to him, and turned to shake hands with the lady who could have been his age. She was sitting, but on a folding chair. She had a four-legged aluminum walker beside her.

"Zachary, this is Mollie St. Ives." The senator said it like I should have known the name, and it did ring a vague bell. The senator laughed at my awkwardness. "You're too young to remember. She was in a couple of movies with Gable and Stewart and them guys."

"Of course," I said.

"Hello, young man," said Molly St. Ives with a thick voice. Her eyes were tired, though. "What are you doing here? You're not ancient like us." At her throat hung a wattle of skin.

Now this was something worthy of remark: here were two people who didn't know me, or of me. Meaning that the employees had all been briefed, my presence and status and name, rank, and serial number were known only to those involved, I wasn't just a bit of gossip about whom the word had gone out. Also, both had referred to me as young. The thought brought up the fear I'd found when I looked in the mirror after my shower a few short minutes ago. I'd recognized me, but I wasn't somebody I was comfortable with seeing in the mirror. I'd seen that me before, but not in twenty-five or thirty years. I was running out of time.

Not knowing how to answer her question, I said flippantly, "I think I'm a guinea pig from Florida to see how flatlanders can adapt to mountains and atmosphere with less than ninety percent humidity."

The senator said, "Whereabouts?"

"The Suncoast, Senator. Sarasota."

"Palmer Hibbs."

"Palmer T. Hibbs," I said. "You know him?"

"Hell, I knew him when he first come to Congress, still in diapers."

"He's a good man," I said, glad to get the conversation away from my reason for being here. "I saw him the other day. He's retiring after this term."

"About time," the senator said. He looked up at me from his wheel chair, and swiped the few hairs on his hear to the side. "You know Palmer?"

"Yes, sir." I saw no reason to go into my political background and possible run for congress. "Actually, I played racquetball with him." I managed to look sheepish. "He beat the socks off of me."

"Well, I will be triple damned," the senator said. "Small goddamn world."

"Senator!" Mollie St. Ives scolded. Skin hung from her cheeks and jaw line. Off hand I'd say she'd outlived several plastic surgeries.

"Your first husband was a foul-mouthed son of a bitch," said the senator, "I went fishing with him oncet off Cuba."

Rhonda appeared at my elbow like Scotty had just beamed her down.

She wasn't wearing glasses, so she must have contacts in.

"I need to steal Ethan for a minute. I want him to meet the guest of honor."

Neither said anything for a moment, then the senator said, "Nice boy."

"Thank you, sir. You're always the gentleman."

"He is, isn't he, sweetie," said the actress.

Rhonda took my arm and gently guided me away. She wore jeans, and did so well, and a white silk blouse. Her eyes were unusually hooded. Being an observer of eyes, I saw her eyes were not their usual penetrating and knowing selves. As we neared the circle of people around the child, her features softened. Motherhood is an autopilot and dictates its own response.

"I see you've met our other patients."

"Not a real large client base."

"I'm not in administration for the billing," Rhonda said, "but I'd say St. Ives is into us for twenty, twenty-five million."

"Well, I'm in the wrong business," I said, almost meaning it.

Raleigh was standing to the side and glared at me. His dislike was more apparent each time I saw him. It was akin to jealousy and he had no reason for jealousy. Nothing had occurred between Rhonda and me. While I liked her a great deal, and she obviously reciprocated, there had been no reason for an intelligent husband to take offense. There was more to this than I knew and understood.

The kid was sitting on a metal folding chair.

"Rolly," Rhonda said to Raleigh, jr., "I want you to meet Mr. Ethan Zachary. Ethan, this is our son Rolly."

The boy dutifully got off the chair with an obvious effort.

At first I thought the joke was on me. That all this had been staged to screw with me.

The seven-year-old boy was actually an aging midget.

"Hi, Mr. Zachary," he said like a little boy, and I knew something was dead wrong.

He was wearing jeans and some kind of special designed shoes. He had on a tee shirt with a big number 2 race car, a Dodge I thought, with RUSTY WALLACE scripted on it and a NASCAR logo in the background. An old shirt: Rusty was retired now.

The same car appeared on his baseball cap pulled down tight. The boy was apparently bald. His face was wizened and, by eighty years, prematurely old. His body appeared to have not grown since about the age of four, but his head was disproportionately large for his body. His eyes were tired and old.

While I was shocked, I knew I hadn't been warned what to expect. Maybe Raleigh had set me up. Maybe they just didn't want to talk about it.

But they forgot I was a politician and a bright guy. I've kissed a lot of hands and shaken a lot of babies, so to speak. I stepped forward and grasped Rolly's brittle hand. "How are you doing there, young fellow?"

"Fine." It was awkward for him, too.

"Happy birthday."

"Thanks. I like your shirt." He sort of leaned against his chair.

Rhonda was hovering like a mother hen. Raleigh, senior, had walked away a few feet.

I looked down at my Richard Petty jersey. "I got it from the King personally." Richard Petty was the winningest driver in stock car history and would never be surpassed.

"Wow, when?" He squirmed back on the chair as if very tired.

"A couple of times. Years ago before he retired, he made a personal appearance at Desoto Speedway, which is in Bradenton, Florida near where I live in Sarasota. Another time, when he was running for Secretary of State of North Carolina I attended a fund raiser for him and he personally signed this shirt." I pointed to an unmarked spot above the number 43 racecar. "But I've worn the shirt so much, the signature finally washed out over the years."

"Too bad," said the old kid.

"Yeah, but Rusty's cool, too. I saw him race at Daytona a few times."

"Rusty was in the 27 car, then he went to Penske racing in the 2 car." The kid had his racing lingo and Rusty Wallace history down.

"You go to school around here," I asked, and seeing the look on Rhonda's face, added, "or are you home-schooled?"

"Yeah, that," he said, obviously glad I wasn't pandering. "I got a teacher here and a nanny, too."

"Thanks to Mr. Justyn," Rhonda said, trying to tell me something about Justyn Tyme.

Rolly nodded.

"You drive any of these golf carts?" I asked with an inspiration.

"All of 'em," he said proudly.

"Me, too," I said. "I'm a golfer and I'm professional at driving golf carts." I paused. We talked NASCAR for a few minutes more. I treated the kid as a bright kid and got along fine with him. I remembered when I was a kid, as long ago as it was, and that I hated being talked down to. Kids are people and want to be treated as such.

You knew that no child of Rhonda's would use terms such as "you know" and "like." They'd have been talking in compound sentences to him and never, ever used baby talk. Because of his condition, he was more mature than his years should allow. I felt a kinship with him. One look at him and it was obvious that he was going to die of it. Just as I was going to die of my condition. His disease had a name; I just couldn't recall it. I wondered if he knew about me, that I was different, just as he was. That I was probably dying, too. Thinking about this, different things began to add up and start to make sense.

The nanny came over to check on Rolly and I stepped aside for other well-wishers. I had an idea and went and found Hallelujah Gertz. I outlined my idea and he was enthusiastic. Hell, everybody loved Rolly.

In five minutes, we had two golf carts with sheets of paper taped to all sides of both. On one, we'd marked number 2 in black magic marker, one the other was, of course, number 43.

I drove the 43 car and Hal drove the 2 car through the crowd beeping the horns, Hal shouting "Make way!"

When I got to Rolly and Rhonda, I edged my golf cart around. "All right, Rolly, let's see how good you are."

Hal stepped out of his golf cart, eyed Rhonda with a droopy eye, and walked away to another nearby cart.

Rhonda looked alarmed. "But…"

Rolly ignored her. "But nothing, Mom. You're on, Mr. Zachary."

"I'm Ethan. Or EZ."

"You're wasting time, EZ." He climbed awkwardly into his cart and started moving. "Where?"

I pointed to the floor of the valley. "We start at the helipad. Hal's going to be down the road where it disappears into the mountain. That's turn one and two. We come back around the helipad, those are turns three and four, and run it one more time."

He'd already grasped the idea was steering carefully through the growing crowd.

I followed him through the people, maybe fifty by now, and down the ramps to the helipad. Hal was already in position with his golf cart, about a half-mile down the gravel road I'd run earlier this morning.

We lined up side by side and I said, "Go!" and we took off.

Rolly surged ahead at first, probably because of my greater weight. He made the first turn around Hal sitting in his golf cart too fast and so went too wide. I made a tighter turn and came out of it ahead by a nose. The batteries were valiant, but mine carried more weight and soon Rolly outdistanced me. He learned from the first turn, so when we went around the helipad, he slowed properly and made a better turn. He outran me fair and square, taped sheets of copy paper with big 2's all flapping.

When he crossed the imaginary finish line the crowd above roared and applauded.

I pulled up beside him. "Good race."

"You didn't let me win?" His face was flushed.

"Hell no. You're a damn kid and you were carrying a lot less weight."

He thought about it for a moment and grinned. "Beat you, fair and square."

"I hate to admit it, but you got witnesses." I waved to the side of the mountain above us. I saw the smoke rising from the charcoal. "And that made me hungry." Actually, I was starving.

Rolly led a procession of three golf carts up the ramps, grinning like he hadn't had any fun in years. I wondered if his years were as short as my years. Dog years were seven to one. EZ years were beginning to look like a hundred to one, in a backwards sort of way. Rolly years? If he was seven now, ten to one? If you don't want to know the answer, don't ask the question. He'd had his problem for years, probably. I'd had mine less than a couple of months. That I knew of.

We topped the final ramp and everybody sang happy birthday

to Rolly.

Rhonda hugged him and gave me a look that told me she didn't care if I'd contrived to lose or lost legitimately. For the rest of the party, you couldn't pry Rolly out of his number 2-racecar golf cart.

My idea had been spontaneous, but it was obvious I'd built some good will. Be that as it may, I was still uneasy about this place, this secluded valley. It wasn't just about my cell phone conveniently self-destructing.

CHAPTER TWENTY-THREE

I was sitting on a rock, my legs dangling down the mountainside and eating a grilled half-chicken when Raleigh came over and sat down next to me.

He said, "I was going to introduce you to Justyn; however, he's not feeling well and they took him back inside. But he saw the race."

"Okay." I didn't know what else to say.

"I owe you this, Zachary—"

"You owe me nothing, Raleigh."

His head whipped around at the edge in my voice and he looked me in the eyes for a change. "For Rolly—"

"It was just something between me and the kid, Doctor. You owe me nothing."

"I didn't like you," he said carefully, "but you offered a possible antidote for Rolly. That's what I saw in you. Our tests on you show nothing to date. And your blood type isn't his and never the twain shall meet." He breathed deeply. "You will never know the height of elation, the pinnacle of hope that followed when we first heard of you and your problem. It was as if you were God-sent specifically for Rolly. What a let-down."

Something scratched at the back of my mind.

"I can understand that," I said, and thinking about it, he made sense. The one wild card, me, in the deck and he drew it and it didn't work. He must have been terribly disappointed. No wonder his dislike.

"I'm not sure you can understand. You've never had a child.

You don't have to reconcile your own son's imminent death."

"I have to reconcile my own imminent death," I shot back at him.

"That I concede," he said, putting a hand into his blond hair. "But I submit it's not the same thing, for in a heartbeat I'd trade my life for his."

"Point taken," I said. I wanted to tell him it wasn't my fault.

"Progeria." He said the word like a death sentence.

"I've heard of it." I just hadn't been able to recall the name.

"Progeria is rapid aging of children. It begins right away in the first year or so of life. The consensus is that it is genetic, which is—" he stopped talking.

"Why you and Rhonda will have no more children," I finished for him.

He nodded. "Sometimes they can live up to thirty years of age. Most make it into their teens. I don't think Rolly is going to get that far."

"Shit," I said.

We sat for a minute.

It occurred to me to wonder why I ever wanted children. I think I still did, but my problem made the whole idea academic anyway. I had guilt feelings about thinking of myself while Rolly was a few yards away dying.

"It's also known as Hutchinson-Gilford syndrome. Do you want to know what kills them?"

"Tell me." He was going to anyway.

"Heart problems. Stroke. From progressive atherosclerosis. Atherosclerosis is also a term that usually covers arteriosclerosis. Hardening of the arteries. Just as if he is aging at a super fast rate."

I didn't know what to say so I didn't say it.

Raleigh went on. "He doesn't have all his full range of motion in different functions. I thought he was going to kill himself racing that golf cart." Raleigh shook his head. "Then I thought, what the hell, he's dying anyway, let him have some fun."

"Life sucks."

"Yeah, it does," he agreed. "See, you've run most of your life's course; Rolly has not. It's not the same."

Finally, I put two and two together. "It's not a coincidence you're a doctor here at this place, whatever the hell this place is."

He nodded. "Not at all. Justyn pays us a ton, each. We live here and have no expenses to speak of. He also foots the bills for Rolly; all the latest medical attention, research, whatever is new, we get it first, thanks to Justyn. Periodically, he flies the world's best specialists in for consultation. And it isn't doing a damn bit of good for Rolly."

Left on my plate were some grilled vegetables. Emeril had grilled broccoli, carrots, mushrooms, cauliflower, and different kinds of squash. He was a super chef. I ate a broccoli stalk.

Raleigh picked up a pebble and flipped it with his thumb like a marble down the hillside. "Should Rhonda and I predecease Rolly, or Justyn pass away, it's in Justyn's will that Rolly is provided for in this manner until he's gone. Justyn also hired the nanny and tutor. And they live here. Can you begin to understand the expense Justyn has gone to on behalf of our son?"

"Extraordinary," I agreed.

"Just so you know."

"Why?" I asked.

"I ride for the brand."

What the hell was he trying to tell me? "Fine," I said.

"Point is," Raleigh said, choosing his words carefully, "that you did something wonderful for my son today."

I didn't say anything. Let him say his piece.

He didn't.

Toying with a carrot I started nibbling. Okay, add it up. Raleigh felt a compulsion to owe me something for the race today and making his son's birthday a wonderful happening. But Raleigh had gone to lengths to show me how much he owed Justyn Tyme. In my mind's eye I could see the blind lady with the scales hanging there unevenly. I got the message. But so what?

"All right, Doctor. Did you bring me up here for Rolly? I'm sorry it didn't work out. Or did you bring me because Tyme's a philanthropist and wanted to help me out, too? Or, number three, are you working on me for research purposes associated with this clinic on aging?"

"I pick door number three. It was coincidence that we had a child afflicted with progeria. But, by God, I wasn't going to miss any opportunity that presented itself. Unfortunately, none did so."

He still didn't like me, a fact that could be attributed to that unusual but obvious bond Rhonda and I shared. When word first arrived here about me and their initial research began to unfold my condition, Raleigh's hopes for his son skyrocketed. At first, I represented the only positive hope he had ever found; even the slimmest of possibilities was better than the inevitable downward slope into death Rolly faced.

Without a word, he pulled himself up by one of the walkway cover posts. He didn't look at me again as he walked away.

These thoughts only stoked the fires of my uneasiness. Right that minute I had felt great; I'd had a superior run tuning my body to a higher peak; I'd eaten a fine meal and my metabolism was for once lately sated; and I'd accidentally pepped up a dying boy. So why was that lady tap-dancing on my last nerve with a vengeance?

CHAPTER TWENTY-FOUR

The party was over and a few people were cleaning up. Everybody else seemed to be taking a siesta. Nobody told me to do anything and I needed some thinking time.

I had to have a thinking cigar, so I got a Don José made in Honduras. Serious tobacco, it'd take an hour to smoke for it was close to nine inches long. Since the rain earlier, probably before dawn, had made the forest above wet and drippy, the only place to walk away from people was the exit road. I went down the ramps from my room ignoring the adjacent stairs. I was a walker, not a climber. Down past the chopper helipad I poked a hole in the end of the cigar with the kitchen match and paused to light up. In the wind, I used three matches to get it going just right.

As I was walking out of the parking lot down the gravel road, a golf cart came flying up and swung to a stop. Rhonda stepped out, stripped her white doctor's smock off and dropped it onto the seat. "God, I need a smoke."

Dutifully, I handed the Don José to her and she sucked in a large lungful and handed it back to me. I puffed a bit. We started walking. Rhonda wore jeans and a Big Bird sweatshirt. She changed clothes frequently.

"Thanks." It was all she had to say.

"The kid needs to be a kid sometimes."

"Sorry you had to encounter him and our problems."

Sometimes when you get insight, you shouldn't share it. But I did then.

"I'm sorry I had to see the fires of hell in your eyes, Rhonda. I'm sorry for the torture your soul is going through. Hell, I'm sorry for Raleigh, now. That's really something. I'm most sorry for Raleigh, junior. No kid should have to go through that."

"We don't want your pity."

I put bite in my words. "You don't have it. You have my sympathy. That shouldn't happen to anybody, especially somebody I like."

She put her hand on my arm. "Thank you, dear."

And I think I now understood why she maneuvered to share my cigars rather than ask me for one for herself alone. And I understand now why she was never worried about contagion from me through sharing the cigars.

She saw that understanding in me and smiled wanly. "Sometimes I don't care if I'm going to live or die—that is until my son passes on; I want to live for him. After that…."

I nodded my sympathy. "I am beginning to understand. Your urgency in the research, in my condition. My blood is not compatible with his is it?"

She inhaled deeply again. "No. It was the first thing we checked."

"Too bad."

"Raleigh was so disappointed."

"You, too, I bet."

"I was that. I was that."

We were walking along the road through the cut in the mountains. We passed the arbitrary turns one and two we'd established for the race. The terrain rose a bit and we walked on. The cool, clear air smelled just fine; but somehow mundane pleasures weren't as special as they'd been earlier.

She kicked at a rock. Now, I thought, we'd never know if my extraordinary condition had infected my blood and could be used to reverse progeria.

"You could still find another kid with progeria someplace who has my blood type."

"Probably," she said. "I'd try anything here where I have

control and there are no other medical or scientific controls. But elsewhere? Not likely. The state and the feds would be all over the experiment before we hardly started. And....” Her voice trailed off with some regret.

“I might be dead in a matter of weeks or months.”

“Now that you put it that way, yes. We have to work on you and you only; we haven’t even gotten to first base on your problem yet.”

“And might not anyway.” I paused. “But my problem sort of pales, what with Rolly and all.”

“I used to believe in God. Now I’m not so sure.” She handed me the cigar. “I never understood how God could do such horrible things to an innocent child.”

“Sometimes life doesn’t make any sense to me either.” I checked the ash and knocked it off.

“Lemme tell you about it,” she laughed, hysteria under the surface. “Look at the juxtaposition of life. My son is very young, and he’s dying by rapidly aging. You’re older, late fifties, and you’re dying by getting younger.”

“Yep.” I calmly puffed.

“You made the connection almost immediately, didn’t you?”

“I did.”

“And you are so calm, so cool, so easy about it. You didn’t react when I said you were dying.”

I shrugged. “We don’t exactly know that thing.”

“No, we don’t, do we?”

“Though I will admit it’s the likely outcome.”

“And you’re okay with that?” she asked.

“Not really. I’ve thought about it a lot, and I’m reconciled to it. I’ve lived my bit, done my thing. If it’s time, I’m ready.”

We were going downhill now, through the cut, and the guard shack was in sight.

I handed her the smoke.

“But you know what, Rhonda? My greatest regret?”

“Tell me, Ethan.” She took the cigar.

“I never had a child, a son, a daughter. Nothing. Good, bad, defective. I never had that chance."

"Oh." Her sapphire eyes pierced me.

"I used to say that I always only wanted two things: a daughter and a Harley-Davidson. Now I don't even want the motorcycle anymore."

"Are you trying to make me feel better?"

"Maybe. Maybe I'm trying to make you and me feel better. Maybe the point is only that life ain't fair. Gimme a hit." I took the smoke and inhaled. "Then again, maybe I'm trying to say that bond we share and don't address is sorrow." I surprised myself by saying it, admitting it.

She nodded wisely. "You're very intelligent, Ethan. I know you can follow my logic jumps. Think about this, and I mentioned it partially to Raleigh." She paused for a moment as we walked together. Way above a jet made a lonely contrail.

"I want a child so badly. I want to prove Raleigh, junior is an accident of nature, not a genetic result from Raleigh and my genetic combination. But I can't, I'm a doctor, a scientist. I simply cannot bring another child like him into this world. I cannot do that to another child. I *cannot*." She took my hand. "But you know what I could dare attempt?"

I could guess. But I let her explain.

"We've checked you out exhaustively. There's nothing wrong with you. Nothing intrinsically. Medically, you have a problem. But I'd bet it hasn't had time to impact your genes. You are very intelligent, very attractive in a masculine way. I would take a chance and have your child." She was squeezing my hand and pulled me to a stop. She turned me to face her. "I'm getting back to that undercurrent between us, the thing you termed our 'bond'. Surely you've made the jump in logic to know what I'm going to say?"

"Some. But I see several avenues."

"Aye, that's the rub, isn't it?" She dropped my hand. But we stood looking at each other and occasionally smoke from the cigar in my hand wafted between us eerily. "When I broached it with Raleigh, he said he'd consider artificial insemination from you." She laughed. "Oh, he doesn't like you. You're too much of a threat to him. But he's a scientist and intrigued with the prospect and he wants to have a child, too. A regular kid. He said it was okay with him if you were to jack off in a mayonnaise jar and we'd inject me at the best time."

"So that's how you do it."

"Not in a mayonnaise jar. We've special condoms to keep as much air away as possible. You could have sex or masturbate or think off, nobody cares. But you know what, Ethan?"

The bond between us had already told me. "What, dear?" I reached up to her forehead and tucked a wisp of hair back.

"There is a better way." Her shiny brunette hair bounced a bit.

"I know," I said. But I also knew she'd already decided against it or she wouldn't be talking about it.

"The old-fashioned way you're supposed to do it, the strongest and best sperm surviving by swimming upriver."

"I think I would have enjoyed it." I studied her eyes, and fought losing myself in them.

"Me, too," she said. "But that's the problem. Raleigh wouldn't have to know. We could do it both ways and he'd never know." She'd have sex with me and do an artificial insemination, too. That would double the odds.

"But you would know," I pointed out.

"And that's the problem. I would have liked it too much." She shook her head wistfully. "Goddamn life sometimes." She raised my hand and puffed on the cigar while I held it and blew a mouthful out. "How about you?"

I sighed, not wanting to think about it. "Rhonda, under normal circumstances, I would never have considered it. Never. Hell, I got my own problems."

"Mary Lou?"

"Among others," I admitted. Carrie Jean, Elena Rodríguez, Mary Lou Zachary. "But now circumstances are special. I'd have said yes, hell yes and helped you have a child. But only because I like you and I'm ostensibly dying. And it would give me the kid I've always wanted. Why not help out? And fulfill a dream at the same time."

She crinkled her eyes. "Why, thank you, dear."

If my prospects didn't include imminent death, I'd have been of a different mindset. Rhonda was one hell of a woman. The possibilities were intriguing. But I wouldn't have agreed to her unspoken proposition for the very reasons of complications. I don't just hop in bed with anybody, even a lady as attractive and compelling as Rhonda. Commitment is the key. And I didn't think I could commit to her, or she to me. Not that it mattered anyway.

"I was considering seducing you," she said. "I'd sneak into your room late at night—"

"Even though it's under surveillance?" I asked before I could stop myself.

She eyed me askance. "I told them you weren't stupid. Yes, but I can control that surveillance. I know where and how to turn it off. Then again, perhaps I'd have seduced you outside in the woods somewhere." She laughed again, more genuinely. "Or in the office, in an examining room. I'd have found a time and place."

I laughed at the mental picture. "In one of those machines going around and scanning us together."

She got the picture too, and turned to continue the walk. "I don't like the direction this conversation is taking. It's too easy to talk to you. I'm getting too comfortable with you. That's not wise. That's not helping matters."

Something else was troubling her. We were so attuned that I sensed her mood blacken.

"See, there's another problem. Your biological clock has long since passed thirty-five," she said as we walked. "Studies show that's the age that genetic damage to sperm begins to occur. Infertility creeps in on you. That's when it begins to be more difficult for men to father children. That's when statistics show fathers contribute more to birth defects. After thirty-five, your sperm doesn't swim as well. And the natural selection process breaks down, bad genes don't get weeded out as they do when you're younger and your system is more geared to that sort of thing. It's as if nature doesn't care for people after their prime child bearing years. Then, it's up to science and medicine and nutrition." She jerked her thumb at the valley behind us. "That's why we're here, now that I mention it."

"Ah, I'm glad we've found scientific reason to keep you and me apart." I scanned the lay of land.

She gave me a quick smile. "Yes, there is that. After thirty-five, maybe a third of the potential infertility is attributable to the male."

I glanced at my watch and showed it to her. It was spinning counterclockwise, of course. "All right, Doctor Smarty Pants. How old am I? I think I just passed thirty-five going the other way. What do you think?"

She stopped again and took both my hands. I had to drop the cigar to the side. It was down to about one inch anyway.

Rhonda stared into my eyes. She studied my face and looked up and down my body length. "Yes, I'd say clinically speaking you are thirty-five or less. Since your body repairs itself and from observation of you, I'd say you were aging backwards and your body functions and parts are aging backwards, too. It would not surprise me to see your genes were those of a man twenty or thirty years younger than your biological age."

"Meaning my genes are now acceptable?"

She stepped close and kissed my lips lightly and moved back before I could react. "You, my dear, are a devil."

"Rhonda? I think I could fall in love with you. I really do. But I ain't gonna. I will not let that happen."

"You do love another?"

"I do. I just realized that thing." I grabbed her and kissed her hard on the mouth and released her. She tasted like cinnamon, in spite of the cigar. I didn't taste the cigar. Then my own mood darkened. "Not that it matters anyway. Hell, I'm not going to live long enough for anything to matter."

She looked at me speculatively. "You know something,

Ethan? I'm thinking about you. You're quite a man, you know that? Let me rethink the part about taking some of your sperm. We can freeze it and one day decide whether to use it or not."

"You mean if I live or if I die?"

"No. If I still want your baby after all this is over."

"Oh."

She took my hand again and headed back down the road. "We're wasting time out here."

"Um, a few seconds ago, we were, ah, kind of familiar with each other?"

"You mean when I kissed you and you kissed me?"

"That would be it," I said. The woods had been close from the hills sloping down to that point. "From my observations, much of this way is covered by video cam. We were on Candid Camera and your husband is going to get his gun and shoot me dead. Not that it makes any difference, you understand."

"Did you notice me guiding us, maneuvering about?"

"I did."

"Blind spot, we were safe."

"Good for you," I said admiringly. Women, go figger. But I turned around and glanced at the area anyway, fixing it in my mind.

On the way back, I thought about Rhonda and her becoming pregnant with my baby.

It was a measure of my desperation that I didn't perform my usual calculations. Politicians have to project what-ifs far into the future. Suppose I was wandering around Washington some years hence, as a congressman or senator, and in walks a half-grown kid with familiar piercing eyes. "Hi, Daddy." It would shoot one promising political career right in the butt. However, right now I didn't care. Actually, the prospect of sharing parenthood with Rhonda Smith was flattering. It seemed lately that my middle name was "Regrets." From what I knew and felt about Rhonda, she was one to spend a lifetime with. And, no, the fact that she was beautiful wasn't a major factor. Her attitudes, her quick smile, her brains, the way she handled herself, her concerns, those were all reasons to choose her. Upon reflection, much the same could be said about Mary Lou, Elena, and Carrie Jean. I'd spent most of a lifetime with Mary Lou; when she was younger, she had been voluptuous. And we'd grown together over the years, generally sharing the same intellectual interests. Elena Rodríguez was openly trying to catch my attention, and she had. In today's vernacular, she was hot. And she'd be an asset to my political career, not to mention my ego. Even her frequent use of an inhaler was endearing. Her only downside would be that she'd appear to be my trophy wife. But when she opened her mouth and people heard how intelligent she was, that would change. Carrie Jean Billingsley? Every time I tried to label her, she'd surprise me. Talk about somebody with a future.

We left my Don José stub dying there on the roadside.

I performed a final look around, as usual studying the terrain.

As we walked back, I had more to think about. Raleigh. He was tougher than I thought. I had a new appreciation for him, even though I didn't particularly like him. For one thing, he'd won and kept the lovely Rhonda. If nothing else, that was a major plus in his column. But he was doing what he was doing for his kid and maybe the advancement of science. And he was doing it with a single-minded commitment and to hell with all else, including me. He had good reason to be as he was, cynical, bitter, and standoffish.

I couldn't believe what they did to me next.

CHAPTER TWENTY-FIVE

I was waiting in Rhonda's sitting room, standing in front of the plate glass window looking out over Justyn Tyme's valley. I thought I could grow to like this place. While it wasn't Florida, it had a certain charm I was beginning to appreciate. And, I could become accustomed to running up here. Running on flat and level surfaces was all I was used to; however, mountains and hills offer a change in that humdrum. I'd found it was more difficult to run downhill than uphill. You use different leg muscle groups.

Rhonda walked in wearing her doctor's smock again, but still had her jeans and Big Bird sweatshirt on underneath.

"This is a long day," she said.

"The longer the better for me," I pointed out.

She favored me with a smile.

"I am glad," I said emphatically, "those tests are all done."

"Those tests? You're going to do them all over again. Each one, even blood tests for the lab."

"Do-overs? Damn."

"On our walk I indicated we've found nothing so far, Ethan. Tomorrow we'll start the tests again to see if there is any significant change. Certainly, some of the results will be worthless, but we cannot miss any possibilities."

"Even the bone marrow biopsy?"

For the briefest of nanoseconds she looked startled and then shook it off.

"Even the bone marrow biopsy," she said.

"Damn," I said to stay in character.

"At some point we're also going to complete the comprehensive interview we started but never finished. Raleigh and I had a command performance for Justyn."

"When will I get to meet the man?"

"When he wants you to."

And that was that.

"I'll have Sis get you started testing again," Rhonda said, reaching for the phone on the table.

"Before we start? My cell phone crashed or whatever they do. Could I use your phone to make a couple of calls?"

"Of course," she said neutrally. "This phone doesn't have a direct outside line, but I'll get you one." She picked up the handset and hit the zero. "This is Dr. Smith. Mr. Zachary is going to make a few calls." She handed me the phone. "Just tell her the number."

"Thanks." I never used numbers, just the auto-dial; however, I remembered the numbers correctly.

Rhonda courteously went out of the room.

My home phone rang twice, and then Mary Lou's voice came on the machine and told me to leave a message. I told her I'd be here a few more days and would try to call later.

The operator came back on and said, "Another call?"

On a whim, I gave her Mary Lou's cell number. I'd talk to her anyway, whether she was at home or not.

Mary Lou didn't answer her cell either, and I didn't leave a message on that phone.

Then I had the operator dial Carrie Jean Billingsley's cell. I didn't want to call her house particularly and talk to Jack if he happened to answer the phone.

She answered.

"Hey, it's me. Do you miss me?" I said.

"Bet your butt, Ethan. Why haven't you called? I called you and the service said you're not available."

"My phone broke."

"How are you, Ethan?"

"I feel younger every day."

"Damn," CJ said. "When you left, I tried to talk to Mary Lou about you and that place you went to, but she wasn't very communicative."

"Last time I saw her, she wasn't very happy, either. Did you remove your flamingoes and rabbits?" I smiled at the memory.

"That's when I saw her. She had pulled them up and put them in the garbage in your garage and I had to go into the lion's den to retrieve them and it was a pain in the royal ass and she wouldn't hardly tell me nothin' and why did you have to leave me?"

"I love you, too, sweetie. Don't let Mary Lou get to you. She's going through some trying times."

"*You* are going through some trying times. She could be more supportive."

"I didn't call you up to argue about my wife."

"Where are you?"

"Apparently somewhere outside Lansing, North Carolina."

"What do you mean 'apparently'?"

"It's a long story. They've quite a complex way out in the mountains. Very high tech, state of the art medical institution. They deal with aging."

"Can they help you?"

"Nobody knows yet. I'm still doing tests."

"Is your watch still running backwards?" A euphemism for am I still aging counterclockwise.

"Definitely. I went running earlier and I think I can give you a run for your money, so to speak."

"Yeah, right." She mumbled something.

"Say again?"

"I was just eating a banana. Carbs and potassium and stuff. Um, so how much longer you gonna be up there?"

"Beats me. They are giving me the same tests over again starting in a few minutes."

"That means they didn't find anything the first time?"

"Right, CJ. Also, they want to see if they can find any differences, even tiny ones."

"What are they going to do after that?"

"You must be referring to treatment. Frankly, CJ, I don't know. I don't think they do, either. I'm not sure there is a treatment anyway, even if they find some anomaly."

"Well, you just make them repair whatever's wrong with you, buster. I need you back and healthy."

For a minute the ether between us was silent.

"I thought you were leaving for Seattle or someplace out there." I kept my voice neutral.

"I was. Friends don't run out on friends, especially when those same friends are dying off—oops."

"Thanks, I think. Don't worry about what you say. I'm glad somebody is honest with me."

"How's your golf game? Any good looking women up there?"

"I haven't played. And, hell yes."

"Look here, Ethan. I'm really worried about you. I'm worried your condition will deteriorate and nobody will care. You'll just become some clinical abnormality for show and tell at doctors' meetings."

"I can take care of myself." I wondered if that were true. I was putting an awful lot of trust in Tyme, Inc. and those medical people here. Then the refrain I was beginning to hate just popped right up into my mind. *What choice did I have?*

"All the same, I still worry about you."

Thinking of something else, I said, "Do me a favor?"

"Sure. Anything for you." Her voice turned saucy.

"It's about Mary Lou—"

"No."

"I haven't asked the favor yet."

"Don't ask me to do something for her, Ethan." She sounded like I'd just killed any good will I'd built up.

"I can't get hold of her—"

"What's the downside?"

"Like I said, I can't raise her on the phone. Have you seen her lately?"

"No, and it ain't my day to watch her."

"Pretty please? Just go over there and make sure she's not lying dead on the floor or something?" It had not escaped my attention that Mary Lou would make a good hostage to insure my cooperation.

"There's an incentive. You made the paper this morning. Want me to tell you or did you read it online?"

"I've haven't been online since I got here. Tell me."

"Front page story, Ethan. Mysterious absence, nobody knows where you are. You missed an important commission vote last night. Vince MacLean had a couple of nasty things to say about you."

"That doesn't sound like the kind of story Elena Rodríguez would write." Elena would cover for me if she could. A thing which a good reporter would not do, but a friend would.

"She didn't write it. Buried in the local section was a three-sentence story that she had been dismissed from the paper."

It didn't take much to add it up. "When they publish a story on firing a reporter, that's bad. Normally, they wouldn't say anything. Just give her her walking papers. But to print it tells me they're slapping her with some kind of scarlet letter. Telling the world and likely blacklisting her."

"Jeez," Carrie Jean said. "Public humiliation. Couldn't have happened to a nicer twit."

"Stop being catty, will you? It's not becoming. There's an outside chance she got fired because of me."

"What do you mean?"

"I'm not sure. She could know about my condition. She knows enough herself and knows most of the people who know me to interview and deduce that something is dead wrong with me. She was already suspicious right after I got out of the hospital. And being somewhat loyal to me, not writing the story. Or stonewalling it. Some variation on that theme."

Also, I speculated that Vince MacLean had something to do with it. MacLean never got good press from her, and I did. While I thought Elena's coverage was fair, MacLean certainly did not. And the paper and its offspring, LNN, were MacLean backers. Their editorials usually reflected his views and they'd endorsed my opponents. With Elena moving into my camp and not doing a hit piece on me, the *Sarasota Star-Banner* could conceivably have canned her. I fervently hoped they didn't have access to her notes or computer files. For surely she'd put her thoughts or preliminary story points down for reference. And Mac had seen me with Elena enough; maybe he was jealous, he'd certainly made enough cracks about it.

Then my other refrain kicked in. Since I was probably going to be dead anyway: *What difference did it make?*

"Ethan? Are you there?"

Somebody cleared her throat and I glanced up and Sis was standing in the doorway, hands on hips with an anxious and impatient look on her face. They must teach impatient body language in nursing school. For some reason, this made some neurons connect in my brain. Finally. So I decided to tell Carrie Jean something. No one else I knew could handle this right.

Ignoring Sis, I said to Carrie Jean, "I'm here. Just thinking. Listen, something else just occurred to me. If we talk again, keep at the top of your mind that we're probably being recorded and listened in on, both."

"Ethan!"

"Yeah. Think it through, darlin'." I was telling her right then to watch her words.

For a moment she didn't speak. Then she said, "Good thing you didn't tell me that thing *first*."

"You're beautiful and I do love you." I was acknowledging her correct response. She'd connected the dots. If I'd opened the conversation with that, we might have gotten cut off and she'd come to that conclusion.

"I love you too," she said, "I'd be blue without you."

Right there I wondered if we were being ridiculous like a couple of kids. Blue meaning law enforcement or the cavalry, she was asking if she should call one or more of them in.

"The way I see it is three days repeat testing and then decision on treatment. I'll call you in three or four days. I should have some news by then." If she didn't hear from me in that time, it was up to her. Who could she contact with some wild story? Some local sheriff who had no dog in this fight? FBI? With what story and corroboration? "If you run into Palmer, give him my best." Translation: Palmer T. Hibbs was a heavyweight and could command attention. Law enforcement would respond to him with alacrity.

"Will do," CJ said.

"They're waiting on me in the lab," I told Carrie Jean. "I don't know if I'm gonna have any bone marrow left." Prophetic.

"Poor baby."

"So I gotta go."

"All right, Ethan. Take care of yourself."

"I am."

I hoped I was just being cautious, that I was overreacting. I hoped. I'd just picked up a few off-key signals, a couple of things that didn't fit right. Logic told me I was seeing conspiracies where there weren't any. Tyme, Incorporated had already spent tens of thousands of dollars on me, maybe more. Since Rolly couldn't benefit from my blood or me, what had they to gain except a rapidly disappearing research subject?

And if I were dying, what difference could any of this possibly mean? One thought did nag at me though. How could anyone benefit from my death?

One additional chilling thought struck me then: What if I had just put Carrie Jean in danger? Suppose they used her against me? I was already worried about Mary Lou.

CHAPTER TWENTY-FIVE

After another three days, I no longer cared what a positron emission tomography was, I and don't think I cared about the metabolism of my frontal lobe or my gizzard. Or thyroid function tests checking the level of something called thyroxine. Why, I wanted to know. Because the thyroid controls the metabolism, they said.

On the third day, when most of the testing was complete, I was waiting outside the lab where they take blood and other body fluids thumbing through *Discover* magazine, trying to absorb new science and technology. I was sitting in a chair next to a desk upon which rested a ubiquitous computer monitor and keyboard. And a telephone. Sis was in the lab with another nurse setting things up.

Nonchalantly, I reached over and picked up the telephone. Some intercom looking buttons and what looked like an outside line. I started punching in CJ's number and it didn't work right. This being an institution, I reasoned, you probably have to dial for an outside line. I punched in the traditional 9 and got a different dial tone. Then I punched in 941, the Sarasota area code, and CJ's number.

Nothing happened. I held the line open for a moment.

Then a female voice came on the line. "This is not a preauthorized number. Is this Mr. Zachary?"

"How'd you know?"

"On my screen it shows the number you're trying to reach is the same number you called the other day, so it had to be you.

Just a second, I'll get authorization, you don't have to bother."

"Thanks a lot." I think.

She came back quickly. "You're clear, Mr. Zachary. If you need to call, just hit zero and tell me, I'll take care of it."

"Okay." Carrie Jean's number was ringing. I didn't think these people worried about long distance bills, not at a nickel a minute or less. Not with all the money they'd already spent on me. It could be they simply wanted to monitor who I called.

CJ's service answered leave a message at the tone. "Hi, it's Ethan. Just checking in. Everything is fine. Still testing. Will call again in a few days."

I hung up and hit the zero again and gave the nice lady Mary Lou's cell number. I got her service, too, and left a similar message.

Then I called the Sarasota County Administrator and told him I was stuck in North Carolina and was trying to break loose. I did not tell him why nor did he ask me why.

After that I called Miles Tonchot, the Sarasota County Attorney, who was my friend and political ally.

"I'll tell you, Easy, we've got a problem."

"Why should you be any different," I said.

He ignored me. "The FDLE has an investigator nosing around. The Fed that was here disappeared days and days ago."

I'd decided against telling anybody about it, but I had to now. "Miles, that was C. Roger Pinella. I talked to him and straightened him out. He went back to where he came from." No need to point out that where he came from was the CDC in Atlanta.

"Fine, Easy. Things are serious. Stories about you in the paper. MacLean raising hell. You're not here to defend yourself. Now this FDLE investigation."

"Vince MacLean must've initiated that," I said. The implications were vast.

The only reason the Florida Department of Law Enforcement, state cops, were investigating me was because the governor had to have asked them to do the investigation. In order for the governor to ask the FDLE to investigate a public official, somebody had to have made an allegation about illegal or immoral activity, mental instability, malfeasance in office, payoffs, that kind of thing. The governor has broad powers in those instances. Depending on the results of the FDLE investigation, he can remove an office holder or official and appoint replacements.

That is, this was bad news. Major bad news.

"Do what damage control you can, Miles," I told him. "I have absolutely no choice in this. I have to be here for now and don't particularly want it broadcast far and wide." Breathing deep and making a decision, I continued, "They shouldn't find much of anything except peculiar personal behavior which, last time I checked, isn't against the rules. MacLean will try to pin the Kennedy assassination on me, but it shouldn't stick."

"I guess we have no choice."

"Absolutely and irrevocably none, Miles. I do thank you for bailing me out on this if you can. But you've got to trust me, I have to do this thing I'm doing."

"Easy, I don't know, I don't want to know. I can guess a bit but won't. Be advised, the governor will review whatever the investigation turns up. At that time it becomes critical mass. On the other hand, things here are already in the major damage mode. Especially with MacLean and his big mouth and the newspaper."

"Yeah, I heard they fired Elena."

"They did, the bastards." My mind's eye could see him scratching his head. "Aren't you and Governor Burwell tight?"

I grinned at the phone wryly. "That doesn't matter. He'll do his job as the law states and as he swore and all else be damned."

Poor Elena Rodríguez. She was probably at Wal-Mart buying inhalers by the case. After a few more pleasantries and gossip, we hung up. I tried Mary Lou at home and on her cell again. I left the main number for the Tyme Institute and told her to call any time day or night.

My career was going straight down the toilet. That fact gave me a new sense of urgency here. However, if I was going to die, my career didn't matter.

But most of all, I began to worry about Mary Lou.

They poked and prodded and x-rayed and scanned and drove me crazy.

So crazy, I ran a couple of times a day. I ran out the front gate again, and sometimes I ran on the hiking path. I got so I could pick up the cameras on the outside of the hiking path. Barbed wire and video surveillance filled in the places where you could walk off the property. Or climb away. The rest was almost unscalable cliffs up or down.

One location just off the hiking path offered a possibility of escape to the north. You'd have to climb a tree and maybe disable or avoid the surveillance camera. At any rate, I was rather familiar with the surrounding terrain.

On the fourth day, they told me the bad news.

CHAPTER TWENTY-SIX

To put it charitably, Justyn Tyme had a "lived in" look.

His hospital bed angled about forty-five degrees, so he was almost sitting up.

When they escorted me into the room, Tyme was watching a giant screen television that took up half the wall across from his bed. The picture was so high definition I doubted you could buy it on the open market.

He fumbled with the remote and Jackie Chan froze on screen, airborne and smiling, atop a towering building, where bad guys lined up to take him on.

"If there is a message in Jackie Chan, I believe that it is to not take yourself seriously." Justyn Tyme dragged a clear oxygen mask to his face and breathed deeply.

Hal had retrieved me from the clutches of Sis and her imaging machines. He delivered me to the ornate Tyme residence, on the edge of one of the terraces. Inside, Hal led to me what appeared to be a study, but was an office.

Computer monitors and keypads sat on a credenza behind the desk. The desk was some kind of cherry wood. Sort of a tasteful command center.

The woman was standing behind the desk, chair pushed aside out of the way. She stood with authority, short, heavyset, blunt jaw. Her gray hair fell half way to her shoulders, and a pencil protruded from that hair where her left ear would be. She wore the khaki slacks, but had a matching jacket on. I thought it was cool in here.

And she had linebacker eyes. To those not initiated, that means a combination of killer, carnivore, predator, intimidator, vampire, and saber tooth tiger rubbing hands together in anticipation of ripping your throat out and dining upon your warm entrails.

"Glad to finally meet you, Mr. Zachary," she said, not meaning it and not hiding not meaning it. "I am Belinda Foursleeps, chief of staff." Okay, so no wonder Custer lost.

I gave her a big wide smile and stuck my hand out across the desk. She took it, and her own hand was dry and cardboard like. "So you are the one pulling the strings around here."

"I plead guilty. This enterprise requires someone at the helm, a pilot as it were, for the disparate elements would all be going in different directions." Innocuous words, but she catalogued my friendly smile and my observation about her pulling the strings. Her eyes acknowledged my recognition that she was the power here. If there were a root of all evil in this place, it resided within her.

I suspected she was an enforcer in addition to piloting this enterprise. About her was a focus of purpose.

"Though it wasn't necessary, I wanted to meet you in person." Her voice was flat and non-committal, but her words told me that she already knew more about me than I wanted to know she knew. Subtly, she was exerting her power to include me. "I certainly hope our medical personnel will be able find some avenue of assistance to you." And not so subtly.

Perhaps under different circumstances, I would have been somewhat intimidated. But I was convinced I was dying, and doing so quickly. Therefore, someone of her power and threatening presence didn't concern me. It did not, however, escape me that she had input into a possible treatment for my counterclockwise aging.

We stood silent for a moment and Hallelujah Gertz slunk out of the room.

"Come with me, let us see if Justyn is awake."

She turned and went out the door and down a corridor that

went straight away from the entrance. The corridor was longer than it would seem and then I realized we were walking into the side of the mountain. This wasn't just your run-of-the-mill billionaire's standard residence perched on the side of a mountain; much of it was dug into the mountainside.

Now I was standing at the bedside of Justyn Tyme. He patted my hand and then took another drag on the oxygen like a person smoking a cigarette. More medical equipment rested behind his bed than they had in most hospitals. Interestingly, the place was not opulent. It was just a big, high-tech, state-of-the-art hospital room. A nurse in an official nurse's outfit hovered, her eyes flitting to monitors and the patient.

Belinda Foursleeps said, "If you don't need me, Justyn, I've a million things to be doing."

"Fine, thank you, Belinda."

When she was gone, Justyn Tyme said, "She's a hardass, but it takes a hardass to run my empire." He smiled benignly. I noted the imperial use of "empire." They had to be a "good cop, bad cop" team. Tyme was the nice guy part, and Foursleeps the enforcer. Deducing from the old man's apparent incapacities, Belinda Foursleeps probably ran the day-to-day operations of this aforementioned empire.

The old man indicated the wall where Jackie Chan was still frozen in midleap. "Jackie is instructive. He came from more than humble beginnings. Yet now he not only is the star, but he runs the production, makes the decisions—all that upper management crap, Hollywood style." He paused for oxygen and the nurse checked a monitor, and pulled an alligator clip off one of his fingers. "Jackie went through the trial of fire when he was young—as did I. Now he has more money than he ever dreamed he would—although not as much as I. Not many do." Tyme rolled his head toward me and continued.

"I understand we're making little progress for you." The death sentence. Nobody had officially told me that fact, but I had pretty well guessed it.

"Apparently not," I responded, not knowing what to say. I

decided I needed a long run or a short cigar.

Justyn Tyme looked a thousand years old. A few long wisps of crystal hair lay across his scalp. His ears stood out. His face was ancient. An IV dripped into the arm he was using to swing the oxygen mask. An old fashioned comforter lay across his legs.

He saw me eye the comforter. "Rhonda gave that to me. It was her grandmother's." He coughed lightly. "Rhonda speaks so well of you, Mr. Zachary."

"Given the opportunity, I would speak well of her also."

"Twenty years ago I personally recruited her down in San Antone, her and her high school sweetheart. I sent them to school over in San Diego. We're like family. I have made their son Rolly an heir, or sort of one, to my estate. It will do him no good. He's as dead as you are. Like you, he's marking time until it arrives."

I had a snapshot of a mental picture of Rolly in his same small body, aged to death, lying there dead, dwarfed on a gurney. And me next to him, body somehow crushed from the inside, sucked in upon myself, brain frazzled from reverse aging.

Suddenly, it hit me. Justyn Tyme wasn't putting me down. He was welcoming me into the club, one that he was the founding member.

"So now it's you, Rolly, and me."

He nodded. "Rhonda assured me how intelligent you were." He smiled grimly. "The Chinese have a saying that goes something like 'An inch of time is an inch of gold.' I wish it were so, for I have much gold and not much time." He waved the nurse aside.

"I don't have much of either substance."

He ignored me. "It was at that point I told her, if what she said were true, that you would tell her to shove the psychologist up her lovely ass."

"It hasn't come up yet." Whatever he was talking about.

"It will. They're flying one in, just for you."

Another leap in logic. Another possibility to explore. Must

be next after all the tests were completed.

"I must thank you formally for your interest in me and your efforts to help me in my time of need with this, this condition." It sounded bureaucratic, but I wanted to say it.

"Rhonda wanted to name it the Zachary Syndrome, but I pointed out we don't know if it's a disease or not."

"I'm flattered, but I did wish to express my appreciation."

"Your appreciation already extends to helping us. When you die, we get your body for research." The release I'd signed. "While we do wish to help you, we also want to explore whatever it is you've got, what happened to you to generate this so-called condition."

They wanted me as a guinea pig. Was there more? If so, he wasn't saying so yet.

"Widdershins. Have you ever heard of that word?"

"No."

"It's a word. It means contrary, wrong, counterclockwise."

"It fits, Mr. Tyme."

"Let me tell you why I established this clinic, this Tyme Institute. Twenty-five years ago I was young and full of life. I was seventy years old and I decided if I didn't want to die, then, by God, I wouldn't. I'd do everything I could to prevent dying." He inhaled more oxygen and rested his head back on the pillows for a moment.

Jackie Chan remained poised to strike.

Tyme's watery eyes locked on me again. "I founded this place to keep me alive, in essence. Coincidentally, it has saved or prolonged the lives of many very wealthy people. You'd be amazed at what leading edge technology and nutrition can actually do. Nobody walks in my front door without a ten million dollar deposit. They become eternally grateful for their enhanced quality of life, if not extension thereof. And I am eternally grateful for my enhanced wealth. You, my friend, are the first person to come here for free."

His statements had me thinking again.

"Over the years we've had a procession of rich and famous,

but mostly rich, troop through here. You wouldn't believe the absolute junk they'd been eating their whole lives; you wouldn't believe the alternate medicine they've tried; you wouldn't believe the exotic herbal treatments they were undergoing; you wouldn't believe the idiotic herbal junk they were stuffing in their bodies. They've injected their bodies with plastic, with toxins, with silicone, and they don't understand why they have to age." He coughed and the nurse gave him water through a bendy straw. "All they had to do was walk and eat their broccoli. And not smoke." He smiled. "And we help them. It's not magic either. Our refrain: nutrition, moderation, exercise. The problem we haven't licked is mental: dementia, Alzheimer's, mental breakdown and degradation. Those are the things I've avoided, that's why I'm still kicking." The comforter flapped a bit where his feet were.

I nodded.

Off to the side of his bed stood an IV tree. Two bags of clear liquid fed into tubes running to his bed. Also hanging was an ominous bag of blood.

"We've dabbled in things like stem cell research, family genetics, DNA research; but the logistics are far beyond us, so I maintain a research wing which monitors all such medical science advancements. Perhaps one day those things will open new doorways; when they do, we'll be right there." His head rolled aside and his thumb must've hit play, because Jackie Chan leapt into action for a few minutes. Then Jackie froze again. "What do you think, Mr. Zachary?"

What was I supposed to say? He'd pronounced the death sentence on me and said not much else. He'd just wanted to take my measure, for what that was worth.

"Is Justyn Tyme your real name?" Actually, I really wanted to know.

"It is. I suppose you could call it kismet, you could. I think having that name sealed my destiny. Over the years it led me to think I could live forever, or put off dying at the last moment, time after time. To an extent, that has occurred. At one time I cared if people believed that or not; no longer do I do so."

Tyme appeared to me to be already dead; he could be called "Marking Tyme."

I would have only one chance, and that was right now. I had to jump at the opportunity.

On the floor next to the IV setup laid a discarded tissue. I appeared to spot it for the first time and moved casually, bending to pick it up. Straightening, I looked around to find a waste can. In that quick scan, I ran my eyes over the blood IV bag.

O positive.

Somehow I'd already known it.

Spotting a nearby medical waste bucket, I dropped in the tissue. Mission accomplished, for what it was worth.

The nurse ushered me out as Jackie Chan flew and leapt and kicked and struck and pirouetted like a ballerina. I wanted to stay and see him win in the end.

My visit with Justyn Tyme gave me mixed feelings; but one thing was obvious. Inescapably obvious.

My rush to the end had begun.

CHAPTER TWENTY-SEVEN

I needed information.

Rhonda was in her office, ballpoint in her mouth, right hand on a mouse chasing something across her screen.

"How about a smoke?" I asked.

She pulled the pen out of her mouth, eyeballed me over her glasses on the tip of her pert nose and smiled. "You're on." She could tell I wanted to talk.

We found a picnic table out alongside her building. I offered her a miniature García y Vega to smoke on her own. "I only want a couple of puffs," she said. I lighted it for her and she dragged in. "What's up?"

Taking the cigar from her, I said, "I'm out of time, I know that." I held up my watch as it wound backwards with increasing speed. "I need to shit or get off the pot." I fingered my jaw. "Hell, I've got wisdom teeth growing in."

She nodded. "X-rays and cranial scans showed that."

"So, right now I'm officially inquiring as to what the plan is for me. And, also, I've a couple of questions."

She raised her eyebrows and took her glasses off. "Questions?"

"Who does what to whom around here."

"Justyn owns and operates this clinic."

"Who is he? Who's this Belinda Foursleeps?"

"Belinda was, or is, which doesn't matter, Justyn's companion. She was his personal secretary for ages. When Justyn's wife passed away, Belinda became his companion. Most people tiptoe around her."

"I saw that potential."

"Yep. Justyn has a trust set up for when he passes. Belinda is forever the executor or administrator of that huge trust. It contains most of his money and his assets and his possessions. Except for a couple of things. Rolly is an heir until he passes." Rhonda made an effort to say that without emotion, but her voice broke and she exerted an effort to control it. "The other interesting point is the inheritance. Justyn has it in his will that Belinda inherits two percent more of his assets for each birthday he reaches."

Brilliant, I thought. The longer he lasts, the more money Foursleeps inherits; thus insuring her stake in his continued good health.

"I'm not certain that matters one way or the other," Rhonda went on, "for Belinda controls everything and makes most of the decisions anyway. Her business acumen is unsurpassed and she earns Justyn more annually than the GNP of many small countries."

"I know Mr. Dithers is a rich man, and I accept it, but I don't know what business he does."

Rhonda laughed. "Dagwood doesn't do anything to tell us, either, does he?"

"Accounts is about all."

"All right, Ethan. Nowadays, like all wealthy enterprises, Tyme, Incorporated invests venture capital, buys and sells companies, corporations. Mix and match, cut and paste. Belinda has a team in New York that has a million databases and researches everything. They can tell you projections for next year's price on cowrie shells on Guam."

"The genesis?" I prompted.

"Where'd Justyn get his start?" She folded her glasses and put them on the picnic table. "He was from Michigan. A pilot in World War II. I want to say fighters like P-38's or P-51's. After the war, mass production of houses and neighborhoods started. Others did the building and selling. He put together groups of investors, and did the financing of these new row houses.

The Veterans' Administration was insuring loans by the thousands. He got in on that boom. For years he controlled most of the containers for the shipping business. And he was always fascinated by high tech. He got in on the financing of a bunch of these dot com companies and got out in time. He held IBM and Microsoft stock galore. Add it all up. Then he founded this clinic for his own purposes and it has more than paid for itself a thousand times over. Not coincidentally, this clinic has kept him alive the last few years."

"Most of that appears artificial now," I said.

"He still hopes." Rhonda looked out over the valley below and I couldn't see her face.

"Me?"

"Yeah."

"Am I going to help him?"

"We don't know."

"All those tests have told you nothing?"

"We have not yet finished reading, analyzing and comparing."

A woman drove by on a golf cart and waved.

I drew on the forgotten cigar, found it dead, and relighted it. "I do not sense overwhelming enthusiasm and hope in your voice."

She took the miniature cigar from me and inhaled. "No, Ethan, you don't." She sighed. "I don't wish to erase any hope you have. You can rest assured that we have the best experts available reading the results and making suggestions. But…."

"I'm a big boy, I can take it."

"Do not give up. I certainly am not surrendering. You're about finished with the testing. We never did return to finish the interview we started. Let's do that so we can correlate those answers with the data and tests. You never know."

"I think I do know, Rhonda. It ain't looking good."

She reached out with her left hand and pushed my shoulder with energy. "No, you don't. Suppose we can tie some combination about rattlesnake venom and cigar smoke and cat hair. That's what our synthesis of all the data will show. Not to mention that it's possible one of those scans or tests will turn up something special in your blood, on your brain, in the cellular structure in your liver. I don't know. But we need to find out." Her eyes blazed.

I touched her hand. "Thanks, Rhonda. I needed that, I think." I could see her as the sole ray of hope for Rolly. Whom did she turn to? I always thought I had that kind of inner strength, but now I wasn't so sure. It had to be a million times tougher if it was your son dying, not you, not somebody else.

She leaned back and regarded me. "Sometimes I want to get drunk for a week and not know anything. Perhaps smoke some fine cigars, maybe a few joints. Just let the world go on without me."

I suspect that was as close to self-pity as she'd ever get. The more I knew about her, the more there was to like. As comfortable as we were with each other, it had been my intention to ask her about carrying a handgun and anti-bugging devices with her in Sarasota. That did not fit her character, as I knew it.

"You're one hell of a person, Rhonda Smith. In another life, another time, another place...."

She studied me intensely. "Thank you, dear. I think I'd have liked that."

CHAPTER TWENTY-EIGHT

"No, negative, disapproved, no way, José. Not me. I will not do it." I was adamant.

We were in the middle of the oft-postponed formal interview.

Rhonda sat on one side of the coffee table, and I lounged on the other. The session was being recorded.

Looking out the expansive plate glass window, I watched a golf cart speed through the cut toward the sentry shack at the main entrance. Shift change, doubtless.

"It would really, really help," Rhonda said. She'd been trying to persuade me on and off.

"I don't believe that."

"We might find some answers." She took her glasses off and rubbed her eyes with exaggerated exasperation.

"So what if you find an answer, then it doesn't do us—or me—any good." I made my voice equally exasperated.

"Nuh-uh," she said.

"Uh huh," I said.

"Never mind," she said.

"Good," I said.

She glared and then I felt guilty. "If you only knew the expense that went into this, you'd cooperate."

"It doesn't matter." I folded my arms symbolically. Suppose she was right and we would find the answer if I cooperated. If that were the case, then I didn't want to know. It was that easy.

They'd flown in some world famous shrink from San Francisco. And certainly they were paying his hourly rate.

"Ten thousand a day plus expenses," Rhonda said, reading my mind. "He had to cancel appointments."

"Suppose I am nuts. I don't want to know the answer to that, so I ain't asking that question."

"Suppose your mind has convinced your body to age backwards and you are doing so?"

"It isn't," I said. "That's totally implausible."

"So is getting younger in some exponential fashion," said Rhonda pointedly.

She had me there.

I had no answer for that one.

"Maybe he can find the answer in your unconscious." She was driving home the point.

Of course, I had no choice. Logically speaking. Here's my point: Already I was having some misgivings about Tyme, Inc. and their altruistic attitude toward me. If it cost ten million to walk in the front door here, why let me in free? Easy answers. To help Justyn Tyme, and to help Rolly. But we all knew the shrink wasn't the answer. One thing *I* knew. One of the top psychiatrists in the world would be able to hypnotize me. And I sure as hell wasn't going to open myself to post-hypnotic suggestion or whatever the hell they call it. No mega-pro head doctor was going to mess around in my head. I kind of thought that I'd need all my faculties. I didn't even want to be in the same room. But I was bright and they knew that, and to avoid this onrushing death looming over me, they'd expect me to capitulate eventually.

So I had to be cagey.

"Even Justyn said he knew I wouldn't cooperate with your imported psychiatrist."

"Oh."

"And he said he told you that, Rhonda."

"Well, yes."

"So there." I stuck my tongue out at her and realized that Justyn might have figured that I thought what I did for the same reasons: that I didn't want to surrender any of my consciousness to them and give them an opportunity at influencing or changing my behavior. I had to regroup and seem to capitulate. "Look, let me think about it. Let's use psychological evaluation as a last resort. If we don't find anything, don't have any clues whatsoever, I'll do it. After everything else is exhausted." I sat back as if to say, "That's my final offer."

She knew she'd won a scuffle, not the battle. But she agreed immediately because it was the closest to agreeing she'd ever get from me. "Fine, let's get back to the interview."

"Fine," I said with equal emphasis. We were going through my life step by step. Military service, my family, my marriage to Mary Lou. We'd gone over my life much the same way I had with the onset of this counterclockwise death attack. I'd discarded genetic problems. None of my relatives had ever died backwards. And the Tyme Institute was having professionals go over my genetics, DNA, for whatever good that would tell them. Rhonda had asked probing questions.

At one point earlier, I'd laughed when she asked about our wedding. Considering my marital problems it was funny. But I didn't want to admit Mary Lou was leaving me.

"What's funny?" Rhonda had asked, picking up on a discontinuity.

I had to tell her something. "Now I'm stuck. See, Ricky Nelson had a song called 'Hello, Mary Lou, Goodbye Heart.' That was our song. So now it's going to run through my head all day. It's one of those kinds of songs." And it was.

"Okay," Rhonda said, satisfied. Then we went into our second argument about the San Francisco shrink—or whoever he or she really was.

"Now we're to the point where you went from running your own law firm to becoming a member of the county commission."

"Thirty years as an attorney was long enough for me. Never mind the lawyer jokes. I was just tired of it, got a super offer, and retired."

"My research showed there was another trigger."

Rhonda and Raleigh had been thorough researching me, I recalled. She knew enough about me to keep me from skipping. "Yep."

"I don't think it's pertinent to our search, Ethan. But I'm curious. Garbage?"

"Yard waste," I said, leaning forward watching out the window. The regular security sweep of the hiking trails was happening now. I could see the John Deere Gator utility vehicles and golf carts moving in and out of the trees on the ridge above that was in my field of vision. I checked my watch, but of course it was merrily winding away backwards. An electric clock on the wall filled in. "The county is in charge of garbage, recycling, yard waste, all that. I'd done a lot of work in the yard one day, and I had a bunch of tree branches, shrub-prunings, yard waste, in a few garbage cans for pickup. Well, they weren't picked up. The yard waste pickup truck kept passing it by."

Rhonda laughed, and I felt we were away from the awkwardness of the psychiatrist issue. "I saw the pictures in the newspaper. You put the stuff in your pickup and dumped it on the county building steps at high noon one day."

I nodded. "It just so happened the local television and print media were there to cover a county commission meeting. A rookie reporter named Elena Rodríguez ran over and interviewed me live. I merely gave my side of the problem that I didn't exactly meet the strict requirements for pickup, but my yard waste was in garbage cans and easier for pickup than the rules at the time required. At that instant, a commissioner named Vince MacLean walked out of the county building and demanded to know if I thought I could do a better job running things. I said 'Hell, yes.' And that launched my political career, right there on the steps of the county building, my pickup illegally backed over the curb, and I'd dumped the old by-now stinky stuff out of the garbage cans loose onto county property."

"And they arrested you."

"For littering. Big trial, media event. But they were dealing with an attorney, an angry attorney. First day of the trial, the judge threw it out. She said the same thing happened to her and the county darn well better get organized. It all worked to my advantage. Talk about free air time, free publicity."

"It shows you are a take-charge kind of man with more than his share of initiative." Rhonda cleaned her glasses.

In a little while we finished my personal history.

"That's about it," I said.

"No, it's not." Rhonda's voice was sharp.

I looked at her. "What do you mean?"

"Rattlesnake," she said.

"Oops." I hadn't wanted to talk about that. But, I recalled she'd seen the scar when she first examined me at Dexter's office in Sarasota. "Oh, yeah, I got bit by a rattlesnake."

"How? What size was it?"

"I just sort of stuck my hand in front of it and it struck," I said. "Maybe a four-footer. Pretty big."

"Why on Earth did you do that?" she wanted to know.

I didn't want her to know. "I was golfing and not paying attention," I lied.

"Did you ever notice all the bad things happen to you when you are golfing?"

"Yeah," I said dryly. "Including my stupid handicap and losing enough balls to start a driving range." Maybe I'd diverted her.

"So," Rhonda said, "you just go bitten by a snake playing golf?"

"I did."

"What about the alligator and somebody named Carrie Jean Billingsley?"

"Shit." She knew something. I felt like a vampire was applying the alcohol swipe to my neck. Why? I thought furiously. And worked to cover my emotions and keep my face locked tight. Something was wrong, dead wrong.

"What difference does it make, Rhonda? A damn snake bit me; I lived." I didn't cover the irritation in my voice.

"I'll tell you, young man." She wagged her pen at me like

a lecturing professor and fixed her eyes on mine. "We have to know everything. Suppose your condition is a result of, or augmented by, snake venom, anti-venom, and alligator saliva. All triggered by the lightning. We won't know unless you tell us."

I'd been teaching a sixteen-year-old Carrie Jean how to play golf. We'd parked near the lake on the back nine for me to hit my shot. I hit a 7-iron and headed back for the golf cart. Carrie Jean was standing at the edge of the lake furiously throwing rocks at a big old alligator that was busy eating a turtle. Well, she didn't see this rattler. Apparently, picking up rocks, she'd disturbed the snake, and her back was to him. He was weaving about; tongue lashing like a frog catching flies at a picnic and his head was drawing back. I shouted for her to freeze. Carrie Jean is bright and quick. She froze at the panic in my voice. She turned her head slowly and saw me staring at the rattler. Her eyes got as big as hubcaps. She swallowed hard and I could see the lump go down her dry throat. I ran that way. What she didn't see was the angry gator flipping his tail, powering his way toward her. Gators usually are afraid of people. But sometimes people erroneously feed them, which takes away that natural fear and thus the gators become dangerous. Especially if they're pissed off because a young lady hit them in the eyeball with a rock or three. I slowed as I got real close, not wanting to trigger the rattler. CJ's eyes were larger now, fixed on the snake. The snake had to be close to deciding whether to strike or not. I sort of waved my hand to get his attention but it seemed to only confuse him, not that I know what a confused snake looks like. So I slowly stuck my hand in between his head and CJ's bare legs. It was a tough decision, but one I had to make this way. My hand was wider than the 7-iron, and I might need the golf club for the alligator in a few seconds. Well, the alligator snaked up on the grass, probably looking for a free meal, with his mouth opening wide. That movement triggered the rattlesnake and he struck, chomping onto my hand. Simultaneously, I closed my hand over his serpentine head, not wanting him to strike twice and maybe hit CJ. And I thrust hard with the 7-iron around Carrie Jean, ramming the club down the gator's throat. His mouth snapped shut as I withdrew my hand, scraping it on his teeth. I'd like to address the terrible odor of decay coming from an alligator's mouth and his lungs. Decidedly unpleasant to say the least. Already in position, I followed through jamming my shoulder into CJ's midsection, bending her over my shoulder. And with her over my right shoulder and a surprisingly strong rattlesnake in my left hand I ran us out of there. I put CJ down in the golf cart. The snake was writhing all over my arm and she watched it with fascination. I think the fangs scraped the inside of my hand again, but I held on, wound up like Randy Johnson on a three and two pitch at the bottom of the ninth inning and the bases loaded, and flung the snake away. He was too disoriented to bite me on the way out. He bounced near the edge of the lake and coiled defensively. I grabbed a spare driver and walked that way. Carrie Jean demanded to know what I was doing and I pointed out I was going to kill the bastard and she said, "Why?"

"And you know what, Rhonda?" I said, finishing up. "Carrie Jean was right. The snake was just doing its job. At four feet plus, it was relatively old, why kill it? It didn't need to be on the golf course, but there are snakes on all golf courses. The gator disappeared with my 7-iron. Hope it worked better for him than it worked for me."

"Would the alligator have attacked her?" Rhonda asked.

"That was my opinion at the time. He was aiming for her and chomping down. It was spring and it was a bull gator. That's their mating season and they're nasty then. They move at night between waters. This one would have eaten most of the turtles he could catch out of that small lake and found another lake to fish out until he ended up in a large enough environment to support him or located a suitable female."

"And Carrie Jean Billingsley didn't panic."

"That's her," I said, careful to keep my face straight. "She even had her wits about her sufficiently to keep me from killing the snake. So I went to the hospital for treatment, end of story."

The problem was that except for CJ and me, no one else knew of the story. The only thing people knew was that I'd got snake-bitten while playing golf. Except: Rhonda had known more. To this date, nobody knew about the alligator. Except Rhonda. Which led me to think if Rhonda knew, then other people here knew also. Which wasn't really a problem, not about the snake and alligator, it wasn't. But if they knew that, what else did they know? The how was seeping into my mind and scaring me.

They could have interviewed Carrie Jean herself and found out that way. But, one, CJ wouldn't talk, and, two, what would have pointed them toward her? I hadn't mentioned it so that CJ's name was involved. And, three, CJ would've called me immediately.

When Carrie Jean went off to college, we corresponded regularly by e-mail. I had a hazy recollection of her making a passing reference to the incident in one of those e-mails. Which I'd deleted after reading. No need to anger Mary Lou should she happen to log on—not likely, but anything's possible. A good computer tech could dig anything off a hard drive, and I hadn't deleted anything out of my deleted file, making it simple to retrieve.

Two plus two equals four. They'd wanted to go through my computer when they were taking samples at my house. I remembered being asked and refusing. Then Rhonda and I had driven from my house to my office downtown. Raleigh had been at my house along with their team. If none of them could do the deed, all they had to do was go online to some in-house computer wizard up here and in two shakes they could suck my hard disk dry.

And install permanent access to it using their own tracking spy ware.

Right then I recalled my lighthouse screensaver running just before we left. I'd thought the machine was on hibernate. Now I understood.

Note to self: get a new system and don't transfer anything from the old one. Of course, if I died, this wouldn't matter a bit.

I was going to accuse Rhonda of invading my privacy. Then a couple of things occurred to me. Suppose Rhonda was sending me a subtle message? She was intelligent enough to do so in a way so subtle that nobody here in the mountains reviewing the tapes or her behavior would be any wiser. Or, and more likely, the glitch in logic which had caused me to catch her mistake was unintentional. And if they were willing to go to those lengths, maybe I shouldn't let on I'd figured them out. I'd already determined there was some other agenda at work here. Now wasn't the time to tell them I was on to them. I needed a hole card. Let them think I was fully cooperative and not suspicious one bit. And this added to my determination not to be interviewed by their tame psychiatrist—or psychologist, I never did know the difference. Bob Newhart was one or the other.

Interrupting and saving me, Raleigh slammed into the room like he owned it. "Hey, doll," he said to his wife. He had a sheaf of papers in his hand and held them out to her.

She gave him a swift smile and took the papers.

"Just faxed in from the Pentagon," Raleigh said, putting his right foot on the coffee table and leaning on his knee.

Before we left Sarasota, I'd printed another copy of the list of my units and assignments in the military.

"Anything hopeful?" asked Rhonda.

"His units were clean. In the sixties and seventies, there were a series of twenty-eight chemical and biological tests using GI's and their units. Mostly in Alaska, Hawaii, Florida and Maryland. The DOD estimates maybe three thousand troops and sailors. Something called Project 112, and Project SHAD, translating to Shipboard Hazard and Defense. Big Tom was a test in 1965 where they sprayed bacteria all over Oahu simulating biological attacks. While Zachary passed through Honolulu enroute to the Republic of Vietnam, he wasn't anywhere near when that test was run."

"How about the CDC?" Rhonda waited expectantly.

I remembered C. Roger Pinella investigating me.

"I checked with Atlanta," Raleigh said. "They didn't want to talk, but I pulled the right strings and found out that they were simply acting on a tip from DOD. They didn't put any credence in the story, but they had to check out the report."

This told me that Palmer Hibbs' contact in the DOD wasn't as confidential as Palmer thought. But, I had to admit, they were likely simply doing their job. They couldn't ignore warning signs.

"That leaves Agent Orange exposure," said Raleigh. "From our tests on the samples taken from your house, we can rule out all other environmental factors." He was talking about exotic or alien spores but neither Rhonda nor I was paying attention.

Rhonda shot me a startled look. As I looked at her trying to figure out what was wrong, something live fled from her eyes. She sat her glasses on the table and pushed Raleigh's foot off and onto the floor. He stopped talking, knowing something was afoot but couldn't identify what.

"But I have none of the symptoms or the diseases which have developed from exposure," I pointed out. Dexter had told me to research Agent Orange and I had read up on the possibilities. And I knew there were a ton of them. Many of my fellow veterans were suffering and dying because of Agent Orange.

"As I've said," Raleigh told me, "it could be a contributory factor."

Something was going on within Rhonda.

"Too many possibilities with Agent Orange," Raleigh pointed out. "Think respiratory and prostate cancer, diabetes, myeloma, Hodgkin's disease, Spina Bifida, brain seizures, birth defects. Some they haven't yet made the connection to."

A stricken look had settled over Rhonda. She shot me an intense glance, one the writhed with meaning—and regret.

Ah, got it. Birth defects.

I watched her with open frankness. Raleigh was pensive, still involved in the flow of the conversation, still on subject.

Neither Rhonda nor I was. She was struggling internally. We both needed to share a smoke; it was almost an imperative.

I guessed that now I wouldn't have to provide sperm in any

fashion, fresh or frozen.

Rhonda slowly regained her composure. I decided that I'd review my regrets later. That list was lengthening; maybe it was endless. But I will say, that given a second chance, I'd still try to have kids. A vast majority of Vietnam vets exposed to Agent Orange had children and those were born whole and healthy. I didn't recall the amount of exposure, probably just in passing. I'd been in treated areas, and I'd been near a spill on the flight line and Da Nang. For all I knew, I'd been out there in the jungles or hills of IV Corp and been sprayed. Lots of aircraft were flying over and I'd been otherwise occupied. I clamped down on speculation and went through the same sort of internal reconciliation that Rhonda had, and redirected my thinking back to the conversational thread.

"All these possibilities," I said casually, knowing the answer, "exist, but have you a way to identify them as part of the problem?"

Raleigh shook his head. "Not many of them. But at least we know for future reference. If we find something weird in your DNA or a virus in your brain, then we can make some attribution. For instance, the field of research into the brain is exploding lately. Researchers are chasing special molecular pathways in the brain, electrical switches. One of hundreds is something called LVGCCs—"

"L-type voltage-gated calcium channels," Rhonda put in.

"Anyway, scientists have found certain chemicals can affect switches and pathways. So can electrical shock." He paused for effect.

"I suppose lightning comes under the heading of electrical shock. This would include the quote mysterious ball lightning end quote." I was beginning to see the unlimited possibilities, scientifically speaking. They were looking for a needle in a haystack, to coin a phrase. I said as much.

"Exactly," Raleigh replied. "It would have been nice to find a tumor or a chemical or some haywire brain function. It would have been. Now we're at this point, a ton of data correlation."

Rhonda held up her supple hand. "Justyn is funding research at a major university to the tune of twenty million a year, just for stem cell research. If you're looking for results, that's more promising."

She didn't say than what. But she meant the long term research into my "widdershins." Another reason they wanted my body.

"So soon somebody's going to be studying the genetic makeup of alligator spit and rattlesnake venom and plugging it into a program with my name on it?"

"Close enough," said Rhonda.

"What's he talking about?" Raleigh asked.

"More input. Ethan was bitten by a rattlesnake and almost lost a hand to a gator." Rhonda's look of admiration almost made the ordeal worthwhile.

"He is snake bit," Raleigh said as if I weren't there. He snorted. "Would've saved us a ton of trouble and money."

"Well I am terribly sorry to inconvenience you, Doctor Smith."

"Now there's some venom," Raleigh said and walked out.

"You have every right to be angry, Ethan," Rhonda said. "He's insensitive sometimes."

"I can tell he doesn't like me a lot."

"It doesn't matter," she said.

She was right. And now it was obvious they had no real answers. "You-all don't have a clue, do you?"

"We're hopeful."

"Jesus. All this and nothing."

Rhonda Smith leaned forward and rubbed my arm to calm me down. "We might not know the answers, but we have a recommendation for treatment."

"What is it?"

"I'm not prepared to say right now. It's late and we should finish up here. Then tomorrow morning we'll get together and make you a proposal for treatment. Maybe you could talk to the doctor from San Francisco."

"As a last resort only."

"We're almost to the last resort option."

"I need a smoke."

"Me, too."

Again at the picnic table, again smoking away, me not so happily.

And again Rhonda surprised me. "This Carrie Jean seems to be a really special person."

"She is." If Rhonda had read through all my e-mail, then she would already know how really special CJ was. Apparently, Rhonda wasn't going to admit that fact. If she said any more, it would be obvious to me she had another source of information. And I wasn't going to let on that I knew she knew. Mentally I shook my head at these needless complications.

"Rhonda, there is another possibility which just popped into my mind."

"And that is?" She sat up on the hard bench and looked interested. She could tell from my voice I had something.

"My mother's ashes. When I was a kid she told me there was an old gypsy curse on her family. She never told me exactly what it was. My wife believes the curse resides in her ashes there in the urn." It was one reason Mary Lou had turned to the psychic kind of stuff she was in to.

"You are serious?"

"I am."

"All the while we're running a chemical analysis of those ashes, you expect me to believe some Stephen King genesis for your syndrome?"

"I don't expect you to believe anything. You wanted to know everything. I told you something we haven't addressed up here yet."

"I'm a doctor, a scientist."

"Yet you want me to let a shrink take me apart to find the genesis?"

"Touché." She smiled.

"Not for reasons of a long ago curse I don't believe. My

mother had specific directions for the disposition of her ashes, but they disappeared in the shipping or packing of her belongings. I never saw them, so I've kept the ashes, not knowing what she wanted done. I hoped the papers would show up one day or somebody would find them in an attic someplace. Such has not yet been the case."

"My turn for a wild surmise," Rhonda said. "You, your family. We've checked them out. Nothing outright weird, so such as I'm about to say is not the case."

"Maybe I'll understand when you say it."

She ignored me. "Clones."

"Clones?" I asked stupidly.

"Clones," she said. "Cloning isn't what the movies make it out to be. Cloning so far has guaranteed plenty of genetic problems. You, the you I'm talking to, could be the clone and gone haywire at this point."

"Yeah, right."

"It is too farfetched. But again, so is your condition. It's one reason we had to do an in depth personal workup on you."

Staring at her, I just shook my head.

"Rhonda? I never thought about the Agent Orange stuff. Forgive me?"

"No, I don't. I was serious about having a baby with you." Sadness eked through her words.

I'd thought that the idea had been shelved. Had I remembered to bring up the Agent Orange subject earlier, she'd never have considered it enough to explore it.

We sat and smoked for a few minutes. Rhonda quickly handed me the cigar stub and fumbled in her pocket and came up with a stick of cinnamon gum, jamming it in her mouth.

Looking around, I saw Raleigh hurrying down the walkway.

"Raleigh was a good man," Rhonda said with resignation. "Until our son was diagnosed with progeria. He's still a good man, but he's bitter about life. This has grown us apart." Her stare nailed me. "Can you comprehend the ups and downs of hope we've gone through?"

"Because of me?"

"Because of you."

I thought about it. "I don't know what to say, Rhonda. It ain't my fault—unless you count me being too stupid to get out of the rain." I glared at her. "Can you comprehend the ups and down of hope I've gone through?"

"Because of us?"

"Yes. Because of you." I waved my hands inclusively. "And this place you represent."

Raleigh neared us.

"I guess there are sufficient regrets to go around." Her eyes clouded.

"You bet," I said, and couldn't read her.

He came up and gave me a look I couldn't interpret. "We have a meeting with Justyn and Belinda right now." He turned his head to me. "It's late. First thing tomorrow, what we'll do is have a formal debriefing with you. We'll go over everything we know and try and figure out what to do next. We should have most of the test results back by then." Apparently even here, they had to send out for special tests.

"All right."

Rhonda patted my hand maternally as she got up. "We'll think of something." But she didn't look me in the eye, as was her custom. I attributed this to Raleigh's presence.

I had a great deal of thinking to do, so I went to my room and got a cigar and took a long walk. Since it was still light, I headed up the hiking trail. I took a García y Vega English Corona out of its tube and put it in my mouth without lighting for a while. They taste good, even without the smoke. Surely though the taste of Rhonda on it would make it better yet.

Rhonda wouldn't budge and tell me what treatment they had thought up. And why the word treatment? Were they going to try some out-in-left-field, non-medical idea? And Rhonda had said a "recommendation" for treatment. Were they going to say, "Maybe you could try such and such" and send me on my way? Cut me loose, as it were? All indications told me this wasn't going to be the case.

Which was fast becoming a big time worry for me. Too many unanswered questions. Too many things that didn't add up. The guns and electronic devices. Their background research on me. Their unauthorized scouring of my entire hard disk. The miraculously inop cell phone. They wanted to know everything they could about me.

Why hadn't they simply asked me? I had nothing to hide.

Or did I?

One possible answer to this mystery was that there was something about me that even I did not know. And they could determine this unknown factor by putting together information they dug up. This sounded absolutely ridiculous, so I discounted it. Scientific methodology, yep, that's me.

The other possibility that explained their behavior was they were looking for something, some information, that I would not, or had not, told them. To counter this, I'd have everything to lose by not telling them. If I knew something that would have a bearing on my problem, I'd tell them or face what I was facing right now: death. So I'd have every reason to cooperate and no reason to hide anything.

Night was falling and the air had a bite in it, so I lighted the García y Vega and began to befoul the clear mountain air. Of course I'd stopped at a strategic location. I studied the terrain and trees and fences and the now familiar electronic warning devices, cameras. This was the one location, so far as I could tell, which, with a fair amount of trouble, you could find your way off the Tyme Institute property without surveillance.

A bird rustled in the undergrowth. I looked at the oak and thought I could climb out on the branch and drop clear—if I had to.

A pair of security guys on a 4X4 Gator Utility Vehicle came whipping around a curve in the path, saw me, and slowed. They continued on the path.

Resuming my walk I thought that if this were Florida at this time, gnats and mosquitoes would be announcing their presence with authority. I resumed my thinking, also.

So why dig into every corner of my life, and why bother to hide the fact they were doing so? A couple of leaps in logic told me they could be looking for something I wouldn't tell them. Meaning something illegal or immoral, money problems, vulnerabilities, or the like. Troubles that would have no bearing on my physical condition, so I wouldn't have been inclined to include it in the info I'd given them. Perhaps they bought into what Dostoevski once wrote: "Behind every great man is a crime." The "great" part would be arguable.

Why? Add that to a professional shrink who could likely hypnotize me. What did they care if I had something to hide?

One obvious conclusion: blackmail, extortion, leverage.

Accept that premise for a minute. How can you blackmail a dying man?

And more important, why?

Dark seeped over the valley and I made my way down the trail toward my room. The cigar butt no longer glowed, so I fieldstripped it and tossed away the remnants.

And one more thing: why sabotage my cell phone?

As I walked down the trail into the compound in the valley, the security guys on the cart came down behind me.

CHAPTER TWENTY-NINE

It promised to be a fateful day, so I didn't run in the morning wanting to save my strength for later. I did have a large breakfast, jamming in as many carbs and as much protein as I could. And that was plenty for I still had a never-ending gnawing hunger.

On the way out of the dining room, I looked down at the valley floor. Noise of the chopper had attracted my attention. I saw Hallelujah Gertz helping the senator and the actress onto the helicopter.

Emeril came out the door and stopped by me. "That leaves you as the only client on station, Mr. Z."

I'd already guessed. "Well, I feel important," I replied.

Raleigh sped up on a golf cart and gestured for me to get on board. He took us to the doctors' office building and we ended up back in Rhonda's conference room.

Rhonda looked drawn. She wore no makeup and her hair appeared more severe this morning. Maybe they'd had a bad night with Rolly. She wasn't wearing official Tyme, Inc. garb; she had on a for-real dress, dark blue and the hem around her knees.

I sat opposite Rhonda and Raleigh paced, assuming the chairmanship of the group.

"The purpose of this meeting," he said, "is to formally address the findings of our medical investigations into your strange case."

"And to review a few other things," Rhonda put in.

"Be advised," said Raleigh, "our examinations and testing, while exhaustive, were not necessarily all-inclusive. That is, we did what we could. Ordinarily, we'd continue some of the tests and repeat them at periodic intervals. However, we don't have the luxury of that time allowance."

Sure you do, I thought, until the day I die. Their sense of urgency was alive and well.

"Hey, Raleigh," I said abruptly. "Cut to the chase. What's wrong with me?"

He stopped pacing. "We don't know."

All was dead quiet for a minute.

Then Rhonda cleared her throat. "Because we don't know doesn't mean we can't take some corrective action."

Ah.

"We had hoped originally that it would be a matter of some unknown or reverse form of progeria," Raleigh said. "Considering our family, that would be the first thing we'd investigate. Unfortunately, we had to rule it out."

Again I didn't know what to say, so again I didn't. Rhonda looked out the window.

"We did discover an anomaly or two," Raleigh said, picking up his interrupted place. "We've isolated a few seemingly random electrical signals—"

"Traces, really," Rhonda said.

"We can't identify a source or a reason," Raleigh continued. "The source could be chemical, it could be affecting some neural pathways, it could be residual from the lightning strikes—"

"Still?" I asked. "That'd be a stretch."

"It would be incredible," he agreed. "In that one little piece of evidence could lay a million explanations. Wild ones such as the lightning strike, the ball lightning hit, broke a barrier between universes of some kind. Theories abound of anti-universes. You could have a touch of anti-matter screwing everything up, namely your biological clock."

He echoed some of my thinking. "I've thought of things like that. Anti-universes, anti-matter, anti-gravity, anti-venom, anti-some-damn-thing. Parallel universes where I'm the guy from the other universe and we switched at the convergence of universes, portal provided by your basic mysterious ball lightning. Some bleed-over from elsewhere or elsewhen."

Rhonda appeared enthusiastic for a moment. "Me, too. Think about the energy field that surrounds each of us. Some call it an aura. Suppose your energy field interacted with the magnetic force lines of the Earth, enabled by the lightning strikes. The outcome? One backwards working Ethan Zachary."

"That is far fetched," said Raleigh.

"So is a parallel universe." She had him. "A disrupted universe and the ball lightning is a function of local disruption and Ethan was in the wrong place at the wrong time."

"You can say that again." I didn't try to hide the sarcasm.

Rhonda eyed me with enthusiasm. "Taking off on what you said. Of course, you think, we think, in terms of lightning. Most people would. Think about this. You could be the aforementioned anomaly from another universe—" She held up a hand to forestall what I was going to say. "—An antimatter universe where things are opposite. Suppose that ball lightning was composed of or had some antimatter properties. String theory tries to incorporate everything into one theory, something to do with 10-dimensional space-time accounting for the matter-antimatter symmetry...." She reacted to my look and trailed off. "I'm just saying that maybe there's a leak, maybe mind you, from another universe which explains your condition. In antimatter universe everything is opposite, positive is negative. One of these which would be time, or clocks going backwards." She shrugged evasively. 'I don't know if I believe that or not. I am saying, however, that you do fit the conditions I've outlined."

While I had mentioned it in passing, *me in a different universe?* I didn't really believe that one—or want to, anyway. But I do read *Discovery* and *Scientific American*. "If I'm a bleed-over or an anomaly here, do you reckon in the antimatter universe there is a me whose personal clock is going clockwise? I mean, in a yin and yang fashion to preserve the matter-antimatter symmetry?"

"You know what, Ethan?" asked Rhonda. "You continue to surprise me."

"I can read," I said with fake smugness. "Are boys girls over there and vice versa? Dogs are cats?" This speculation was becoming ridiculous to the extreme. Both Rhonda and I seemed to realize this at the same time.

"Somehow I don't think so," she said.

Raleigh fingered his lab smock. "Maybe it was a function of a mobile time warp and the ball lightning was a manifestation—"

"What the hell is a mobile time warp?" I asked.

"I don't know, but it sounds good." He was defensive, but at least he was thinking, and that was only to my benefit.

"It still seems most reasonable," Rhonda said, "that the condition is a result of cause and effect. The cause, the trigger, likely was the lightning, regular or high-test ball lightning. The receptive conditions would be set up my some combination such as Agent Orange, rattlesnake or viper venom, nicotine, and cat hair. There isn't enough computer time to figure the odds of all put together."

"Don't forget capricious gypsy curses, voodoo spells, and/or psychological trauma," I said, trying for a little humor.

Raleigh jumped on it immediately. "What trauma?"

I shook my head. "That's my point. There isn't, or wasn't, any. My life isn't any different than anybody else's."

Rhonda said with a smile, "You know, we haven't brainstormed this well. We haven't explored alien tampering or some kind of actual time travel in depth."

"And maybe Tinker Bell hit me with pixie dust."

"Point of order," Raleigh said. "The DNA testing will tell us if Zachary has any alien blood. They couldn't fake a whole person to the nth degree."

Of course, I didn't tell them about the remote viewing. I wondered how the FarReaching Institute was coming along in their search for the genesis of my problem. They were fast becoming my only and final hope. To find out how they were doing, I'd have to call them, something I certainly refused to do from here.

"Makes me wonder what kind of DNA Tinker Bell has."

Rhonda scolded me. "This is serious, Ethan. Sure the odds to these possibilities are a jillion to one. Answer me this, mister smarty, what are the odds out of the billions of people alive and who have been alive throughout the history of the planet that you alone would age backwards? And compound those odds exponentially that you would age backwards as opposed to some other effect."

"Your point," I admitted. "And a good one. I concede the possibility. It seems to me the odds of aliens landing on Earth are better than the odds of me aging backwards."

"There you go," she said, leaning back as if winning the fight.

Raleigh sat down, getting into the mood of the group. "I'm medically certain as I can be that what you have is not a disease. If you pin me down, I'd say your condition was nature gone amuck."

"Wow," I said. "Considering I'm one of nature's creatures and all, you might have a point."

Raleigh appeared taken aback. After a minute, he agreed. "You're right, Zachary. That makes you a freak of nature."

"Raleigh!" Rhonda admonished.

"Here's one for you," I said, thinking in the spirit of things. "Suppose, just suppose, the lightning killed me. I'm on the way to wherever I'm going to end up. And this is all a quickie universe my dying and misfiring neurons have created. I'm the real spirit and you all are constructs. When I wind down to nothing, this, my ephemeral moment, is gone, this construct universe, you all, everybody, everything is gone. Nothing remains."

That was pretty heavy. Nobody said anything for a while.

Then Rhonda sighed. "If what you say is correct, you certainly assigned me a few hellacious burdens, my friend." She was referring to Rolly.

"If," I said carefully, "that is a correct assumption of what's going on, why should this universe be any different than any other? Can it not have sufficient detail, sufficient life? It's a universe unto itself. So the hell what?"

Raleigh rose and started pacing again. "That's what I say. So the hell what? It doesn't change things any. The problem is in this universe, so we're stuck with it."

I took a deep breath. "Something useful finally said." It was my life in balance. Well, it wasn't in balance. My life was forfeit. Done and gone. We were just now haggling over the "how come" part.

Rhonda peeled and chewed a stick of gum. "You're both back on track. Let us just say that what Ethan has is some kind of imperative virus, or electrical problem that maybe is genetic or imbued at the lightning strike. This is my opinion, or one of them, for what it's worth. It could be genetic or a freak of nature. But the lightning, probably the ball lightning, triggered it. It might even be some smaller cellular inhabitant we have not yet discovered, haven't known even to look for, and this is the first case."

What she said actually made sense. I had my own thoughts, but I wasn't scientist or medical professional enough to articulate them as she had.

She went on. "I haven't voiced this yet, but I've read of natural lasers occurring in the atmosphere. Ball lightning could have generated—nah." She shook her head vigorously. "Genetic, virus, cell division, electrical charge—for that matter, didn't you tell me a pine tree fell on you?"

"My head hit it or it clipped me, I was already out of it. My head felt like the clapper in the church bell on Christmas."

"See, there I go again," she said slumping back. "Problem is we don't know what we're looking for. So we haven't found it. Or we have found it, but we don't know what it is. Am I making sense?"

"Too damn much," I said sincerely. I explained Mary Lou's tarot cards. "She believes in gypsy curses," I alabied. It occurred to me that the FarReaching Institute might have finished and they had been trying to contact me.

"Emotional, mental trauma," Raleigh said. "We still have the San Francisco psychologist standing by."

They both stared at me as if willing me to cave in and agree with using the shrink. I admit I was wavering. "Hell, I don't know. Maybe. Let me think about it some more."

"A psychological profile would help complete the medical workup," Raleigh said casually.

"One thing I want to be is helpful."

Raleigh eyed me, telling me he was getting tired of my irreverent mouth.

Well, I was getting tired of games.

I didn't say anything. I guess we were all lost in our own thoughts. I spent a few moments staring out the plate glass window, looking out over the compound. A man in a security golf cart was cruising aimlessly. It seemed to me that when I first arrived I hadn't seen any security presence at all. Now it was everywhere.

My mistake was in thinking they wanted to keep me here for my dead body. All signs pointed to that fact. Well, most signs. Probably, I reasoned, if I was long gone back in Sarasota, they'd have a difficult time prying a public figure's body away from the grieving widow. And, toss in the fact they'd miss first hand observation of my demise. So, it stood to reason they wanted me here, backing into death while under their microscope.

"How long do you reckon I have left?"

Raleigh didn't hesitate. "If you continue to accelerate your reverse growth and aging, maybe thirty days to crunch time. Your physiology will have to change and adapt to the new conditions, and that is physically impossible. We can talk about all these alternate universes, but I will tell you right now, biology is biology."

We were quiet.

Into the silence, Rhonda said oh so softly, "I pray it will stop at that time. Perhaps having run its course." The anguish in her voice told me she'd prayed for that thing before, and many times. For Rolly.

Again we were silent. I don't think any of the three of us really believed that whatever was ravaging me would just up and quit. But for a brief second, I believed it was possible. If the human spirit could prevail, then it would be so. Rhonda's open soul projected such.

Then the moment went away.

I said, "Somebody mentioned a recommended treatment?"

Rhonda stood, glanced at me for one searing moment and said, "I have to go check on Rolly." Without another look, she walked out.

Raleigh watched her with irritation. Maybe you get that sometimes when husband and wife work too closely together. And maybe not.

He started pacing again. "It's a variation of chelation therapy and hemodialysis. In chelation therapy, they run your blood through filters and cleansers and what not and return it allegedly more pure." He turned and walked the other way. "They use something called EDTA. That stands for Ethylene Diamine Tetra-acetic acid. It's been around for years and was originally designed to remove impurities, pollutants like plaque, aluminum, cadmium, and other things from the body. Some in the medical community look upon chelation therapy as quackery. Hemodialysis is a mechanical procedure used to clean the blood, too. Think kidney dialysis. This gave me the idea."

I didn't know what to think. "And?"

"I proposed this and no one has yet come up with a better idea. I propose to pump your blood out, give you new blood, and do the process over and over until there is no chance that any contaminants remain."

"Remove and replace my blood supply?" It sounded like something a mechanic would do. It sounded last resort. I said as much.

"You bet. But it's the best we can come up with. Think about it. Your entire body is responding to some stimuli. The blood might well carry the signals and instructions to your cellular structure. That's one of the functions of the blood anyway. So remove the messenger, solve the problem."

I'm not certain he believed it himself. It appeared to me that he was trying to convince himself as well as me. I'd heard of chelation therapy, sort of an alternate return to health procedure. And it might explain why Rhonda left: she didn't want to associate herself with this plan.

"How long do you think this would take?" I asked.

He looked at his watch. "I'll do the first treatment this afternoon, change out some of your blood, dilute it if you will, see how you tolerate the procedure. It would probably take a few weeks to do a complete flush safely several times. And we'd know in those few weeks if it was working."

O positive.

I looked at my watch and observed the second hand speed backwards. No blood was touching the watch. On the nineteenth hand, Raleigh had a point. What could it hurt to change out my blood? It did not escape my attention that the treatment time might span my likely remaining days. I wasn't certain for whom this was convenient. But it kept me here for that time frame—until I died or lived through this thing. I already knew they wanted my body, now they wanted to make sure it was here when it officially became a body.

That lady who keeps tap dancing on my last nerve? She went into high gear.

Just then the phone rang; Raleigh picked it up, nodded to himself, and said, "He'll be right there." He dropped the receiver into the slot. "Let's go, Belinda Foursleeps wants to see you."

Standing, I said, "What for?"

He shrugged. "She'll tell you herself, I'm sure."

Raleigh personally escorted me to Justyn Tyme's building. This time there was a security guard at her door and he silently triggered the door open for us.

Belinda was seated at her command center. She was still wearing her uniform of the day, khakis and jacket. She stood and said, "Thanks for coming, Mr. Zachary. Please sit down."

Something significant was going on, something about to happen. There was an air of expectancy about Belinda and Raleigh.

I sat in one of the chairs in front of the desk. Raleigh sat in the other.

On the green blotter in front of her, Belinda rearranged two stacks of documents. Next to them was a single envelope. She sat and lifted the envelope. "How much did you propose to Mr. Zachary?"

"How much?" Raleigh leaned forward. "We just discussed the blood replacement therapy, that's all."

"Finish the rest now," she told him. She scooted her roller chair under her and sat. The chair made her appear taller than she was.

Raleigh looked at me. "Zachary, if removing and replacing your blood is not effective in treating your condition, then you are going to die a horrible death. I think we've pretty well established that."

Raleigh had made a point to assure me that I was going to die by contraction or some damn thing, growing younger, bone structure growing smaller. Whether that theory was true or not, I hadn't yet decided if I fully believed it or not. But it was a logical extension of what was going on inside me. See "incoming wisdom teeth."

"At least I have something to look forward to," I said flippantly. I recognized a setup when I saw one. What was their game?

He went on. "When you begin to regress too far and death is imminent, I thought we could do some transplants to keep you going. Internal organs, liver, lungs, pituitary gland, the like. From children, compatible to your O positive and other factors. They'd be smaller and fit better and you wouldn't die from organ compression. We have access to the transplant priority lists and can guarantee you'll receive the transplants when they become available. Consequently, you'd have to be here on site and ready. The Tyme Institute carries a great deal of clout."

It sounded logical and desirable.

"And donation money," Belinda added. "We've been funding Angel Flights or whatever you call them for years. Also, Tyme's corporate jets participate frequently. The system owes us and will respond. You will receive the first organ available. And so on."

It was consistent with the blood replacement theory. It was scary. Now I was thinking about swapping out perfectly good innards for those of children? If it worked, it would prolong my life. I will say that I have thought and thought about my life expectancy lately. I had thought that it would be just fine to die in my teens as my organs began to squish, my brain squash as my head allegedly grew smaller. But I didn't believe that part. The physics and biologics wouldn't work. I think I'd just sort of croak one night and wake up dead. I didn't believe my bone structure would shrink. Though with my impossible condition, anything else was certainly possible.

"Jesus, you've got it all planned and figured out," I said incredulously.

Belinda Foursleeps gave a tight smile for the first time. I'd complimented her. It was what she did.

She handed me the envelope. "Open it."

I took it and pulled the flap out. Inside was a single sheet. I took it and read it.

BANK OF AMERICA
CERTIFIED CHECK

Pay To The Order of ETHAN ALLEN ZACHARY

$50,000,000.00

FIFTY MILLION AND NO/100 DOLLARS

I pointed at the two stacks of documents. "And those would be releases."

"Smart man," Belinda beamed. She was happy as a wild hog in an acorn patch. "One set for us, one set for you."

Too many O positives running around, I thought.

"Sign the paperwork and you can cash that check right now," Belinda said.

I tossed the check on her desk. "If I'm dying, this means nothing to me."

She nodded sagely. "That's one reason we decided on that astronomical amount. You can set up your family and friends for life."

Arm-twisting without the pain.

"See, Mr. Zachary, think about it this way. If you're going to be dead anyway, why not make it pay?" Belinda stood and leaned over her desk. She held out her hand. "Sweet, loving wife Mary Lou Zachary. She'd be happy with twenty or thirty million, don't you think?"

I said nothing, dreading what was coming next.

"Sweet young thing, Carrie Jean Billingsley. Whom you probably knew in a carnal fashion when she was under legal age and still—" Belinda saw the look of thunder upon my face.

"We never...." I was angry and sputtering. But they didn't care whether CJ and I had ever had sex or not, just that they could generate the idea that we had. More of CJ's long deleted e-mails, more of her swearing her undying love for me. To see her innocence touched by this, this—

But they were playing hardball now.

"Carrie Jean Billingsley could live her life out on twenty, twenty-five million." Belinda straightened. "And if rumor has it correctly, you have a dalliance with another young lady." Belinda leaned over and scrolled a screen on a monitor. "Ah, Elena Rodríguez. Quite attractive."

From an angle I could see there was a head and shoulders shot of Elena.

"A few million here and there would certainly ease your conscience, Mr. Zachary, she being unemployed likely because of you." She scrolled some more. "There are a few Zachary kin left. You could bequeath them quite a bit." She laughed. "We'll even set your cat up for life. Wouldn't you like that, Mr. Zachary?"

I laughed out loud. "Old Budweiser's dying, just like me. He wouldn't care if he lived in the Taj Mahal or a dumpster."

"It was the point I was making, Mr. Zachary, not the fact. I don't care if you eat the goddamn cat; I never liked them in the first place. Do you see any cats around here?"

"And my part of the bargain is to stay here, to get transfusions, to allow organ transplants, and then to die under your supervision."

"That's right." She sat back down. "You're dying anyway, Zachary. And please be advised we've spent a considerable amount on your behalf already. I don't know exactly how much, but a few hundred thousand at least."

"Your altruism overwhelms me." But she was right. Sending Boeing 737 aircraft about the country for me wasn't cheap, nor was the specialists and the equipment and the tests. Somewhere they were decoding and recording my genetics, my DNA and comparing and analyzing it. "You can afford it." I wanted to sound as if I didn't care one way or the other.

She pushed both stacks of paper toward me. "Start signing. The lawyers put arrows where they want your signature."

Raleigh was sitting quietly. At least he wanted to think he had scruples.

And now I knew why Rhonda had abruptly left.

I sat back and folded my arms, ignoring the check and the paper work.

Belinda had a pen in her hand and was extending it to me. After a moment, she withdrew her arm.

O positive.

"So, tell me Belinda, sweetheart. What happens to my old used organs?"

Another tight smile. "For fifty million dollars, it's none of your concern." She tapped one stack of papers. "It says so right in here." She leaned back and crossed her legs. "Since you'll be dead it shouldn't matter to you, either. However, I will confirm what you've obviously already deduced."

"He has?" Raleigh was surprised.

"That is why I insisted we pay him the fifty million," Belinda said. "He'd figure it all out before he died. I want his cooperation."

"No." Raleigh didn't think I would have come to the conclusion I already suspected.

"This afternoon," Belinda continued, "when you're hitching him up to IV's in one of two interconnected surgical theaters next to Justyn's room, you think about it."

"Oh." Raleigh figured it out.

Belinda eyed me. "What's it to be, Mr. Zachary? Have you come to a favorable decision yet?"

"No."

"You do not approve of my methods?"

"No."

"It's how I operate. I perform in the most efficient fashion."

"That's obvious."

"Perhaps I could have approached it in a nicer way, Mr. Zachary. But I have no time. Keep in mind I'm the one who devised the plan. You've thought it through and you can see I could have done this in different ways, many of which did not include fifty million dollars. Or even one dollar. I'm being generous and above board."

I turned to Raleigh. "Do you really think my organs will help Justyn?"

"They can't hurt," he replied. "They might have enough of the residual whatever is in you to help him, to make him grow younger, to keep him alive. Any of those would be acceptable. His own body is failing him and we're keeping him alive with machines."

Then what I thought was the last piece of the puzzle fell in place. "Not to mention complete transfusions of my blood."

"Yes." His voice was very low.

"I have to know this, Raleigh. Was Rhonda a part of this?"

He met my eyes and didn't speak.

"Did she know?" My voice was demanding.

"What is it with you and my wife?" His eyes were dark, hooded.

"Nothing. Not a goddamn thing. But she's the class of this outfit."

"In a month it won't matter to you."

"Did she know?" I insisted.

"At the last. After it was conceived and put into play."

CHAPTER THIRTY

Hallelujah Gertz.

I went for a walk up and down the ramps, to the ends of each terrace. Where I thought the residences were, none of the buildings were marked. So I kept wandering around, smoking, until I spotted Hal running his golf cart from one place to another. I contrived to intercept Hallelujah.

"Hey, Hal."

"How you, Mr. Z.?"

"Good as can be expected. Which one of these places can I find Rolly?" I was asking where the Smiths lived in a roundabout fashion so my curiosity wouldn't alarm him.

Gertz checked his watch. At least his watch was reliable. "He'd be home for lunch now." Hal pointed up a level and to a two-story building two removed from that of Justyn Tyme.

"Thanks." I turned and then, as if spontaneously, asked, "by the way, did Justyn's body reject your kidney? Or does he still have it?"

"Oh, it's still tickin'—" He realized he might be giving away a company secret and stopped. Then he shrugged to himself. "Guess I don't talk about it much. Sorry."

"No big deal, Hal. I was just curious. You didn't admit anything to me."

"Sure thing, Mr. Z." He sped away, left foot outside the cart and almost dragging along beside him.

Live and learn, Hal. Why wasn't I surprised at the obvious revelation?

The residence of the doctors Smith was just another Tyme, Inc. building. But this one had only a single front entrance and a for real WELCOME on the entrance mat. Not seeing a doorbell button, I banged on the front door.

A woman I barely recognized as a face in the crowd at Rolly's birthday party answered. "Yes?"

Not knowing what to say, I said, "Can Rolly come out and play?"

"What?" She was young and had long, brown hair, and a chiseled chin.

"You the nanny?"

"Yes, sir."

"Is Rolly home?"

"Yes, sir."

"Well, I came to visit."

"Oh."

She just stood there.

"Well?"

"Oh. Nobody ever...I mean, I've never...."

"Is Rhonda home?"

"Yes, sir."

"Why don't you go ask her?"

"Yes, sir." She disappeared and the door swished closed.

In a moment it reopened and Rhonda stood there. "Ethan?"

I looked around behind me. "None other."

She smiled and stood aside. "Come in." She was still wearing the dark blue dress.

The entrance floor was parquet. Fresh flowers sat on a side table. I followed Rhonda inside. The living room was downstairs. A large television connected to Playstations or whatever was against one wall. The furniture was tasteful, top of the line brand names people in the know would recognize, especially since North Carolina was the home of most of the furniture on the east coast.

Bookshelves lined the wall above the television and held plenty of hardbacks; the colors diverse enough to be lights on a

Christmas tree. On the wall, which met the one with the shelves, about twenty pieces of white and colored construction paper were taped and tacked up. They were all a child's art. Crayon, finger-paint, pencil drawings, brush pictures. Rolly was just like any other kid. But somebody was proud of his art.

"What's up?" Rhonda asked.

"Just wanted to say hi to Rolly."

"He's coming down." The nanny must have gone to get him.

"I talked to Belinda Foursleeps. With your husband."

Rhonda wouldn't meet my eyes for a minute. Then she squared her shoulders and glanced at the stairs at the side of the room. Her voice was hushed and she locked her gaze onto mine. "Did you agree?"

"Not yet." I kept her gaze. Her eyes were deeper sapphire blue now than I'd ever seen them. We were a couple of levels deeper than we'd ever been. "I told them I needed to think it through. Everybody's waiting on me. This afternoon I undergo my first blood treatment or replacement or whatever the hell it is." I paused. "I just wanted to know if you knew about the whole thing with the fifty million and the transplants for Justyn."

Rhonda glanced at the stairs again. She moved her face close to mine. Her voice was harsh. "Only this morning. But know you this, Ethan. I would do *anything* for my son. Anything."

We were silent for a moment.

I wanted to ask her if she knew Foursleeps was going to use Carrie Jean Billingsley against me, the accusation that we'd slept together. But I didn't ask; if Rhonda had known, I didn't want to know. Upon reflection, I don't think she knew.

Then she continued. "Just so you know, Rolly has not been threatened, his circumstances will remain the same with or without you. Justyn likes him, he likes me, and he likes my husband. We are loyal employees who could never possibly repay him for what he's done for our son. I was not consulted on the plan. Had I been, I would not have recommended it."

So she didn't sell me out. But all things being equal, she was loyal to Tyme, especially for what the old man had done for her son. She wasn't signing on to either side. Her main concern was her son. And never mind what she thought of our relationship, or me, her focus was Rolly.

"Fine," I said because I couldn't think of anything else to say. Then I thought of something. "If you were me, would you take the fifty mil and give them your body parts?"

Her eyes showed strain first then her face. "I don't know." Her voice was a harsh whisper. "God, Ethan, I don't know." She was speaking as my friend and as a doctor. She reached up and cupped my face with both hands. "You've changed in the short time I've known you. I can almost see you grow younger before my eyes." A strand of her hair fell across her left eye and she did nothing to remove it. "God, Ethan, I don't know."

"EZ!" Rolly came down the stairs slowly, taking one at a time, putting both feet on each stair, and then one foot at a time to the next.

Rhonda snatched her hands from my face.

"Hey, boy."

Rhonda dropped my gaze and walked away. The nanny was standing atop the stairs watching Rolly with concern.

He made it down and came my way. I shook his hand. It was dry and shaky. And light as a gum wrapper.

We sat and talked a bit. He showed me the Speed Channel on the satellite television. It had an old formula-1 race on and we both made fun of the open wheel racecars. I spotted a Frisbee against the wall.

"Want to go outside and toss the Frisbee around?"

He wanted to, I could tell. "No. I'm too tired."

Oh, shit. God damn nature. Why couldn't it restrict bad things to us adults?

Rhonda was sitting on the carpeted stairs about half way up. I could see her legs below the landing above through the railing. Her unclad legs were every bit as attractive as the rest of her. The nanny was nowhere to be seen.

We talked about books. I remembered some of the books Carrie Jean was reading at that age. But Rolly was into more adult books.

"I like Louis L'Amour westerns," he told me. "They don't have a lot of big words and they're about the land. And I like Harry Potter books. I'm glad she ended the series, um, in time." His face was wistful.

"I know a young lady lawyer that loves Harry Potter," I said. You couldn't shut CJ up about them. I'd even watched one of the movies on DVD at her suggestion. "She says the movies are very faithful to the books."

Rolly nodded solemnly. "They are."

"Look, kid, I just wanted to come and say hi." I didn't tell him I might not be around much longer. Especially since Rhonda was certainly listening. So I didn't make like it was goodbye on my part. "Maybe we could have lunch tomorrow. Emeril won't mind."

"Golly. I'd like that."

I felt like a friend just died. It wasn't my intention to mislead him, and doubtless they'd think I'd come over here to do that thing and lull them into trusting me at least through tomorrow lunchtime. The invitation had just slipped out; I was fooling myself as well as them. Not that it mattered, it occurred to me, because even if I'd made it a formal goodbye, Rhonda might not reveal what she guessed from my words. And maybe she would think that I thought I was going to die or go into an induced coma this afternoon when they started pumping out my blood and replacing it. The likely scenario as I envisioned it: Keep me alive, strapped to the operating table, but unconscious. A human organ farm to be harvested at their leisure.

I levered myself up, nonetheless feeling like Benedict Arnold. "Got to go, kid. Don't want to interrupt your nap. They never let me sleep in the afternoon."

His smile was wan. He pried himself off the couch and I fought the impulse to help him. Let him keep his dignity.

We walked slowly to the stairs. "See you kid." I shook his hand again.

I could see Rhonda now. She was leaning forward, head

buried in her arms on top of her exposed knees. I almost bent over and whispered to Rolly that he had a good mom, but I didn't want to patronize him.

"Hey, Rhonda, see you around, sweetheart."

I shouldn't have said that, but I did and I'd do it again. There had to be closure between us. That was more important to me than what I was going to do that afternoon.

She raised her head so that I could see only one eye. One striking, beautiful sapphire eye. One sad and wet eye. Then she buried her head again. If she didn't know this was the end, then she certainly suspected it. But from whose perspective? Did she know it was the end for me due to Raleigh and Foursleep's scheming? Or did she know the end was near because she knew me well enough to read my intentions?

Rolly said, "Mom?"

Goddamn.

I chucked him on the shoulder and left.

For a change, I knew what I was going to do.

I just had to figure out how I was going to do it.

And when.

CHAPTER THIRTY-ONE

My mistake was curiosity.

I stood outside debating with myself. A cool breeze blew and I needed a smoke badly. But I had other things on my mind.

A security guy I hadn't talked to was standing in position in front of Justyn Tyme's residence. He waved at me and walked over. "Mr. Zachary, Ms. Foursleeps and Mr. Tyme are looking for you."

He led me into the building and down the corridor. Two more security personnel stood in front of Justyn's door. My guard nodded to them and one knocked on the door and swung it open.

I walked over to Justyn's bedside. The nurse hovered in the background as usual. Belinda Foursleeps was standing alongside Justyn's bed and both of them watched me walk over to them. About ten feet to the side of his bed and past the IV tree, a framed child's painting hung on the wall. I continued over to look at it. A lot of red, it was obviously a couple of stick figures representing Rolly and Justyn standing together on the top of a mountain. It was signed ROLLY SMITH.

Nodding my head, I went to the bed. "Hello, Justyn." I had to step around a machine on wheels. I'd been through a whole lot of medical analysis lately and knew a lot of machines, but I didn't know this one. It was on a cart of its own and had tubes leading under Justyn's covers. It was probably a kidney dialysis machine.

Nobody complained that I didn't call him "Mr. Tyme."

"Have you decided yet?" Belinda stared at me.

"I think I'll sleep on it tonight, and probably sign off tomorrow morning." My voice was "practiced casual." A little delaying and misdirecting tactic.

Belinda nodded as if my answer was something she wanted to hear.

"Zachary, you're a strange bird," Justyn said with a dry cough.

Supposing he was referring to my failure to jump at fifty million dollars, I said, "I'm an attorney," as if that explained everything.

Apparently it did. Apparently attorneys take their time and review all options before they sign anything.

"Therefore," Justyn said slowly, "you're on board."

I didn't affirm. I said, "I don't want a certified check." It could be taken while I was under their control and cashed in. They knew as an attorney I'd think of things like that.

That got their attention.

"Tomorrow," I continued, "when I'm ready to sign, we'll get on the phone and I'll obtain some account numbers. You people deposit the amounts I tell you into those accounts. When those deposits are confirmed, I'll sign." More obfuscation. They would expect an attorney to cover possibilities and not be so trusting. So, I was playing to their view of the lawyer stereotype.

I'd sold Belinda Foursleeps obviously. I'd done what she'd likely expected me to do. However, she looked at Justyn for confirmation and he glanced at the machine alongside his bed and turned to her and nodded. He appeared very tired. If that was a kidney or hemodialysis machine, the treatment had him in a weakened or groggy condition.

The nurse moved over to us nervously.

Belinda said, "All right. Let's go." No wasted chatting with her.

She went out the door ahead of me.

It was the last time I saw Justyn Tyme.

Belinda turned right toward her office complex and strode off.

I glanced to the left and stepped around the security guys.

About twenty yards down the corridor, farther into the mountain, were two doorways alongside each other. I headed that way, curious.

"Ms. Foursleeps!" said one of the security team, his voice urgent.

I increased my pace. Both doorways were double doors with windows in the top half.

Belinda's voice was alarmed. "Zachary, where are you going?"

I said nothing but stopped and looked through the window of the first door.

I'd been told in a roundabout manner that this was where I would undergo the blood replacement therapy. The room was a complete surgical theater. Chrome and steel glistened. Machines and electronics and monitors lined the walls. It could be a control room over at NASA.

"Zachary!"

Glancing down the corridor, I saw Belinda and the security guys heading my way in a hurry.

So I stepped over to the next set of doors and looked in.

An exact duplicate operating theater. Plumbing, electronics, surgical tools on adjustable swing tables covered with plastic. Between the two rooms, I saw, was a pair of double doors, so people could go from one operating room to the other.

Six feet were closing down on me quickly.

It occurred to me that in the paperwork Belinda had prepared, there was no timetable referring to the removal and transplant of my organs. Something I had known percolated to the surface of my brain: I would be at their mercy when undergoing my first blood treatment this afternoon. Hallelujah Gertz had only one kidney and was doing fine. They'd think I could do without one kidney. Why not start the treatments on Justyn immediately? If necessary, they could drug me when they gave me the first transfusion and go on about their plan?

But I'd thrown a monkey wrench into their plan by stalling

my signature until tomorrow. Unless I was drugged this afternoon and then I'd do whatever they told me to do.

I'd just thought I'd bought myself some time when I'd told them I'd sign the paperwork tomorrow. They could go on their own timetable. Justyn didn't look good, was probably on kidney dialysis.

Belinda knew I was smart and prone to figuring things out on my own; therefore, she didn't want me making judgments based on what I was seeing right now. That's why she was alarmed at my viewing the surgical rooms. The already-prepared and set-up operating rooms.

Several other things all of a sudden added up. Some of these I had already considered and had caused me to make the decision I had regarding this whole mess. Most of all, right now, was a bad taste about this place and these people.

I heard heavy breathing and a hand took each of my arms and tried to lift me away from where I stood.

I windmilled both of my arms and broke the hold, spinning both security men away. I was off balance and as I regained my feet, the one on the left leaped for me. I dodged, elbowed him in the kidney and sent him sprawling. Continuing my turn from the elbow strike, I lashed out with my right heel and knocked number two into the far wall.

The first one was bent over, but he was game. He came for me grunting in pain, hunch-fashioned. Deftly, I slipped aside and clipped him on the back of the neck with a quick chop.

Number two rushed in with an over hand right aimed for my head. I ducked and jabbed him twice in the abdomen with a left-right combo as his right slashed over my shoulder. His eyes bulged out and he stopped cold. I teed off on his chin with an All-American haymaker and he went down like he was shot.

Number one was on his hands and knees just crouched there as if he didn't know where he was or what he was doing.

Taking a couple of deep breaths, I relaxed and turned to Belinda.

She was standing as a spectator. A fleeting look of alarm

about her own personal safety flitted across her face and then disappeared.

"You're good, Zachary," she said with appreciation.

Damn.

That was my mistake.

I'd sent her and them a message.

She already knew I wasn't fooled by much of their song and dance. Now I'd tipped my hand somewhat. I needed to stall, buy time. An old attorney trick: play ignorant.

"What the hell, Belinda?"

She stood straighter. "Those rooms are sterile. I was afraid you were going in and they'd have to be sterilized again." She gestured. "You can see they are makeshift operating rooms, for emergency, for Justyn. We didn't have the physical space here to design and build them into their own contained units with inner doors and intermediate decontamination areas. So we had to build them right here off the main thoroughfare."

Looking up and down the corridor, I doubted whether there was any travel other into Justyn's room. But, I had to admit, she was good. It was all probably true to a certain extent.

She gave a disgusting look at her two strong-arm guys. They were still where I'd left them. She looked up at me speculatively.

I shrugged innocently. "I don't like to be grabbed from behind. I'm sorry I overreacted." I doubted if we were fooling each other. My gut level reaction to the situation had endangered my safety and my plan. "I need to cool off. Hell, I need a smoke." I walked off down the corridor past Justyn's room patting my pockets for a smoke and not finding one, even though I had a García y Vega miniature in my pocket.

If Belinda decided to get reinforcements and forge ahead with her plan, I was finished. I wasn't panicking, but I had a severe case of "hurry the hell up you're one step ahead of disaster."

Once outside, I stopped and looked around. Raleigh Smith was walking away from his residence. An idea hit me. "Hey, Raleigh," I shouted.

He turned and I waved for his attention and fast-walked over to him.

When I neared him, I said, "Jeez, can you believe what just happened?"

His eyebrows went up.

"Foursleeps just sicced two goons on me."

"What did you say?"

"I don't know what the hell kind of place you're running here, Doctor Smith, but I'm not sure I like it a lot." I explained a version of what happened close to the truth. "Like they thought I was stupid enough to break sterile barriers and all. Can you believe that?"

"What happened to the security team?"

"They surprised me and I overreacted and knocked them on their ass." I shrugged as if it were no mean feat.

He did what I wanted him to; he remembered my reaction on North Beach on Lido Key in Sarasota. So he knew I was capable of some action. "They weren't expecting me to go apeshit, Raleigh, so I caught them unawares."

He nodded knowingly. He also eyed me with his own specu-lation, wondering if he could take me. I could sense him roll the idea around in his mouth like tasting a good cigar before you light it. The idea appealed to him, especially since he didn't like me and now knew that Rhonda and I shared some kind of bond.

"Now," I tossed in casually, "I'm too upset to do the blood thing right away. I'm going to take a walk and have a long smoke, then I'm going to have Emeril fix me lunch and then I'll be over to your office. Damn, I'm upset. Why'd they have to try that on me?"

He shrugged himself, secretly amused. I was playing to his intellectual arrogance. He thought he was smarter and better than I and therefore did not even consider that I was using him.

"I don't know," he said. "People have been on edge lately." He looked at Justyn's place. "Lemme go check it out." He started walking that way.

Wrapping my arms around my torso, I mimed a shiver. I wanted somebody to know why I was going to come out of my room with my jacket on. I didn't want to spend the night in these mountains wearing only a shirt. Not that anybody would notice, but I was trying to cover all the bases. My mind was working overtime. "The hell with it," I said. "I'll see you after lunch." I walked off rubbing my shoulders and heading for the up ramp.

At my level I went down the walkway occasionally scanning the territory below. Several golf carts had sped to Justyn's residence; but so far nobody was hustling after me. I could acquit myself well; however, they had me with sheer numbers—and weapons, if necessary.

In my room and mindful of the cameras, I changed to my best running shoes and stripped my shirt to keep them from guessing what I was doing. In the closet and away from the camera, I quickly donned three pullover shirts, tucked two of them in and left the outer one hanging over my beltline to disguise the fact I was wearing three shirts. Layered clothing is the best in cold weather and my jacket was lightweight.

Stuffing a few cigars in my jacket pocket, I looked at the *Guns, Germs, and Steel* book by Jared Diamond that Carrie Jean had given me. I'd have dearly loved to take it with me. But it was too big and too heavy for the trip upon which I was embarking. I'd have liked to take my inoperative cell phone, too, to be tested, but if they were watching on the surveillance cameras, that action wouldn't make sense and might trigger a response from them. So smokes, matches, and jacket. Just like I was going on a walk in the woods. I went to the bathroom and drank about a quart of water from the bathroom sink. It might be a while before my next drink and I didn't want to dehydrate.

There were two options for my walk. One, above me on the hiking trail. I'd have preferred the second option, the road to the main gate where I knew a location that was a blind spot in their security camera coverage. They'd expect me to go that way and maybe hitchhike my way out. Not to mention that I'd have to run the gauntlet of gathering troops at Justyn's residence.

I turned and headed up to the ridge. Their helicopters could locate me immediately if I was walking or running along one of the country roads and then they'd hunt me down like a dog with vehicles.

Briefly, I thought about stealing a pickup or SUV below and making a run for it. It was an attractive idea, but it was high in danger. I was being subtle and should continue. This plan had the best chance of success.

I started walking casually up the trail. I paused and turned to survey the valley below me. To cover, I peeled the wrapper off a miniature slowly. Lighting up, I saw several of the golf carts and four-wheel ATV's below separate and head different ways. Two started running up the ramps. Puffing on my smoke contentedly, I headed up myself like I had all day long to wander around up here.

It was plain that within hours I was supposed to be virtually dead, devils with sharp knives and stuff whacking into my new young body.

For better or worse, I was going to miss Rhonda and Rolly.

And Emeril's cooking. I was still full from breakfast, having carbo-loaded. I didn't think I had time for another meal. Eventually, somebody down there, most probably Belinda Foursleeps, was going to decide to have me watched full time—if they had not already done so.

The air was clear and brisk and I increased my pace immediately when I crossed into the tree line.

I turned left at the T-junction on the ridge. I found a place where I could see through the vegetation to the trail below. A golf cart was sitting outside my residence and two security men were standing there talking on a hand held radio.

So my mistake compounded. That is to say, because I'd decided to go look at the operating rooms, Belinda's action followed; because of my ruckus with the security team, I'd talked to Raleigh. And because of that, I'd incited Raleigh. He'd had to confirm for himself that I had bested two security men. He didn't believe me. And he sure didn't like me. And since he thought he was better than I was, he'd have to test me. I'd seen it before in him. His natural dislike was egged on by my more than friendly relationship with his wife. That all added up to: I shouldn't have made that original mistake a little while ago.

Because right behind me topping a rise was Raleigh Smith on his golf cart, blood in his eye.

CHAPTER THIRTY-TWO

Sometimes it ain't worth getting up in the morning. This had been due for a long time. I never wanted it to happen. I'd like to think I was more of an adult to have it happen.

But a secret part of me welcomed it. Raleigh and I had been at odds since we'd met. I'd unconsciously challenged him; and he was more open in his dislike for me.

He slid his vehicle to a stop and stepped out.

"Who'd you think you were fooling?" He slowly unbuttoned his smock and carefully set it on the seat of his golf cart. "I told them I thought you went another way, maybe down the ramps. When they can't find you, they'll check the tape if nobody was monitoring you." He grinned without mirth. "By then it will be too late." He started circling me.

"You want to be grown up about this, Raleigh?" I asked. I puffed nonchalantly on my cigar. I didn't thank him for diverting the posse for a little bit.

"Don't try to dissuade me, Zachary. I owe you for myself and for your advances to my wife."

I ignored him and walked over to his golf cart. There, I took the cigars out of my jacket and sat them atop his lab coat.

Turning back to him, I said, "I like her, Raleigh. I like your son. Almost by definition, you must have some redeeming qualities."

That stopped him momentarily.

"But I will be damned if I can find any," I said. I stood there watching him circle me in some kind of martial arts dance.

Except I'd stayed near the golf cart and that interfered with his stalking. I tried to stop this one last time. "Raleigh, think if you lose to me. What will Rhonda think? And you won't be able to live with yourself."

He stopped moving and nodded. "You know, Zachary, that's the wisest thing you've said. And I thought about it. But right now it's the other way around: I can't live with myself if I don't do this." At least he was honest about it.

I felt time slipping away. Security teams were probably boiling out of the valley below.

"This machismo bull shit ain't gonna get it, Raleigh," I said and looked down to study my cigar and flipped it into his face.

Instead of going for the KO as anybody would expect, I kicked his legs out from under him. I recalled his response to María and their standoff. That meant to me that Raleigh was highly proficient, so I needed to do something unexpected. And I was in a hurry to end this. He hit the ground and rolled— an intelligent move for I was leaping with both knees at his abdomen. So I had to do a paratrooper tuck and roll and wound up on my feet again. All the water I'd just drunk sloshed around in my stomach.

He was up easily, leaves and small sticks flying off his back and shoulders. He moved in purposefully, his guard up, not as confident as he had been to start.

Suddenly, he was airborne, both feet lashing out for my chest. I leaned aside and kept my position, giving my arms leverage. I swung under his sideways lancing legs with my right arm, caught them, swung them up and flipped him 180 degrees.

He hit the ground face down with a thud. But his arms broke his fall.

So I kicked his arms out from under him as he attempted to push himself up and escape my certain kill shot.

He bounced off the ground again, knees scrambling to get purchase. I let him partially rise again and clipped his chin with a sharp right. That put him down again and I dropped onto his back. He didn't respond probably because the shot to the chin had made him groggy. So I moved aside, lifted him, and hit him alongside the jaw.

Very pretty.

It put him out. There would be a bruise and swelling on his jaw line for a few days. A little reminder from me.

"Raleigh, you gonna play with the big boys, you better be ready next time." But of course he didn't hear me. I rolled him over and checked his breathing. It was fine. Only in Hollywood does a mere punch put an opponent out for hours. But I'd tagged him well a couple of times and he'd be unable to function for a few minutes.

I searched for a moment and found my small cigar. It had gone out. I relit it and retrieved the rest of my cigars from his golf cart.

I went back to Raleigh, squatted next to him, and checked his breathing again. I didn't want to kill off Rhonda's husband

Or did I?

Nah. She'd never forgive me.

He seemed to be coming around, but he wouldn't be up and fully aware for a while yet.

My considered opinion was that it had been too easy. Then it struck me that had I still been heading north towards age sixty instead of heading south to thirty years of age, I might not have pulled it off. I smiled. There was an upside to this counterclockwise aging.

Puffing from my smoke, I said, "Raleigh, this was childish. But I thank you."

I patted him on the shoulder. "I'm getting too experienced at this closure business." I rose to my feet and glanced down the trail. I imagined hot pursuit. Whether they were there or not, I knew full well they were on the way. Belinda Foursleeps was an organizational genius and they'd figure it out in minutes. "How many transplants has Tyme undergone?" If Raleigh heard me, he didn't answer.

Then through the foliage, I glimpsed the metal of something heading up the trail. I heard engines, the ATV's scurrying around the valley. It was an out of place sound, one I hadn't heard often. It leant wings to my flight.

Had Raleigh delayed me too long? I cursed myself. Just for a little ego, I'd spent time testing myself against Raleigh. Dumbass move, Ethan. Hope you feel better, because you're going to pay for the dalliance.

I started running on the western leg of the ridge trail. Then I stopped.

CHAPTER THIRTY-THREE

Turning, I trotted to the eastern leg, scraped some leaves to show a recent passing. With enormous regret, I took a cigar from my jacket pocket and tossed it farther along where it might lead someone to think I'd dropped it there in my haste—heading the opposite way.

I retraced my steps, hoping I'd bought some time.

When I got to the location I'd previously scouted which was not under direct electronic surveillance, I puffed my cigar into life and threw it as far as I could farther down the trail. Maybe they'd see it and think I'd gone past this particular place on the trail. And maybe not, but it was worth a try. Could they be suckered twice? I didn't know, but anything I could do to confuse the pursuit would help.

I heard the crunch of tires climbing the trail behind me and scaled the trunk of the oak tree in front of me. Then I scooted out on the big limb that hung over a three hundred foot drop.

The golf cart came blasting along the hiking trail and slowed. I froze and looked over my shoulder. There was no way to tell whether they'd bought my fake trail along the other fork of this trail. My blood chilled, for probably they had two or more teams chasing me and the others had taken the false trail.

"Look, smoke," said the guy riding shotgun and his arm extended and pointed down the trail. They went out of my line of sight and I could hear the golf cart slow and then accelerate. They'd bought my ruse.

I looked for my next step and tried to avoid glancing down

the cliff face. The wind was cutting into me here twelve feet above the trail. I leaned over and grasped the bole of a pine tree, which was growing right at the edge of the cliff. I skinnied down it wasting no time.

Shortly, I was perched on the overhang. The fence made a barrier between the oak tree and me.

Sounds of a rushing golf cart told me they were coming back this way. I levered my body over the edge of the outcropping, found a foot purchase and lowered myself below the edge of the ridge.

The golf cart stopped and voices came to me. I scrambled on. The voices got closer and I envisioned them walking around the trunk of the oak tree. My mind's eye showed them stopped and looking about.

I held my breath.

It did not escape my notice that all this attention did in fact mean their intentions were nefarious. It confirmed the conclusions I'd been making.

"The fence and the cliff," another voice wafted over. "No way." I heard the click and noise response of a handset radio. They must have been walking back to their transportation, because I couldn't hear the transmissions any longer. Doubtless, they were checking in with the search coordinator.

Hoping they were too far away to hear my travel, I began to move again. I scurried along the face of the rock wall, heading downward and to my right. I clung to the rocks and found holds for my hands and steps for my feet. It wasn't hard, just slow and tedious.

Then a background noise lent a great amount of urgency to my progress. It was the sound of a helicopter lifting off.

Above me the sky was clear and blue; what the hell was wrong with North Carolina in the mountains? Couldn't they have the common courtesy to boil some clouds up and produce some aircraft-grounding thunderstorms? If this were Sarasota, I could almost conjure a thunderstorm or two up at will. No such luck here. The sun warmed my back and the rocks chilled my front.

A crumbly ledge appeared around the next corner and it ran downwards for fifty feet. I still had to maintain a grip to avoid overbalancing and falling, but I traversed the ledge swiftly. Out behind me was a large valley; trees covered the entire floor and the slopes of this valley.

The chopper noise had faded and now it was returning.

At the end of the ledge was a real slope, not a cliff face. I didn't have to cling to it and locate each following step. But I did have to maintain a minimum grip and back down, for it was an impossible slope to walk upon. Nonetheless, I scooted down it as the chopper sound grew. Upon frequent occasion in the past, incoming chopper noise had been welcome relief—not so this day. I felt naked upon the slope.

Then the situation reached critical. I was level with the tree-tops, but the slope had disappeared into another sheer drop. I needed to stop, breathe a bit, and cogitate.

But I could hear the helicopter heading this way. The pitch and echo changed, telling me there no longer was mountain between the two of us. I scrambled down as far as I could go. I was adjacent to a tall pine, but the tip of it was too slender to support me.

The steady quivering of the air because of the chopper slashing away at the local atmosphere reached me and I knew it had lifted over the ridge top.

Leaning way out, I grasped the top of the pine and pulled it over me. It didn't feel as if it was doing a perfect job of camouflage, but that would have to suffice. My jacket was a neutral khaki. I wrapped my jeans clad legs in between limbs and lay back to hope. At least it was providing me opportunity to breathe and rest.

I should have realized something was askew when Dexter had called me and asked what my blood type was. He hadn't recalled my blood type at the time—so what; it was simply that somebody had inquired of him obliquely. That had to be the first contact from the Tyme Institute. At that point, they didn't know of my condition, but they knew or suspected enough to raise hope of succor for Justyn and/or Rolly.

The helicopter passed directly overhead. That was fine with me; the angle would make it more difficult to spot me. They would be watching for movement, for color discontinuity.

A series of thick roots grew from the mountain face below me so I rolled over and lowered myself to a set of them. Hand over hand, I climbed down twelve, maybe fifteen feet, using roots and rocks as a purchase. At that point, a boulder protruded from the earth and I perched on that.

The chopper must have been making a precise grid search, for I heard it coming back. Taking a deep breath, I leaned out, grabbed a pine branch and swung myself to the main trunk of the thing. I tasted pinesap. I made a Herculean effort to descend, but the branches were too thick here. So I swung the top of that old pine back and forth until it encountered the branches of an oak that was growing from higher up the slope below.

From there, I edged along a thick branch to the trunk. The good thing about that oak was that the tough ridged bark scraped the pinesap off my hands.

The floor of the valley stretched broken for a mile. The walking was up and down through thick scrub, ferns, and rock. For a while I followed a small brook to the spring from which it originated. The exercise felt good and I wasn't thirsty yet. I had to walk around rocks and trees on rough ground, and most of it was up one hill and down the following slope. But the woods covered me well. They couldn't have infra-red capability in their helicopters—could they? My intention was to make it out of this valley before the sun fell so I could plot my way. I reached the far side of the valley and headed north where I'd spotted a shoulder of the mountain that would be easier to surmount and get out of here. When I reached the slope, I made sure to zigzag under the best tree cover. Off in the distance, I thought I recognized Phoenix Mountain someone had pointed out, but I saw no ashes out of which to rise.

It had been a long day and promised to be a long night. The

sun ducked below the crest of the mountain to my left and I wound my way upwards in shadows. Without sunlight, temperatures had dropped to maybe sixty and would hit forty-something tonight. Not too uncomfortable, except I'm from Florida. I had a jacket and a couple of shirts on as protection. The air was clear and cool and pure and needed one cigar worth of smoke to season. Instead, I burned a tick off my ankle.

Throughout the afternoon, the helicopter had continued its grid search. Now, I heard the sounds of another chopper. So they'd recalled the second machine from wherever it had been. Likely, Greensboro.

That made me wonder how long they would continue their search. There had to be a point of diminishing returns.

Once, I scared up a doe and two smaller deer. They leapt out of the brush and pounced off, just as startled as I was. A ragged patch of mushrooms growing alongside the path reminded me I should be hungry. I wasn't yet, not exactly; and this was contrary to the demands of my counterclockwise metabolism.

Carefully I climbed to the shoulder of the mountain ahead and slunk over it in as much shadow as I could manage. A good commander would have an alert sentry atop an overlook where I'd escaped, and kept him on station scanning the territory with his binoculars all day. Before I exposed myself, I sat in a shadow of a tree and studied the terrain on the far side of this valley. I saw no telltale light reflections off binoculars lenses.

Then I found a rock cleft somewhat higher I could climb through with far less chance of exposing myself. At the apex I paused to study what unfolded before me.

A farmhouse. It sat on a terrace a third of the way up the far side of the valley ahead. A wisp of smoke came from the chimney and I dearly hoped that didn't mean it was going to get really cold up here tonight. An asphalt lane led from the farmhouse to the southern end of the valley and on out after that.

It was very tempting; but I had to pass. This place was too close to the Tyme Institute. And residents probably wouldn't trust some guy who wandered out of the forest in the early evening. So I had to avoid these people. And, more importantly, their likely dogs.

So I skirted the valley from above. It was more difficult, but I did so. There was still sufficient light on this valley since the far side wasn't high at all. I headed for the point where their asphalt driveway disappeared. That meant a road somewhere ahead.

But I didn't make it before full dark. I had to decide whether to descend to the asphalt trail or continue up here. But I was making little time now. A dog barked way behind me at the house and told me I was probably far enough away to chance it.

So I dropped down, wending my way through trees. My good shoes were clotted with clay, but I scraped them as well as I could. Once I got moving on pavement, the clay and mud would dry and knock off.

The road dropped to a twenty-degree slope and I chose to walk on the asphalt. It certainly was easier. After about a half-mile, this encountered four other lanes at a junction, driveways really, and they tied together and kept going downhill.

So did I.

Starlight was sufficient. Occasionally, some wildlife, a squirrel or fox, would stir in the underbrush. Once, I heard a motor and hustled into the brush myself. Nothing came my way, so I went back to the road and continued down.

While I was in excellent shape, I was getting tired of going up and down and down and up. I'm wont to say that I'm a flat-lander and this ordeal certainly confirmed that once and for all. All things must end, and this asphalt roadway did. It dead-ended on an actual, for real, official road. The concrete surface reminded me of the road I'd encountered upon which I'd seen the sign indicating Lansing. At the intersection on this side was a long two by four stretched across three fence posts. Atop that rested fifteen or twenty mailboxes.

If I remembered correctly, Lansing was to the right. Not knowing any better I headed that way. In about ten minutes, I heard a motor and saw the approaching headlights. Discretion made me hurry off the road and hide among the brush. I just couldn't take a chance. Sometimes on the hillsides off the road, were houses. Twice, dogs ran inside the fence line barking at me. One thing these hills had an over abundance of was rocks and all dogs have an atavistic reaction to rocks thrown at them. They go away after a couple of close calls.

When vehicles came along, I hid. One pickup, with a diesel sound, cruised slowly and occasionally a powerful light scanned the brush line. I saw it nearing me and hit the ground, rolled into a ball next to a rock outcropping and pretended I was part of the natural environment. I wouldn't win an Oscar, but the spotlight missed me.

Resigned to dodging people all night, I made my way back to the road and headed up a hill. The roadway twisted and turned and went up and down to distraction; I'd have traded my last cigar for straight and level.

About midnight several vehicles came from the direction of Lansing, so I found a boulder off the road and rested for twenty minutes. My legs were sore from all this up and down travel, but since I'd arrived here, I'd been walking or running several times a day. So I was still strong.

Resuming my travel, I found a fork in the road and didn't know which to take. I flipped a mental coin and started down the right fork. A truck rounded a turn on the left fork and when it passed, I reversed direction and took that fork. Shortly, I encountered a road sign that told me Lansing go thataway.

Hell, I could do that in my sleep.

After midnight, there was only one car an hour on the road.

The temperature had continued to drop all night and I guessed it to be now in the mid forties, another reason I preferred southwest Florida.

I lighted a good stick, I couldn't tell which one—it tasted like a maduro wrapper, but I appreciated it more than I'd appreciated any cigar lately. My walking pace was around twelve to fifteen minutes a mile so I'd make Lansing in a couple of hours, even on this twisted, bunched up ribbon of a road, depending on how long I had to hide from traffic. At this time of night, that wouldn't often, if at all.

Blood types, transplanted kidneys, busted cell phones, secrecy, inordinate security—these things all made sense in context now. These and more had triggered my growing concern and distrust. Their technicians stealing into my hard drive and sucking the guts out of my computer confirmed my distrust. Everything was adding up now.

Everything they said sounded good. Blood removal and replacement, Chelation therapy, hemodialysis, whatever. I wondered once why they didn't suggest wild treatments such as chemotherapy. But no, not if they wanted my blood and my organs. They didn't want to fry those things and then transplant them into Justyn.

The whole problem was electrical, not blood, not organ—for all I knew. And the lack of confirmation to the contrary from all their tests reinforced that theory.

Then they hit me with a fifty million dollar offer. This would cover a myriad of sins had they ever tripped and some of what they intended surfaced for public or legal scrutiny. That they wanted all my internal organs I had little doubt. Justyn Tyme must have been on his last legs and thus propelled Belinda Foursleeps into action. And it explained their sense of urgency, even when they'd discovered I'd be of no help to Rolly. That was a major tip-off. Raleigh and Rhonda being armed and carrying electronic detection equipment highlighted the importance and urgency. They were paranoid. It made me wonder how many transplants Justyn had already bought. Hal was certainly one, if not the first. At least Justyn had paid his way.

I puffed on my cigar and strode along the highway. A rabbit or something similar, I couldn't tell, scooted away in front of me.

And finally, it explained Rhonda. She had to stay. She'd told me.

The efforts of the Tyme Institute were stellar. They helped people stay alive.

For a price.

And their research would pay off one day if it had not already. They were embarked upon a noble cause. If occasionally, they stepped over the strictly legal or medically ethical line, so be it.

Rhonda had told me: she'd said she would do anything for her son.

I didn't blame her. That should have been a major warning. Rhonda had compromised herself and her son by telling me that much. Had she been sending me some kind of signal?

At that time, I thought I'd never know. But it well could have been suspicion on her part for they not told her everything, and had just informed her of their offer that morning.

And the synthesis of all this cogitating told me what Belinda and Raleigh were going to do.

They were going to take all my blood out and transfuse it into Justyn Tyme. They were going to harvest my organs. Perhaps they hoped that my condition would prevail in his body and begin to age him backwards, make him younger. At the least, they likely hoped it would arrest his aging and, I was certain, his imminent death. So, bottom line, Justyn had nothing to lose, since he was dying anyway.

Another thing which explained their sense of urgency: They'd run me through a million tests; and these were for the advertised purposes of trying to find out what was wrong with me. But suppose this: suppose those tests also were to insure compatibility with Justyn, and to insure there was nothing inimical in me which would threaten Justyn Tyme. Now that made sense.

It wouldn't surprise me if they were going to take my heart, too. Justyn hadn't looked well at all when I saw him yesterday morning. It was hard to imagine that it was only yesterday, but it was. And if they'd not had a replacement organ for me, so what? I was dying had had signed releases allowing the transplants, and removal and replacement of my blood. So who cared what they were going to do with my ex-blood? Certainly not me, not if I was lying in an operating theater being kept alive by machines and transplants, a fertile field of regenerated or healthy and renewed organs. Something struck me right in my brain where I should have thought of it earlier. Suppose they whacked out a kidney and did not replace it. Were they going to watch and hope I'd regenerate the organ—grow a new one? It might have been a consideration. Nobody knew what my body was doing anyway.

And they had gone about it all so subtlety. One logical step after another.

And, it occurred to me, that while I'd escaped their dastardly clutches—and I wasn't out of the metaphorical woods yet—I still had the original problem.

Ahead I saw the echo of lights in the sky.

Lansing.

Well, what was I going to do?

I couldn't very well go to the police and file a complaint.

"What's the problem, sir?"

"Well, see, officer, there's a mountain hideout of a bunch of nasty old bad guys holed up in the mountain and they wanted to—"

"Wanted to what?"

"Um, save my life."

Nope, that wouldn't work.

Houses were all around me now. My watch still didn't work. But I knew it was at least a couple of hours until dawn.

And I was on foot in a strange town.

CHAPTER THIRTY-FOUR

Well, I hadn't expected everything to go perfectly. That clump of houses I thought was leading into Lansing?

That was Lansing.

Toss in a few buildings and a small post office, and that was about it.

There was a mom and pop store and at this hour I couldn't tell if it was open or not.

A bread truck was parked in front, and I guess if it wasn't open, then early morning jobbers were stocking shelves.

Not being familiar with the geography hereabouts, I needed information. I needed a way out of here.

But I wasn't going to find it in Lansing, North Carolina. Not at two or three in the morning.

From the dark roadside I watched the store.

And wondered why there was a big Lexus SUV parked alongside the store, very out of place. Hadn't I seen it before in the parking area near the helipad?

Belinda was smart enough to put watchers at key locations in the closest towns. A town like this—a few hundred?—it was easy to wait and watch at the most logical of places. The only place showing activity during the night.

If they were watching for me, I could probably sneak up behind the vehicle and con whoever was inside out of the vehicle, disable them, and steal their SUV. Now that was sorely tempting. I was sick and tired of all this walking.

But my discretion prevailed: should I jump them and steal

their Lexus and then run for it, they'd know where I started and where I was headed. I preferred to continue afoot and not concentrate their search. An old war axiom: keep the enemy spread out and guessing.

So, I worked my way around the mom and pop store and took up my early morning jaunt.

Around many curves on a long uphill stretch, I heard a laboring engine behind me. Climbing an embankment, I squatted behind a convenient tree. A long, silver gasoline tanker truck lumbered toward the crest of the hill. As it passed, I scrambled down, sprinted alongside the right side of the truck and swung onto a foothold at the very rear of the vehicle. For fifteen or twenty minutes, I rode until the tanker pulled into a gas station in a small town the sign told me was Warrensville. Hopping off, I walked down the main drag of Warrensville, North Carolina and was promptly outside the town limits. The residents hereabouts all had well kept yards and property with lots of flowers everywhere. I didn't know a rose from a rhododendron but they had plenty of the latter.

In a while, I came to an intersection. My tired mind told me I'd had enough and suggested Plan B. A sign indicated West Jefferson and Jefferson thataway so I went thataway about a hundred feet. The clean skies allowed me decent nighttime vision. I located some trees to hide behind if necessary and lighted a cigar to pass the time.

Theoretically, traffic would have to stop at the intersection and therefore give me time to check the vehicle out. If I determined it was safe, I'd try to hitch a ride. Old American tradition. And more safe than jumping aboard and stealing a ride.

Convincing myself I might have a long wait, I cleared my mind to enjoy my last cigar. I couldn't tell what it was, but it was a ring size over fifty and maybe five inches.

Immediately, motor and lights approached the stop sign. I should have figured. It was none other than the bread truck on its way someplace from stocking the little store in Lansing much earlier.

Stepping to the edge of the road, I dropped my cigar. I wouldn't expect anyone to give a lift to a smoker these days. The bread truck didn't really stop at the stop sign, not at this time of night. He sort of gave it a glance to the left, and turned right, my way.

I popped out my thumb and pasted a hopeful look on my face and forced a shiver over my body. I'd take a pity ride, what the hell. I was tired of walking.

He slowed immediately. The door slid open. "Hey, partner, you're out late." North Carolina twang never sounded so beautiful. Warmth and the smell of fresh baked bread: I thought I'd died and went to Heaven. In a while we were entering West Jefferson, North Carolina.

He dropped me off at the 24-hour Super Wal-Mart with a couple of fresh and warm croissants. People in North Carolina are eminently hospitable. While I always carry a few hundred dollars and had yet to spend one cent, I hit the ATM inside Wal-Mart with a few of my credit cards and soon had two thousand dollars cash and felt better. Inside the Wal-Mart I bought a Coke and cigars and went outside and sat on a bench. The croissants were still warm and the Coke was cold and I was in Heaven.

Dawn rushed upon the land and I went inside and asked the night manager if he knew where I could rent a car.

He told me he was going off shift in an hour and there was an Enterprise agency near where he lived down the road in Wilkesboro, just off Interstate 77. He gave me a ride and soon I was ensconced in a luxury car. The late Paul Harvey was right: Wal-Mart people are okay.

I didn't worry about Tyme, Inc., tracing me via credit card use; surely they could do that thing, but by the time they could react, I'd be long gone. And it wouldn't take a Mensa geographer to guess where I was headed.

While I was dead tired, I didn't want to stop anywhere near here. But I did take time to buy and activate a prepaid cell phone. Then I headed down I-77 for points south and Savannah.

I thought that would be far enough away to be safe. Six hours from here and six hours from Sarasota.

Finally free, and safe for now, I was on my way. But I was still dying.

But I felt a new sense of freedom. Rhonda, I'll miss you, darlin', but damn I'm glad to be out of there.

And it was time for one each Ethan Allen Zachary to go on the offense.

After all, I reasoned, things couldn't get any worse.

CHAPTER THIRTY-FIVE

It didn't seem logistically reasonable for Belinda's goons to tap as many phones as I might be calling. And it didn't seem reasonable they'd want any kind of public confrontation. Logic told me that once I was free and clear of North Carolina and back in my own home ground that I would be more or less safe. I didn't know this, but I hoped it would be so. But with satellites and microwave relays across the land, it might be possible to intercept cell phone calls by just running some super-duper computer programs and breaking into the right connections. The NSA could do it; maybe Tyme had the right programs?

So, I was determined not to call cell phones. And they couldn't possibly know my new cell phone number; especially since it was a renewable phone, one not registered, just like a phone card.

I called my house and, of course, no answer.

Belinda Foursleeps would expect me to call home, probably even to call Carrie Jean Billingsley, so I didn't have to play games by hiding the fact I was wandering around the country free and clear.

Of course I was worried to death about Mary Lou. I tried to tell myself if the bad guys had her, they would have used that against me already. Or so I hoped. I hadn't heard from her nor had she returned any of my calls. Since the Tyme Institute had allowed me to make outgoing calls, surely they wouldn't have prevented any incoming calls for me. I didn't want to, but I had to, so I called her cell phone. Just the generic answering voice. I didn't leave a message anywhere.

It was during the day, so of course no one answered Jack Billingsley's phone—and apparently Carrie Jean wasn't home. If one cell phone would be monitored, it'd be hers. But I had to contact her; else soon she'd have the cavalry headed for the Tyme Institute in the mountains near the border of Virginia and North Carolina. And they'd start asking questions that Belinda could answer and I couldn't.

"Gee, we don't know where he is. We were treating him, free of course, and he got cold feet and ran off and didn't have the common courtesy to say goodbye. Some people are like that, they get spooked at all this electronic gear, and they don't pursue the full course of treatment. See we have some of the highest qualified and most preeminent medical personnel in the world." Belinda would do the talking smoothly and refer the investigating law enforcement to high priced law firms. The past clientele, a virtual who's who, would vouch for them. She might trot out Raleigh Smith as an expert witness. They wouldn't chance putting Rhonda in the spotlight; her empathy might well flummox things for a bit, but why chance it?

Driving south now on I-95, tired and not even hungry anymore, I dialed Carrie Jean's cell phone.

"Ethan! I'm so happy to hear from you I could pee my pants."

"Well, now I feel all warm and fuzzy. I miss you, too." I tried to think of a code to tell her someone might be eavesdropping upon our conversation; then I decided it didn't matter. "Our conversation might be monitored, CJ. I don't know why they'd bother, but be advised. So I'm not going to be very specific."

"You're not running from the law are you?" She knew better; she'd have extrapolated from our earlier telephone conversations.

"No, we kind of parted up there without formal goodbyes." I was telling her I was enroute.

"So, I'll see you when I see you."

"That's it. Have you seen Mary Lou?"

"No. But I have Budweiser over here."

"Explain, please?"

"I did what you wanted; I went over to your house and checked. I used your garage code on the outside keyless pad. She wasn't home and the mail was stacking up in the mailbox. There were several bowls of water and your wife had a giant Tupperware bowl full of Purina cat chow next to the litter box."

Carrie Jean was telling me Mary Lou had been gone for a long time. No wonder my phone calls went unanswered.

CJ went on. "Dad doesn't like cats, so I'm keeping Bud in my room." Jack Billingsley and Mary Lou had that in common.

"You could return him to my house now, if you wanted."

"There's a plan."

After disconnecting from Carrie Jean, I called Major Yaroslav at FarReaching Research. Even though I had dialed their number only one time, I still remembered it.

"Mr. Zachary, it's so good of you to call. I've been trying to reach you. Your emergency case, remember?" His voice was dryer than ever.

"I do, major." I thought for a moment how to put it. "I've had medical problems."

"We know." He paused. "More precisely, that's what we foresaw. Your case was one of the more—. Disregard, I shouldn't refer to other clients."

"Any answers?"

"Yes and maybe. I will explain. Your major concern, if I recall, was that you had a problem and were looking for the genesis of that problem. Almost your exact words."

"Correct."

"My man traced it back to a blinding light. Or a combination of brilliance, those were his words. Does that help?"

"As far as determining the cause of my condition, yes. How about other results? Anything about my future? The eventual resolution of my problem."

"That would be the maybe part. We accept physical laws and scientific fact, most of the things we all learned in school. My man encountered something out of the ken of his scientific frame of reference. Not," he cautioned, "necessarily a limiting factor. But the further he got involved, the more disoriented he became. I think dizziness is not the right word, but it is part of his explanation. So he discontinued his attempts at discerning the endgame you requested."

"That was it, then?"

"Not at all. Against some protocols, I assigned the same case to another viewer. I don't like to do this because one can taint another, but this one had been on vacation and had no contact with the first viewer."

Hope grew in me.

"She encountered a wall," Major Yaroslav told me.

"A wall?"

"Each of our people is different, obviously," Yaroslav said, and their mental approaches are myriad. This lady got a variation of the blinding light, but that was it. It was as if there was a wall, a bright wall, interfering with her search." I heard paper rustling on his end. "I have here a sketch. Black ribbons, asphalt?"

"Yes."

He described the clump of palm, pine, and brush in which I'd been looking for my lost golf ball. And he described a box vehicle, obviously my golf cart.

We went over more of the same. Frankly, I was disappointed. I'm not certain I'd put a lot of hope in the scientific remote viewing; however, as time went by, this had fast become the last resort. And, as Major Yaroslav pointed out, their approach was not to suggest a fix for the problem; it was simply to see what had happened or what was going to happen, when and where. And they'd mostly failed at a big part of their task. It had been a legitimate attempt and, upon reflection, I thought it was amazing they'd come up with what they had.

"Listen, Major, I have an idea in the back of my mind that you have inspired. I need to think about for a while. Could I call you again for another session, this time to provide specific time and/or place?"

"You can, I have to pay the rent, thank you."

In Savannah, I drove off the Interstate downtown and found a new hotel overlooking the river. And I slept until the next morning. By four in the afternoon I was driving into Sarasota.

Carrie Jean was in the middle of cutting my overgrown lawn. I guessed Mary Lou didn't live up to her promise to mow it.

I stepped out of my car and into a swarming armful of Carrie Jean Billingsley. She felt good, hot and sweaty from the pushing my lawn mower around a long overdue yard. She wore shorts and a tee shirt and no brassiere and her traditional ponytail. I gave her a brotherly peck on the cheek and she stepped back and looked at me quizzically.

"My God, Ethan. You've changed. You're harder to recognize. Even with that scruffy beard." Maybe three day's growth. "You are, um, younger, leaner, and tougher. Did I say younger?"

"You did."

"Some people are not going to recognize you. And you got the look of a hawk."

"I have been doing a great deal of exercising lately."

"Tell me about everything."

"Lemme make a phone call first."

Still outside, I called the sheriff's department and asked for a certain lieutenant before duty hours were over.

"I might not be here, but the garage is open, tell them to go right in."

"Somebody will be there in twenty minutes, EZ."

I wanted a professional to sweep my house and phone for hidden microphones, cameras, and phone taps.

Disconnecting, I turned to CJ. The air was hot and humid and the land was flat. Take that, North Carolina.

Having heard my half of the conversation requesting an off-the-record bug sweep of my house, Carrie Jean was expectant.

At that moment, a Lincoln Continental swung into my driveway. Kendall Oh got out of his car. His family had run restaurants in the Chinese section of Vancouver, British Columbia and he'd broken with tradition and become a statistics professor at one of those California universities. And then retired to sunny Sarasota. I don't know what that said for sunny California. He was now president of the Bent Tree Homeowners Association.

"Hello, Commissioner, I was driving by and saw you standing here."

We didn't see eye to eye on many issues of our neighborhood and therefore had a standoffish relationship.

Oh stopped suddenly as if startled. He ran his eyes over me to make sure I was who he thought I was. I didn't respond. He was your traditional hall monitor, the one everybody in school hated because when he got a little bit of power, he lorded it over one and all.

Oh glanced at Carrie Jean as if he didn't want to speak in front of her.

I still said nothing and let the uncomfortable silence grow.

"Commissioner, I'd like to take up two issues with you." He pointed at the front yard in which rested my lawn mower. "Your lawn and landscaping have not been up kept in the fashion outlined by the deed restrictions."

"I've been out of town and it's being taken care of right now."

"I can see that, Mr. Zachary. But the point remains it was an eyesore for—"

"You have another point?" Hall monitors always pissed me off. Though, he was just doing his job as he saw it.

"There have been eye witness accounts of strange goings-on here."

"Like what?"

He shifted feet uncomfortably. He looked at CJ who offered him no support.

"I was told about men in chemical or biological protective suits going through your property and your house."

"What's your point?"

He paused. I wasn't being responsive, so he wasn't sure how to proceed. "I must ensure there is no danger to the neighborhood."

"None."

When I didn't elucidate, he said, "What was it all about?"

"Nothing that needs to concern you." I was becoming angry.

"Wasn't that the radon test you were talking about?" Carrie Jean said. She was trying to keep the peace.

"Yes, that must've been it," I said.

Oh paused. "So you're blowing me off. I can live with that. But can you live with a formal ethics complaint to the county attorney's office? Or in open commission session?"

Why did everybody feel obligated to threaten me? I don't react well to threats. "Do what you want, Oh. I've got important things to do now." Just what I needed, more pressure.

I turned away and Oh got in his car and left.

"Help me turn in my rental," I told CJ. Then I had an idea. "Let us leave the lawn half-mowed for a couple of days."

"Living dangerously, Ethan."

I dropped off the car at Enterprise and Carrie Jean picked me up. In her truck, I felt safe to brief her on what I'd gone through at the Tyme Institute.

"Those sons of bitches," she said. "They only wanted you for organ and blood donations to the old man?"

"More or less. I think if they'd have discovered some base cause of my counterclockwise aging, they would have pursued that thing with vigor, it only stands to reason. But they didn't find much if anything at all. And nothing electrical." I stared out the window at the intersection I seem to spend half my life, Bee Ridge Road and Cattlemen Road. "I suspect they hoped some residual counterclockwise element stayed in my organs and made Justyn grow younger. Since he's dying anyway, it makes little difference if he grows younger and then dies. And, to continue their supposition, if he in fact did begin to age in reverse and eventually ended up as I did, then perhaps by that time they'd have discovered how to control the backwards progression. Sort of a no lose scenario for a dying man." I laughed. "He'd probably have given all of his jillions of dollars just for a couple of weeks of being younger." Finally, we moved past the intersection on under the Interstate. "The fountain of youth has always had its pitfalls."

She was driving with one hand. She put her other hand firmly on the steering wheel, hands at eleven and one, almost stiff-armed. "Are you going to die soon?" Like me, she preferred to drive as far back as the seat would allow.

I touched my head. "I don't know, it doesn't feel like it right now."

"What did those doctors up there tell you?" Her voice was harsh.

"They think I'm not going to make it."

"Shit."

"Yeah." I pulled out a miniature and lighted up. Only fleetingly did I think of Rhonda Smith.

Carrie Jean was fighting to control herself. Her voice held a tear in it. "If you're going to die off, why aren't you smoking expensive cigars?" She gave me a wan smile.

"Because I didn't think of it."

CJ drove effortlessly. "I'm wondering why they didn't attempt some kind of treatment. I can't get away from that one."

"I can. For the same reason they did what they did: Justyn. They didn't want my organs, my glands, whatever they were going to transplant contaminated in any fashion. Had they given me radiation, chemo, some experimental treatment, those things could well have either delayed or totally precluded transplants to Justyn Tyme. It took me a while to extrapolate this." And it explained, perhaps, Rhonda Smith's angst, anger, and eventually, her removal from the medical decision-making. Rhonda well could have been urging such treatment and finally, because of their delays or denials, figured the whole thing out.

"What can we do?" continued CJ. I kind of liked the "we" part.

"I'm not mentally bankrupt, I've a couple of ideas."

"What are they?" Her voice brightened. "Now that you mention it, you never know if chemotherapy or radiation or that total blood transfusion might work or not."

"I don't want to jinx them by saying them aloud." Besides they were so ridiculous no rational adult would think them viable. Actually, they were dangerous. Life-threatening dangerous. "But I've got a lot of preparation to go through first." I'd had plenty of time lately to think. "I will try those other treatments—through Dexter—if these things don't work first." Like hell. My gut told me radiation or chemo would only fry me or hasten my already imminent demise. On the forty-eleventh hand, what did I have to lose?

We got back to my house and an unmarked sheriff's car was leaving. The driver rolled down the window and Carrie Jean leaned back so I could talk past her. "Hey, Al, find anything?"

"Two," he said, "buried in the phone." He held up a tiny electronic somethingorother. "Expensive, it is, and very state of the art." He eyed me suspiciously. "You under investigation, Easy? Or is this some political thing?" He was giving me an out. Theoretically, he should report these kinds of things. His eyes kept drifting to Carrie Jean as we talked across her. "And two," he dangled a tiny mini-cam, "in the bedroom."

"Probably Vince MacLean, Al. I'd like to keep this confidential for now."

"That man is one first class son of a bitch," Al said cheerfully.

I thanked him and he drove off.

"That's encouraging," I pointed out.

"I'd think they'd still have an academic interest in you, Ethan. They sure must want to know how it all turns out."

"They'll find a way." So soon Belinda Foursleeps would know her bugs were inop. A fact that might well precipitate some other action on her part. These considerations lent more urgency to my actions.

We walked in the house and it smelled uninhabited. CJ had brought Budweiser back and he spent a minute rubbing a hole in my leg until he decided that was enough and headed someplace for his traditional nap.

"Let me show you something." Carrie Jean led me to my bedroom. She opened the walk-in closet. My side was full of my clothes hanging neatly. Mary Lou's side was empty. In the bedroom, I checked her chest of drawers. Empty. I went into the spare bedroom where she'd been sleeping. Same. So much for the kidnapping theory. No hostage Mary Lou.

No notes in the kitchen. The telephone answering machine was blinking steadily and I didn't want to listen to all the messages—including several from me.

"I'm sorry, Ethan." Carrie Jean squeezed my hand. "She… well, here you are dying and…." CJ shook her head. She was being charitable, something Mary Lou wouldn't have done. CJ didn't want to speak ill of Mary Lou. Hell, I didn't want to think ill of Mary Lou, but—damn. A funny thing was happening to me: dying was giving me a new perspective. People gotta do what they want. So what? Maybe it was a measure of the finality of our marriage that I didn't find any real anger at Mary Lou deserting me in my time of need.

CJ had to run some errands, so I got to work. I used my laptop instead of my tainted PC. The very first thing I did was to go online to Amazon.com. They were selling the Segway Human Transporter, the world's first "dynamically stabilized, self-balancing human transporter." It looked like a cross between the old-time push lawn mower and a scooter. I had them deliver it to the Tri-City, North Carolina Airport, Tyme, Incorporated hangar facilities. And mark it for a certain Rolly Smith. In a couple of weeks I either wouldn't need the money or, if I did, Mary Lou would have half or more of it anyway. And I thought Rolly would have a ball running that Segway all over the valley. And his mother would pull her hair out worrying, yet when she thought about it, she would think of me, and maybe she would smile.

As I worked, I had the television news on to LNN, and immediately missed Elena Rodríguez. She was going to be one of my priorities.

But I did sit up and pay attention when I heard my name in a promo. After the commercial break, they came back on with their top story.

The anchor spoke breathlessly as if this were an announcement of the Pearl Harbor attack. "Today, the Sarasota County Commission voted to censure county commissioner Ethan Zachary for repeated absence, nonattendance at mandatory meetings, and a failure to respond."

I wondered what a "failure to respond" was. Not wanting to hear any more, I hit the button on the remote and killed it.

There were too many problems to solve, but I was going to try. Especially the Mary Lou problem. I had to find her. But how? She hadn't left a note, not that I knew of, nor had one of the dozens of telephone messages been hers. Nor was there a sign of her on my e-mail. A puzzle. A puzzle I could solve by calling around; I'd eventually find her. But if I called a lot of people inquiring over the whereabouts of my wife, it would look stupid. Maybe that was what Mary Lou wanted. Maybe she wanted me to look stupid. Maybe she wanted me to exert a maximum effort to find her. Hell, I didn't know. I'd put my mind to it. Maybe there was another answer. If I had law enforcement looking also, that would compound the embarrassment. Typical Mary Lou: she thought she was going to humiliate me before she nailed me. Well, I never responded well to that kind of leverage, either.

Dexter had no new information, but he clamored to know about my trip and what treatments I'd undergone. I made some arrangements with him, to his surprise, and told him I would brief him when I saw him.

Trying to avoid the hard phone calls, I made the easy ones first. I called the FarReaching Institute remote viewers with a request. I called Palmer T. Hibbs. I called Miles Tonchot the county attorney and my friend.

Miles was discouraged. "It's over, Easy. The governor's running a full investigation on you. He's going to be up in Tampa tomorrow and wants to talk to you, but his investigator wants to interview you first."

"Gimme names and phone numbers, Miles. I'll let you know what happens."

He did so. "And take your lawyer with you, Easy. Don't admit anything that might come back to bite you in the ass."

"I am a lawyer, Miles. Hell, we all are."

"You've heard the quote, Easy, about the man who acts as his own lawyer has a fool for a client."

"I know, Miles. I'll handle it."

"You sound more confident than I feel, my friend," he said.

Me, too, I thought as I hung up. Hell, I was dying and worrying about this kind of crap?

Then I got to the hard phone call.

I punched in the numbers I remembered with the North Carolina area code. When that operator came on, I said, "This is Ethan Zachary. I need to talk to Belinda Foursleeps."

"Well hello, Mr. Zachary," said the voice I'd never met. "She doesn't take phone calls this late and especially without giving me specific instructions."

"Fine. Tell her I called." I'd hear from her all right.

"Mr. Zachary? With the bloody Cain you caused around here? I'd better check with her. Standby, please."

Even spoken in passing, that thought gave me great pleasure.

In less time than I thought would happen, the operator came back on. "She will talk to you, Mr. Zachary. Let me transfer your call."

After the electronic clicks, Belinda came on. "Zachary?"

"You do remember me."

"Not all that fondly. What is it you want?"

"I've got a deal you can't pass up."

"I doubt that very much, Zachary, but try me anyway."

CHAPTER THIRTY-SIX

I refused to talk to the governor's henchman.

"Is he at the hotel?" I asked. Meaning his own hotel. The governor's family was in the hotel business; they owned a fleet of them.

"Until noon."

"Good. Tell Jeff I'll be up there in about an hour."

The phone was quiet. The governor's aide wasn't expecting this kind of interview. "Commissioner, I won't tell the governor any such thing. He has a full schedule."

"Yet he wanted to see me."

"Well, after I talk to you and make recommendations."

"Like I said, tell Jeff it takes about an hour to drive from Sarasota to Tampa. I'm on the way."

The aide read the tone in my voice. "All right, Commissioner Zachary, but I can't guarantee he'll have time."

"Fine. I'm on the way."

An hour and ten minutes later, the aide ushered me into the penthouse suite. The panoramic view of Tampa was, as always, full of traffic and old cigar factories and off in the distance I saw the Skyway Bridge towering over the mouth of Tampa Bay.

"Ethan, nice of you to come," said the governor. Jeff Burwell was mid fifties, balding, and was wearing his trademark suspenders, no suit jacket, and long sleeves rolled up. He told his aide to leave. He was cut from the same mold as Palmer Hibbs, an old time politician adapting to a new day and time.

We sat in a couple of easy chairs, Jeff drinking coffee, me

drinking diet Coke.

"What the hell is going on, Easy?" He'd been staring at me since I walked in. "You need to shave, son."

"Down and dirty, Jeff. Vince MacLean sees an opportunity to take Palmer's seat in Congress, so he's stirring up trouble."

"He might have a point." Burwell drank some coffee. "His charges are serious."

"Jeff, I have a medical problem he's using. I can't shake it."

"Some damn thing sure is wrong with you."

I gave him a thumbnail version of my problem.

"Damn, boy, I ain't never heard of that one."

"Me, neither, Jeff. It's tough." Floaters danced at the edge of my vision.

"How's Mary Lou taking it?"

"She's not. She left me."

"Your luck ain't runnin' very good, is it?"

"No."

"What did the doctors say?" He looked skeptically at me.

I shrugged. "Nothing they can do."

"You gonna die?"

"Nobody knows. It doesn't look good."

"Damn, boy. I hate to lose one of my best fund raisers." He sort of smiled to show he wasn't serious.

"Me, too," I said.

"And you was a lock for Hibbs' seat in congress."

I had hoped so.

"I have a formal request for investigation which could result in me removing you from your position, Easy. I don't want to, but I got to. And if you go down, there ain't nobody in our party with a high enough profile to beat MacLean for the congressional seat. Shit, you got us in a crack."

"Hell, I'm sorry, Jeff. It isn't like I want to go through this."

He eyed me. "I know you well, boy. You got a answer already."

I nodded. "I do." I paused. Over in the bay, tugs ushered a giant cruise ship into the channel towards the docks.

"Well, what the hell is it?"

"I resign my seat. You appoint Elena Rodríguez to replace me until the election. Miles Tonchot will be campaign manager for her and she will run for congress."

"Who the fuck is Elena Rodríguez?"

"Cuban-born, ex-television reporter, high name recognition."

"Good demographics, but probably not enough to beat MacLean."

"There is more. Suppose she has unlimited funding, and Palmer Hibbs endorses her. With your backing she'd have a good chance." I didn't say I had other plans to deal with MacLean.

"Starting to sound good. I'll have to run it by the network. But you leave a vacuum, Easy. That could cost us the election. Even with our backing. I control the state party mechanism, but that don't translate to enough votes sometimes. And, damn it, man, you are the power of the party in Sarasota." True, I was the one who had been holding it all together. Hibbs was always in Washington and couldn't do it, the sheriff was apolitical, and the Sarasota party chairwoman was there because I pushed her into it. And, probably, the most important thing: I was the best and biggest fundraiser on the Suncoast. A couple of local representatives to the Florida State legislature weren't ready for prime time and our state senator was in the other party.

"MacLean is playing dirty politics right now, Jeff. Suppose we let it ride past the filing deadlines and close to the election. Surprises happen."

"If you got something on MacLean, I don't want to know about it."

"Would I do that to that fine gentleman who's been kicking me around so much while I've been down? Not to mention stabbing me in the back and selling me down the river. And plotting against me."

"Naw." He sighed and pushed himself up from the chair. He adjusted his suspenders.

I rose.

"Look here, Easy. I'll check this Elena Rodríguez out. If Palmer gives his approval and she don't have any dirty laundry,

I'll buy off on it. You've scared off all the big dogs down there, nobody else has dared express a interest in Palmer's job. But you never know."

"May I?" I pointed at his computer.

"Goddamnit, I hate this part of the job. Okay, do it."

I sat and got into the word processing program, typed out my resignation, dated it a few days hence, and hit print. Typing wasn't as easy as it used to be because of the floaters swimming around in my eyes. I printed a second copy in case I needed one. Pausing for a moment, I reflected only how much work and effort I'd put into my job as county commissioner. I'd enjoyed most of it; commissioners have a direct impact on people's everyday lives. Damn. I signed them both and handed Burwell one.

He glanced at it. "Shit. Done, boy." He shook my hand. "You line up Palmer Hibbs. My guys will check out Rodríguez and then I'll appoint her to your commission seat. She live in the right district?"

"She does."

"Then I'll make it public." He stuck his hand out and I took it. "You need anything, you tell me. I got connections over in Gainesville at Shands." He was referring to the University of Florida teaching hospital.

"Thanks, Jeff."

Jeff Burwell might sound like a good old boy at a dairy farm, but he played political hardball and he would live up to his agreements. He and Palmer Hibbs were old time politicians, a vanishing breed.

To angry looks in the lobby, I lighted a Macanudo Portifino, "The ultimate cigar," or so they claim. I walked outside and inhaled deeply. If I didn't die from impending reverse aging, then I was going to croak because of inhaling smoke. And I no longer had a job. Well, so much for my career. Even if I lived through this, I was pretty well done with my life, as it existed now. I suspected the next time I'd hear from good old Mary Lou was from her attorney, whoever that was, with a handful of legal papers. If I was going to be dead, then I was simply policing up loose ends before the fact.

Somehow a weight had seemed to lift off my shoulders. As I drove home I appreciated the sun and a fine cigar.

CHAPTER THIRTY-SEVEN

A wave of dizziness overwhelmed me.

"Are you all right?" she asked.

Holding onto the table with both hands, I couldn't answer. I had to concentrate and focus on the madness to my method. Or whatever. There was one anyway.

"Ethan, jeez, I'm worried about you." Her eyes showed genuine concern. "You're looking very ill."

"It will pass," I said, having to enunciate each word.

She watched me alertly while I tried to recover from the spell. Eventually, the tightness went away somewhat and I resumed normal breathing, let go of the table, and leaned back for support. Then I picked up the water glass and drank half of it. I gave her a wan smile. "I think it's okay now."

We were silent for a few moments.

"I heard you had a command performance with Governor Burwell today," said Elena Rodríguez. She was wearing a low-cut black sheath dress and my eyeballs were dry from looking at her. When we'd danced earlier, it hadn't been a brother-sister-just-friends slow dance. Her eyes were inviting, her touch light and familiar and very feminine. Unfortunately, I could only manage one dance, but that was enough. My hand still felt the phantom curve of her hip. And her cheek had been warm and inviting.

The disorientation slowly passed. I was staring at the beginning of the end.

Or, more likely, the final phase, the endgame, pick your own synonym.

Elena was eating lobster like a man and thoroughly enjoying it; but, unlike a man, she wasn't dripping anything on her outfit.

We were at the window overlooking the Gulf of Mexico, far above Lido Key. The restaurant sat atop a hotel. Way out I could see the lights of a tanker heading for Tampa Bay.

"It didn't take long for the word to get out," I said.

"It's my job—my old job," she amended. "I still have contacts." She looked over at me, demure eyes blinking under dark eyelashes. "Ethan," she blurted, "the gossip also has it that Mary Lou has left you."

I nodded.

"And you asked me out, formally, to this high priced affair. Here we are, and people are seeing us together."

"You can say that again," I said, noting with regret Jack Billingsley and a very attractive woman sitting at the bar watching Elena and me.

Earlier, the chairman of the Sarasota County School Board and his lovely wife had stopped at our table and said hello. His eyes told me "What a babe!" Yep, people were noticing.

"All right, Ethan. You make me ask, I will. Is this about us? You and me? Or do you want to discuss the governor's official investigation and interview?"

I had been afraid Elena would interpret my invitation in a similar manner, but I hadn't known how to address it in our brief phone call.

"I am formally passing the baton. I wanted us to be seen."

"Enigmatic," she said, raising those lovely Spanish eyebrows.

"Do you know what's wrong with me?" I asked bluntly.

She ran her dark eyes over me and gave me more regrets. "Nobody's told me. You hear whispers, rumors. My eyes show me a remarkable transformation. You are years, decades younger than you used to be. You've been away for weeks, mysteriously so. Makeovers and facelifts?" She shook her head slowly. "Somehow I don't think so. My research and investigative reporting, if I may be so formal, was turning up more strange whispers and outlandish speculation."

"That's why the paper fired you?"

"No," Elena said. "They fired me for not reporting the story."

"Well, dear, I owe you."

"You bet your sculpted ass—excuse me, too much wine already."

"It's from running and racquetball," I said.

"I don't care where it's from."

"Fine." The subject made me uncomfortable.

She continued to eye me. "Well?"

I said, "Um...."

"You know I'm available for you, I've said that in many ways, Ethan. Does that make it easier?" Her smile was wan. "Ethan and Elena, it has a certain ring to it."

Toying with my fillet, medium rare, I finally pushed it aside. I wasn't at all hungry. Which, in itself, was an alarming development.

"Elena, there's not much doubt. I'm dying." It wasn't an easy thing to say, but I did. I went on with a rush. "Something that probably came from that lightning strike. I'm aging backwards and the pace is increasing. Now I have nowhere else to grow. My body is out of control." I paused to gather my thoughts. "So, let me say, that if I weren't in this condition and Mary Lou was no longer an issue, I'd be chasing you around this table right now. You are most attractive and right now you're driving me crazy."

"Oh, shit," she said. From nowhere she came up with an inhaler and took two puffs. "Excuse me." She rose unsteadily and headed for the ladies' room.

I thought I'd make a point, so I went to the bar and Jack got off his barstool. "Hey, EZ, this is Valeska." Valeska nodded a head full of piled-up blonde hair and a lot of high-priced surgery jiggled.

We exchanged pleasantries until I saw Elena returning to our table. Jack hit me with an elbow. "Mary Lou?"

"Gone," I said.

"I heard. Not wasting any time, are you?"

"This is a business dinner."

"Yeah, right." He saw the look on my face. "Jesus, EZ, you sure have changed." He grinned. "I can guess at the business."

It was time to leak the word. "I'm trying to convince her to be my replacement."

"Heir apparent?"

"Yep." His business tendrils were extensive. The word would travel far and wide now and, in doing so, would be self-validating. I excused myself. CJ's father was my age, but still a child at heart.

I got there in time to seat Elena.

"A traditional gentleman."

I sat and looked wistfully at my steak. Elena appeared to be no longer interested in food, either.

"You are going to die?" She had a handkerchief wrapped around her right fist.

"It looks like it. Listen, Elena. I'd like to keep my privacy."

"I won't tell. Promise. Tell me what I can do to help you?" She smiled and inhaled a puff of whatever is in those things. "When I was in the bathroom, it occurred to me that I was making this about me. Durn. I'm just out of a job and a prospective husband just dumped me like a feather. But you're, you're dying. It should be about you, not me." Then, surprisingly, she giggled. And then looked embarrassed at the outburst.

"What?" I wanted to know.

"Sorry, Ethan. I couldn't resist that. At your expense, too. They always said jogging and running and stuff was good for you." She smiled and shook her head. "Living proof, right in front of me."

Suddenly, I felt better and the darkness receded a tad. I grinned. "Well, I like running anyway. Endorphins and all."

"To each his own." Her smile went away. "How can I help you, Ethan?"

"Do what I ask."

"Ask away, honey. The condemned man should get his last

wish." She leered and squeezed my hand.

It was late and nobody was at the tables next to us, but I saw Jack still watching us in the bar mirror.

"Maybe if we go to bed together? I can make a difference."

"Ah, thanks. But that's not what I had in mind."

"Pooh." She gave a false pout. "Say it, my dear. I can take anything." She paused. "Now."

"You know that I have some political connections and influence hereabouts?"

"More than influence. You're The Man in this county."

"I need somebody to fill my seat on the county commission and to run for congress when Palmer retires."

"You want my opinion? There are a few possibilities—"

"I want you to do it."

Her dark eyes locked onto mine.

A waiter walked past with a basket of freshly baked rolls, and the smell made me hungry for just a second.

Elena was quiet for a moment. "When I was a child in Cuba, my family, we would all go walking together. There was not much else to do. We always walked past this neighborhood bakery shop and the smell was so wonderful. Sometimes, when my father had the money, he would buy us all a pastry, but I always wanted a big slice of the old Cuban bread and a swab of olive oil. I was different, even then. But the smell of fresh bread brings memories, warm and fond memories." She paused, eyes a million miles away. "My father, he would smoke a hand-rolled cigar." She sighed. "Maybe that's one of the reasons I like you so much. The cigars." Her eyes fixed on me again. "And you can't find anybody *else*?"

"I don't want anybody else."

"I don't have the money, or the connections."

"I have both."

"The connections I know about. But the money?" She grinned. "Unless Mary Lou is going to contribute, along with her lawyers, you better recheck your bank account."

"I've got a rich benefactor. I'm going to establish a PAC, call it something like 'Citizens for Quality Sarasota Government' or something similar. My old law firm will run it. Your campaign will get some hard money and the rest will go to support you and your positions by the PAC."

"And I needed a job."

"You got one: full-time campaigning. You have to start pounding the pavement, neighborhood groups, mobile home parks, you know the drill." I thought about what I was going to do in the next couple of days. "There are limits to campaign donations; however, none on spending your own money." I'd ensure she got some, too.

Elena's eyes were dreaming. Then she turned to me. "Why, Ethan? Why me?"

"It's not a legacy thing," I said, trying to be reassuring. "I can't think of anybody else who can hoe that row. And win. And I sure as hell don't want Vince MacLean and his cronies to take either seat." I took her warm and supple hand. "I know your heart, your values, your political bent. The party needs someone like you, new blood. And I'd like to get personal. You covered for me and it cost you your job. I owe you. Finally, you are my friend."

"Thanks, Ethan." She leaned forward, squeezing my hand, eagerness in her eyes. "So that's what the meeting with the governor was about."

"It was. Pending a couple of things, you'll be appointed to my vacant seat—"

"Do you have to die for this to happen?"

"No, I resigned."

"Surprise, surprise. I bet the paper and LNN would kill for this story."

"It's not public yet."

"Give it to the local broadcast station and scoop the paper." She paused. "Not that I'm vindictive." She batted her eyes, a smile breaking in them.

"You and Burwell's henchpeople work that one out," I said.

"You actually got the governor to buy off on this cockamamie idea?"

"On the date of my resignation, he will formally appoint you. And he will endorse you for congress."

"Jeez."

"It will work out, trust me."

"I don't know what to say. I know my way around, but it's never been me, never been about me."

"If you want, Miles will run your campaign—I talked to him. Trust him. He's a good man. You'll make a fine team."

"Him, I like. He's straight-up." She thought for a moment. "The first part sounds like a slam dunk."

"It is. It gives me time to make some local arrangements, call in favors, stuff like that," I said. "But the hard part is up to you and Miles."

"I can work on Palmer Hibbs," she said, enthusiasm starting to bubble out as she considered the concept.

"I'll prep him. I have a racquetball game scheduled with him in the morning."

"You are in no condition for sports."

I shrugged. "I'll try. It doesn't look like either one of us is going to make it to your news awards dinner."

Elena smiled. "If I win, LNN and the *Star-Banner* will have to accept for me. I will gain some satisfaction."

"You should win the category. You are an excellent writer. You wouldn't have been long at that paper anyway...."

"Thanks for remembering." Elena froze. She looked at me quizzically. "You're not doing well, are you?"

I felt weary. "No, I...I don't feel real good right now."

"Your eyes are haunted, and I ache for you."

My forearms on the dining table held me up. I couldn't speak.

She leaned over the table and extended her fancy linen napkin. "Hold still." I felt her finger in the napkin scrape my left ear. "You're bleeding." She showed me fresh crimson on the clean white cloth.

She picked up the lobster and snapped its head off. The little eyes flailed about loosely. "I don't want you to die." Lobster juice splattered the table and her shear sheath dress endearingly.

"Me, neither."

CHAPTER THIRTY-EIGHT

That night it took a long time to get to sleep. Waves of nausea rolled over me.

I didn't eat breakfast, just met Palmer T. Hibbs at the YMCA over off Bahia Vista Street. I won the first game, surprise, surprise, and then couldn't make it through the second game.

"You don't look good, boy." Palmer wiped sweat off his neck. "You look like death takin' a crap."

"I'm not doing well, Palmer."

"Tell me."

I did.

"Christ on fire, Ethan. You went to quacks?"

"They weren't quacks, Palmer. They were the cream of the crop in what they do."

"They didn't do nothin' for you."

Our voices were echoing in the quiet racquetball court.

"They had their own agenda. I think a pretty girl with a smile, maybe the big money aspect, and the promise seduced me. Hell, I can't think straight now."

"You're a vet, I can get you into Bethesda as a special project."

"Jeff Burwell promised me Shands up in Gainesville."

"Whatever." He swabbed at his eyes. "Just do something, dammit."

"I have a few things I must to do first."

"Your funeral, boy. You're a grown boy. What do you want from me?"

"I'm resigning from the county commission, and I'm not

going to run for your seat."

"Which follows that you're gonna play kingpin and push somebody."

"I am."

"So long's it ain't that goddamn MacLean."

"Elena Rodríguez."

"Jesus. You foolin' around with her? What's with Mary Lou?"

"Everybody asks me that. One, I'm not having an affair. Not with anybody. Two, Mary Lou moved out. I'm going to work on that. Three, Elena Rodríguez is my choice to take the reins."

"You want my concurrence."

"Your endorsement, Palmer. Today I'm calling in favors all over the county. Jeff Burwell bought off on it and when the time comes, he'll campaign for her." I smiled. "And the thing is, I think she'll do a bang up job. Or else I wouldn't want her for the job."

"It sounds as if you're locking it in. Nobody else in the party can compete now."

I grinned. "That's the idea."

"Do I have a choice in this?"

"Sure you do, Palmer."

He eyed me cynically. "No, I don't have a choice. Your way or MacLean. That's what you've boiled it down to." He shook his head. "Machiavelli reincarnated."

"Palmer, listen. You're my friend. You've helped me along the way. You helped me get hold of the remote viewers. You've been concerned with my family and me. That's a friend. I thank you. I am here asking for your concurrence and your endorsement of Elena Rodríguez. You do what you've a mind to." I smiled at him.

"You know, when you started taking over here, I found I didn't have to get involved any longer. That's difficult from Washington City at any time. And it worked out. You done that job well and earned your place. I've come to trust you, boy." He looked at me through sweat as though when he called me "boy" it was automatic and he just realized it was now a fact. "Once it's set in stone, I'll get the congressional campaign committee and the national party involved."

Since I was close to downtown, after my shower, I headed for my commission office. I didn't feel a kinship and was going to pick up a few personal items and not talk to anybody. But you can't sneak in anywhere.

When you're in government, you're not supposed to delete anything off your computer—the open records laws. I was busy illegally deleting things off my computer when the door to my office swung open and Vince MacLean walked in without knocking. A smiling man dressed in a brown suit followed him.

MacLean said, "I heard you were here, Zachary. I want you to meet…."

Suddenly, MacLean registered what he was seeing. "What's wrong with you?" He studied me. "It *is* you. Could've fooled me for a minute. As usual you need a shave." He continued to stare at me. Then he shook his head.

Brown suit asked MacLean, "This is him?"

"It doesn't look like it, but it is. Something's happened to him while he was gone." MacLean stuck a finger down his collar, one closed tightly by a string tie, and scratched absently.

Brown suit nodded, shrugged and stepped over to me. He held his hand out and I extended mine, thinking he was going to introduce himself. Instead he handed me a folded sheaf of papers. "You are hereby served."

MacLean chortled. "Collusion, Zachary. He's with the law firm Mary Lou has retained."

I looked down and then up. "MacLean, get out. You," I pointed at brown suit, "stay."

Vince MacLean looked uncertain, but the lawyer said, "It's all right, Vince. I can handle it."

MacLean went out, obviously upset at being left out.

"What are the terms you-all are demanding?"

"It's right there in the paperwork."

"Tell me, I don't have time to read."

He was uncertain.

"Summarize. I'm an attorney, I understand."

"All right, Mr. Zachary. In summary, Mrs. Zachary wants half of everything, including future earnings, including residuals from your law firm. And expenses and attorney fees, of course."

"Of course. Let me tell you what. Here's my response: I agree. In place of my half of my future earnings, I will give her the whole house, all stocks and bonds, and all of the annual payments from my law firm. That will keep her comfortable for the rest of her life."

"And attorney's fees?"

"That isn't going to amount to much now that I'm agreeing to everything. She can pay that."

"I see a problem with your failure to share future earnings."

"One, I'm almost sixty years old and I just resigned my job. Two, I'm dying, if nobody bothered to tell you."

He looked startled. "I am sorry, sir."

"Two other conditions."

"And they are?"

"Have the paperwork ready to sign tomorrow. Expedite the court procedures so this can be done immediately. Deal with my law firm for that, and a few judges owe me, whomever you draw. So that should help."

"Those conditions are more than acceptable, sir; however, I haven't the authority to commit right now. I must consult with our office and Mrs. Zachary."

'Fine, but my timetable is the important thing. And I've one final condition."

"And that is?"

"Tell Mary Lou I want to talk to her."

"Yes, I can. This all sounds doable."

"Fine," I said, "remember the operative word is expedite, hurry, get with the program, immediate urgency."

"Yes, sir."

"Without that, you might never have a deal."

He shrugged. "If you are trying to tell me that you will pass away before we complete everything involved, then it doesn't matter to us, for Mrs. Zachary will inherit it all then."

I grinned. Trumped me. Found the one weakness in my approach.

So I nodded in agreement. "You know my law firm?"

"I do, sir."

"Then you are aware of their tenacity, their reputation?"

"I am."

"Good," I said. "Be advised if this agreement I have outlined fails or doesn't go down as I want, I will devise a last will which gives Mary Lou less than she will get right now. In the long run you might be able to contest that will and win; but the legal fees will take most of the cash and securities, I promise you. And think how my law firm will wave the flag of her deserting me as I lay dying."

"You have a valid point."

I had run one hell of a bluff, because I wouldn't do that to Mary Lou. But it was the only leverage I had.

"Then you need to be getting judicial holy water and having secretaries typing up papers."

"I am on the way."

Brown suit left and I didn't even know his name.

I ran into the bathroom and vomited.

After I gargled and cleaned up, I went to MacLean's office. But I saw him going down the corridor carrying his Stetson and talking to brown suit. So they were leaving. Vince doesn't lock his door during the day. And this would save me a trip back during the night.

I walked into MacLean's office like I owned it. Even though things were ragged for me lately, I was prepared as usual. The Seven P principle. Proper Prior Planning Prevents Piss Poor Performance.

Vince had a habit of sliding his center desk drawer in and out. I had friends who owned banks. I pulled two robbery dye packs out of my pocket and inserted each into a corner of his center drawer. Old Vince was going to have a major surprise later when he returned. Recalling his hard and fast rules of first-thing-n-the-morning constitutionals, I went into his bathroom and put two more dye packs under the pads of his toilet seat. There were people, me included, who'd kill to witness old Vince having a seat with the sports page. While I didn't feel like it, I allowed myself a self-satisfied grin.

Usually I do not engage in retaliation. However, he'd gloated when he set me up for brown suit and was taking advantage of my condition. He'd ratted me out to the governor. He needed comeuppance.

Additionally, I had to insure he wouldn't win the election. A few points would make the difference between victory for Elena and defeat for MacLean.

Like an investigation by the governor for violation of the Sunshine Law.

Quickly, I started his computer. I typed his password in: NUMBER1. Then I sent me an e-mail offering a deal on the Midnight Pass issue, and hinted at a conspiracy against the other commissioners who were not in favor of reopening Midnight Pass. From his viewpoint, I hinted that we'd push through a development project for him in return. That ought to do it. After my resignation, somebody would go through my e-mail and discover this message from Vince MacLean. Not only would it nail his ass to the wall, but also it would lend impetus to my side: opening Midnight Pass. By the time they untangled the webs, it would be too late.

Glancing at my watch to see how much time I had before Mac returned, I saw it running backwards like a propeller.

It was possible that after MacLean's violating e-mail was discovered that the FDLE would confiscate his machine and go over it with a fine-toothed comb. So while on-line to send the note, I started surfing through every porn site and associated link I could find. I signed up for daily e-mails from some of them. Vince MacLean would have to get a professional computer expert to remove all the spam, popups, and spy ware that would result from my little trip down porno lane on his equipment. Finally, I shut everything down and left.

I hoped I was going to live long enough to see this through. Besides nausea, I fought the thoughts that I should have ignored Tyme, Incorporated and gone to some research hospital. Life is full of "What If's?"

CHAPTER THIRTY-NINE

Abandoning everything, I left the office and found my pickup. I drove south on Tamiami Trail heading for Bee Ridge Road. There were better ways to get there, but my thinking was fuzzing up and that was the easiest.

Traffic was better than usual. On my cell phone, I hit the preset for Dexter and muscled past his receptionist.

"Dexter, I'm on the way."

"I have patients. Appointments."

"Sorry my friend, I don't think I'm going to make it much longer and this has got to be done while I have any strength left."

"Meet you there."

Again, the Cattlemen and Bee Ridge intersection. Dexter's office building. Which I walked into, took the elevator to his floor, and went to the stairs in the back, walked down the stairs, and went in a side entrance to Doctors' Hospital. I walked through a couple of floors and down several corridors. Nobody was following. Just being careful. Hate to have the whole thing fall apart because of a small lapse.

Dexter met me outside a small operating room. I changed into a hospital gown and hopped up on the table.

"My friend, you are certifiably crazy to take two pints of blood and a bone marrow donation at the same time."

"That's me," I said wanly.

He gave me a quick checkup then got to work.

While they took the blood, I briefed him on what I had gone

through up in North Carolina.

"So it was all for naught," I said.

"That's not the case," Dexter said. "I'm going to give you an IV because you look dehydrated. You're very weak and I don't want to do this, but I will." He hung two bags from the hooks and attached one. It started pumping or dripping or whatever the hell those things do. The other bag was blood, O positive, doubtless. He didn't hitch that one up. Not yet, that is. "Anyway, it sounds like they followed scientific method exhaustively. I'm saying, Easy, they ruled out everything they could."

"They did that thing, Dexter. But they didn't fix anything."

He nodded and dropped the operating table from recline to full down. "On your stomach," he ordered, "I'm giving you a local anesthetic."

The sting didn't bother me at all. The lack of blood was getting to me. I felt faint and told Dexter so.

"It stands to reason," he said. "Pituitary, thyroid, adrenal glands. Makes sense. They'd be logical to transplant. They all pump out hormones and stuff into the bloodstream. The pituitary is called the master gland. It regulates other endocrine glands and body processes. It's tiny at the base of the brain attached to the hypothalamus."

"I need to know this?" Dizziness clouded my thinking.

Dexter went on, ignoring me. "It especially stimulates the thyroid and adrenal glands. We already know the thyroid controls metabolism. The pair of adrenal glands perches atop the kidneys. They have two—count 'em, two—major functions. Jump right to the adrenal cortex and you got your corticosteroid hormones—we're speaking energy storage, food use, and body shape. And, not to be ignored, the adrenal medulla, affecting nerves and secreting epinephrine, that is adrenaline and neoepinephrine. Now you've got me thinking. Suppose you, Ethan Allan Zachary, have a specific comprehensive interaction of these things *and* an electrical interaction."

"You're trying to say it puts me right here on this table right now?"

"Anything's possible, and that makes more sense than most of what I've heard up to now. It's not widely done, but these glands can be transplanted. I can see where Tyme would be willing to chance it—especially if he's thinking fountain of youth. Human growth hormones drop as you age. Perhaps lightning triggered extra production in you."

"They did not really discuss this with me."

"Not surprising," Dexter said. "Had they done so, you might have been onto them sooner." He continued to work and I remembered giant needles and didn't want to know. "I'm aspirating about a thousand milliliters of bone marrow from you. After bone marrow donations, there is usually some bone pain for a few days or a week or two. And it takes four to six weeks for your body to replace the bone marrow." As he worked, I could feel an occasional movement deep down in my back, his instruments or collection needles probably. "But in your case, I have no idea how you'll recover—or if it makes a difference. A month or two ago you would recover immediately. But now...?"

"Another thing they didn't address with me was shocking me." I wasn't all that articulate right then.

"You mean ECT?" said Dexter, still working.

"Electroshock is what I mean."

"The old term is ECT," he pointed out, "for electro convulsive therapy. And they did right not even suggesting it. It was designed to improve severe cases of mental illness. I think it's still used on a limited basis these modern days, but they use anesthesia to preclude the attendant spasms and frequent bone breakage."

"Oh," I managed to say. Frequent bone breakage?

Consciousness came and went and I was gone. I didn't know if 1,000 milliliters was a bucket of bone marrow or a teaspoonful.

I awoke in a hospital bed, not the same room in which I started this mess.

Shortly, a nurse brought me medicine and food on a tray. "Spinach, double order of liver and gravy for blood renourishing, and noodles with more gravy for carbo-loading to help you regain your strength."

I drank all the orange juice immediately and started feeling better. I wasn't hungry at all, but I forced myself to eat.

Dexter showed up as soon as I was finished. He checked my vitals and he shook his head. "I don't like what I'm seeing. I want you to stay here. We need to do something and do it now."

"What?"

"Treatment."

"I say again, do what?"

"Damnfino."

"Nobody knows."

"We have to try something, you're dying. I'm thinking about transplanting a few glands we talked about yesterday. But I can't convince myself that has a good chance of working."

"I got stuff to do, Dexter. If I make it, I'll let you send me to Gainesville. If I need it." Shards of darkness gathered about me.

"What are you talking about?"

I shrugged and lay back. Bone marrow donation and two pints of blood gone, that took a lot of energy out of me. I didn't know if I was up to what I planned. "How much is a thousand milliliters?"

"Consider it a quart." He put a clamp on my finger. "Your oxygen level is better than I expected. We can fix the fluid loss. Your fast recovery or regeneration condition is kicking in already."

"Great. Time heals all wounds," I said, not hiding my sarcasm. That same biological counterclockwise condition was going to kill me real soon.

I drowsed and slept for a couple of hours.

Then I made several phone calls.

One last time to North Carolina. The same operator's voice.

"Ethan Zachary one last time, darlin'. Put me through to Belinda Foursleeps?"

"Yes, sir, Mr. Zachary."

"Hello, Zachary."

"Time to do it or get off the pot, Belinda."

"You got a deal, Zachary."

"Can you be here in the morning?"

"I will."

"The Tyme, Incorporated jet?"

"One of them."

"Good. Carry a cell phone and give me the number. I want you driving around downtown Sarasota at noon. Alone."

"I don't drive."

"Give me strength. Okay, you can have someone drive you. I'll call you at noon."

"Fine." She gave me her cell phone number and brusquely hung up.

I called my friend María and a couple of other people. Then I crashed and woke up the next morning. I found myself more rested, but still not hungry. I dressed and walked out of the hospital without checking out. Not that I'd ever checked in to begin with.

Still very weak I drove home, not a long drive. The answering machine was blinking away trying to impart to me the urgency of dozens of telephone messages. I checked the caller ID history and saw that CJ had called, among others. I called her but she must have been out running so I left a message myself.

Feeling good about one thing, I lighted a cigar inside and puffed smoke in all the rooms in the house. Take that, Mary Lou.

Knowing I needed strength, I cooked a half dozen runny eggs sunny side up and a pot of grits for carbs. I couldn't eat much, but I sure tried.

Inwardly smiling at her discomfort, I smoked another cigar inside the house. Even Budweiser took offense.

At 11:30 I climbed in my truck and headed downtown. At noon I was standing alone at the corner of Washington and Ringling. I'd already programmed Belinda's cell number into my own cell phone. I pushed the preset numbers.

CHAPTER FORTY

"Belinda, where are you?"

"Just a minute, I don't know this city—town."

Her voice went away from the phone and I heard her talking to someone, probably her driver.

I lighted a García y Vega English Corona and waited.

"Sixth and the Trail," she said without preamble.

"Tell your driver to head for Ringling and go east. When you see me, stop and get out. He circles the block or something."

Belinda grunted and disconnected.

The cigar tasted good, smooth and mild. An excellent morning smoke.

Standing across the street from the county courthouse, I watched traffic and kept my eye on the vehicles coming up Ringling. Right down Washington to the south was the Dairy Queen and I had an urge to walk there and have lunch. I hoped I wasn't hallucinating. I smelled ozone and carbon and burnt diesel. People who knew me waved and I returned the gesture. Across the street leaning against the courthouse reading a newspaper stood María. Occasionally his eyes roamed the area. I picked out one more of his cronies sitting in a car in the parking lot behind me. There probably would have been two more but I couldn't locate them.

Presently, I saw a long white limousine coming towards me on Ringling. I had little doubt this was Belinda Foursleeps.

It took two light cycles and the limo pulled up, stopped, and Belinda stepped out without the driver's assistance. She slammed the door and stepped up on the curb. She wore the basic Tyme, Inc., garb, blazer and silk shirt and matching skirt. She didn't offer to shake hands.

She paused to look around. "You chose an interesting location for highway robbery."

"A commodity is worth what someone is willing to pay."

"Shall we get this over with?"

"Did you bring it?"

"I did," she said and pulled a large envelope out of her pocket. "I do not see evidence of your side of the bargain."

"I have it, you have to trust me." I blew smoke nonchalantly.

"Have I any choice?"

"Everybody has a choice, including life and death," I said, my voice harsh.

She saw the look in my eyes and shivered. Then she handed me the envelope. I opened it and checked the contents. "Just as the doctor ordered." I put it in my pocket. I took out my cell phone and punched in another preset number. When the woman answered, I said, "Do you see a big 737 out there, it might have Tyme, Inc. on the side?"

Belinda, listening, said, "It does."

"I've been watching it," the woman told me.

"That's it. Deliver the cooler to it. Somebody in the crew will meet you and check it out."

"It's over by Jones aviation. It'll take me about two minutes to get there."

"Thanks, hon. I appreciate your help."

"Anytime, Easy."

I punched the disconnect and told Belinda, "In two minutes an airport security vehicle will pull up to your aircraft. The woman driving will have the cooler and will hand it over."

Belinda whipped out her cell phone and began barking orders. She put the cell away. "An ingenious plan. I have an expert on board to check the contents. We shall wait."

"I'm curious," I said looking down at her, "is Raleigh going to give Justyn a bone marrow implant, or is he going to do something fancy with the stem cells?"

Belinda ignored me.

So we stood there. I had nothing to say again, so I didn't say it again.

Belinda did, though. "I wouldn't have trusted you, Zachary. Except you know why?"

"Tell me." I waved at a Sarasota city police car, and Belinda eyed it suspiciously. "Routine patrol," I said.

"Two days ago the chopper run brought a Segway to Rolly. For that, you have my temporary gratitude."

"The kid needs to be a kid."

"But I still might have you killed."

She said it conversationally and I had little doubt she meant it.

"I don't think you will," I said.

"Give me a reason."

I puffed on my cigar. "I'm dying. What Raleigh extrapolated would happen is happening."

She eyed me. "You don't look very healthy at that. But you never know, you might live through it. Stranger things have happened."

"That confidence will give me strength for a long time."

Belinda snorted.

"I'm going to trust you to keep your bargain," I said. "If I'm alive, I'm still manufacturing blood. And your doctors might still have an academic interest in my continued survival."

She actually spat on the ground like a man. "I don't indulge myself at all. I haven't bought myself a present, spent any money on me alone in years. See, my clothes are even company." She smiled but didn't mean it. "It would please me very much to have you killed. I would indulge myself this one pleasure."

She meant it. But death threats don't mean much to a dying man. This thought was reinforced by a wave of nausea and abdominal cramps.

Belinda's cell chirped. "Fine." She disconnected and hit another key. "Come and get me now." She pocketed the phone.

"It checks out. The deal is done."

The limousine had circled the block and must have been waiting for word because I saw it appear from Osprey Avenue and turn right on Ringling and head toward us.

Belinda pointed at María across the street. "Your man?"

"He is."

"Smith described him well."

"I had to show you I was prepared for anything."

"Trust is a wonderful thing, Zachary."

"I trusted some professionals up in North Carolina recently." My voice had an edge that I couldn't make go away. "And I found deception."

Belinda nodded and looked up at me. "Then perhaps we're even now."

"We'll never be even, Belinda. I'll be dead and you'll be going about business as usual."

"With a dying old man and a dying child."

"Be that as it may."

The limo pulled up and Belinda didn't wait for the driver. I opened the door for her and she stepped in without looking at me. And the limo turned right and accelerated down Washington.

And my head began to ache.

CHAPTER FORTY-ONE

I checked my watch to see how long until my scheduled meeting with the lawyers and Mary Lou. My heart froze. The hands were racing backwards at a rate I hadn't yet seen.

I was already convinced I was dying; there was nothing medical science could do for me. There always had been some slight chance Dexter could fry me with radiation or microwave me or some damn thing. But now I knew there was no time left. Nausea, pain, and cramps told me I had but a few days, if that. And I would soon become incapacitated. I was walking south on Ringling and spotted a clock. I had half an hour before the meeting. The time with Belinda had been brief.

Dairy Queen wasn't crowded, surprisingly. I got a chocolate shake I didn't want and sat at a concrete bench under an umbrella and thought about my life, what had been, and what might have been. The cool milkshake soothed my now sore throat.

Feeling sorry for myself, I recalled many lunches here with Carrie Jean. She'd always burst into my office and demand I feed her.

María sat down across from me. "Hey, boss. Usually you a chick magnet, first time I seen you with a not so hot woman." He performed a double take. "You don't look so good, man."

Blowing cigar smoke, much to the disgust of a retiree who was standing at the order window, I nodded. "I don't feel so good."

"That short lady made me, din't she?"

"It's what I wanted. You did well. I owe you."

"Naah. We all do for each other when it's needed." He glanced around nervously, doubtless not wanting any street people seeing him talk to me.

"Good. You know Elena Rodríguez?"

"Hell, yes. She babalicious."

"María, I'm done. I'm outa here. She's taking my place. How about look after her some? She's one of my favorite people."

"Jesus, boss. You sound like you checkin' out."

Wearily, I said, "I am. It's all over but the shouting." And that was coming soon.

I dipped into Belinda's packed envelope and pulled out a smaller one. I gave it to María. "A full scholarship to Stetson Law School and expenses."

"A full boat? You win the lotto?"

"I wish."

"I already owed you, man, not the other way around."

"María? I had the opportunity and could not pass it up."

"You pulled some shit with the short, ugly broad."

"I did. And it felt good doing it, too."

"Shit hot. I thank you."

We shook hands and I threw away my unfinished chocolate shake and walked away from that Dairy Queen for the last time.

My abdomen hurt worse and the little milkshake I'd drunk wasn't settling well. But the cigar tasted excellent. Death gives you a weird perspective.

My ex-law firm was a five-minute walk and I'd parked my truck there. I went to the truck and got the Ricky Nelson album out of the cab. Then I went in the back entrance of my ex-building and down the corridor into my ex-conference room.

Mary Lou and her lawyer sat there without talking to each other. Mary Lou looked tired. But she was dressed superbly.

"Ethan, my God!" She pushed her chair back and stood. "Look at you."

Brown suit had another brown suit on today.

I was still standing in the doorway to the conference room. Down the hall, a handful of the people I'd hired and worked with were gathered and staring at me. My ex-secretary had her hand over her mouth.

Nobody said anything about me smoking a cigar indoors.

Pointing at the conference table where a couple of dozen papers were spread out, I said, "Ready for signature?"

"Please read them first." Brown suit was the only one sitting down.

"No thanks. They reflect what we agreed to?"

"Yes, they do."

"Ethan, I—" Mary Lou started to say.

"We need witnesses, fancy stamps, holy water, whatever," I said and waved at the secretary with her hand over her mouth. She scurried down the hall.

Smoke made my eyes tear up as I leaned over and signed the documents. I didn't care. Mary Lou signed.

"Let's go outside," I said. "They can finish up here without us."

Pausing, I retrieved Belinda's envelope. I opened it and pulled out a Bank of America cashier's check made out to THE ETHAN A. ZACHARY MEMORIAL POLITICAL ACTION COMMITTEE FOR BETTER GOVERNMENT. I handed it to the secretary. "Take care of this, will you?" Her eyes grew wide at the million-dollar amount. I handed her another check made out to Elena Rodríguez for a cool million. Elena was now set.

Mary Lou led the way. Once outside, we stood under a live oak behind the building. Traffic sounds were muted. Occasionally someone would look out a window pointedly.

"Ricky Nelson," I said, handing her the album. "Hello, Mary Lou."

She took it. "Why didn't you call me?"

"Not much to say, and I've been busy." And I hadn't been thinking right. I'd figured it out last night. Her note was in the Ricky Nelson album.

"If you'd called even a few days ago," she said slowly, "I was waiting and waiting."

"I was out of town," I said and wobbled, unsteady on my feet.

Mary Lou reached out to hold me steady. She seemed to see me again for the first time. "It's you but it's not you. You look deathly ill. But you can't be the Ethan Zachary I've known for so long."

"One and the same and short on time."

"Ethan, I still love you. But I can't be married to you any longer."

"Fine."

"We grew apart, our interests veered away from each other."

"Fine."

She eyed me as I swayed.

"For a long time we grew together," I managed to say.

"Nowadays, I don't even know if we're growing. If so, it's away from each other."

"Fine."

"You haven't shown that you need me in so long."

"Sorry." Maybe she was right. But I just couldn't put things together right then.

Waves of nausea rolled over me and I held onto the oak with one hand and my cigar with the other.

"Ethan, maybe I should call an ambulance."

"No."

"You are dying, aren't you?"

"I am." And swiftly comes the scythe.

"Oh, no, Ethan."

I took my hand off the tree and grasped her shoulder and then hugged her.

"I'm truly sorry, Mary Lou. May God be with you."

I released her and turned to walk off. Somehow I'd dropped my cigar. I took a couple of steps and fell flat on my face.

Mary Lou was immediately beside me. Slowly, I pushed myself up and she helped me stand.

"Almost forgot," I said.

She was crying openly.

Struggling, I pulled Belinda's envelope out of my hip pocket. It was wrinkled now, but so what? I fumbled out a piece of paper and handed it to Mary Lou.

She held it close to her eyes and said. "Where did this come from?"

"I sold my soul and my life." I was groggy and didn't know what I was saying exactly. "That's what I got in return."

"Oh, my God. A cashier's check to me? Two million dollars?"

"Yeah." I stumbled across the grass to the parking area and got in my truck. I spat out the window and it didn't make it all the way and dribbled down the side of the truck and the saliva was tinged with blood.

I could hear Mary Lou crying until I got out in traffic and then all I could hear was the phantom echo of her weeping.

CHAPTER FORTY-TWO

I don't know how I made it home. A traffic deputy followed me partway up Fruitville thinking he was following a drunk driver, and then he recognized my truck, pulled up alongside me to make sure it was me, nodded and turned off. It was easier to drive on Interstate 75 because all I had to do was point the truck and stand on the accelerator. Bee Ridge Road was tough to navigate, but it was straight and only a couple of lights to negotiate. Midafternoon traffic was light, thank goodness. Old women and children dove for cover when I drove down Bent Tree Boulevard. I managed to veer onto my cul de sac and wheeled into my driveway and stopped half on the grass.

Opening the door, I fell into CJ's arms.

She held me upright. "Mary Lou called me." In itself, that spoke volumes.

Carrie Jean half carried me through the house, past a wondering Budweiser, and sat me on the bed. She pulled off my shoes, lined me up, and eased me down.

"Dexter is on his way," she said and I passed out and dreamed I was going through a rock crusher.

A sharp, striking pain woke me.

Dexter was leaning over me, syringe in hand, and needle still in my arm. He saw that I was conscious. "A little highball I worked up," he said. "Steroids, vitamins, and some illegal stuff I'm not telling anybody."

"Thanks," I mumbled and fell back asleep, more comfortable already.

It couldn't have been much later, but I woke. Dexter was lounging in the chair drinking water and CJ was sitting cross-legged next to me watching me. She'd covered me with a blanket and the air conditioner was going full blast.

"I'm going to admit you to the hospital," Dexter told me once he saw my eyes flickering.

"No." My voice was hard, commanding.

Carrie Jean sat there; big eyes wide open, squeezing my hand.

"I need a day."

"You do not have one day to need," Dexter said.

"Oh, well, gimmie another shot then."

"That might kill you. It sure jumpstarted you earlier. I want you in the hospital."

"For what purpose?"

"I can do some things. I can treat symptoms immediately. I can try experimental meds. I can send you to Gainesville."

"No time left for that." I was so weary.

"It's the only thing left, Ethan."

"Let me die with dignity."

"Ethan, I need you," said Carrie Jean at the edge of my consciousness.

"I just need rest, God, I'm tired." Whatever Dexter had given me had been chock full of painkillers, for I felt like I was drifting on clouds. I rolled over and put my head in CJ's lap and fell asleep.

When I woke, it was dark and CJ was grilling steaks on the barbecue grill on the patio. Budweiser followed her around like he was on a leash.

"You need food," she said.

I nodded but didn't think so.

A hot shower and clean clothes helped. Then I sat outside smoked a cigar and watched CJ cook.

She served us outside, steaks and salad and Gatorade. CJ reminded me that Gatorade was invented at the University of Florida. Surprisingly, I ate a few bites of everything.

We didn't talk much and afterwards, we sat in lounge chairs

and I smoked silently. CJ sat there with me.

"You're not going to leave, are you?"

Big wide smile. "Nope."

I stubbed out my cigar, went inside and fell into bed in my clean clothes.

The bedside CC Radio clock said 5:12 AM when I awoke. It was very quiet, but I knew something was wrong. Pain began to seep into my being, maybe that's what woke me up. I was still dressed, but under the covers, however she did that. A warm, comfortable spot glowed on my left side, a thing that turned out to be Carrie Jean curled up against me. The night was cool, so she had all the sliding glass doors in the back and the bedroom wide open. I could feel the air I was breathing, another thing separating us from North Carolina.

But something was abnormal; something triggered me.

Budweiser was not a watch cat. But the old feline stood next to the bed with a low almost inaudible whine.

Thinking about North Carolina gave me a chill. Belinda Foursleeps wasn't trustworthy. It wouldn't surprise me if her goons showed up to kidnap me and sneak me back to the mountains for some transplants. I didn't think she'd have me killed. Not yet. But it occurred to me that right damn now Carrie Jean was in danger. It didn't matter what happened to me, hell I was a dead man already. My body was just waiting for its last breath.

The pool screen door creaked open and slammed shut. Footsteps scraped on the patio as I struggled to get out of the covers. Lights flared.

I was clawing in the bedside table's drawer for my .357.

"Goddamn you, Easy." A giant hand lifted me out of bed and slammed me against a wall. A painting of the black and white barber-pole lighthouse at St. Augustine slid to the floor.

Carrie Jean was sitting up in bed wiping sleep out of her eyes. She was still dressed in jeans and a pullover University of Florida jersey.

"Daddy!" she said.

Jack Billingsley was holding me up against the wall. I

couldn't do much, especially in the weakened state in which I found myself. Plus, Jack had two inches and forty pounds on me.

"First you run Mary Lou off," Jack said, voice accusing. "Then you're out with all kinds of different women, including that teevee reporterette. Now you're in bed with my damn daughter? I don't think so." He launched a blow for my chin but he telegraphed it so far in advance, I just moved my head aside and his hand smashed into the wallboard, cutting a fist-sized hole right where my head had been. I kicked out and knocked him onto the bed.

Immediately, Carrie Jean jumped on his chest.

"Get the hell off me," Jack screamed and pitched her aside.

CJ rolled off the bed and landed on the floor. She scrambled up and dove at him as he was levering himself off the bed. They hit the floor on the other side of the bed in a tangle of limbs and bedclothes.

Budweiser wailed and scrambled out of the mess.

"Go back to your bimbo of the day," CJ said hoarsely.

"I will not have my daughter sleeping with my friend. Not my friend, not any more," he stammered and stood.

I was staggering and fell onto the bed.

"Kill me now," I whispered to the ceiling.

"Daddy! Ethan is dying. We didn't sleep together." She turned on a light.

"Malarkey. You were in bed together." Jack loomed over me and looked down. "Jesus, look at him." He stood there staring down. Then he looked between CJ and me. Again and again his eyes swung between us. Then he scratched his head. "He looks like he's already dead."

"If you've killed him, I'll never speak to you again."

"What the hell is wrong with him?"

"Nobody knows."

We were all in the breakfast nook, CJ and Jack drinking coffee, me drinking a real Coke, sugar and all when Dexter came in. He carried a bottle of water and set his traditional doctor's black bag down.

"I'm on the way to the hospital to make my rounds," he told us. "I'll make the arrangements for a room." He looked at Carrie Jean. "Can you get him over there or should I call an ambulance now?"

CJ switched her gaze to me. "Ethan?" She had figured I was up to something.

Unnecessarily, I looked at my watch. It was racing backwards faster than ever. My mind was foggy. I knew it didn't matter. Dexter and medicine could no longer help. Some part of my brain told me I was going into mental degradation. Neurons were fizzling or disappearing or dying or whatever the hell they do when you're checking out. I'd be dead by nightfall. I felt ice in my veins and pain everywhere. "Let me have another shot, Dexter."

"No."

"The pain is bad and getting worse."

"Even I can see that on his face," Jack said.

"He won't live through this if you don't," CJ said, her own face tied with worry.

"Here's the deal," I said, fighting to control my voice and my body. "I have a few things I must do. Everybody leave me alone. Carrie Jean, come and get me at noon." If I weren't done by then, it wouldn't matter anyway.

"Give him the shot, Dexter," said CJ, her words urgent.

"Do I have a choice?"

He opened the bag and out came the syringe. I didn't feel the sting. "My special Easy cocktail." Finished with that one, he removed another from his bag. "For pain. Can you take morphine?"

"Does it matter?"

"I guess not." He cleaned my other arm with an alcohol swab and I didn't feel that one, either. Within a couple of minutes I began to perk up. It was noticeable to them all.

"Noon, or I have deputies and an ambulance over here. You are no longer accommodating the changes. Strange things are happening within your body."

"Tell me about it. Thanks, Dexter."

He left and Jack left.

CJ showed no signs of following.

"Carrie Jean? I need some time alone."

"I don't trust you."

"If I live through this, dear, I pledge my troth to thee." Those words echoed from somewhere in the past. My brain wouldn't download the memory.

"Those are words I would have killed for. But it doesn't matter now, does it?"

Breathing deeply to control the returning pain, I said, "It does to me. It was meant to be."

"Destiny shattered," she said, her eyes locked on mine.

"Out and leave me."

"I love you, Ethan. Will I ever see you again?"

She knew I was up to something. I wouldn't lie to her.

Choosing my words carefully, I said, "If it is humanly possible. Know you now that I have one hell of a reason to make it?"

She locked onto my eyes for a long moment. "Yes, I know that." I could tell she wanted to cry but wasn't going to.

We stood and she came into my arms. I held her for a few minutes.

She saw the trickle of blood from my nose as I felt it run out. She leaned back and wiped it off with the neck of her shirt.

"I do love you."

She tilted her head to see my face. "I know. I've always known. I think Mary Lou knew, too. I love you, Ethan." She kissed me lightly, a singular kiss. She disengaged herself from my arms and turned to leave. She walked out the front door and I heard her truck start.

Remembering, I hurried outside, the movement hurting me. I pulled out another check from Belinda. "Here." It was almost mortally wrinkled.

She took it. "Bank of America, cashier's check, three million dollars, made out to Carrie Jean Billingsley." She looked at me. "I don't want your fucking money."

She handed it back.

"It's not my money, it's yours. I extorted it from Justyn Tyme. Small enough amount for what they were going to do to me and what they did not do to me."

"I don't care."

"Which is a good reason to take it."

"Nope."

"In legal terms, call it defamation of character."

"You're talking riddles now, Ethan."

"Listen, CJ, I went through hell and I want somebody to collect. If it was in my name," I lied, "then Mary Lou would have a claim on it."

"Let her have it."

"I got her some, too."

CJ shrugged, touched my cheek, and folded the check. "Dear, sweet Ethan." She tucked the check down her shirt. "For our honeymoon."

"Goodbye, Carrie Jean Billingsley."

"Don't you sound so goddamn final. See you at high noon."

Or in the next life, I thought as fog tugged at the edges of my awareness.

CJ drove away from the front of my house.

CHAPTER FORTY-THREE

Madness clawed at me. I found a cigar, what kind I don't know, and lighted it and smoked away. Mary Lou would have to air the place out for a month.

I called the FarReaching Institute but it was well before business hours and I had to leave a message, which I did, stressing the urgency. Then I sent them a priority immediate attention e-mail in case they didn't get the voice mail. Not that I had much hope in a solution to them. But I had a couple of questions. Questions that were becoming more and more difficult to remember.

Then I went into the garage and got my wire strippers and came back into the living room. The lamp was some fancy lighthouse I couldn't remember that Mary Lou had bought me years ago. Knowing her it probably cost five hundred dollars. I put my cigar down, pulled the plug and cut the wire so that about twenty-four inches of cut wire remained. I plugged it back into the socket and jammed the two exposed leads against my arm.

Bam. I was so weak, it knocked me on my ass. The wire was smoking on the carpet. I crawled over and snapped it out of the wall. I didn't want to burn Mary Lou's house down. Especially with me in it.

The pain had disappeared, but now returned. The electric shock only served to paralyze my system. Webs of fog edged into my mind. I checked my watch and it was racing backwards at breakneck speed. Not to mention I was still weak from the blood and bone marrow donation.

Well, the hope had been nice while it was there. I figured if I had an electrical problem, then maybe I could shock myself back on kilter. I would not be denied.

Budweiser shadowed me as I went about the house, doubtless thinking I'd turned crazy. I had not. I was going mad, though. I speculated that I would become completely and stark raving mad before my body imploded or exploded or shut down or whatever.

Mary Lou's expensive hair dryer was next. Mary Lou never bought anything cheap. She'd never been to Wal-Mart or Sam's. Hell, Wal-Mart sold cigars cheap, though I was wont to say that wouldn't last long in this day and age of political correctness.

I didn't change or take off my shoes. I merely plugged the hair dryer into the wall socket outside on the patio and stretched it. But it was not long enough to reach the pool. It took me agonizing moments to find an extension, but I finally did, ripping it off some ornament Mary Lou had bought to spruce up the living room. After connecting everything, it did finally reach the pool. I walked into the shallow end down the stairs fully clothed. Then I hit the switch and the hair dryer whooshed on. I sat on the bottom step holding the hair dryer out of the water. Apprehension swept some of the madness away for a moment.

You just don't electrocute yourself. Something, some survival mechanism, refuses to let you do that thing. I inhaled deeply on the cigar and tossed the hair dryer out in front of me a few feet. I probably wore three inches off my teeth clenching them while the appliance was arcing toward the water's surface. The cigar fell into the pool, chopped neatly off.

The hair dryer hit, bounced once off the handle and sank into the water. An immediate great cracking sound came and went in a nanosecond and the hair dryer sank, extension cord and all. I felt nothing.

What happened was obvious. GFI. Ground Fault Interrupter. Built into outside circuits. One whiff of a short and it kicks off the circuit breaker. Groaning, I climbed out of the pool, retrieved the hair dryer, and went shedding water through the house into the garage. Sure enough, the breaker was tripped.

"Goddamnit." The cat was standing in the doorway to the garage watching me. Animals must be able to sense madness. I flipped the circuit breaker back to on. I saw my leaf blower hanging on the sidewall past my golf cart. I got it and the outdoor fifty-foot extension. "This ought to do it." I plugged the extension into the kitchen socket, where hopefully there was no GFI and trailed the extension outside. This had to draw enough amps to do the job. I connected the leaf blower into the extension.

Again I walked slowly into the pool, down the steps into the shallow end and sank down to a sitting position on the bottom step, the leaf blower high above my head. I flipped the switch and a great plume of water danced in front of me where air blown from the blower was hitting the water.

Again old Budweiser crouched in the sliding glass doorway watching.

Up in Raiford, north of Orlando, near Starke, we have a prison in which used to reside Old Sparky. Until the PC crowd decided if you have to execute somebody, do it in a genteel fashion; just give 'em an IV and let them sleep off into eternity. Well, I felt like the last guy walking up to Old Sparky.

The leaf blower was kicking up a hurricane and I was losing my nerve. Enough madness crept in past my mental barriers to give me the insane courage. I tossed the leaf blower out and it hit the water and exploded. Plastic parts blew everywhere and I felt the tingle of shocks going through me and all the electricity in the house went out at once.

The first thing that leapt into my mind was that Mary Lou was going to kill me. She'd need an electrician now to rewire the circuit breaker box. And then I noticed I was still alive. Maybe all the water diluted the electricity, not that that made any sense whatsoever.

Once more I dragged myself out of the pool and the pain and fog returned. I looked at my watch and it was spinning counterclockwise. So much for faint hope.

"Fuck it," I said, resigning myself to a horrible death.

When I went to the bathroom, I peed blood.

I went and got some cigars and sat in my seat outback on the patio and smoked. I chose another Macanudo Portifino, it being the most expensive one I had. Hell, it was so good it was nutritious. It didn't matter anyway, I could hardly think. I knew I had had some other bright idea but it didn't seem important. Ennui settled over me and I just smoked.

Budweiser sat and watched me, half afraid, half curious. For a while nausea attacked me and I vomited a couple of times. Cramps bent me in half. All of my bones no longer ached: they hurt with flashing pain. Eight o'clock came and went, I knew, because I had to go into the house for more matches. Birds and squirrels normally about and noisy this time of day strangely absented themselves. I watched plastic pieces swirl about in the swimming pool, blown by the Florida morning breeze, certainly not the pool pump.

Sitting in the chair I was facing east towards Arcadia, where I always said you could almost order up a thunderstorm. The sun raced toward the west, and the lighthouse shadow moved slowly on the sundial. Some morning thunderclouds began drifting in from the east, too. The lighthouse at the end of the tunnel?

Even in my stupefied, petrified brain two plus two equals four. Without thinking, I tossed that cigar butt into the pool and got up. That was a measure of how bad off I really was. It was my job to clean the pool and keep it clear and properly dosed with chemicals. Any other time, I wouldn't have dreamed of befouling my swimming pool.

Even though I was dying, I stopped to light another cigar, possibly the last rational action I'd take in my life. And my last smoke. *The condemned man has his last smoke.*

Remembering was a chore, but I grabbed my cell phone and stumbled into the garage like a drunk on Saturday night. I pressed the automatic garage door opener and lurched into my golf cart. Budweiser trailed me and jumped aboard like he always did. What the hell, give him his last ride, nobody else would. He sat alertly upright on the seat beside me. The garage door opener didn't work: no electricity. Good thing it had counter weights and springs. Groaning, I climbed out of the cart and pulled the disconnect cord. It took all my strength to manually lift the garage door. Backing out I ran into the grill on my pickup. The damage was mostly to my pride. I drove around back and stopped at the sundial. It came apart, the stand and the sundial round surface itself. I had enough sense to eyeball the time it showed. I managed to load it onto the back after dumping the golf clubs on the ground. I kicked them around until I found my new 9-iron, the S & W prototype CJ had given me after the lightning had fried my other one.

Like a drunken sailor I sped to the golf course, not a block away and down a fairway scattering a foursome. Within sight of the clubhouse stood the fateful copse of trees that started the whole damn thing.

Budweiser whined, knowing something terrible was about to go down.

The cobwebs of fog of madness no longer attacked me; they were firmly digging into my brain overwhelming my thinking, my rationality, my logic.

But it was locked in now. Nothing could stop me. I slammed the golf cart into some palmetto brush, the swords slicing at me and piercing my stomach. Budweiser mewled.

It took a superhuman effort to set up the lighthouse sundial. I adjusted it at a few minutes later than when I first dismantled it.

Pain lanced, no longer confining itself to my body. My head felt as if it would explode. I stood exactly where I was the first time. I puffed on the cigar, refusing to put it down, and grabbed the sundial.

Nothing seemed to happen. But clouds raced from the east and loomed thickly. Wind burst about me. Budweiser was so afraid he jammed against my legs. The shadow of the lighthouse indicating the time inched forward, and then seemed to stop. That might well have been a symptom of my madness.

The golf course warning Claxton wailed away, a familiar

sound in the midst of madness. The piercing sound cut through the racing thunder.

Rain forced itself into my world stinging, blinding. I lifted my head and lost my cigar. Flashes of lightning from afar edged into the range of my vision. The offbeat thought that North Carolina couldn't match this shot through one lucid port in my brain.

Belatedly, the warning Claxton continued to blare.

The shadow of the lighthouse necessarily disappeared and the storm raged about me, but the lightning danced elsewhere. Suddenly, I remembered and reached over for my 9-iron. I held it aloft, willing lightning this way.

For several minutes the storm raged and then seemed to dissipate somewhat.

It wasn't working. The madness surged ahead, overwhelming me. The storm abated more. In a lull I heard my cell phone. Stupidly, I pulled it out of my pocket.

"Mr. Zachary?"

"Yeah," I said, my brain not working well, words coming out thick.

"Major Yaroslav here." The remote viewer guy. "We ran it for you. My best man says he thinks a set of trees four hundred yards to the east of the original location shows more promise. He describes three palm trees, a couple of oak trees, some pine and a confluence of two strips—asphalt?"

"Golf path," I said. "I know it." It was on the back nine.

I dropped the phone on the ground and labored the sundial back onto the golf cart.

As I took off, Budweiser leapt on board. He wasn't going to be left alone in a storm. Rain still streaked and lightning flared but not here. I sped across Bent Tree Boulevard from the front nine to the back nine, cutting over bunkers and sand traps and ignoring the lake where CJ had challenged the gator and rattler and down the fairway to where they had to be referring. I slewed to a stop and the wind and slick grass turned the golf cart over, me and the cat sprawling onto the soaked ground. The sundial rolled like a Frisbee.

It didn't matter because there was no sun to set it up and recapture. The rain was stinging my eyes and I fought my way to the center of the trees, and jammed myself against the tallest tree, a long-leaf pine. Somehow, I had maintained a madman's grip on the 9-iron. The wind pinned me against the tree and lightning sprawled all around me, teasing me. Budweiser inserted himself, soaked and thoroughly angry, behind my legs against the tree where he thought it was most safe.

I smelled electricity and no longer knew what the hell I was doing and didn't give a damn either. I knew the enemy was out there and dared it on. A bolt slammed into a tree fifty feet away and I felt the residual flash, but my atavistic mind knew that wasn't what I was looking for. The immediate crack of the lightning ripped the fabric of this universe asunder. I held up the 9-iron taunting nature. "Come on you sonofabitch!" my voice shouted and I wondered what the hell I was doing and wondered where was Carrie Jean and what the hell was going on and God help me now what???

The gods struck the land with vengeance and the ground its very self danced and rolled like Armageddon. And hell, this was fun. I flaunted the 9-iron like the madman I was, daring and challenging.

An errant bolt struck the tree across from me, bounced off other trees, ate holes in the ground and raised a furrow there, too, as it tore towards me and I smelled my hair burning. Another struck above us and I could feel sheer power of the universe flowing into the earth itself through the tree behind me. We grew into one, the tree and me, and my arm tingled like I stuck it in a flame and a solid ball of living light spiraled above me and down into me. I sensed something ancient, something primordial, a kinship of agelessness for an eternity or a nano-second. The ball of plasma flung itself in and out of my vision, toyed with the ground, and played havoc with my immediate universe.

Budweiser howled like a werewolf at midnight and that

scared me more than anything. Hell, I didn't care. I was mad, I threatened the universe with my 9-iron and found it was no longer in my hand and that my hand was blackened and charred. I could no longer hear. Budweiser would have to wail at the cosmos alone. Poor sonofabitch.

A strange thing happened then, amongst many others, but I could feel smoldering pine bark scraping my back as I slid down the trunk of the tree to the ground. Carrie Jean, where are you when I need you? Huh? Goddamn.

The last thing I remembered thinking was that now would be a perfect time for a fine cigar.

CHAPTER FORTY-FOUR

I remember flashes of awareness. At the time, a stray thought from the past suggested it was my neurons disassociating, dying, me on my way to eternity.

Carrie Jean was there again, screaming into a cell phone, pounding my chest, breathing life into me.

Another flash was in the ambulance, some uniformed guys sticking things onto me, barking orders, sides of the vehicle swaying in the wind and the rush for the hospital and Carrie Jean sitting there watching everything, damn cat on her lap, the whole world wet and smelling like burned out wiring.

I remember passing out watching her and the stricken look on her face and her warm eyes.

I remember fighting the fog of madness for an eternity, to the exclusion of even new and old pain. Compared to the pain, the lightning hadn't hurt a bit.

I remember Carrie Jean holding my hand checking the time on my wrist. Didn't she have her own watch?

This was where I came in.

I woke up in what could well have been the same hospital room. And Mary Lou was sitting next to the window staring out.

Surveying the room with one slatted eye, I peeked around. No flowers this time. Maybe I hadn't been out as long. I assessed my physical condition. No broken bones that I could tell. Or, more accurately, I had no splints or casts cluttering any body parts.

An intriguing thought struck me: I was alive. Or, I amended, more appropriately, I wasn't dead yet.

I popped both eyes wide open and dragged my arm out from under the covers and felt sore. My eyes leapt for my watch face and had a difficult time focusing. Finally, I convinced myself which way was actually clockwise. The hands were going correctly. But, I thought, maybe the latest lightning incident really broke the damn thing and it was moving clockwise because it was twice broke. And this kind of logic would kill me. At least the hands were not racing around the dial, never mind which way they were headed.

"Ethan?"

"I'm awake."

"Thank God. We were beginning to worry."

"We being?" I asked.

"Dexter. Me. Your sweetie."

I didn't respond.

"I sent her off for some rest. She's been sitting here for two days." Mary Lou smiled wanly. "Oh, to be young and in love again."

I waited, knowing she had to get through this.

Mary Lou was on her feet and slowly walked to the bed. She took my hand and twisted it so she could read my watch. "Carrie Jean set it on the right time forty-eight hours ago." Mary Lou checked her own watch and then cross-referenced the clock on the wall. "And Carrie Jean also coined the term we're all using. True time. Not real time, you have your own lexicon, Ethan. As long as you're running true time, you're looking good."

"Dexter?" I croaked.

"He'll tell you himself. But he says you're recovering, that's why you slept so long."

"Recovering from?"

"The lightning attack and whatever was wrong with you."

"I'll be dipped in sh—"

"Spit." She smiled again, something she hadn't been doing a

lot of recently.

"Am I injured?"

Mary Lou shook her head. "Not as much this time. Apparently, practice makes perfect. You've some burns and bruises, but that's about it. And—"

She said nothing for a few moments.

"And?" I prompted.

"You, according to Dexter and my own observations now, you appear to be a healthy young male in your mid-twenties. Dexter doesn't know if you will start to age chronologically like everybody else or on your own timeline. It's not as if there is a lot of medical research in the subject."

My heart froze. My blood chilled.

"Ethan! Are you okay?"

Shaking my head to clear it, I said, "Yes, I think so. I just had a chilling thought. There are some people who'll be terribly interested in my alleged recovery, and they might not be so nice this time."

"Your sweetie told me," Mary Lou said. "We've had some time here together." Mary Lou's tone, surprisingly, was not snide. "We established a cabal and included Dexter." She grinned, and it was genuine. "You're dead."

"Okay." I had to think it through and then understood.

"It's a secret. Not even your other sweetie knows."

"I don't have sweeties, Mary Lou. Could you be somewhat less cryptic?"

"Elena Rodríguez. On the news of your death, the governor appointed her to your county commission seat."

Knowing this was fine, but I didn't really care. I felt weak and tired and sore and beat to death. But there was urgency within me growing.

Mary Lou still held my hand but was no longer looking at the watch. "Would that I could be young with you again, Ethan. I'd try harder this time."

"You did fine. You were fine, I mean. Hell, you are fine. The fault was with me." My voice felt dry, raspy. The urgency was burning a hole in me.

"No, likely it was mutual," Mary Lou said shaking her head. "I sort of redesigned you in my mind and ignored the real you. You no longer met my expectations."

"We grew apart," I said.

"Did we ever. Dolly—remember the tarot reader?"

"How could I forget?"

"She said she saw a dark veil about you, a dark side. I believed her. I believed in that shit then."

Lying on the bed made it difficult to shrug, but I did so anyway.

"Maybe I didn't have anything else to do," Mary Lou continued. "A lot of that psychic shit was beginning to make sense. I thought if we got divorced it would change things."

I remembered having an epiphany about that at the time. "I think the aforementioned dark side was whatever was attacking my physiology counterclockwise," I pointed out.

"Well, I chose to believe that you didn't need me, you no longer sought my counsel, my opinion." She dropped my hand and smoothed her dress. "Now it's too late."

It had been too late for a long time; we just hadn't recognized that fact.

She went on, "Star alignment, psychic healing, none was helping. I thought that divorce would reverse the negativity between us." Her voice choked. "Now look at us."

I didn't want to do that thing, but I did. I remembered the good times, when we started out, how we'd gotten through the tough times together. "Jeez, Mary Lou."

She rested her hand on my arm. "Two different paths now, Ethan. Nothing can change that." She grinned, once again the old Mary Lou. "And now, here you are, dead." She sat on the edge of the bed.

"Mary Lou? Don't ever let anybody know I'm alive? Promise me."

"Who the hell cares, Ethan?"

"Some people with more power than you would believe. If

they think I'm still alive they will want to witness my death. You better shake and bake me."

Cremation would get rid of the evidence and preclude Raleigh Smith from performing an autopsy. It was good I was dead, so to speak, for doubtless Raleigh would want to follow the progress of my counterclockwise demise for many reasons, all the way from professional curiosity to necessity in case Justyn Tyme responded to the blood and/or bone marrow or stem cells or whatever the hell they gave him from me. For a brief moment in time I wondered how Rhonda would react to the news of my death. "Put my mother's ashes in another urn. If we're lucky, they won't check the DNA. If they do, maybe her remains will fool them."

"Okay." Mary Lou sat silent for a minute. "That would explain Carrie Jean."

"Meaning?"

"She told me to cash in the insurance—and sell or throw away your stuff. I do not need the life insurance money, by the way, thank you very much. She said if you recovered, you-all would start fresh, without even your toothbrush."

Carrie Jean had figured it out and done the planning while I lay comatose. The urgency welled up within me. If Belinda Foursleeps or Raleigh Smith had any inkling I was recovering and not dying or dead, they'd hunt me down like a dog and dissect me like a frog in biology class.

"Hello," said a voice from the door. "I bought some clothes and cigars and a new toothbrush. They're in my truck right now along with a cat named Budweiser." Carrie Jean filled my eyes, fresh and lovely and my heart soared.

Mary Lou stood quickly as if caught in an illegal act. "Damn it all. I will miss you, Ethan Allan Zachary." She bent over and kissed my lips. "Even though you're dead, I'll insure the divorce is legally consummated, retroactively or whatever. It shouldn't be long."

Then Mary Lou was gone, edging past Carrie Jean.

Carrie Jean hurried to the bed. "How do you feel?"

"Like a million dollars now."

"Maybe three million?"

EPILOGUE

"Hi, honey, I'm home."

"I'm out by the pool."

Fast forward.

It was our rental house in Las Vegas. Not a palace, but close. Thanks, Belinda.

I went through the house and out the back onto the patio. Carrie Jean was floating face down on a plastic raft and blew me a kiss. Like everything else she wore, she looked good in a bikini.

She cocked an eye. "Any luck?"

"No." I shook my head wearily. The desert sun had been hot, but not enough to stop me from running. And searching. We'd both go out on a long run before dark and continue looking. We'd been at it for two weeks.

We'd come to Vegas for one purpose: to get married. No, not at a drive-through Elvis wedding chapel. To avoid bigamy even though I was legally dead, we'd checked the Sarasota County website and the *Star-Banner* website daily to check for divorce announcements. And the day after it appeared in the announcement section, Carrie Jean Billingsley became Carrie Jean Zachary.

I went inside to find a cigar. A good one. Thanks Belinda. I kicked off my running shoes and went and sat on the edge of the pool and dangled my legs in the cool water.

"Feels wonderful." I was content as I clipped the end off the smoke and lit up.

As content as I could be until I reconciled my loss.

CJ paddled over and grabbed my knee. I patted her curvaceous rump. She purred.

She slid off the raft and hung in the water next to me.

We hadn't made it to Seattle or wherever, not yet. I wasn't certain we were going to go there any time soon if at all. It wasn't as if one of us had to earn a paycheck any longer.

"Your damn cat is interfering with my honeymoon," Carrie Jean said. But she didn't mean it. She'd put more hours in searching the neighborhood than I had.

"We'll keep looking," I said firmly. "But it is in my heart that we won't find him. Um…."

"Um, what?"

"We don't know but that he might have disappeared into another dimension."

"You never did," CJ pointed out. "Budweiser is simply following his natural cat instincts. He's out cattin' around."

"I hope that's all it is."

"He's been old for too long, Ethan."

Not long after we got married, Budweiser had disappeared. But not before we noticed major changes. His feluke disease went away mysteriously. His fur was slicker and shinier. He lost weight and was suddenly healthy. He had a big appetite he hadn't shown for years. His hearing was back to cat normal. He actually *played* with CJ like a kitten.

Doubtless right now that lady cat was tap dancing on his last nerve. And he was out there alone, without our support in his coming trauma. On the other hand, until then it was more than likely he was having a ball.

Budweiser's misfortune was, in fact, my own good fortune. Look at it this way: his own counterclockwise condition proved that mine had not been hereditary or from some other source or combination of factors as Rhonda had at one time speculated. If I'd had the condition all along and a bang on the head or electricity from lightning had kicked it off, then Budweiser wouldn't have gotten it from the same lightning, ball lightning or whatever, that reversed my race toward death. So I was pretty safe now—or so I hoped. I'd certainly stay out of the rain. I wasn't superstitious, but three strikes and you're out. Another reason for dry, not-rainy Vegas.

Habitually, I glanced at my Seiko. Still cranking along clockwise at the correct pace. True time. I'd worn out my eyes on that watch lately. Trusting my trusty Seiko, I was having a second chance at life. The mystical fountain of youth was not handing me immortality on a platter.

So far so good.

Carrie Jean saw me looking at my watch. I nodded to her reassuringly.

"See, Ethan, you do not understand. You are fine; you will be fine. You will no longer grow younger. You will be back on track. With me."

"My pleasure, sweetheart." I was beginning to hope I would live a normal life. So far my physiology was looking good. Not everybody gets a second chance at life. I kept telling myself that.

She dimpled. "The universe, Ethan, nature its very self, bent to my will. It enabled *us*."

I couldn't convince her otherwise. And it was as good an explanation as any.

"I already ran the websites."

"Thanks," I said and tipped a particularly long and perfectly rounded ash into the ashtray.

Daily we scoured the web for obituaries. Google searches. Half dozen North Carolina newspapers. News searches on Drudge.

So far no Justyn Tyme.

And no Raleigh Smith, Jr. Thank God.

Her really fine runner's legs scissored in the water.

I tugged on her left ear.

She looked up at me.

"Not everybody," I said, "gets do-overs in life. I will do better this time around, and I am thankful I have you to do it over with."

Her eyes said it all.

We had decided on having children. But not when. I remembered Dolly the Tarot reader seeing children in my future. And, in a secret part of my soul, I'd thought she'd foreseen *me* turning into a child. We were going to chance the Agent Orange curse of genetic disruptions. Maybe my quick-heal regression had corrected any genetic damage caused by Agent Orange. I was determined to keep trying until we had a daughter. I was thinking about what kind of a mother CJ was going to make.

And the doorbell rang.

"Who could that be?"

Shrugging, I levered myself up, put the cigar down so I wouldn't stink up the house, and headed for the door dripping a bit.

It was our rural mail-lady, we being so far out.

"Express package for you to sign for."

I signed a pink piece of paper and took the package. "Thanks."

She was already climbing into her truck.

A discordant note began clamoring in my mind. The package was addressed to me.

Carrying the package out back, I noted it had no return address.

On the patio, I said as much to CJ.

"Nobody, I mean nobody, knows we're here," she said, heaving herself out of the pool to a standing position without using her knees. As my new ways dictated, I paused to admire her suppleness and grace. There has to be a God, for certainly He was smiling upon me.

Then my brain kicked in. As far as the world knew, I was dead. Everything here was in CJ's name.

I began worrying.

"Open it."

"Suppose it's a bomb or anthrax or something?"

"That would be a waste of effort. Open it."

I was still dubious.

She snatched the package from me and tore off the brown shipping paper. Inside was more paper, wrapped as a gift. She tore that off, too.

It was a box of cigars. And an envelope. The cigars were Arturo Fuentes, Canones of the Gran Reserve line, Cameroon wrapper, big ones at eight and a half inches with over a fifty-ring gauge. Big, gaudy, expensive smokes.

I took the manila envelope and opened it. A whiff of cinnamon chilled me to the bone.

No letter, just a yellow sticky note in a familiar handwriting. *Thanks!*

The sticky note was stuck on the face of an 8 x 10 photograph of Rolly gleefully riding his Segway along the walkway in front of his home in a certain compound in the middle of the mountains in very northwest North Carolina.

CJ was looking at the picture. "Rolly? Jeez, Ethan, look at him."

Rolly was smiling for the camera and waving gleefully.

I saw the kid, CJ saw a shriveled tiny old man.

So I explained the look on his face.

"You did a really good thing for that kid, then, Ethan. You're a saint."

"I feel like one lately, hon—oh, my God."

"What? Tell me," she demanded.

My mind was blazing a million miles a second.

"Ethan! What's wrong?" And then her face showed understanding. "Slow down, there's more to this. A step at a time, dear. Chill out for a minute."

The tap dancing lady was back and tuning up some nerves.

I went over and got my cigar and had to relight it.

"Follow the logic here for me," CJ urged.

I puffed and inhaled for the first time in weeks.

"Right. It's from Rhonda. Surface meaning: Thanks for a super present, Rolly is having a ball and I thought you'd like to see a photo of him having the ball. And she's right. The kid's enjoying himself, locked up there in the middle of nowhere, not really a kid, not an adult. No note, so he's doing about the same, not on death's doorstep." Or she wasn't able to get a note through.

CJ had an arm around me and was squeezing to keep me on an even keel. My brain continued to burn.

"Next level. Rhonda is telling me they know I'm alive."

"And our location." CJ shrugged it off. "So what?"

I thought about it. Some of the tension went out of me.

"My first thought was that we were in danger."

"Me, too."

"But knowing Rhonda—"

"Women throwing themselves at you again."

"That would be flattering, Carrie Jean, but not the case." I didn't think so anyway. However, for the rest of my life, each time I smelled or tasted cinnamon I would think of Rhonda.

"Actually, you dumb man, it is the case. But, from what you've told me, sort of."

"Nope. It's not to plant a jealous seed in your brain, either, darlin'. For I have eyes only for you—"

"Cut the crap and tell me."

"She is our guardian angel. That's what."

"Meaning?"

"Rhonda Smith is telling us that they know where we are and, likely, how I am doing. But that is not the important thing. She's telling me that we are safe—for now. Think about it. We're not playing witness protection program here, so we aren't that hard to find. Especially since you're using your real name. Credit cards, motel bills, gas stations. They can track us anywhere."

"And did."

I nodded. "Rhonda is telling us they know. But to watch over our shoulder."

"Well, then, let us go about our lives and not worry."

That's what we'd do. It also gave us time to build some new identities should we need them.

I searched the photo again, this time for visual clues. I saw none. Rhonda would have found a way to indicate they had

Budweiser.

    Wouldn't she?

AUTHOR'S NOTE

A few years ago, the DQ mentioned within was torn down for "progress." I left it in the story for nostalgia and because it belonged there.

ABOUT THE AUTHOR

JAMES B. JOHNSON has written five novels: *Trekmaster, Habu, Mindhopper, A World Lost,* and *Daystar and Shadow.* *Mindhopper* was optioned twice for a movie, and two were translated into French and German. He has also penned numerous short stories and articles. Jim has sold advertising, worked for the Post Office for fifteen years, and spent eleven years in the Air Force. He lives in Sarasota, Florida, with his wife Beverly.

www.ingramcontent.com/pod-product-compliance
Lightning Source LLC
Chambersburg PA
CBHW022144010726
47493CB00002B/330